He leapt, catching her arm before she reached the far side of the bed . . .

Aidan rolled her over and held both wrists above her head as he lowered himself on top of the struggling woman, crushing her into the mattress. Her face relaxed with shock, and he was darkly pleased to see the fear behind those aqua eyes.

He wanted her to feel a portion of the fear her captives felt before being hanged . . . the fear he had felt. Only then would he turn her over to the authorities.

He reached down and lifted her skirt, telling himself that it was necessary, crucial, that she be searched. His hand caressed her calf, then drifted up the outer portion of her right leg as the lady stubbornly held his gaze. Aidan's fingers skimmed her inner thigh until he encountered the sheath for her deadly knife.

"Do you have any other weapons?" he asked, holding on by the fingernails to his gentlemanly ideals by giving her the opportunity to end the search.

She said nothing, and he cursed her stubbornness. He placed his hand on the delicate bone of her other ankle and started drifting up her leg. Aidan looked into his enemy's eyes, and his baser instincts took over, much as they had on the peninsula, much as he feared they always would.

He fought against it, his hand pausing on her upper thigh. "Do you have any other weapons, Lady Rivenhall?" He stared at her lips.

"No," she breathed, staring at his.

It was more than he could take.

"Damn you," he whispered, unsure if he was cursing her or himself, then dropped his head to taste the traitor who had haunted his dreams and nightmares . . .

The Lady Lies

Samantha Saxon

BERKLEY SENSATION, NEW YORK

THE BERKLEY PUBLISHING GROUP
Published by the Penguin Group
Penguin Group (USA) Inc.
375 Hudson Street, New York, New York 10014, U.S.A.
Penguin Group (Canada), 10 Alcorn Avenue, Toronto, Ontario, M4V 3B2, Canada
(a division of Pearson Penguin Canada Inc.)
Penguin Books Ltd, 80 Strand, London WC2R 0RL, England
Penguin Group Ireland, 25 St. Stephen's Green, Dublin 2, Ireland
(a division of Penguin Books Ltd.)
Penguin Group (Australia), 250 Camberwell Road, Camberwell, Victoria 3124,
Australia (a division of Pearson Australia Group Pty. Ltd.)
Penguin Books India Pvt. Ltd., 11 Community Centre, Panchsheel Park, New Delhi—110 017,
India
Penguin Group (NZ), Cnr. Airborne and Rosedale Roads, Albany, Auckland 1310, New Zealand
(a division of Penguin New Zealand Ltd.)
Penguin Books (South Africa) (Pty.) Ltd., 24 Sturdee Avenue, Rosebank, Johannesburg 2196,
South Africa

Penguin Books Ltd, Registered Offices: 80 Strand, London WC2R 0RL, England

This is a work of fiction. Names, characters, places, and incidents either are the product of the author's imagination or are used fictitiously, and any resemblance to actual persons, living or dead, business establishments, events, or locales is entirely coincidental.

THE LADY LIES

A Berkley Sensation Book / published by arrangement with the author

PRINTING HISTORY
Berkley Sensation edition / June 2005

ISBN: 0-425-20358-1

BERKLEY ® SENSATION
Berkley Sensation Books are published by The Berkley Publishing Group,
a division of Penguin Group (USA) Inc.,
375 Hudson Street, New York, New York 10014.
BERKLEY SENSATION and the "B" design are trademarks belonging to
Penguin Group (USA) Inc.

PRINTED IN THE UNITED STATES OF AMERICA

10 9 8 7 6 5 4 3 2 1

To my husband, Gaston,
for showing our children what a man should be

Acknowledgments

My eternal gratitude to my agent, Maria Di Giovanni, for hearing my words, and to my editor, Louisa Edwards, for easing my path.

Prologue

LONDON, ENGLAND
SEPTEMBER 24, 1794

The first thing he saw was feathers.

The man wearing the ornate hat, he knew, was Christian St. John's father, the Duke of St. John, home from a rousing victory as Commander of British forces at the Battle of Lincelles. The sun glinted off numerous medals as the duke emerged into the garden, making the uniform and the man that much more impressive, that much more heroic.

"Pay up, Wessex," Daniel McCurren demanded, drawing Aidan's attention toward his auburn-haired friend whose blue eyes were lost in the sky above him. "I told ya Christian's father would na miss his birthday celebration."

Resigned, Aidan reached into his pocket and fished out a farthing. His own father, the Earl of Wessex, had sent a letter saying the regiment would be home in October, so it had been a sound wager. But if the Duke of St. John was home, his most trusted officer, the Earl of Wessex, would be too.

"Here." Aidan tossed him the coin, smiling at the thought of seeing his father again, before punching the arrogant Scot square in the shoulder. "You skirt-wearing blackguard."

"It's a kilt, you English puff." Daniel hit him threefold as hard, knocking him out of the tree they had been climbing and very nearly causing him to land on John Elkin's chestnut head.

"Apologies," Aidan grunted as he lay sprawled across the grass.

John did not lift his eyes from the pages of his current read before giving Aidan a swift kick in the backside. "Think nothing of it."

The force of the kick rolled Aidan on his back where he lay, trying to remember why he had befriended such a motley crew.

John Elkin was a cynic whose warring parents had driven him firmly into the pages of his beloved books. But to a privileged few, he was a fiercely loyal friend with a sardonic wit and a heart as soft as strawberry jam.

His brawny assailant was Daniel McCurren, a charismatic Scot who made people grin when they saw him and laugh when they chastised him. The word *fear* could not be found in his vocabulary and, unfortunately, neither could humility.

Christian St. John was the youngest son of the Duke of St. John and heir to absolutely nothing. He was carefree, gullible, and astonishingly naïve, believing the best of people until proven otherwise. All in all, he rather reminded Aidan of a pup.

"Oh, nicely done, John." Daniel laughed overhead.

"Careful, Daniel." Aidan tossed black strands from his eyes and glared up at his large friend. "Or I'll not allow you to marry my sister."

"Sarah?" John asked, surprised. "Daniel wishes to marry Sarah?"

"He told me his intentions last week." Aidan smirked.

"A bit young to contemplate marriage, aren't you, Daniel? Well, never mind." John was so amused by this revelation that he slammed his book closed. "I suppose I should offer my congratulations to the bride."

"Take one step, Elkin, and I'll throttle ya," Daniel promised, his eyes turned to slits, but Aidan could see the hurt beneath the anger. Guilt washed over him and Aidan felt a child for allowing his annoyance to break the confidence of his closest friend. "Aidan, you should na divulge a man's private affairs."

"Man!" John chuckled. "You're ten, same as us."

"I'll be eleven in two weeks' time," Daniel boasted, leaping on the change of subject. "A full year older than Christian."

Aidan sat up, reclining on his elbows and squinting in the direction of his fair friend as Christian greeted his illustrious father. The duke clasped his youngest son's shoulder and bent to whisper in his ear. Aidan watched, curious, as Christian's Nordic blue eyes turned and locked on him.

"Aidan Duhearst," the duke called across the garden.

His heart bumped with excitement. He knew then that he was correct, that his father was indeed home. Aidan rose, praying that it was his father himself, and not a footman, who had come to fetch them from the party.

He dusted off his breeches and walked toward the duke, motioning to his sister where she sat on the lawn playing with the sixth of the seven McCurren boys. Sarah kissed the four-year-old on the cheek before sliding him from her lap.

She began to rise but the duke stopped her, saying, "Just Aidan."

Her dimpled smile faded and her green eyes met his.

Aidan indicated his ignorance with a discreet shrug and walked toward the Duke of St. John.

"Will you join me in my study?"

Stunned, Aidan could do nothing but give one brusque nod. He followed the duke's broad back, listening to the rhythmic clicking of his Hessians on the white marble, a disconcerting contrast to Aidan's lighter footfall.

The footmen opened black double doors at the end of the hall, closing them the moment they passed into the room. He glanced around, nervous and more than a little curious.

As many times as he had visited Christian's townhome, he had never set foot in this room. Not that they hadn't tried. Christian had devised a scheme to pilfer a cheroot or two, but when the time came and the footmen distracted not even McCurren could muster the courage to turn that doorknob.

"Aidan, have a seat."

He did. His lanky legs stretched to reach the carpeted floor as he settled in the enormous leather chair opposite the desk. He waited, watching as the duke stared out the tall windows with his hands clasped behind his back.

"You are aware, are you not, that I have just returned from Lincelles?"

"Yes, Your Grace." He sat up, determined to sound more dignified, more mature. "All of England is aware of your victory."

The duke turned to face him, laughing at some private amusement Aidan did not understand.

"Yes, well, 'twas not *my* victory," he said, sitting at his desk and placing his forearms on the polished mahogany.

"No, Your Grace." Aidan grasped the padded arms of the chair, afraid that he had offended in some way.

"We were outgunned at Lincelles." The duke lifted blond brows. "The French had column after column of cannons." He sighed. "I've never seen such a force."

The duke stared through the wood of the desk and Aidan waited, not sure what to say.

"As our troops assembled, the French fired their cannons, confident that we would not charge. But we did." He nodded. "The first line of infantry was cut to ribbons, and when the second faltered . . ." He paused, taking a breath before starting again. "A lone dragoon officer rode to the front of the line, his sword drawn as he charged into the fray."

Aidan's heart stopped.

"Nothing touched him. And when he reached the French

line, he sailed his mount over the cannons as if borne on wings." The duke was lost in his memories, narrowing his pale eyes as if he could see them. "I have never seen anything more glorious in all my days.

"Wave after wave of British infantry charged the French line to assist the brave officer who rode, cutting down their gunners as they reloaded their cannons. It was this unrelenting resolve that broke their line, and their will." He met Aidan's eye. "A resolve carried across the battlefield of Lincelles by your father."

Aidan's chin quivered, and he could not breathe, his nostrils flared as he struggled to take air into lungs locked by shock.

"I have never met a finer, braver man than your father was."

The duke's words faded as Aidan braced himself against the pain of knowing it was his fault, knowing that he had not been enough to keep his father home. If he had been a better son, a better brother, then perhaps his father would not have left them.

"The Earl of Wessex was the noblest of gentlemen, and I suspect that I shall never have the privilege of knowing another man like him."

Aidan stared at the carpet until the meticulous pattern blurred. He heard a metallic ping and absently glanced up, only to see his father's gold ring shining against the dark wood.

"I know this is difficult, Aidan, but as of this moment . . . *you* are the Earl of Wessex."

Aidan had always known that one day he would be required to fill his father's shoes, to ascend to the title he had been bred to. But not yet.

He wasn't ready.

He reached for the Wessex signet and placed it on his middle finger, then watched in horror as the weight of the cold metal caused the ring to slide off. With a shaky hand, he pushed it up and clenched his fist, terrified that he would never grow to fit it.

One

LONDON, ENGLAND
APRIL 20, 1811

At a small desk buried in the depths of Whitehall, an old man sat staring at three well-worn dossiers. He reached for the first, as was his ritual, and reread every detail, every event concealed therein. And when he was finished, he closed his eyes in the silence that was only obtainable in the wee hours of the morning . . . and prayed.

He prayed for protection, he prayed for guidance, but most importantly, he prayed for forgiveness.

He repeated this process with each subject of his well-maintained files and then slowly rose, picking up the papers before walking to the fire. He stared into the flames, hesitant to let go, and with a heavy sigh, let the women of Whitehall slip from his fingers.

The fire flared, and the papers curled, charring at the edges. He stabbed with the poker, stirring the flames and meticulously burning the papers until nothing remained but ashes . . . ashes and his tortured conscience.

Two

Aidan did not know where he was or how he had gotten there.

Cool air rushed past his face, a welcome confusion to his warm skin. He cracked his eyelids, shutting them when light sliced through his already throbbing head, tenfold worse than anything he had experienced after a night of excess.

He tried again, slowly this time, blinking, straining to focus. Dirt. He could see the ground, but the ground was moving. No, wait. He was moving, but his legs were not. His hair felt wet and sticky, black clumps stuck to his forehead. Dropping his gaze, he tried to comprehend the blood spattered across the front of his uniform.

And then he saw her, and he was no longer confused.

An angel.

His angel.

He would have thought an angel would have wings and yards of billowy white cloth, but his angel wore an ice blue ball gown. God must have known he was an Englishman, creating the perfect emissary to meet his tastes.

A sense of peace washed over him, and he smiled to himself, pleased that he had died alongside his men. His head bobbed as he struggled to remain conscious. He lifted it with a jerk and noticed the beautiful blond angel was speaking.

To him? What would his angel want to know? What could he tell her? How could he explain what had happened at Albuera? Explain how he had failed his men?

He could not.

Guilt stabbed at his gut, and he groaned in pain when he was unceremoniously thrown on a hard wooden chair, his wrists burning as a rope cut into his flesh.

"Idiots," she snapped in French. "Unbind him."

His angel looked angry, but not at him. A soldier to his right cut the ropes that were securing his wrists, and the tension in his shoulders eased. He felt two drops of blood slide down his cheek, competing to drip on his already soiled jacket. But he had no idea from whom it had come.

Confused, Aidan struggled to listen to his seraph, but the words meant nothing and his attention wandered to the dim room in which he now sat. Two men, dressed as French infantry soldiers, stood on either side of him, and a third guarded the door. To his left was a functional sideboard with a pitcher and several glasses.

In front of him, a colonel of the French army sat behind a battered desk talking to his angel. French and English merged in his mind, and he was unsure which language they spoke.

"Where was he found?" The angel's tone was curt.

"Albuera. He was found with one leg pinned beneath his horse and seven of our soldiers surrounding him. All dead."

"And the horse?" his angel asked in French; he was sure.

"Dead. Impaled with a lance."

Aidan grimaced, the screech emanating from Thor when the lance pierced the stallion's chest playing in his head. The horse had nearly drowned in a puddle where he fell.

Drowning would have been so much faster, so much easier.

"No, you fool. Obviously, the horse was dead," the seraph said, dissolving the memory of his loyal stallion to that of a carcass. "How else would he have become trapped beneath the animal? Describe the horse. Its quality? Its tack?"

Why she would want to know, Aidan could not fathom.

The colonel sputtered. "He . . . the horse . . . the horse was a very fine quality."

Aidan smirked at the enormity or the man's underestimation, but then again, he was French.

"And," she prodded when the soldier did not continue. He sensed urgency in her tone as her fair brows lifted with irritation. "The tack, Colonel!"

Aidan stared, never having seen an angry angel before, but concluding that he had neither the training nor temperament to judge angelic behavior.

"Also of high quality with no markings of any kind," the colonel reported.

"Hmmm." The angel walked toward Aidan, tapping a delicate lace fan in the palm of her left hand and cocking her head to one side as she looked down at him.

He stared, captivated.

Her eyes were huge. Green with blue flecks, or was it blue with green flecks? He decided they were green and very beautiful. Her golden hair was piled high atop her head in an elegant coiffure, as if she had just waltzed off a ballroom floor. Aidan had no doubt that she would dance beautifully, and he suppressed the urge to take her in his arms and do exactly that, but he was too tired. So he contented himself with a good, long, thoroughly delightful look.

The ethereal woman's nose was small and tipped up ever so slightly at the end. And her mouth, God, her mouth was the perfect width, and her lips were full and so damn succulent. His chest tightened. He had not had a woman in seven long months, and this heavenly creature would tempt a saint, much less a sinner like himself.

"What is your name?" the angel asked in English with not one hint of a French accent.

His name?

Blood dripped from his chin, and his brows furrowed as the fog began to clear. Aidan looked about the room, at the colonel, at the bars on the windows of the dirty chamber. He listened to the clank of metal and the distant cries of men on the other side of the heavy oak door. He blinked. Albuera! He had been fighting at Albuera with Beresford.

Damnation! He had been captured!

His head snapped up, and his body tensed with the instinct to fight his way out of the room, but the sound of a pistol being cocked behind his head held him in his chair.

That was it then; he was a dead man. But he should have died with his men . . . in battle.

Guilt feasted as the seraph leaned closer to get a good look at him. He lowered his gaze, fearful that she would see it. His eyes continued their downward descent, coming to rest on her breasts, now spilling from the bodice of her gown. Desire crawled in his chest as she squinted, peering through the mud and blood to the man beneath.

"Bring me your handkerchief, Colonel," the woman commanded.

She held out her hand and waited, still looking down at him, and asked once again, "What is your name, sir?"

Aidan straightened himself and lifted both brows, saying with that air of condescension only the English possess, "I'm afraid I have forgotten."

With the handkerchief now in hand, the woman took a step forward, taking his chin in her left hand and tilting his head upward. He flinched at the gentleness of her touch as she wiped away blood and dirt from his features, while boldly holding his gaze.

He sat impassive, giving no indication of the effect she was having on his senses, no indication of how her feminine scent caused his heart to race, no indication of how her touch burned him.

The angel leaned toward him, inspecting him as she

turned his face from side to side. He watched her consider. What she contemplated, he hadn't a clue, but her touch was becoming unbearable, and just when he felt his eyes drifting closed with pleasure, she was gone, dropping his chin from her soft hands as if he were a vermin-infested guttersnipe.

"Remove his jacket," she ordered, retreating toward the desk. "And give me the contents of his pockets."

Aidan rose to his height of six feet one inch and towered over the two soldiers at his side. He grit his teeth against the pain from his injuries as they cruelly yanked off his coat, pulling his shirt open in the process. His hands balled into fists, but he did not use them.

It was not the time.

When the soldiers had finished, he looked down at the woman who was clearly in command of the room. Their eyes held, and she observed him in return, waiting for the search to be completed. And when it was, the impatient rustling of silk petticoats was the only sound in the small chamber.

Exhaustion drew air deep into his lungs, expanding his aching chest. He knew they would find nothing to identify him. The only item he carried into battle was a miniature portrait of his sister holding his niece and nephew. Reminders of why he was fighting this godforsaken war.

The stunning angel, his enemy, came forward to take the miniature. She held Sarah's portrait in one hand and placed the palm of the other against his exposed chest, running her fingers beneath his muddy shirt and awakening his flesh with reminders of long-ago pleasures. Pleasures he hungered for, pleasures that provided, for a fleeting moment, a respite from the harsh realities of war.

Aidan closed his eyes and cursed himself for tensing, for revealing the effect she was having on his body. She was lovely, and she used that beauty, wielding it like a saber, and he was too weak to defend himself against her.

She continued the sensual assault, asking, "Are you injured, my lord?"

The use of his title stopped his now-shallow breathing. He forced himself to regain his composure, and when he was once again in control, he said, "I'm afraid to disappoint you, my lady, but Frenchmen are notoriously bad shots. I believe I was merely grazed."

Her feminine laughter was out of place within the filthy walls of the prison. She applied pressure to his shoulder in a silent command to have him resume sitting on the hard chair. He remained standing, but he was tired and saw no benefit in resistance. He glared at his stunning captor and then took his seat.

"Oh, but you English are refreshingly arrogant, and you more so than most, my lord." Her smile was dazzling, as if she were flirting with him in the midst of some grand event, not in a filthy French prison. She walked to the desk and picked up a sheet of paper, reading to herself.

"You fought at Albuera under the command of Lord Beresford." She nodded to the colonel in an unspoken communication, and the man began to take notes. "You were in command yourself of a small regiment, most likely, and from your accent are most assuredly a peer of the English House of Lords. The only question remains as to which one."

Impressed by her accuracy, he watched as the treacherous seraph walked toward him, stopping close enough that her skirts obscured his filthy boots. Aidan lifted his chin and looked into her mesmerizing eyes. She allowed it, invited it. He held her gaze, continuing their mental swordplay. After several moments, the woman sighed and took a step back, looking as though she might expire with ennui.

"When I was a child, I had a horse." She paused, smiling at her memory before continuing to pace the small room. Suspicion narrowed his eyes as he contemplated her reasons for revealing such personal information. "This horse was so stubborn that the more my father beat him, the more my horse refused to do the work that was required of him."

•

Aidan's eyes slid to the colonel, who was looking at the lady's backside with undisguised lust.

She continued, "Fearful that my father would kill my beloved horse, I enticed the animal with a carrot." She stopped in front of him and laughed. "And do you know, that horse did anything I asked of him from that moment on?" The woman waited for a response, and he enjoyed taking his time in giving it.

"Enchanting tale," he finally said. "But I fail to see the point of your little recitation."

The woman lifted a brow and grinned. "Ah, but the tale has a point, my lord." Disquiet crept up his spine. "You strike me as a man with whom a beating would have little effect." Aidan set his jaw. He knew all too well the amount of punishment his body could endure during the heat of battle.

"However," she said, placing her legs between his knees and spreading them wide, brushing his inner thighs as she stepped between them. Caressing him, knowing the effect the movement would have on him, on any man. The siren looked down at him, smiling as she bent forward to give him a long look at her breasts before her jade eyes met his.

Her face, her mouth were a mere six inches away. His hands itched to touch the enticing mounds so elegantly displayed before him. He battled, but lost. His shaft was hardening, and his gaze fell to her lips when she breathed, "A carrot, you might just take into your mouth for the pleasure of tasting it."

She leaned closer. He could smell her, feel the heat rising from her creamy skin. Aidan clenched his hands into fists and stared at the wall, but despite his effort to ignore her, he could feel her breath on his neck just behind his ear.

"And I know just what you want to bite," she whispered, drawing the lobe of his ear between her teeth. Aidan closed his eyes as ripples of pleasure washed over his traitorous body.

"Mmm, and I might want to . . . bite . . . back," she finished.

Desire flared in the pit of his stomach, consuming his entire body. She stepped out of his reach, and relief flooded him. He looked up and forced himself to smile his most charming smile when he said, "I dare say you had a French horse, my lady. English mounts are not so easily led by such common enticements."

Anger flashed in her beautiful eyes, but when she turned to look at him, he thought, for the briefest of moments, that he saw surprise. No, something more than surprise, different than surprise. He studied her, trying to identify the emotion. But she recovered quickly, lifting her delicately pointed chin as she spoke.

"Well, my lord, it seems we need offer you neither the stick nor the carrot." The angel walked toward him, placing her soft hands on his cheeks. He could feel them shaking as her thumbs traced the location of his dimples now hidden beneath the stubble of his fledgling beard. Her mood was light, her eyes sparkled. His blood ran cold as he identified the emotion as excitement.

"Lord Aidan Duhearst, Earl of Wessex," she proclaimed in triumph. Aidan flinched. He grabbed her wrists, pulling them away from his face as shock relaxed his features. The soldiers moved toward their lady protectively, but the woman shook her head as she stepped away from him.

"Come, come, my lord. Did you think we would not hear of your exploits both here and in England?" Her lips curled with giddy amusement. "You have killed so many Frenchmen that you are becoming a legend."

The woman's hips swayed as she walked forward and wound a finger around a lock of his hair. "And as for England, well"—she bent toward his ear—"let us just say that the ebony-haired earl has kept many a lady of the ton entertained over the years." She circled Aidan, coming to settle in front of him. "Is that not so, my lord?"

He smiled, raising one brow and not bothering to conceal his hatred. "Quite true. However, I would wager a great deal of blunt that I've not entertained as many ladies as you have entertained men."

His head snapped to the right with the force of her hand against his cheek, splattering blood on the delicate silk bodice of her costly gown. Her eyes narrowed to slits, and for the first time, Aidan saw her as a very dangerous woman.

"Take care, Lord Wessex," she hissed through clenched teeth. "I could have you hanged tomorrow if I so wished." The lady held his gaze to make sure that he understood his precarious position, and when they both knew he did, she said, "Take this English filth to his cell." The two soldiers were flanking him and Aidan had no choice but to comply when they wrenched him to his feet. "Colonel, have his wounds seen to. If he bleeds to death, I will hold you personally responsible. *Tu comprend*?"

The colonel understood quite clearly. "*Oui*, Mademoiselle." His reply was a bit anxious as the soldiers moved Aidan toward the door.

"Hold." The woman spoke to the soldiers, both of whom came to an immediate stop with a crisp click of their boots against the wooden floorboards. "Colonel, please inform the general that I shall be unable to dine with him this evening." She glanced down at her blood-spattered evening dress and looked at her captive. "I seem to have ruined my gown."

Aidan felt a mean spurt of satisfaction to have been the cause of her inconvenience. The striking woman walked toward him, holding out his miniature as if it were rubbish.

"You may have your portrait of your sister, the Duchess of Glenbroke, Lord Wessex. It should comfort you on your walk to the gallows," she sang before spinning with a dismissive swish as she left the dank room, the colonel at her heels.

Three

Celeste paused at her bedchamber door and turned to face the French officer.

"Colonel Meillerie, I would like the Earl of Wessex ready to travel by morning." She smiled sadistically, saying, "The earl will be quite a prize for the emperor."

"Yes, Lady Rivenhall. He will most certainly delight Emperor Bonaparte, but the general will not be pleased at having him removed from his custody." The young man's lips rolled in French, his gray eyes reflecting his concern.

Celeste lifted her hand to the colonel's sunburned cheek. She smiled, filling her lungs to draw attention to her full breasts.

He noticed.

"But you did not tell the general of the Earl of Wessex's capture. Did you, Philippe?"

His brows furrowed, darkening his mood. "No, however—"

"Then do not tell him," she cajoled with a dainty shake of her head. "You would not have known who the man was if not for me, and you know of my relationship with the emperor." She shrugged. "I will inform Napoleon of your hand in this matter, and he will most likely promote you. Making you an advisor, which means . . ." She paused, stroking his lower lip with her thumb and letting her gaze linger on his mouth. She watched him shudder and try to conceal his desire. He failed. "You will be nearer to me."

The colonel turned her hand, pressing a kiss into her palm. "As you wish, *ma cherie,* but give me a memory to hold while I await our next meeting."

The man surged forward to capture a kiss, but Celeste smoothly retrieved an unmarked lace handkerchief from the folds of her gown, blocking his advance. He accepted her token with obvious frustration.

"Have the Earl of Wessex ready to travel by daybreak. My escort will come to you in the morning." She smiled, dragging her hand down the front of his jacket to lessen his disappointment. The man was very nearly undone, and guilt pressed on her chest. "Thank you, Philippe," she said, fluttering her lashes and slipping into her rooms.

Madame Arnott rushed in from the bedchamber when she closed the heavy door. Worry clung to the older woman's features as her eyes took in the blood spatters on Celeste's silk gown.

"What did the colonel want of you?"

Celeste grabbed the desiccated hands of her old governess and the only mother she had ever known. "I am fine, Marie, but you must pack," Celeste announced before crossing through the sitting room and into the bedchamber. "We are leaving at first light."

"Why?" Madame Arnott asked as she followed. "The emperor wishes for you to evaluate the general and the garrison's efficiency. We have not been here long enough—"

"The colonel has captured the Earl of Wessex," Celeste interrupted, scarcely believing her own words.

The Earl of Wessex had for so long been her hero, and

in the dark hours of the night, her fantasy. She could scarcely believe that he was here and in very real danger.

"No!" The old woman gasped, as if denying the man's capture would make it untrue.

"Yes." Celeste turned her back toward her servant to receive assistance in removing her ruined gown. The older woman's hands moved deftly over the tiny buttons. "And I'm taking him with me at daybreak."

Marie's hands stilled. "You are not serious, *ma petite*? Do you have any idea of the dangerous position in which you are placing yourself?"

Celeste's temper flared. She grabbed the bodice of her now loose gown and tugged it roughly from her slender body. "Of course I am aware of the danger. But I am sick of death, of watching brave men hanged while I look on, a pretty ornament in Napoleon's court."

Old hands grabbed her shoulders and gently turned her to face faded blue eyes. She looked away from her companion, not wanting to be comforted or absolved.

"You have helped so many. Albuera would not have been won if not for the troop locations you gave Lord Beresford. You saved hundreds, perhaps thousands of English lives. Not to mention the other instances where you sent information across the Channel. You cannot save every man, *ma petite*."

"I can save him," Celeste said fiercely. "I am taking Wessex with me, and then I will allow him to escape." She twisted out of the old woman's grasp, full of determination to aid the English war hero.

"No, no! You must not," the older woman implored. "They will begin to suspect you, the daughter of an Englishman."

"And the daughter of a French woman, born and raised in France. I will not be swayed. I need this victory, Marie. Please." She begged her confidant to understand as she sat on the lumpy mattress that had been her bed for the last four nights.

"Why this man? This Wessex?" the old servant asked.

Celeste turned away in confusion, her heart pounding in her chest. She had all but swooned when she realized who sat before her in the interrogation room. How could she explain her connection to the Earl of Wessex? How could she explain that she silently savored his exploits as they were reported in the ballrooms of Paris? Her admiration for a man that fought against his enemy courageously, openly, while she was forced to hide behind a pretty veil.

She could not.

"I don't know. He's so strong and alive. I simply cannot witness, moreover, aid in his destruction." She buried her face in her hands, suddenly overcome with exhaustion. "Not him," she whispered.

Madame Arnott sat on the bed and held Celeste's hand, stroking her back, soothing her. And for a moment the world lifted from her shoulders.

"All right, my sweet. I shall help you free the Englishman, but if we are discovered . . ."

Celeste pulled away from the comforting embrace. Her eyes cooled as hatred clogged her throat. "I know very well what the French do to their enemies." Images of her father being dragged down the stairs by French soldiers rushed back with painful clarity, hardening her heart and her resolve.

"Falcon will not like it," the old woman said.

Celeste felt a flash of trepidation, but she had not remained alive these past four years without developing the ability to push fear aside.

"Falcon will never know. The earl will merely have escaped from the stupid French," she said, untying the dagger she wore strapped to her inner thigh and rolling down silk stockings from her shapely legs.

"But if Wessex returns to England and Falcon questions him about his escape . . ."

"Falcon will never know," Celeste repeated, "and neither will the earl," she said, hiding behind her veil once more. "Now let us pack and get some rest."

•   •   •

Aidan did not sleep. His head was pounding from the slap-dash sewing that had been done to his scalp. He rubbed his temples in a futile attempt to ease the pain as he sat in the dampness and stench of his prison cell, awaiting his fate.

The gallows.

He did not mind the dying. It was the missing of things to come that tightened his chest. No children to play with their cousins. No teaching his son to ride. No giving his daughter's hand in marriage. No wife . . . no wife to welcome him home and ease the emptiness that consumed him.

At least he was not leaving any children behind to grieve him, leaving children to survive his reckless pursuit of glory.

Guilt washed away his bitterness. His father had been the best of men. Noble, generous, loyal—everyone Aidan had ever met confirmed his memories. He rubbed his disloyal thoughts away from his brow with the palm of his right hand. No, his father was a war hero, and Aidan's anger was misplaced. His father had loved him, had loved both his children dearly—but he had loved England more.

That was only right. Men of his position had responsibilities. He alone was responsible for protecting the land entrusted to him by his father. He could not bear the thought of a Frenchman stepping foot in Blackmore Hall. His father had died to prevent that from happening . . . as would he.

Aidan reached into his jacket and pulled out the miniature of Sarah and the twins. His sister would be inconsolable, but her husband, Gilbert, would help her through the worst of her suffering. He smiled as he ran his finger across the image of his niece and nephew. At least he had done his part to ensure that they would live in a free England. The twins would inherit his and Sarah's childhood home. He had made sure of that before leaving for the continent.

His throat constricted as melancholy settled in his chest. He swallowed and stared at the chubby cheeks of his young nephew, wishing he had a son to watch grow to manhood, wishing he had a son to leave the estate to—but it was not to be. He would die for his country, like so many men before him.

Aidan sighed, regretting not dying in battle rather than swinging from a rope. He was not a particularly vain man, but he had killed quite a large number of Frenchmen and would prefer to be remembered for those feats and not his undignified demise.

A legend, the woman had said. He smiled at the thought. Well, the legendary Earl of Wessex had one last duty to perform. Aidan rose and walked to the water basin, carefully removing the bandage that covered the stitching in his head.

He stripped and began to wash himself and his uniform of as much mud and blood as his water basin would allow. If he were to be hanged this day, he would bloody well look like an English gentleman.

At dawn, the doors at the far end of the corridor clanked open. Aidan rose, shaking the stiffness from his legs then straightening his damp cravat. His uniform looked remarkably better after hours of his ministrations, and he was rather pleased with the result.

Two soldiers followed the jailor to his cell, both in dark blue uniforms and both very young. Irritation burned away his fear when he realized the commanding officer had not bothered to escort him to the gallows.

"Follow these men," the jailor ordered, opening the cell. Aidan set his jaw and glared down at the small man who stepped back instinctively. "Watch him carefully," the man cautioned the soldiers.

One of the men pointed toward the entrance of the prison, which was set aglow by the morning sun. Aidan took a step toward the door, only to be shoved in the back by the now-brave soldiers. He stopped in the narrow corridor and turned, warning them with his eyes that another push would not be tolerated.

Aidan straightened himself, determined to die with dignity as he emerged into the sunlight of the muddy courtyard. But his left brow arched when he saw not a hangman, but a demon of darkness masquerading as an angelic blonde.

Surely even the French would not allow a woman to command the garrison. Aidan wondered for a second time who she was.

Beside her stood an old woman dressed entirely in black, and his fair enemy smiled at her, saying, "Did I not tell you that the earl would be a fine prize to present to the emperor? It will be quite entertaining to see this tall tree fall at the foot of France." The young woman's disdainful gaze lingered on him while her troops chuckled at her words.

Aidan smiled with a dark amusement of his own. "Not bloody likely," he sneered, knowing that he would never bow before Bonaparte.

The stunning woman walked toward him, her hips swaying enticingly, her jade eyes sparkling. "When you are a corpse, my lord, you will have very little to say in the matter." Her smile was sweet and swift, dying as she swung around to give instructions to her troops.

"Load him, and guard him well, or you will have me to answer to." Aidan noted the wary looks on the faces of her young soldiers before the ruthless woman climbed into her ornate carriage with the old woman following after her.

Lady Rivenhall was shaking when she settled in the comfort of the garish carriage that had been given her by Napoleon. "Pull the blinds," she said, a bit breathless, as Madame Arnott seated herself opposite her.

Reaching out to pull the thick velvet across the windows, the old woman whispered, "I do not like this. You did not tell me he was so . . ."

Celeste's heart was pounding far too rapidly, which only added to her irritation with herself. "So what? Handsome? I had no idea. He was covered with blood and dirt last night. All I could really see was his size. However, it changes nothing," she said firmly.

"As long as your interest in Wessex is not personal. It does no good to wish for things that will never be, my sweet."

Celeste shook her head as the carriage lurched forward. "Wish for what? I do not expect to live through this war! Much less can I imagine a home with a husband and children."

"Do not lie to me, Celeste," Marie said in clipped tones that revealed her anger. "You fight to end this war so you can have exactly that. The handsome earl is the embodiment of all those hopes and dreams you have buried in your heart. And if he lives, so too will your hopes of that life."

Celeste's chin quivered, and she knew she would soon cry. She closed her eyes to stop the tears and let the numbness take over. "I am going to sleep," she said.

But Celeste did not sleep.

Her mind was filled with the image of the Earl of Wessex as he regally stepped out of the prison. The man had taken her breath away. He was every bit as handsome as she had dreamt him to be. His black hair, now clean, contrasted with his light skin to capture the eye and hold the spectator enthralled. The sable locks were in disarray and curled at the collar, but far from detracting from his looks, it enhanced them, making him more dangerous, more masculine.

And his eyes . . . his eyes were so green the grass would envy them. But when he drew the corners of his lips up to expose a mouth full of white teeth, the appearance of deep dimples had all but made her weak in the knees.

Then she remembered the feel of his bare chest. Surprisingly smooth skin covering hardened, battle ready muscles. Celeste was accustomed to seducing men, to teasing and touching to make them comply with her every wish.

Yet never in her life had she felt such a burning need to

touch a man as she had last night, to unnerve him as much as he did her. True, she had needed to discover his identity, but she need not have been so wantonly seductive in the process. And he had wanted to touch her. They both knew it, and it was that thought that kept her awake most of the night.

Marie had been right. She wanted Wessex to live, wanted to know he survived because of her. The fact that he would never know it was she that had arranged his freedom was of no consequence. The legend would live, and she could dream, and that would be enough. Celeste closed her eyes, filled with new resolve, and slept . . . and dreamed.

It was spring and night still came early.

A large flock of birds echoed from the trees just north of the encampment. A small deserted cottage had been commandeered to sleep the ladies, while the remainder of the guards slept in wagons or tents in the fields surrounding a small garden.

The earl studied the troops. Young and untried, and most assuredly devoted to the beautiful witch that had cast her spell on their young hearts.

"What I wouldn't give to be in that cottage," one of his guards lamented in French as he passed Aidan his dinner, stew and a stale baguette.

"*Oui,* but I think the emperor would object to your enjoying his mistress." The shorter man laughed, and Aidan looked down at his food to hide his shock.

The men left him to eat, which was rather difficult in shackles. But Aidan's mind was not on the tasteless stew, his mind was busy mulling over how to use this new information to his advantage. He broke the stale baguette in half, hoping that the center would prove easier on his teeth. However, his hand stilled when he caught sight of a shimmer of black buried deep in the heart of the loaf.

He glanced at the soldiers seated by the fire several yards away, and removed the gleaming metal. A key? His heart seized, and his brows furrowed in confusion. He looked up and counted his guards, hope swelling in his chest as he slipped the key into the pocket of his trousers. He would need to wait until they slept, which would give him time to plan a stratagem for his escape.

Aidan rolled his blanket into a makeshift pillow and lay down, causing his shackles to sound his movements. The guards glanced in his direction before resuming the game of hazards being played by the campfire. He smiled to himself, filled with the knowledge that he would survive, that he would once again walk the grounds of Blackmore Hall, but all the while wondering who would have given him that key . . . and why?

He considered the question for hours, listening as conversations died, to be replaced by the sound of crickets and a soft breeze. Aidan fished for the key in his pocket and unlocked the shackles on his hands and then his feet. Lifting his head to check that his guards were indeed asleep, he rolled unobserved over the side of the wagon facing the woods. And then he was gone, swallowed by the dark.

Four

❧

Celeste waited anxiously for the sounding of the alarm, but it had not come. *What was Wessex waiting for?* Didn't the man realize he was wasting valuable time? She shifted impatiently in her bed, and then she heard him. He entered the bedchamber so quietly that had she been asleep, she would never have known he was there.

She stifled a scream, but realized he would expect a struggle. Celeste flipped over and reached for her knife, but Wessex was too fast. He had her pinned beneath his powerful thighs with one hand over her mouth and the other clasping her wrists.

"What were you reaching for, Mademoiselle?" he hissed, skimming over the small table to the side of her bed. Then he saw it and released her left hand, oblivious to her blows as he retrieved the knife and held it to her throat.

She stilled.

"You're a deadly one, aren't you? But then I'm sure many of my countrymen have learned that lesson far too late. How many men have died by your graceful hand, I wonder?"

His face hardened, and even in the dim light she could see the rage that he struggled to control.

"I should kill you now," he spat, pressing the tip of the knife into her throat. She winced as the blade pierced her delicate skin, leaving blood oozing from the wound.

Celeste closed her eyes, strangely calm, ready for the final thrust. Penance for all the men she had been unable to save. But if this man, this myth could escape . . . she would happily die for that.

But what was he doing here?

"You . . . you English are more foolish than I had thought. You escape and wander into the middle of the camp you are fleeing from," she whispered. "You will be captured by morning."

"I think not," Wessex said, glaring down at her with contempt. "When the alarm sounds, you will order your men to search the woods and the surrounding areas. When I am not found, they will assume that I have slipped through them. No one would consider looking for me in their own camp."

"And in the morning you will be found and then hanged," she said, hoping for him to see the error in his plan.

"After the forest has been searched, I can escape quite easily."

She admired his logic. None of the soldiers would explore an area that had already been searched. "Leaving me to sound the alarm."

His smile became feral as he bent down over her body. His face was mere inches from hers, causing her breath to shorten considerably.

"You shall not be able to sound any alarm," he whispered.

She shivered beneath him. "Why not just murder me now?"

He laughed softly as he sat back on his haunches. "I need you to speak with your men, both now and when they return from their search of the forest. And if we are discovered . . ." His eyes glittered coldly. "Napolean's mistress will make an excellent hostage."

Celeste inhaled her shock, and in the next moment they heard shouts coming from the direction of the encampment. Before she knew what was happening, he was off the bed and dragging her with him. He twisted her arm painfully behind her and pulled her back into his chest. Her forearm was trapped against the hard contours of his abdomen and the twisted muscles of her own shoulders.

Celeste felt his muscles bunch as he bent down and hissed in her ear. "Order them to search the woods and surrounding areas. Give them two hours, no more." He pressed the knife further into her neck, adding, "One sound and your pretty little throat will be slit, and you will be dead before you hit the floor. Do you understand?"

She nodded and jerked her arm away from his punishing hold. "I need my dressing gown." She took one step toward the garment.

"No. Light that candle," he ordered.

"What do you mean? No!" Celeste felt her face pale. "I cannot allow my men to see me in such a state of undress."

The Earl of Wessex lit the candle and held it up as he circled her, openly and appreciatively examining her body beneath the thin muslin chemise. His smile was lazy, and the hair at the nape of her neck prickled. *Lord, he is handsome.*

"When you open that door to receive the news of my escape, I can assure you that your sergeant will not be looking at your face, mademoiselle, and therefore will see no signs of distress that would force me to kill you both."

His gaze slid to her eyes, and she knew that he would indeed kill them. But then his brows furrowed with confusion. He reached up, touching the wound on her neck. Celeste winced at the sting of it and watched in disbelief when he turned his hand over to examine his bloodstained fingers as if he had not been there to inflict the injury.

Celeste very nearly laughed at the absurdity of the

situation, saying with sarcasm, "Knives are for cutting, my lord."

His eyes locked on hers, but just as she began to read them a crisp knock sounded, causing her to start. Wessex slipped behind the battered door with his knife at the ready, nodding for her to open it.

Celeste grasped the rustic wooden handle and sighed loudly in frustration when the soldier's eyes immediately settled to her breasts.

"Yes, what is it?"

"The prisoner has escaped, Lady Rivenhall."

"You imbeciles," she spat. "How did a man in shackles escape his guard?"

"We do not know, mademoiselle," the man said with a twinge of embarrassment.

Rolling her eyes dramatically, she ordered, "Search the woods and fields. You have two hours. Find him!"

The threat of the consequences of failure sent the man running down the hall. She closed the door and lifted her chin. The earl arched a black brow and stalked toward her.

"You're quite the actress . . . Lady Rivenhall, was it? You're English." She compressed her lips with determined silence, intimidated by the suppressed anger in his voice.

"A traitor and a whore." Wessex lifted her wrists and bound them with the sash of her dressing gown. "My, you are a busy woman," he drawled, then grabbed her chin and stuffed a washcloth in her mouth, cutting her lip on her own teeth in the process.

Her handsome hero lay down on her bed, pulling her after him. Her heart was pounding with fear, and she found herself more afraid to touch him than she had been of his knife. He pulled her flush against his lean body, back to chest, backside to groin.

His large hand splayed over her stomach with the weight of her breasts resting heavily against his thumb. He pressed himself against her derriere, and she heard a soft sigh of satisfaction escape his lips, the undeniable evidence of his desire hardening against her backside.

"Now, isn't this preferable to sleeping in the woods?" he whispered into her hair, his lips almost touching her ear.

A shiver skidded down her spine, forcing her to close her eyes at the incomprehensible pleasure of being held by the Earl of Wessex.

The man did not move, and Celeste remained paralyzed with fear as she contemplated the possible outcomes of this night. But then she felt his even breathing as his arm relaxed against her hip. Her eyes opened wide in disbelief.

The man was going to sleep! A hundred soldiers swarmed around him, searching for him, and he slept!

Lady Rivenhall lay awake for two hours, unjustifiably annoyed with the man that slept beside her. Then the expected knock at her door roused the earl to wakefulness.

She opened the door as before, and the nervous soldier's gaze slipped down to her breasts as he bowed his head in an attempt to look submissive.

"We have searched the woods and the outlying areas, Lady Rivenhall, but have been unable to locate the prisoner."

"Have the guards responsible for the prisoner ready for my inquiry tomorrow morning. There is no use in posting guard tonight. The man will be a great distance from here, unless he is as stupid as our night watch. Leave me." Celeste waved the man away with an air of disgust and slammed the door.

"Well played, Lady Rivenhall. Now, don your boots and, your dressing gown," he commanded, blowing out the candle that had illuminated the small bedchamber.

When she had complied, Wessex lifted her with ease through the window and followed quickly behind. Celeste's fear was overshadowed by anxiety for the earl's safety, knowing that her men were encamped no more than one hundred yards to the east of the cottage. If the guards chanced to look their direction as they ran toward the forest . . .

The earl grabbed her painfully about the upper arm, interrupting her thoughts. "Stay low to the ground and walk, don't run. If you disobey me . . ." He paused, and crouched to the ground when a group of soldiers burst into laughter.

It was difficult to disobey since the man had re-bound and gagged her, but she was amazed by his boldness. Walk! As if she had spoken aloud the earl added, "Any sudden movement or noise will draw their attention, so keep your progress fluid."

They stalked across the open field, clinging to tall grass and the occasional tree. The earl was acutely aware of their surroundings. Every noise or movement drew a turn of his head, along with his attention.

The edge of the wood lay just ahead, and Celeste prayed, for his sake, that he would leave her and take flight. But he did not. They continued walking for what seemed like hours before he stopped and removed the muslin sash and gag.

She drew in a deep breath as if to scream, but he stopped her with his words. "Your troops cannot hear you." She sensed his satisfaction. "The only things that will respond to your cries are wolves."

Celeste laughed out loud. "Wolves are hardly more dangerous than my present situation, my lord."

"Quite true. Nevertheless, deserters and criminals might venture into the forest to locate the source of such a feminine howl." He threw something at her feet, and the moon captured a glint of steel.

Her knife.

Wessex turned to leave, but hesitated. He stalked toward her, grasping her about the throat with his right hand and thrusting her against the nearest tree.

Celeste's heart slammed against her chest. Her hero was going to murder her after all. It came as a bit of a shock, even though she had known it to be a possibility.

"If you were not a woman, I would kill you for what you have done to my men." And then his lips were covering hers, punishing her as he pressed them painfully and purposefully against her teeth. She thrashed from side to side to catch her breath, but he held her.

His enemy.

But with a suddenness that took her breath away, the kiss altered. His lips softened, became supple, pliant. They moved over her leisurely, drinking in the contours of her mouth. She was shaking with pleasure, and she sensed his understanding, his concurrence that at that moment in time they were simply man and woman.

He lifted his head and peered down at her, his eyes shielded by the darkness.

"Au revoir, Lady Rivenhall," he whispered, still holding her by the throat. "May you burn in hell for what you have done to my countrymen."

Her enemy once again.

The Earl of Wessex stepped away and began walking in the opposite direction of the camp. Frustrated by the knowledge that he would never know it was she that had freed him, Celeste reached for her knife and hurled it at the tree to the left of his head. The sound of the knife embedding in the wood caused Wessex to stop and turn to look at her standing thirty odd feet away.

"Quite deadly," he said with a contemptuous sneer.

Lady Rivenhall watched her hero turn and disappear into the dense underbrush of the forest, waiting until he was out of sight before she gloried in her victory. She grinned, feeling more relief and joy than she could have imagined. The Earl of Wessex would live, the embodiment of masculinity, integrity, courage, and honor . . . in short, an English gentleman.

Five

✦

LONDON, ENGLAND
JUNE 23, 1811

Aidan Duhearst, Earl of Wessex, stood propping up the gilded walls of the gaming room at Lord Reynolds's annual ball.

Since his return from the peninsula, he had been recuperating at his estates in Wessex, and it had nearly killed him. If his physicians had their way, he would be there still, but Aidan could no longer sit on his backside, quiescent as the French swept through Europe.

He looked about, tugging at his black evening jacket and thinking how much more comfortable he felt in his uniform. His sister had hounded him into attending the ball in the hopes of raising his spirits. But the grand events that had for so long been a central entertainment of his life now seemed insignificant and hollow.

He lifted his champagne flute to his lips, wishing it were filled with something stronger. Aidan sighed and studied the crowded ballroom. Beautiful women scurried past him, adorned with a king's ransom in jewels and silk. He smiled politely, knowing the ladies had no idea what was befalling their brothers and sons on the battlefields of Europe. Men were dying so that the privileged London elite could continue living the opulent lifestyle they now enjoyed.

Aidan stared at the fastidious dandies who were so careful to wear the latest fashions. He wondered how the pink-waistcoated gentleman to his left would react to blood seeping through his precious silk as a bullet lodged in his chest. But, of course, none of these men would ever know, as they made damn sure to pay other men to fight for their estates.

Men Aidan had watched die.

Disgusted, he took another sip of champagne, contemplating how soon he would be able to leave without increasing his sister's concern for him. All he wanted to do was drain himself between the thighs of the most readily available woman, and then return to his own bed.

"Damnation," he swore under his breath when silver eyes locked on his.

Aidan pushed away from the wall, his first instinct to make a dash for the door. However, he remained where he stood, waiting for the man who was so intent on speaking with him to arrive at his side.

"Wessex," the huge man acknowledged, peering into his eyes as if he might find the answers he sought.

"Glenbroke," Aidan said, nodding a courteous welcome to the duke. "I don't suppose there is any chance of your telling my sister that you spoke with me and that I am enjoying the ball immensely?"

Gilbert de Clare clasped his hands behind his back and looked over the heads of the twirling couples on the crowded dance floor. "Not likely, I'm afraid. I have never been able to lie convincingly to my wife, and I fear her wrath far more than I fear yours."

Aidan chuckled, exposing his dimples. "She does have a temper, does she not?"

"Ruthless—she threatened to quit my bed if I did not seek you out." The duke's luminescent eyes held amusement mingled with a deeper affection that Aidan could not help but envy.

"Oh, the little hellcat does know where to hit a man."

Aidan joined his brother-in-law in watching the decorative couples dance past mountains of flowers and food, food he would have killed for on the peninsula.

The duke leaned toward him as the two men stood shoulder to shoulder. "How are you, Aidan?" Gilbert asked, his voice quiet.

Aidan could feel his jaw clenching as he attempted to sound serene. "I am well, Gilbert."

The Duke of Glenbroke was not deceived, and his eyes narrowed with concern. "It is this for which you have been fighting, Aidan. Our way of life," the man said astutely, understanding the bent of his thoughts.

"I realize that, Your Grace. However, one cannot help but wonder if our 'way of life' is worth the cost. And despite Sarah's desire to see me enjoy myself tonight, I cannot seem to muster any enthusiasm for dancing after witnessing my friends' limbs being hacked away from their bodies."

The duke remained silent, for there was nothing he could say.

Aidan turned his head, pushing the memories aside. "Sorry, old man. No need for both of us to be miserable."

Gilbert smiled and gave Aidan's shoulder an affectionate squeeze. "It's all right, old boy. But I must warn you, your sister has decided that you should marry."

He groaned. "Bloody hell."

"She thinks if you marry and begin a family it will lessen the pain of the destruction you witnessed at Albuera. I believe she has even picked your bride."

Aidan's eyes flew to his brother-in-law's. "My bride?"

The duke laughed. "Yes, and I must say I wholeheartedly agree with her selection."

"Dear God, even my own kind has turned against me. You traitorous bastard," he teased. "Very well, who is this paragon of the fairer sex?"

"Oh, no." The duke held up both hands. "Perish the thought that I should ruin all your sister's clandestine plans for seeing you happily wed." Gilbert chuckled. "You shall just have to attend dinner Saturday next in accordance with Sarah's matrimonial schedule."

Aidan took another sip of champagne, murmuring, "Perhaps the French were not all that bad."

"Eight o'clock sharp, and do not even consider . . ."

But Aidan was not listening. His eyes fell on a woman standing on the far side of the ballroom. He could not see her face clearly for she stood at an angle, but something about her . . .

He tensed as the golden-haired woman turned to receive a note from a footman. He watched her read the missive and then discreetly slip the communiqué into the bodice of her lavender ball gown.

"Aidan?"

He realized the duke had called his name several times, but he had not heard him. He continued watching the woman as she looked about then retreated into the recesses of Lord Reynolds's home.

Rage shot through him like a flash of lightning. He shoved his glass at Gilbert, splashing champagne all over the duke's exquisitely cut evening jacket.

"Wessex!"

He ignored the cry as he pushed his way through the crush, focusing intently on the retreating figure elegantly clad in a shimmering silk gown.

Aidan followed with caution, waiting to ascend the stairs until the fair woman had done so herself. It could not be her, his rational self argued. But his senses had been sparked, and now his gut was contradicting his mind.

He reached the second floor of Lord Reynolds's townhome just in time to observe the woman entering the last room on the left of the corridor. The hall was dark, having been made so to indicate that this area was out of bounds to guests.

His booted feet fell silent on the lush chartreuse carpeting as he approached the door and he noticed that it had been left ajar. Aidan glanced down the hall and then listened to the soft noises emanating from deep inside the chamber. He pushed the door open and slid into the large room, twisting the knob before closing the mahogany door and slowly releasing the latch.

His efforts were rewarded. The woman did not hear him as she searched the small writing desk on the opposite side of the room. Aidan surveyed his surroundings, looking to block any possible means of escape.

An ornate four-poster bed dominated the large room, with a massive armoire to its right. A blue brocade settee and a large chair of quality leather sat at an angle in front of the marble fireplace. The long windows opposite the door were flanked by luxurious midnight blue velvet drapes, which mirrored the colors woven into the intricate pattern of the oval Aubusson carpet.

The only other exit from the bedchamber was the double doors that led to the adjoining sitting room. His lips curled in a malicious grin as he crept toward her.

He was surprised by the depth of loathing he felt for this woman, this siren that lured men to their deaths by seducing them with her deceptively angelic beauty.

"I see a frog has leapt the pond and landed upon our fair shores," he said ferociously.

Lady Rivenhall stiffened and bolted for the sitting room doors, but they were locked. She spun, lifting her skirts to run, and Aidan was on her, pressing her into the paneled wood while grasping the wrist of the hand that now held her knife.

Aidan could feel her breast rising against his chest. He looked down into her blue-green gaze and saw no fear, only calculation. He held her cold eyes as he squeezed her wrist until he thought it would break, before she finally relinquished her weapon. There was a reason the French had sent this woman, he thought with reluctant admiration. Aidan was disgusted with himself for admiring any aspect of this traitor, and his revulsion quickly dissolved into anger.

"Why are you here, Lady Rivenhall?" he asked with one brow quirked above empty green eyes.

"I became lost and wandered into this area of the house," the woman replied with no hint of anxiety.

Aidan scoffed, and shook his head. "Why are you in *England,* my lady?" The heat from her bare neck and shoulders rose to warm his down-turned face.

"I am a British citizen, my lord."

"Yet you fight against the freedom that citizenship provides," he stated as a matter of course, wondering who else was fighting against that freedom. "Who sent the note?"

Her eyes remained blank and unreadable. "What note?"

She gasped when his hand dove into her bodice. Aidan traced the curve of her breast as his fingers searched for the concealed missive.

"This note," he whispered, feeling the folded parchment.

He wrapped his finger around the paper that lay beneath her breast then slowly withdrew it, unable to avoid grazing her nipple, which had hardened to an enticing peak. She shuddered against him, and Aidan felt a primal satisfaction at her response before he opened the note and read the brief communiqué.

First floor, east wing, last door on the left.

He pulled himself from her lithe body, gripping her arm as he hauled her toward the bed. He needed to search her, and the bed was the nearest place to conduct the examination. He pushed her down on the colorful counterpane, exactly where he wanted her, then stopped.

He looked down at his stunning enemy and realized that she was indeed where he wanted her. He closed his eyes to purge the seductive image only to open them when he heard her scramble toward the door. He leapt, catching her arm before she reached the far side of the bed.

Aidan rolled her over and held both wrists above her head as he lowered himself on top of the struggling woman, crushing her into the mattress. Her face relaxed with shock, and he was darkly pleased to see the fear behind those aqua eyes.

He wanted her to feel a portion of the fear her captives felt before being hanged . . . the fear he had felt. Only then would he turn her over to the authorities.

He reached down and lifted her skirt, telling himself that it was necessary, crucial, that she be searched. His hand caressed her calf then drifted up the outer portion of her right leg as the lady stubbornly held his gaze. Aidan's fingers skimmed her inner thigh until he encountered the sheath for her deadly knife.

"Do you have any other weapons?" he asked, holding on by the fingernails to his gentlemanly ideals by giving her the opportunity to end the search.

She said nothing, and he cursed her stubbornness. He placed his hand on the delicate bone of her other ankle and started drifting up her leg. Aidan looked into his enemy's eyes, and his baser instincts took over, much as they had on the peninsula, much as he feared they always would.

He fought against it, his hand pausing on her upper thigh. "Do you have any other weapons, Lady Rivenhall?" He stared at her lips.

"No," she breathed, staring at his.

It was more that he could take.

"Damn you," he whispered, unsure if he was cursing her or himself, then dropped his head to taste the traitor who had haunted his dreams and nightmares. But his head snapped up when he heard feminine laughter mere feet from the mahogany door. He leapt off the bed, shoving Lady Rivenhall behind the armoire.

His back pressed against the wood, and his left shoulder fell flush to the stenciled wall. There was a good six inches of the armoire to his right. It should be enough to conceal them, provided the visitors did not venture too far into the large room.

Aidan pulled the treacherous woman into his body, one hand splayed across her abdomen while the other clamped firmly over her mouth. Her back rested against his chest, so he was forced to bend forward and whisper.

"If you scream—" His threat was cut short when the inebriated couple stumbled into the bedchamber.

"Oh, Jonathan. What a lovely room," a woman observed.

"Do you like it?" the man asked, followed by the hiss of a silk cravat being pulled off its wearer's neck. "My wife chose the color."

"It's very restive."

Silk rustled, and the woman giggled when the man said, "Not for long. Come here, you wicked wench." More rustling. "Ahh, Fiona, you have the most superb heavers that I have ever seen."

Aidan tried desperately to block out Lord Reynolds's words, but it was difficult when the weight of Lady Rivenhall's breast rested against his hand.

Lord Reynolds moaned, obviously kissing the objects of his adoration. "You fit perfectly in my hand . . . and my mouth," he said, and the woman cried out in delight.

The traitor in his arms tensed, her breathing becoming low and shallow. The back of Aidan's thumb grazed her breast, and he pulled her closer to his body. He could feel her backside against his groin, but when her nipple hardened at his touch, Aidan forgot why they were voyeurs to this little scene.

"Take off that damn gown," Lord Reynolds demanded, his breathing ragged. "I want to feel your skin warming mine."

Aidan's hand slipped from Lady Rivenhall's mouth to her throat so that the woman might breathe, or so he told himself. But when his fingers felt the heat of her throat, his hand continued to descend until he found himself reaching beneath the bodice of her gown to cup her breast.

Her slow intake of air was only audible to him, but it spoke as loudly of her desire as her nipple hardening against his palm. His movements were languid and silent as he began kneading her. He rolled her peak between his fingers and felt her head fall back against his shoulder in silent encouragement.

"You like that, don't you?" Lord Reynolds asked.

Aidan could only imagine what the man was doing to the lady on his bed, could only imagine what sensual caresses would stir Lady Rivenhall to scream with carnal satisfaction.

"Oh, yes, Jonathan. Don't stop, please," the woman cried.

"I'm so hard for you Fiona. Oh, that's it, yes."

Aidan gritted his teeth. He had been to bordellos that were less stimulating than this. His hand continued cupping Lady Rivenhall's breast as he rocked his arousal against her delectable derriere.

"I need to be inside of you, Fiona. Now," the man begged.

Aidan's lips fell to Lady Rivenhall's neck, as Lord Reynolds thrust into his paramour, eliciting a sensual moan. The feel of her breast in his hand and the taste of her warm flesh set Aidan's heart to pounding.

He kissed the length of her elegant neck, but when he felt her backside rubbing rhythmically against his shaft, he nearly came undone. Aidan bit his lip to stifle a moan of pleasure, and began moving with her, against her.

Lord Reynolds shouted, "Oh, God," when he reached his peak and then fell silent. The only sound in the room was the huffs of exertion from the lovers and Aidan's own heartbeat as it pounded in his ears.

"Fiona, you are the most wanton piece I have ever bedded," their host panted.

"Thank you, Jonathan. Oh, damnation, is that the time?" the woman asked anxiously, accompanied by frantic rustling. "My husband will be looking for me. I was to meet him in the garden at midnight."

"Turn 'round, and I'll lace you." More shuffling. "I want you all evening on Thursday."

A kiss and a giggle. "Very well, my lord."

The door opened and closed, leaving Aidan alone with

Lady Rivenhall. He withdrew his hand from her bodice and closed his eyes, trying to regain some semblance of control. His breathing was becoming steady, but he realized his other hand still held her crushed to his aching body.

The woman was so damn desirable. He trembled with the overwhelming need to drag her to the rumpled bed and make love to her, trembled just as Napoleon must have shaken.

She was the emperor's mistress, Napoleon's woman.

Aidan grasped her upper arm and spun her to face him. "We seem to have a knack for escaping detection. However, I'm afraid I must insist you accompany me to His Majesty's Foreign Office."

He began to step away from the armoire when her hand flew to his chest in frantic appeal.

"Wait."

Aidan looked down at the fair woman and was startled to see desire lingering on her refined features.

"Not yet," she whispered. "Take me in a moment, but not yet." Aidan stood frozen as her crimson lips pressed to his. Confusion, desire, and rage battled for rule of his mind, but then she pressed her exquisite body to his, and desire won the day.

He could delay for a moment—after all, how could she escape if she were in his arms, if she were beneath him? Aidan surged into her mouth, stroking the soft heat with his tongue and reveling in the taking of Napoleon's woman.

She tasted just as he remembered and had spent long nights trying to forget. It had taken nine days to find a British regiment, and nine nights of being haunted by his ethereal captor. His desire for her was reprehensible, and he had convinced himself that it was his months of celibacy that were to blame.

But now, as he held her in his arms, the women who had warmed his bed since his return vanished from his mind. He circled her tongue, the movement echoing his own spiraling desire. One hand drifted to her breast, and the other fell to her rounded backside. He kneaded and caressed, pulling her against his throbbing shaft.

Lady Rivenhall's hands roamed over his chest and abdomen. She stood on her tiptoes, kissing him eagerly, hungrily. The armoire shifted beneath their arduous embrace, and her hands drifted to his neck so that she might have a better taste of him.

Aidan winced at her touch, hissing in pain.

Lady Rivenhall pulled away from his lips, asking, "What happened?"

"Your ring cut my neck," he said as he looked down at the enticing woman's swollen lips, at her full breasts, and the pain retreated into the far recesses of his mind. "No matter. Where were we?"

He took her mouth and invaded her. She made soft mewling noises, as her hands stroked his back and then descended to his backside. Undone by her bold caress, Aidan tore away from her lips and kissed down her neck to the delightful mounds of flesh revealed by her lavender gown.

It would not be long before her tightened nipple was in his mouth as she lay naked beneath him. The thought made him lightheaded, and then the candles flickered. He blinked several times in confusion and then looked at the stunning woman before him.

"You bitch," he mumbled, and just before sinking into unconsciousness, the Earl of Wessex remembered that Lady Rivenhall was a traitor . . . and quite deadly.

Six

❧

"*Well?*"

"Nothing," Celeste said with a shake of her head. She stripped her hands of white gloves and allowed Madame Arnott to unlace her demure gown. "I searched his study as well as his bedchamber and dressing room. There was nothing. And after meeting Lord Reynolds, I would say the man thinks of nothing more than horses and whores. I would be astonished if he were the man we have been asked to find."

"But you cannot be sure."

"I will not be sure of any of them until we have the traitor in custody," she answered, stepping out of her petticoats and laying them on the brocade chair. "However, I'm afraid we have a much bigger problem on our hands."

Madame Arnott picked up the gown, examining the crushed flounces as if trying to understand how so much damage could have been done in one evening.

"Yes, and what is that?"

"The Earl of Wessex."

"What?" The crunch of black taffeta erupted in the room as Madame Arnott walked to stand in front of Celeste, the damaged gown forgotten. "He was reported to be recuperating at his estate in Wessex!"

"Well, he is here, and I can assure you the man is fully recovered." A flash of heat skidded up her spine and deposited itself in her cheeks. "He discovered me searching Lord Reynolds's bedchamber and was quite determined to turn me over to the authorities."

"How did you escape him?" Marie's eyes widened with concern.

Celeste's cheeks turned positively red. "I drugged him," she said. "He should awaken in two or three hours." Celeste sat at her dressing table and began unpinning her golden hair, trying not to remember the feel of his warm lips, his masculine hands. "I shall need to contact Falcon. I see no alternative, do you?"

"No." Madame Arnott picked up the sterling silver brush and stroked the blond strands that fell to Celeste's waist, her intelligent blue eyes considering the possible effects the Earl of Wessex might have on their mission. "You are in a great deal of danger, *ma petite*. We must devise a plan to neutralize Wessex."

"I know," Celeste answered, staring at Marie's reflection in the mirror, but she could not imagine any action that would turn the powerful earl from his course.

However, one thing was certain: She would see the Earl of Wessex again, and Celeste wondered if she would be able to resist her attraction to the very man who threatened her mission and her life.

Aidan Duhearst woke at half past three in the morning, thoroughly delighted to be alive. His mathematical cravat had dissipated into an incongruous mass, and his normally tidy black hair was as rumpled as his clothes.

He pushed himself to a standing position, but had to lean against the armoire when the room began to spin. Aidan waited for the ride to cease before staggering out into the dimly lit hallway, where he found himself face-to-face with Lord Reynolds. The young lord's coffee-colored curls hid eyebrows raised in surprise.

"Had a bit of a romp, did you, Wessex?"

Aidan smiled while raking his fingers through his hair, forming a makeshift comb. "Excellent event, Lord Reynolds," he replied, hoping the evasive answer would satisfy.

"Quite," the older man chuckled. "Had my own sample of muslin a few hours ago."

"If you don't mind, Lord Reynolds," Aidan said, affecting an exaggerated yawn. "I believe I shall retire to my own home."

"Not at all, old man. I'm for bed myself. Good evening."

The men parted company, and Aidan found himself walking out of the large double doors and onto St. James Street. The earl sent up a silent prayer of thanks when he spotted his landau some twenty yards down the road.

"Home, please," he grunted, pulling himself into the luxurious conveyance, and ignored the widening of the coachman's eyes at his master's less than meticulous attire.

Aidan sank into the sage squabs, touching the cut on his neck. It was sore, and he could feel the blood that had pooled at the wound. Whatever drug she had used was very powerful, and she had most assuredly used it before tonight.

But why hadn't she killed him? He could identify her. And while she might not have had a lethal poison on hand, she certainly could have used her knife once he had lost consciousness. She must have been interrupted, for he was sure that Napoleon's mistress would not hesitate to kill a man.

The woman was deadly, and if he did not find her soon she would pass on information that would condemn British troops fighting the French. He did not doubt her ability to extract information from men since she was willing to use her body to lure and entice.

He himself had been weak, overpowered the moment he

pulled her body to his. The moment he felt her breast, her backside, his lips against her silky neck, he'd been lost.

Bloody hell!

Aidan shook away the wave of desire that washed over him. She was beautiful, but she was a traitor, a woman who bedded Napoleon himself, a woman who betrayed her country and led its young men to slaughter.

Blood surged through his body, but this time anger was its cause. He vowed that when he saw her next he would remember his men. Men who fought for England, brave men who lay dying in the filthy streets of Albuera while Napoleon's troops walked among them, skewering the wounded with their swords.

Aidan would never forgive himself for surviving, for being taken captive while his men were robbed and then mercilessly slaughtered. Men who gave their lives to defend the Earl of Wessex; men of lesser title, men of lesser ancestry, but men far more worthy of God's grace.

Yet, he knew why he had survived.

God had given him Lady Rivenhall. Given him the opportunity to avenge his men and protect the crown. And in that moment and before God, he swore that she would not pass information to the French . . . even if he were forced to kill her to stop it.

A banging on his front door awakened the Duke of Glenbroke from an exceptionally peaceful rest. He carefully withdrew his arm from beneath his wife's head in hopes that she would remain asleep. Not that there was much danger of her waking, for his duchess slept like the dead.

The silk of his dressing gown felt cold as he shrugged it over his nude body and stepped into the darkened hallway.

"Who is it, Simkins?" he asked his loyal servant, who had managed to appear in pressed trousers and jacket as if he had never retired.

"The Earl of Wessex is awaiting your presence in the study, Your Grace."

"Thank you." Gilbert's bare feet padded down the stairs and across the marble floor to his study.

He tried to still the anxiety that was pounding at his heart. It was four o'clock in the morning, and Aidan was not the sort of man to interrupt his rest without a damn good reason.

"Aidan, what is so important—" The duke broke off and pulled at Aidan's loose cravat with his fingers. "What the devil?" Gilbert's smile broadened as he observed the rumpled hair and disheveled attire of his handsome brother-in-law. "Damnation, Aidan, you disappeared, and your sister spent half the evening searching for you. She would not be pleased to know that you have been tumbling a lady in Lord Reynolds's own—"

"Gilbert, I must speak with you." Glenbroke's eyes narrowed at the severe tone of his brother-in-law's voice. He waited for Aidan to continue.

"What have you heard of a Lady Rivenhall?"

Gilbert shrugged his large shoulders. "Which one? There are several."

"Blonde, blue green eyes, young?"

"Sorry." Gilbert shook his head. "But she does not sound familiar." He raised both brows, a large grin spreading across his face. "Why do you wish to know, Aidan? Did the lady perchance make this mark on your neck?" He chuckled, but stopped abruptly when his brother-in-law's eyes became as cold as the emeralds they resembled.

"Yes, however, not for the reason you have assumed. Do you recall the details of my escape from the French encampment?"

Aidan watched the Duke of Glenbroke straighten to his full height. Gilbert's jaw pulsed with tension as he waited for Aidan to continue, luminescent silver gray eyes sharpening to give his full attention to the subject being discussed.

"Most of them, yes."

"Napoleon's paramour, who questioned me at Albuera, was none other than Lady Rivenhall." Aidan's lip curled with contempt. "An English-born lady who was searching Lord Reynolds's bedchamber not more than four hours ago."

The duke's eyes narrowed with shock. "Are you certain?"

"Positive." The men stared at one another until the duke's head began to nod.

"Very well, then," Gilbert said, his demeanor hardening. "Give me the details of the lady in question. Tomorrow I shall meet with a man who might be able to answer our inquires pertaining to the Lady Rivenhall. In the meantime, stay on your guard. At present you are likely the only person who can identify her as a French agent." Gilbert held his eyes, both men understanding the seriousness of the situation.

"I shall await your summons, Your Grace." Aidan bowed and left his sister's home in favor of more elusive game.

Seven

❧

When is the admiral leaving?" the dark man asked.

"Tuesday." The woman walked toward him, wrapping her plump arms around his waist. "But I could not wait so long to see you, darling."

The man looked down at the homely chit in his arms as if she were Aphrodite incarnate. Her upturned nose and droopy eyes reminded him of a pig, and her mousy brown hair lacked even a luster that might cause one to overlook the drab color.

Fortunately, the girl had an exceptional body, which was most likely why the admiral had married her. That, and her enormous dowry.

"Where is he now?"

"Do not concern yourself, dearest. Alfred is attending a meeting at Whitehall and informed me that he would be away for the majority of the day." The girl traced the scar on his jaw with her finger and smiled. "We have all morning to enjoy one another."

The man looked into her dark blue eyes as if he adored

her. He placed his palm on her cheeks, wrapping his fingers around the nape of her neck as he drew her to him. If he wanted to search the admiral's study, he needed to get her out of the way, and the fastest way of doing that was to tire the girl out.

"I need you, Sophie," he whispered just before slanting his mouth over hers. He kissed her hungrily in an attempt to hurry the process along. "I love you, Sophie. You are all I think about, all I want."

He placed his hand over her breast, causing the girl to gasp out loud. He caressed her and then pushed the bodice of her gown down, feigning impatience. His nimble fingers unlaced her corset, and he reminded himself to leave her addicted to his touch. She stepped out of her skirts, tossing her gown to the floor, and returned, nude, to his arms.

He rolled her hardened nipple between his fingers as he nipped at her neck. She moaned, as he knew she would, and pressed her hips toward him, offering herself as she always did. The stupid cow thought she was in love with him, and, more foolishly, thought he was in love with her.

She pushed off his jacket and unbuttoned his cerulean satin waistcoat. Her hands tore at his white linen shirt until he stood before her bare-chested. She lowered her mouth to one dark disk, raking her teeth across his nipple. He smiled to himself. He had taught her many things, and what the girl lacked in looks she made up for in enthusiasm.

"Turn around," he ordered.

The woman complied, willing to do anything he asked, just as he had trained her to do. His eyes roved over her elegant back and rounded backside, causing his shaft to harden. He walked up behind her and reached around to grasp her breast with one hand while caressing her derriere with his other.

"You are so beautiful," he whispered as he rubbed the evidence of his desire against her. She shuddered in his arms and he bent his head to her neck. He continued to fondle her and was not surprised when her hand reached back to grab at his cock now straining against his breeches.

"You know exactly how to touch me," he said to the girl as she began rubbing his shaft with unconcealed longing. "Is this what you want?" he asked, pressing his hand to hers as she continued to explore his length.

"Yes," she whispered. "I need you, my love."

He removed his boots and breeches while she turned to watch, her eyes reflecting her lust for his powerful body. He looked at the pink nipples of her generous breasts, and then his eyes drifted to her face. A mistake. His cock began to wither.

"Get on the bed, darling, the way I like to have you."

The chit scrambled onto the mattress and rested on her knees. He joined her on the vermilion counterpane and grabbed both her breasts before gently pushing her forward. Her dark curls glistened with her desire, making it easy to slide a finger into her.

"Have you been waiting for me, darling? Do you think of me when your husband is inside of you?"

"Yes," she breathed.

"Are you ready for me?" he continued, arousing her with languid strokes.

"Yes," she said, gasping, and then pushed herself backward, begging him to fill her.

He placed his cock at the entrance of her sex. The girl shuddered with anticipation, and he waited a moment before he impaled her, sheathing himself to the hilt. She shouted with pleasure, and he began banging away at her from behind, stimulating her body with his hands until she found his rhythm.

The girl screamed with each thrust, and he was sure the servants would hear, but he continued to drive into her until, mercifully, he felt his own body responding. He grasped her about the hips and buried himself, spilling his seed in an uninspired climax.

He pulled the girl into his arms still panting from his exertion. Her back was to him, but he could see that she would not sleep and was content just being held. He gritted his teeth and groaned to himself, knowing she would require more.

"I love you," he whispered, kissing her on the neck. He closed his eyes and imagined the pretty blond whore he had rogered on Saturday.

He rolled the admiral's wife over and took her breast in his mouth. She moaned. He stretched himself out on top of her and was thankful for the difference in height so that he would not have to look at her unappealing face.

He spread her thighs and drove into her, intentionally keeping his movements slow so they would be occupied for an extended period. He did not find it difficult to delay his pleasure.

Sweat began gathering at the small of his back, and he was becoming bored. He nibbled the girl's nipple and began to drive more forcefully. She screamed, and he felt her body clutching at his cock.

He closed his eyes and imagined the blonde harlot and all that they had done together. The places she had put her mouth, the way she had used her tongue. He would visit her again, he decided, as he came into the ugly woman beneath him.

This time she slept.

The man rose and donned his shirt and breeches, quietly slipping out of the bedchamber. He walked cautiously toward the ground floor study, making sure to avoid the household servants.

"What meeting have you gone to today, admiral?" the man wondered aloud, knowing no rumors of invasion had been bandied about Whitehall.

His powerful legs strode toward a large oak desk on the far side of the room. The desktop was immaculate. No letters or calendars to reveal the subject of the admiral's meeting.

The man shuffled the items on top of the desk, and a beautifully carved sterling silver letter opener caught his eye. He grabbed it and shoved it in his pocket—payment for teaching the homely chit how to please a man.

His attention turned to the desk drawers, but he only found references to supply ships' schedules and ship cargo capacity.

"Damn," he said through clenched teeth, knowing he would be paid, but not well, for such information.

He needed to provide troop movements and locations if he wanted to become a rich man. The admiral had proved most disappointing as a source of information. He poured himself an expensive scotch and contemplated how to end his association with the admiral's wife without having the cow blubbering about their relationship to all of her foppish friends.

Thus far, he had simply threatened not to meet with her if she whispered a word about him to anyone. The girl had been so eager to have him in her bed that she dared not even look at him if they were attending the same functions. However, if he were to end their dalliance she would undoubtedly seek him out, perhaps in public.

That he could not allow.

He really had but two options. Invent an excuse for the end of the affair that the girl would accept or . . . kill the stupid bitch.

Eight

"You're not having another one?" the Duchess of Glenbroke asked, appalled.

"I bloody well am," Lady Juliet Pervill nodded, raising her hand to order her second lemon ice at Gunter's.

"Juliet, I wish you would stop using such language," Lady Felicity Appleton admonished. "And if you don't stop eating like this, you will become as big as a house and never secure an offer."

"Another lemon ice please," Juliet said to the waiter, completely ignoring her cousin. When the man had left, she turned to Felicity, saying, "You know I can eat anything and not gain an ounce, and as for a husband . . ." Juliet snorted. "No man has ever looked at me, so perhaps becoming as large as a house will gain me some attention."

"Juliet, you are quite attractive, as well you know," the duchess said.

Lady Pervill rolled her eyes. "I am, at best, average, Sarah, and when I stand next to Felicity, I become absolutely drab. You need not sugarcoat the situation. So, unless small-busted, freckled mathematicians have become all the rage with the ton, I shall count myself lucky that I am rich."

"Oh, Juliet," Lady Appleton said, defeated.

"Some men adore freckles."

"Yes, Sarah, but more men prefer beautiful blondes with spectacular figures and soulful brown eyes." They turned in unison to look at Felicity. "Any offers this week, cousin? Or was that Greek God the last?"

Lady Appleton blushed becomingly. "You know Lord Summers was the last man to honor me, Juliet. Might we forego the browbeating and discuss something else?"

"Delighted." Juliet injected more sarcasm into the one word than most people used in a lifetime. She turned toward Sarah. "I heard that the Earl of Wessex is back in town. I can only assume that Aidan is recovered? You must be relieved."

Sarah's eyes narrowed, and the ever-sensitive Felicity saw it. "You're still worried about him." It was a statement. "Why? I thought the physician said he would recover."

"He has, physically. It's just . . ."

"What?" Juliet prodded.

Sarah sighed. "My brother is not the same man who left England. You know Aidan—elegant, meticulous, generous, controlled." She shook her head, knowing she was not making any sense. "But now, he is temperamental, agitated . . . I don't know—unhappy." Felicity stroked her arm, and tears welled in Sarah's green eyes. "He has lost a stone of weight, if not more." She covered her mouth with her napkin and swallowed a sob.

"Have you spoken with him?" Juliet asked, always the pragmatist.

"Yes, but all he says is that he is well, and he won't speak with Gilbert because he knows Gilbert will relay the information to me."

"What about Christian?" Felicity asked. "I'm sure that Lord St. John would be more than happy to help."

Juliet clicked her tongue. "Christian is not capable of handling a serious situation such as this." She turned to Sarah. "No, better to talk to Daniel. I spoke with his brother Monday last, and he said that Viscount DunDonell is due back from Scotland any day."

"Yes." Sarah began to smile as she thought of their childhood companion. "Daniel would deal with Aidan's melancholy. The viscount can be quite determined when he wishes to be."

"Determined!" Juliet blurted. "The man is the most stubborn Scot to wander the highlands in the last century!"

"Juliet, don't be unkind. Persistence can be a virtue," Felicity pointed out.

"Well, when next I see DunDonell I shall have to tell him that he is the most virtuous man that I have ever met."

"Oh, that reminds me," Sarah said, looking at Juliet as she dabbed at her red nose. "I'm having a dinner party Saturday evening, and you are both invited."

"That sounds lovely." Juliet turned to her cousin. "Doesn't it, Felicity?"

"Yes, it does. However, I am afraid I have accepted an invitation to a soiree that . . ."

"Oh, Felicity, no one will notice if you are not there." Juliet turned to Sarah for assistance.

"Please, Felicity? Aidan will be coming to dinner and I want to surround my brother with friends who will support him during this difficult time."

Felicity's eyes softened to the color of chocolate mixed with a generous amount of cream. She leaned forward. "Of course I shall come, Sarah. It is my honor to dine with such a distinguished hero of the Peninsular campaign."

"Eight?" Juliet asked, smiling in satisfaction but trying to conceal it behind her lemon ice.

"Yes, eight." Sarah glanced at the cousins, thankful to have such loyal friends.

Viscount DunDonell, Daniel McCurren, had been in town for no more than two hours when he received a visit from his lifelong friend, the Duchess of Glenbroke. The beautiful duchess conveyed her concern for her brother's well-being and begged Daniel to speak with Aidan to discover the cause of his distress.

Alarmed, Daniel dashed off a note to his closest friend, informing Aidan of his return from Scotland and requesting his company at their club later that evening.

So, here he sat with a brandy in one hand as he stared with apprehension at the black lacquered doors, mulling over the disturbing information Sarah had confided in him.

"Another," he said to a passing footman, holding up his now-empty glass.

Aidan Duhearst was by far the strongest of them all; he had always been a voice of reason for both Christian and himself. But Sarah had said the war had affected his friend, hardened the once-sanguine Earl of Wessex.

Even the loss of their father, and Sarah's tumultuous relationship with the Duke of Glenbroke had not affected him like this, had not changed him as war had. Lord Dun-Donell sighed, hoping that the blithe Aidan he had once known was not lost to them.

Daniel was absorbed with his own thoughts when the door opened on a small gust of wind. He saw the familiar dimpled grin of Aidan Duhearst, and for a moment everything was as it had been. They clasped hands and pounded each other on the back in a masculine embrace.

"Where ya been, ya bastard? I'm the one that's always late." Daniel's thick brogue was deliberately light as he took in the dark circles under Aidan's green eyes.

"Well, 'bout time you know what it feels like," Aidan said, flopping on the leather chair opposite him. "How are your parents?"

"Grand, although my mother is determined to have me suitably arranged, with an heir suckling the breast of my undetermined wife precisely nine months later." Daniel chuckled, adding, "I think I'll have to do a bit of research whilst I'm in town. Would na want the lad to go hungry."

"Perish the thought!" Aidan said, smiling.

Daniel chuckled and settled back in his chair, placing his right ankle on his left knee. "So, what about you, Aidan? You've been home, what? Six weeks?"

"Seven." Wessex requested a scotch, and when it was delivered said, "Thank you," to the young servant.

"Ya been to Blackmore Hall?" Daniel asked when they were alone once again.

Aidan gave a curt nod. "I recuperated there."

They held each other's eyes, and Daniel was not sure what to say. Never being one to let that stop him, he asked, "What happened on the peninsula, Aidan?"

His gaunt companion stiffened in his chair. "It was war, Daniel. What do you think happened?" He paused. "Men died." Aidan swallowed half his scotch. "My men died."

Daniel's brows furrowed, and he ached for his oldest friend, but knowing Aidan would never speak unless pushed, he pushed. "What happened, Aidan?"

"Leave it DunDonell," Aidan warned, but Daniel saw the pain beneath the hard emptiness of his gaze.

"No." He shook his head. "I dinna think I will leave it, Aidan. Your sister is worried sick about ya, and you've lost a stone since last we met." Daniel took a deep breath and started again. Gently. "Tell me what happened on the peninsula."

His friend looked at the wall, the fireplace, the ceiling, anywhere but at Daniel while he made his decision. Finally Aidan leaned forward, his black hair shielding his eyes from view as he stared at the carpet.

"Beresford . . . Beresford called the charge on Albuera," he began and then closed his eyes. He took a deep breath and opened them again. "My regiment was ordered to hold the road to the village. It should have been a simple task as the French troops were on the far side. But . . ." Aidan paused. "They flanked us, cutting my regiment in half. I turned my mount and headed for the men trapped by the river, but the fighting was fierce, and I didn't get there in time." Daniel felt his friend's guilt, it was that thick. "I watched those men get cut down, surrounded by twice their number of French troops, heard their cries . . ." He stared at the carpet.

Daniel gave his friend a moment. "It was war, Aidan. You said it yourself: Men die in battle."

"Not my men!" Aidan snapped, pushing himself upright. "Not without me."

Daniel sat back, suddenly comprehending. He had never realized how much the death of Aidan's father had affected his friend, never realized the burden of following in the footsteps of such a heroic man. But he saw it now. "Is that how you were injured?"

His friend held his tongue, and Daniel knew that Aidan had tried to defend his men, tried to die with them as his father had.

"The next thing I remember, I was sitting in a room being interrogated by Napoleon's mistress."

"A woman?"

"Yes, she's English, Daniel, and she's here."

"In London?" Aidan must have heard the skepticism in his voice.

"Yes, in London, and stop looking at me as though I belong in a madhouse. I saw her at Lord Reynolds's ball."

"Perhaps you were mistaken?"

"Really, old man, the woman intended to hang me. I hardly think I would forget what she looked like," he said with a tone of exasperated tolerance that Daniel remembered all too well.

The viscount chuckled, "No, I suppose not." Amusement lightened Aidan's countenance. "So, what are ya plannin' to do about it?"

"I don't know, but I do know this." Aidan sat forward again, determined this time. "She's the reason I survived Albuera."

"I thought she tried to kill you," Daniel said, decidedly confounded.

"Yes, yes, yes, she did." Aidan waved off his confusion. "What I meant was, God allowed me to survive Albuera, allowed me to be taken captive, allowed me to escape for the sole purpose of stopping this woman." He waited for Daniel to understand, but when he didn't, Aidan added, "Don't you see, I'm the only one that knows what she looks like, what she is."

"Is that why ya look like hell? You been lookin' for the woman?"

Aidan nodded. "She's in London, Daniel. I know it. Glenbroke is making inquires while I continue to search for her."

Daniel looked at his exhausted friend and said the only thing that would help. "You won't capture her if you're tired and weak. You've got to eat, Aidan."

"I suppose you're right." Aidan wrinkled his nose at the distasteful fit of his impeccable midnight blue jacket. "If I don't regain my weight, I shall be forced to purchase an entirely new wardrobe. It'll cost a fortune."

Viscount DunDonell marveled at Wessex's unwavering practicality. The man was able to go about his day without creasing his breeches; where as Daniel's garments were as wrinkled as a whore's bed sheets.

"Surely, it will not come to that," Daniel gasped with feigned horror.

Aidan did not miss his sarcasm. He gave Daniel a once-over and with a smile said, "Really, old man, you are not in a position to criticize."

Daniel glanced down at his rumpled buckskins and favorite black Hessians. "And what the bloody hell does that mean?"

"It means, Lord DunDonell," Aidan said with a nefarious grin, "that you are slovenly."

The viscount's jaw dropped, and his brows furrowed with indignation. "Slovenly! You bloody bastard. I should throttle ya fer that, but bein' the dandy that ya are, I wouldn't want to disturb your cravat."

"Dandy!"

Daniel chuckled, truly enjoying himself. "Hit too close to the mark, did I?"

"Your verbal aim is about as accurate as your marksmanship." Aidan raised a superior brow, knowing exactly what Daniel's response to that jest would be.

"Care to wager?"

Wessex's emerald eyes positively sparkled as he said, "A thousand pounds?"

Damn!

Daniel bit his lower lip, knowing Aidan was the better marksman, always had been able to back up that bloody arrogance. They stared at one another, and he opened his mouth to decline the challenge, but heard himself say, "Manton's, best of ten."

"Done," Aidan agreed, rising to his feet with a grin that made him look for a moment like the boy who had joined Daniel in a fight against four bullies on their first day at Eton.

The old man leaned heavily on his cane for support as he lowered himself into the crushed velvet chair. He dropped the last few inches onto the cushion with a small grunt and readjusted himself to an acceptable position. His gray-black hair had disappeared with the years, leaving brown spots on the shiny scalp where hair had once been.

The Duke of Glenbroke smiled politely at the older gentleman. He was the type of man who would never be noticed, much less remarked upon. His drab clothing and lack of ornamentation led one to believe him nothing more than a befuddled old man of meager income.

However, Gilbert knew better than to be fooled by the mundane facade. Eyes the color of warm brandy held the sharpness of keen intelligence—although Gilbert had seen them deliberately dulled on more than one occasion. The men were both members of the club in which they now sat, waiting to begin their meeting.

"Evening, Glenbroke, haven't seen you here in quite some time. Must be that stunning wife of yours who keeps you home at night, what?" he said a bit loudly, adding a wink as two gentlemen passed their secluded corner of the great room.

When the men had moved out of hearing range, the old man's jovial tone changed to an authoritative tenor accustomed to making decisions. "What is this about, Your Grace? I am not fond of meetings, as you know."

"Quite. However, it cannot be avoided. The prime minister would like a report on your progress in identifying our traitor. Perceval was not pleased with the loss of *The Minerva*. As you know, the supplies she was carrying were sorely needed on the peninsula."

"Yes, Your Grace. I am well aware of the urgency of the situation. We know that the traitor is going by the name of Lion. He has sold information to the French, information that cost us dearly at Corunna and Saragossa. My assistant, Lord Cunningham, has recently intercepted a missive with the Lion's seal. The information contained in the document was only available to five men holding sensitive committee positions within Whitehall. Lords Reynolds, Cantor, Elkin, Ferrell, and Hambury."

"A peer?" Gilbert could not hide his shock.

"Yes, Your Grace."

"How do you intend to prove which of these men is a traitor?"

The old man stared and then smiled politely. "You may assure the prime minister that the matter is being addressed."

Gilbert smiled, knowing that he would get no more details of the operation. "Excellent. Now if I may impose on you concerning another matter?"

"Certainly, Your Grace."

"The Earl of Wessex has just informed me of the presence of a French intelligence officer on British soil."

The man's left brow lifted with skepticism and a touch of conceit. "Indeed? An operative that I am unaware of?"

"Lady Rivenhall, young, blonde, blue green eyes, five-foot-six? The lady was searching Lord Reynolds's bedchamber when she was discovered by Wessex."

The man showed no emotion. "How did Wessex happen to find her in Lord Reynolds's bedchamber?"

"He recognized her in the ballroom and followed her upstairs."

"How did he recognize her?" the old man inquired evenly.

"Do you recall his escape after having been captured at Albuera? Lady Rivenhall was the woman from whose troops he escaped."

The duke waited patiently, knowing the old man would speak when ready. Gilbert lifted his scotch to his lips and lingered several more minutes before the old man decided to speak.

"If you will forgive me, Your Grace, but your brother-in-law was injured at Albuera, was he not?"

"Yes, he suffered many injuries at Albuera."

"But the most severe was a blow to the head?"

"Yes, however—"

"Oftentimes"—the old man ignored him—"war affects men . . . afterward."

"Are you suggesting, sir, that my brother-in-law is delusional?"

"Of course not, Your Grace, merely mistaken. You see, Lady Rivenhall has already been thoroughly investigated by my office, as her mother was a French noblewoman."

"And the results of your investigation?"

"Lady Rivenhall is exactly what she seems, an English lady whose mother was displaced, like so many others, by the French Revolution."

Gilbert took air into his lungs as he tried to take the information into his mind. "But Wessex was quite certain—"

"Your brother-in-law was mistaken, Your Grace." The old man met his eyes before saying, "Lady Rivenhall has been in London for well over a year. It could not have been she who interrogated the Earl of Wessex on the peninsula. I am sorry."

Gilbert sat back, dazed. He stared into his glass and was surprised when the old man's voice, which had been so grave mere moments before, now became buoyant.

"And the twins? I believe they are nearing one year, are they not?"

The duke glanced up in time to nod at Lord Ferth as he passed. "Yes, the dowager duchess wishes to invite the entire ton to the celebration; however, my wife is standing firm in favor of a small gathering."

"Quite sensible," the old man said, but Gilbert scarcely heard him, so troubled was he by the information he had just been given—and now must conceal from his wife.

Nine

Saturday evening finally arrived.

Not that Aidan wanted to meet Sarah's selection for bride, but he had arranged to speak with Glenbroke after they dined.

He bounded up the stairs of his sister's home looking every inch the English gentleman, just as Sarah had ordered, and was admitted into the drawing room with the other guests. He nodded a greeting to Christian St. John who stood on the opposite side of the room with cousins Lady Pervill and Lady Appleton, then gave his sister an armful of roses as he kissed her dutifully on the cheek.

"Well, when is my future bride arriving, and by the way, *who* is she?" he teased, glancing down at her as her lips pinched with annoyance.

Her green eyes were mere slits when she glared at her husband, who stood blissfully unaware of her ire as he poured himself a sherry from an exquisite crystal decanter.

"I am going to throttle Gilbert."

"Only right the duke should warn me of your deceitful intentions." Aidan grinned, revealing his dimples. Sarah smiled as well and then turned to face him, making him exceedingly uncomfortable.

"It will just be the six of us for dinner, Aidan."

His brows furrowed as his head whipped around to view the two cousins conversing with Christian St. John and the Duke of Glenbroke.

"You're not serious?"

"Deadly."

"Which one have you claimed as my bride?"

Sarah's laughter rang out, causing the others to turn toward the siblings. "Come now, Aidan, you could no more handle Juliet than catch a fly."

"So Felicity is more *manageable?*" he asked with irritation.

"Think of it as compatible. Felicity is a stunning, charming, intelligent lady and would make you a splendid wife. I have thought you perfect for one another for quite some time."

Aidan was reeling. "Have you spoken to her about the possibility?"

"Of course not. What sort of sister do you take me for? Besides"—she grinned—"Felicity would be mortified and would most probably not speak to me for a month. Juliet and I thought it best to just let you handle the matter."

"Juliet!" he hissed through clenched teeth.

"She broached the subject several weeks ago. I think she is concerned about Felicity nearing her twenty-second year with no husband in sight."

Aidan chuckled. "Come now, it is not as though Lady Appleton is a wallflower. The girl has refused six offers for her hand already."

"Seven." Sarah sighed. "I know. She says she is not in love with her suitors, but I was certain she would accept Lord Summers. The man is an absolute pleasure to look at."

"Sarah." The word held his disapproval.

"Therefore, brother dear, if appearance is not a primary concern for Felicity, you might just have a chance," she said with an impish grin.

Aidan rolled his eyes at his sister just as dinner was announced.

The Duke of Glenbroke escorted his irritating wife. Lady Pervill wrapped her arm firmly around Christian's, which, very cleverly, left Aidan to offer his to the elegant Lady Appleton.

He hated to admit when his sister was correct, but he had considered Lady Appleton before he left for the peninsula. She was exceedingly beautiful and by far the most gentle creature he had ever had the pleasure of meeting. Any man would be lucky to take her for his wife.

Dinner was excellent, and his observation of Lady Appleton distracting enough that Aidan very nearly forgot why he had come. Then the ladies were excusing themselves, leaving the three men to their port.

Glenbroke turned to him the moment the doors had closed, asking, "So, what do you think of your bride?"

Aidan's lips quirked as Christian's fair brows furrowed. "What bride?"

The duke's silvery eyes met the Nordic blue of the befuddled Lord St. John. "It would seem my wife has decided that Aidan should offer for Lady Appleton."

Christian's face registered shock. "Lady Appleton? You jest!"

Aidan was mildly insulted. "And what, pray tell, Christian, is so amusing about my paying court to Lady Appleton?"

Lord St. John looked from the duke to Aidan and back to the duke, then rushed headlong into the hole he had dug for himself. "Well . . . well, nothing, old boy. I just never imagined . . . you and Lady Appleton?"

The duke roared with laughter, and Aidan scowled, irritated. "Damn it man, the venture was only proposed an hour ago. Lady Appleton would make any man an excellent wife."

"Yes, she would, but *not* for the likes of you."

"The *likes* of me!"

"You must admit you are a bit of a lecher."

"A lecher!"

"Well, perhaps not a lecher, but most assuredly a rake."

"As are you," Aidan pointed out.

Christian grinned. "That I am, but I am not offering for Lady Appleton."

"Who said anything about an offer?"

"Well, I certainly hope you are not paying court in order to seduce Lady Appleton, because Gilbert and I would be forced—"

"Seduce her!" Aidan's voice was beginning to rise, and the duke's laughter increased with it. "Are you mad, Christian, or merely feverish?"

"Well, then what *are* your intentions toward the girl? It is not as though you need time to become acquainted with her. Either you want to marry the woman, or you don't."

Aidan just stared at Christian's audacity, saying, "Glenbroke, would you kindly ask this meddlesome bastard to join the ladies, because he is most assuredly behaving like one?"

Christian smiled as he rose. "No need to toss me out, Glenbroke. I can only assume that you gentlemen have no objection to a stunning male specimen, such as myself, spending time *alone* with your women?"

The duke nodded his consent, while Aidan vehemently objected. "Felicity is not *my* woman."

"Felicity?" Both of Lord St. John's brows lifted, and he met the duke's laughing eyes. "Such familiarity. Can a ceremony be far behind?"

"Sod off, Christian," Aidan tossed over his shoulder as Lord St. John reached for the brass doorknob.

"And to you, Lord Wessex."

And then he was gone, leaving an irritated Aidan alone with a very amused Duke of Glenbroke.

Aidan rubbed his temples when he felt the twinge of a

headache. He reached for his port and took a substantial portion in his mouth before turning to his brother-in-law.

"Well, have you located Lady Rivenhall?"

The duke sighed with regret, sitting up and leaning his muscular forearms on the polished mahogany table.

"Aidan, are you sure that Lady Rivenhall is the woman who interrogated you in France?"

"What do you mean? Of course I am sure. It is hardly something a man would forget."

Gilbert raised both brows and with great reluctance said, "The Foreign Office has already investigated Lady Rivenhall." Aidan waited. "She has been living in London for over a year, Aidan. She could not be the same woman."

"She drugged me!"

"Perhaps she was waiting for Lord Reynolds, and you frightened her? Did you accuse her of being a French spy?"

Aidan's brows furrowed as he thought back to Albuera. He had been half dead, confused. He felt a moment of uncertainty as he remembered the note. *Last room on the left.* Perhaps it had been a lover's note. Perhaps her reaction was due to fear for her reputation?

And then he remembered her knife, the way she used it. He remembered the recognition in her stunning eyes, the physical attraction between them. He was not wrong.

He knew it, felt it.

"She is the same woman, Gilbert, and every day that woman is allowed to operate without detection is a day she could be passing information to the French. I cannot allow it."

The duke looked at him with alarm. "The Foreign Office has already investigated her, Aidan. There is nothing else you can do."

"I beg to differ, Your Grace. I intend to unmask this traitor and turn her over to Whitehall." Aidan rose and bowed. "If you would relay my regrets to my sister."

"Where are you going?"

Aidan flashed his teeth in a fierce grin. "Hunting."

LONDON, ENGLAND
JUNE 30, 1811

Lady Rivenhall sat in a private box at Vauxhall gardens.
She twisted a black and white mask in her hands as she
awaited the arrival of the English spymaster, Falcon.

He had not been pleased to be contacted, but she saw no
alternative. The problem of the Earl of Wessex would have
to be resolved, and quickly.

"How are you, my dear?" the elderly man asked as he
entered their private dining area. The orchestra became
muffled as the heavy velvet flap fell into place and the old
man settled with a sigh into the seat opposite her.

"Very well, thus far, my lord."

The old man laughed with approval. "You never were
one to beat about the bush, Celeste. I had hoped we could
enjoy a meal before conducting our business." He lifted a
trembling tray of fruit and cheese toward her. She declined
with a shake of her head. "Very well." He set the tray on
the black silk tablecloth. "I know of your meeting with the
Earl of Wessex at Lord Reynolds's ball."

Her blue green eyes opened wide. "How could you
possibly—"

The question was interrupted with a wave of the old
man's hand. "It is of no importance. However, I have just
received information that changes your assignment considerably." His brandy colored eyes locked with hers.

"Lord Wellesley plans to launch a campaign against
Napoleon in one month's time. Ships transporting soldiers
as well as supplies will arrive on the southeastern coast of
Portugal in hopes of trapping the emperor's troops between the Pyrenees and Wellesley. You realize, of course,
what this means?"

Celeste nodded.

"You always were a clever girl, Celeste, but let me be
clear. You must unearth this traitor before Wellesley sets
sail, or Napoleon will be awaiting his arrival." Falcon
paused, holding her eyes until he was satisfied she under-

stood the seriousness of the situation. "You found nothing to implicate Lord Reynolds?"

"No, I have searched his home, and he seems a bit—"

"Incapable." Falcon chuckled. "The man is a complete buffoon. Always thought him highly unlikely. No, our Lion is a very clever fellow. You might never find any documents to prove his guilt."

"Then how am I—"

"His seal. With an intercepted communiqué, Lion has provided in wax the proof we need to hang him. It is his arrogance that will betray him. He might very well leave his Lion's seal with his others."

"Why in heaven's name would he be so careless?"

A smile spread across Falcon's weathered features. "You are very young, Celeste. To Lion it is not carelessness, it is a game. Half the men I employ have been recruited because they enjoy the thrill of the hunt, because they enjoy deceiving people to prove to themselves that they can."

"And the other half?"

"The other half . . ." He placed his hand on hers. "Are patriots, serving their country despite their fears, despite the danger." Her eyes met his, and she was thankful when the old man sat back, saying, "Find the Lion's seal. You have four weeks in which to prove one of these four men a traitor."

"All of four weeks?" Celeste laughed mirthlessly, placing the mangled mask on the table.

Falcon smiled, revealing teeth yellowed by age. "I have seen you bring an entire roomful of men to their knees in one evening, my dear. Four men in four weeks is child's play for a lady of your considerable skills."

"It is not the four gentlemen I am concerned with, it is the one." She fought to conceal her apprehension as she held the old man's eyes, saying, "Wessex will not stop until he has denounced me as a spy." *Or until he kills me outright.*

Falcon eased himself against the plush cushions and ate

strawberries for a good five minutes before answering. "Then you will have to give him a reason to wait until your assignment is complete."

Celeste's heartbeat quickened. "You are not suggesting—"

"Seduce him."

Her heart stopped, and she shook her head, sending her diamond ear bobs swinging. "You do not understand, my lord. The Earl of Wessex is not the sort of man to be satisfied with a stolen kiss in a darkened garden. He will want . . ."

"I know, my dear," the old man said regretfully. "But I see no alternative. Wellesley is relying on us to plug this leak, and you are the only person capable of doing so."

Celeste blinked, trying to rid herself of her lightheadedness. Falcon put a scotch in her right hand, and she downed the contents in one gulp. Her breathing began to slow when the old man added, "I am sorry, Celeste. I have told the Duke of Glenbroke that you have been in London for over a year. Suggesting, even, that the earl's injury has confused his memory. All you need do is nurture Wessex's doubt with your charms." He paused. "It is, of course, entirely your decision."

Celeste swallowed and answered before allowing herself time to think. "It is a privilege to serve the Crown, my lord."

"Excellent. I thought perhaps . . ." Falcon continued talking, but she did not hear him. She covered one shaking hand with the other and tried to control her fear. Tried to understand why the Earl of Wessex threatened her so.

She had been in physical danger before, had allowed men to kiss her, caress her. She had even befriended the Empress Maria Louisa in hopes of gaining information. And while she had been scared, terrified really, for her safety, she had never feared for her heart.

Aidan Duhearst threatened her very soul, and she could not withstand another injury. Her heart had been severed the day her father was murdered by the French and what little remained still bled. She would have to protect her heart from the noble earl and pray that her fortifications would hold.

Ten

Smoke drifted across the flames of the few candles illuminating Dante's Inferno, leaving a haze that mirrored the foggy minds of the patrons of the popular hell.

Aidan had been searching for Lady Rivenhall at every ball, soiree, musicale, opera, and fete for the past five days, and he needed a respite. He tossed a card to the middle of the green baize table and scooped up the trick.

"Have you seen Lady Pervill of late, Wessex?" Lord Robert Barksdale's wide grin was decidedly lascivious.

"Pervill?" Lord Fairfax interjected. "Lady Appleton's the thing, old boy."

"Lady Appleton is lovely, but Lady Pervill . . ." Barksdale shook his head, causing his long brown hair to brush his collar. "Something about that little vixen stirs my blood."

Lord Fairfax shrugged. "Speaking of beauties, I attended Lord Reynolds's event last week and saw a delicious bit of muslin, blonde with enormous green eyes." The man whistled his appreciation. "Damn near caused me to drop Lady Wagner on the dance floor when I saw the girl."

Aidan tensed, his heart pounding in his chest.

"Ah, you refer to Lady Rivenhall," Barksdale said while nodding at a doxy. "Lord Elkin was quite taken with the woman, asked her to his house party at his estate this weekend. Didn't see her myself, but from what Elkin says, I certainly will want to."

"Elkin's back?" Lord Fairfax asked, his brows drawn together.

"Arrived in London last week," the young lord confirmed. "It seems the emperor interfered with Elkin's enjoyment of the continent." Aidan watched Barksdale's hand slip to the young whore's backside. "Have you been entertained this evening, Rose?"

"Been waitin' for you, haven't I, me lord."

"Well, if you gentlemen will excuse me," Barksdale said as he stood. "I could not possibly leave our little flower unattended."

Aidan waved away the strumpets that had descended upon them the moment their card game disbanded.

"Are the twins available?" Lord Fairfax asked the woman with hair a shade too red.

"They're already seeing to the duke, me lord." She giggled. "But me and Sally is just like twins." She paused for effect. "We do everyfing togetha'."

Fairfax swallowed. "Right, I suppose a room is available?"

Aidan sat alone at the corner table, thankful for the dim lighting that hid his black mood. He would have no difficulty in procuring an invitation to the weekend gathering from his childhood friend.

His lips curled in a contemptuous smile as he tried to imagine the look on Lady Rivenhall's stunning face when she saw him. He tossed back the remainder of his scotch and made for the door, carefully avoiding the young buck casting up his dinner in the corner of the crowded room.

"The Duke of Glenbroke's home," he snapped at his coachman when he made his way outside. Detecting the annoyance beneath Aidan's usually emotionless countenance, the man cracked the whip with no attempt at polite conversation.

Aidan sat in the darkened carriage contemplating the traitorous lady. Would the Crown hang a woman? No, there would be a trial, and he would need more than just his word to convict her. He needed proof of her treachery, proof that she was the same woman from Albuera.

The landau rolled to a stop, and Aidan was bounding up the stairs to his brother-in-law's home before the footman could reach for the handle of his carriage. The duke's devoted butler opened the door to the home with a superior tilt of his nose until he recognized the caller.

"Is he in?" Aidan asked as he pushed past the smaller man, tossing him his beaver skin hat and greatcoat.

"His Grace is in the study. However—"

Aidan was at the heavy oak door of Glenbroke's study and pushed it open, anxious to share his discovery with the only other person who knew of Lady Rivenhall's existence.

But he stopped dead in the doorway and stared in frustration. His sister was sitting in the duke's lap as they held one another in a heated embrace.

Aidan slammed the door to make his presence known, saying, "You have fourteen bedchambers upstairs, Your Grace." He shook his head. "I shall never understand your predilection for this particular room."

Gilbert released his wife's lips with great reluctance. He glowered his disapproval. "I believe if I desired to make love to my wife on the entryway floor, it would be none of your bloody affair."

Sarah released her husband's neck and wiggled to face her brother, extracting a muffled moan from the enormous duke.

"Aidan! I have just managed to get the twins to bed!" she said in the precise tone she used as a child when she was on the verge of a tantrum. "What do you *want*?"

Gilbert chuckled and lifted his voluptuous wife from his lap. "Perhaps you should make your way to bed, dearest."

He smiled, adding, "I believe the black lace would be most restive."

Aidan lifted his right hand to stave off the mental image. "Really, old man, she is my *sister*."

The duke held his wife's eyes as she swayed toward the door. "If you did not want to hear such talk . . ." He faltered when Sarah licked her lower lip before slipping from the room. "Then you should not have invaded my study unannounced." The duke's silvery eyes met his. "What is so damned important?"

Aidan grinned like a cat with a mouse between its paws. "I found her."

Gilbert's forehead creased, knowing instantly to whom Aidan was referring. "How?"

"Luck, really. The lady will be attending John Elkin's house party this weekend." Aidan settled into a leather chair in front of the fading fire. "All that remains is to find proof of my claim for the Foreign Office."

"You know Whitehall's position pertaining to your suspicion of Lady Rivenhall. They will not assist you."

"Yes, I know," Aidan said. "But it is of no importance. Whitehall is mistaken, and I intend to prove it."

The duke rose and poured the two men a brandy before seating himself in the chair next to Aidan.

"The Foreign Office has investigated the woman and is convinced that Lady Rivenhall is nothing more than a gently bred lady. So why do you believe yourself capable of proving the woman a spy when they have failed to do so?" Gilbert sighed, swirling his brandy. "Perhaps it would be best to drop—"

"No! The woman is a traitor, and I intend to prove it."

Silence lingered. The duke crossed his legs, his dark brows pulling together as he thought. "Let us suppose, for a moment, that you are correct and the woman is a spy. Would it not be prudent to watch her in order to identify her associates? If she is a French informant and you are determined to follow her, then she can do little harm. But if you observe her contacts, identify the network of French collaborators, Whitehall would have a difficult time refuting your claim."

Aidan was on his feet shaking his head violently. "No, Gilbert. You have no idea what this woman is capable of. She could extract information from Wellesley himself. She is breathtakingly beautiful, charming, intelligent, and able to make a man doubt his own judgment." Aidan swallowed uncomfortably. "She must be brought to heel, and as soon as possible."

"And how do you intend to do that when the Foreign Office will not accommodate you?" The men stared at each other. "If you truly wish to help the men on the peninsula, it is far more important to identify the entire network rather than one agent."

Aidan stared at the carpet, his mind spinning. "The woman is not a simpleton, Your Grace. She is aware that I can identify her."

Gilbert grinned, an idea lighting his luminescent eyes. "Then who better to follow her?"

"What?"

"Follow her to events under the pretense of suspecting her of spying."

"She *is* spying!"

"Precisely," Gilbert said, sniffing his brandy as he allowed the amber liquid to warm in his hand. "That is why the plan is so bloody brilliant."

Aidan glared at the duke, his arms folded across his chest. "What plan?"

The duke leaned forward as he warmed to his subject. "You are the only man who can identify her. Correct?"

"Yes."

"She will wonder why you have not turned her over to the Foreign Office and will make damn sure to stay away from her contacts."

"True."

"So, Aidan, my dear fellow." The duke was smiling, making Aidan exceedingly uncomfortable. "You need to give her a plausible reason as to why you have not turned her in."

"What possible explanation would keep a man, a veteran, from exposing his enemy?"

Gilbert spun his crystal snifter in his hands. "Can you think of no reason?"

"None," Aidan snapped, irritated with this game.

The duke lifted a brow, shaking his head. "You can think of no reason for a man to want to keep a woman out of prison?"

Aidan's heart skipped a beat.

"A breathtakingly beautiful, charming, and intelligent woman capable of making a man doubt his own judgment?"

Aidan was already shaking his head.

The duke shrugged his massive shoulders. "Seduce her."

A burst of laughter escaped Aidan, but he felt as though he had been struck in the gut.

"You do not seduce a woman like Lady Rivenhall. It is too dangerous," he said, shaking his head more adamantly and causing his ebony hair to fall in front of his eyes. He brushed it away. "The woman has been trained to seduce men for the emperor's gain."

"If you do not think you're capable . . ."

Aidan glared at the duke. "Don't think to goad me, Gilbert."

"Then what's your hesitation? This is by far the most logical course of action." Glenbroke's silvery eyes opened in surprise. "You don't . . . you don't *desire* the woman?"

Aidan said nothing, unable to look his brother-in-law in the eye. "I don't know."

"How can a man not know if he wants a woman?"

Aidan placed one elbow on the mantle and stared into the fire, searching for the words to convey his thoughts. "Lady Rivenhall is lovely, stunning even." His jaw clenched to hold in his confusion. "But when I saw her, all I could think of was the death and destruction she is responsible for. She is a whore, a traitor, and a murderess. And the only emotion I feel is the desire for revenge, a desire to take Napoleon's own woman in the basest manner. To use her as she has used men under orders from her emperor."

Gilbert stared, concern creasing his brow. "Do you seek to harm the woman?"

"Do not be alarmed, Gilbert," Aidan said in disgust. "Lady Rivenhall would spread her thighs willingly if she believed she could extract information from me."

"If you are correct and she is the woman from Albuera—"

"She is."

"Then we need her watched. And if Whitehall is unwilling to take on the task . . ." The duke shrugged. "Then I'm afraid that leaves you."

Aidan rubbed his hand over his mouth in an unfamiliar moment of indecision. She was as much his enemy as any Frenchman on the peninsula, perhaps more so because she concealed her treachery beneath a deceptive facade, luring men to their deaths with the promise of comfort from the horrors of war, a siren drawing men to their own destruction.

But now that he saw her for what she was, could he stand aside and watch her call men to the rocks, with the larger goal of silencing her before the entire British navy crashed on her fair shores? Could he suppress his anger, or would he harm her given a chance?

That was his deepest fear.

That he had forever become the brutal warrior that had killed so many men at Albuera. That he would forever be the killer who saw French soldiers and not men who ran red with blood as he thrust his sword into their chests. Would he ever come back from the peninsula? Would this anger never subside?

"I will consider your proposal," he said, then walked out the study doors.

Eleven

❦

Celeste shielded her eyes against the morning sun as she peered into a tobacconist's shop on Pall Mall. The smell of tobacco hung near the entrance of the establishment, and she began to cough when a rotund gentleman departed, blowing cheroot smoke in her direction. She tried to take air into her lungs, but her corset was so tight that she settled for short, cleansing breaths.

Celeste had been following Lord Ferrell all morning and had learned quite a lot about the man now drawing a cheroot under his patrician nose. He did nothing by halves. His dark hair and rich skin drew women in droves, and his wide mouth flashed straight, white teeth over a strong chin decorated with a masculine cleft. He was nearly six feet, if she hazarded a guess, and when Lord Ferrell prowled the streets, ladies' heads snapped round in his wake.

She watched as Lord Ferrell thanked the shopkeeper and turned to leave the establishment. Celeste expelled a breath, hoping to ease her nerves, then adjusted her parcels and made for the door with her head bent as if staring at her feet. Celeste watched from beneath her bonnet and made certain she ran into the handsome lord with such force that her packages went flying.

"Oh!" She stared with wide aqua eyes at the dark man before her. "Oh, my apologies. I'm so sorry."

Lord Ferrell grinned and then perused every curve of her body, coming to rest on her face, which had gone pink with embarrassment.

"Are you all right?" he asked, concealing his carnal evaluation with gentlemanly concern.

"Yes, I believe so." Celeste looked down at the scattered packages, sighing her frustration as she bent to retrieve them.

Lord Ferrell sank down on his haunches in one smooth motion and picked up the lid to a box that had come open. But when he went to replace it, he stilled. A dark brow arched, and a smile tugged at the corner of his lips. He picked up the lace stockings and rubbed the silk between his thumb and forefinger.

The white lace contrasted with his golden skin as he stared into her eyes, saying, "Lovely." The man was not referring to her stockings, and they both knew it. "Lord Ferrell, at your service."

His eyes were locked with hers as he removed the boxes from her hands and rose to his feet. Celeste stood, brushing dirt from her yellow day gown, then held out her arms to receive the packages.

The handsome lord smiled with seductive intent. "I'm afraid you are a menace to the population of London, my lady, and I shall be forced to accompany you to your carriage."

Celeste smiled as they walked, and she kept glancing at him in the way she imagined an innocent would look at a man she found attractive.

He smiled more broadly at her discomfiture, and asked, "Do you always walk about town unaccompanied?"

Giggling like a schoolgirl, Celeste met chocolate eyes that reflected his interest and his lust. "No, my companion turned her ankle at the last shop, and I was forced to finish our errands on my own."

"Your companion's misfortune is indeed my gain." She lowered her eyes demurely as they reached the unmarked carriage. The gentleman continued staring at her with a charming smile that she was sure had seduced many a lady, while her footman jumped down to retrieve the parcels from the young lord.

Lady Rivenhall offered her gloved hand, but not her card. "Thank you, Lord Ferrell. I am forever in your debt."

"Then I shall have to think of a method of repayment," he said, turning her hand over and kissing her wrist as he dragged his lower lip across the exposed flesh.

Celeste felt nothing, not even a twinge of desire. Lord Ferrell opened her carriage door, offering his right hand to assist her up. But as she ascended the stairs of the conveyance, Celeste felt long fingers curling around her waist under the pretense of steadying her. She smiled her gratitude and settled on the velvet squabs.

"Thank you again, my lord," Celeste said, intimating that he should close the door, but he did not.

Smiling, the rake asked, "I don't believe I caught your name."

Celeste smiled brilliantly and for the first time offered the gentleman the full force of her sensuality. "That is because I did not give it, Lord Ferrell."

She could see that he was taken aback and more than intrigued by her seductiveness. The desire in his eyes gave way to amusement, and he closed the carriage door, knocking on the side to signal the coachman to depart.

They stared at one another as the landau rolled forward, and then the dark lord swept an exaggerated bow that made her smile in his direction. She settled against the comfort of the carriage and glanced at Madame Arnott.

"It's done then?"

"Lord Ferrell will have Bow Street runners scouring the city for me by nightfall."

"Three men remain."

Celeste rubbed the back of her neck in an attempt to ease the tension that had built while she stalked her prey. She reached down the bodice of her gown and untied her corset. The laces gave and she took a deep breath, blowing out as she said, "Three remain."

A horse neighed as a rider approached the small grove of oak trees at Hyde Park. It was still dark, so the man's hand fell to his pistol.

"Who goes there?"

The Frenchman's familiar chuckle set him at his ease. "You think me a footpad, no?"

The man rolled his eyes and reached into his saddlebag to retrieve the papers from the admiral's office. "Transport ships and cargo."

The foreigner hissed his dissatisfaction. "This is most disappointing, my friend, most disappointing. The emperor requires the number of troops, and you give him the number of tea bags."

"I have an informant in Wellesley's office that I am working—"

"Work faster, *mon ami.*" The Frenchman sighed his frustration. "I have learned that the emperor is most displeased with our progress and has sent his own mistress to uncover the information we seek. And from what my contacts tell me, Lady Rivenhall is so beautiful that Prinny himself would betray Wellesley for a night in her bed."

"Lady Rivenhall?"

"Do you know of her?"

"No, but the name sounds English."

"Yes, she is half English. I am told she resembles her father, blonde with bright green eyes. Napoleon is rather enamored of her, and as neither you nor I will be paid if the lady discovers the information before you yourself, I suggest you double your efforts." The Frenchman passed him a small brown parcel. "One thousand pounds."

The tall man stiffened in his saddle. "Is that *all* I am to be rewarded for risking my life?"

"When the information is worth paying for, you shall be given enough that you will have no need of working another day." The Frenchman shook his head. "But this . . ." He lifted the papers in his hand. "It is worth a thousand pounds. Contact me when you have the information I require."

Then the Frenchman turned his horse, leaving the tall man to contemplate his new competition.

Twelve

Lady Rivenhall accepted the assistance of her footman as she alighted from the carriage, followed by Madame Arnott. The sky hung low, the clouds threatening to open at any moment, but the gloomy weather did nothing to detract from the splendor of the Georgian manor house.

Two marble staircases curled to a portico covering the massive double doors, where Lord Elkin stood watching her arrival with his hands clasped behind his broad back. His rugged features broke into a polite smile, and she could see from the light in his cobalt eyes that he was pleased she had accepted his invitation.

"Lady Rivenhall, I am delighted that you have honored us with your presence," he said, drawing her gloved hand to his lips.

"It is my honor to have been invited, my lord," she replied with a slight curtsy that provided Lord Elkin a better view of her breasts. He noticed, and was smiling appreciatively when he offered her his arm.

"Adams will show you to your rooms. We shall gather

at seven in the parlor for refreshment before we dine." He held her eyes as he bowed and lifted her hand to his lips in one fluid movement of graceful seductiveness. "Until then," he whispered.

Oh, he was *very* good, she thought as Lord Elkin drifted from the enormous entryway. However, she was better. He obviously intended to bed her, which was rather convenient as she required access to the man's bedchamber.

She turned toward Adams who promptly offered, "Right this way, my lady."

They ascended the staircase that spilled onto the wide corridor of the first floor. Madame Arnott directed the footmen to place the trunks in the appropriate bedchamber of the adjoining rooms, while Celeste enjoyed the view from her Italian marble balcony. She closed her eyes and sighed, suddenly very tired.

"I believe I shall rest before dinner. Would you have a bath drawn for me at five o'clock, please?"

Marie nodded and closed the adjoining doors as she left the room. Celeste peeled her traveling gown from her weary limbs and crawled into bed clad only in her chemise. She closed her eyes and in the next moment was being wakened by the gentle voice of her companion.

"Your bath awaits, *ma petite.*"

Celeste moaned with pleasure the instant she sank into the lavender-scented water. Madame Arnott rubbed Celeste's scalp as she washed her hair, and when she rose from the bath Celeste's tension remained in the tub.

Marie spent the next half hour brushing Celeste's long hair in front of the fire. Once it was dry to a golden sheen, Madame Arnott set it in a chignon that displayed the elegant line of her neck. Lace drawers and an indecent French chemise with equally indecent lace garters completed her provocative undergarments.

Her gown was an alluring creation of gold with silk brocade down the central panel of the bodice. The scooped neckline, which was low but not indecently so, was trimmed with gold ribbon that drew attention to her bosom as well as to her trim waist. Marie laced midnight sapphires through her fair hair, and an enormous teardrop sapphire hung around her neck on a simple gold chain.

When her old friend had finished, Celeste turned to inspect herself in the mirror. The effect was a simple sophistication that enhanced her beauty rather than detracted from it, and she observed dispassionately that the image was breathtaking.

Any other woman would have been thrilled by the result, but she was not, knowing that her appearance was merely a uniform, a means to an end of extracting information. And she knew with all certainty that Lord Elkin would respond to her subtle seduction.

"You are stunning, *ma petite.*"

"Thank you, Marie," she said, wondering for the hundredth time where she would be if she were ugly. She was staring through the mirror when Madame Arnott's soft voice pierced her thoughts.

"Celeste, you must focus on the task at hand. It does no good to regret your decision."

"I do not regret my decision," she replied with a shake of her head. "I merely regret that God has chosen me to bear this burden. I know I have saved many lives, but at what cost?" She studied the brittle smile of her reflection. "I would not change what I have done, but I do wonder what deficiency of character allows me to be so skillful at deception."

Celeste started at Madame Arnott's burst of laughter, and she turned toward the shorter woman in confusion.

"Oh, *ma cherie,*" the woman said, holding her cheeks between her aging hands. "Do you not see it? A person of deficient character would not ponder such things. You are skillful at attaining information because you are clever, and brave . . . and, yes, very beautiful." She paused and looked deeply into Celeste's moist eyes. "But if you wish to turn from your course, we will spend the remainder of the war tucked away in a small cottage on the English moors."

Celeste longed to accept Marie's offer, but images of the men that would die if she were unsuccessful passed through her mind.

She had little time and less choice.

Celeste lifted her chin and pinched her cheeks to bring out a soft pink color. "Pass me my fan, please," she said with determination.

Celeste ran her hands over the bodice of her gown as she approached the entrance of the parlor. She paused to nod her thanks to the young footmen who opened the double mahogany doors in perfect unison.

Conversation in the large room came to an abrupt halt as guests turned to look in her direction. Celeste flushed with embarrassment when she realized that she must have arrived late.

"Lady Rivenhall," Lord Elkin called from the back of the room. Conversation resumed as she walked toward him with butterflies fluttering in the pit of her stomach.

The two gentlemen who had been speaking with Lord Elkin turned to make their introductions. "Lady Rivenhall, may I introduce you to Lord Bower and the Earl of Wessex.

Celeste's eyes flew to the earl's handsome features. His mouth was drawn into an appealing smile with even more appealing dimples.

"Lady Rivenhall," he offered with a gleam of satisfaction lighting his cold emerald eyes.

She remembered to smile, her heart in her throat. "Lord Wessex."

"Lady Rivenhall," the older Lord Bower said with polite interest.

"Lord Bower." She curtsied.

Lord Elkin turned to the disconcerting earl. "Wessex, I do not believe you have met Lord and Lady Paddington?"

The earl's raven brow rose. "Indeed, I have not," he drawled, not sounding particularly interested in doing so.

"Lady Rivenhall, if you will excuse us, I shall leave you in the capable hands of Lord Bower."

Celeste turned to the rotund lord, her broad smile reflecting her relief. "Please do not concern yourself on my behalf, Lord Elkin, I am sure that Lord Bower and I shall find no end of topics upon which to converse."

Lord Elkin propelled Aidan to a discreet corner of the parlor where a potted palm hid them from potentially curious eyes. John halted and turned on him. "You are acquainted with Lady Rivenhall." It was a statement.

"Is that the greeting you offer your childhood friend after two long years?" Aidan asked, feigning injury.

"Cut the line, Wessex. You know the lady."

He shrugged, seeing no reason to deny it. "We've met once or twice."

Annoyed, his friend's jaw tensed. "How well do you know Lady Rivenhall?"

Aidan retrieved a sherry from a passing footman and took his time sipping before answering, "I don't believe that is any of your bloody business, John."

"It damn well *is* when you call upon my friendship and hospitality so that you might be invited to this little gathering. So let us be very clear, Wessex."

"Yes, let's."

John's nostrils flared. "I have gone to a considerable amount of trouble to arrange this event, and I want your assurance that you will not interfere."

The Earl of Wessex perused the room in casual boredom. "No confidence in your charms, old boy?"

"Aidan," his host said through clenched teeth. "I'm quite serious."

He turned his head to meet the midnight blue eyes of his old school chum. "I know you are, John, and I can assure you that my interest in Lady Rivenhall is not of a romantic nature." He swallowed the remainder of the sherry and watched his friend's forehead furrow with suspicion. "Does that satisfy you, old man?" he asked, patting John on the shoulder. "I have no doubt the lady in question will be in your bed by the conclusion of this party."

"I damn sure hope so." Lord Elkin nodded. "Bloody hell, did you see when she walked into the room? I feared it might be necessary to send Adams around to wipe the mouth of every man in attendance."

John's gaze drifted over the figure of Lady Rivenhall with the practiced eye of a consummate rake. "My God, just look at her," he murmured.

Aidan did, but as he stared at the fair-haired siren, he knew his gaze lacked the lecherous glint shining in Lord Elkin's eyes, and held only the cold burn of a rage that had taken root in a prison camp just outside of Albuera.

Thirteen

After a lengthy twelve-course meal, the entire party of thirty-two guests retired to the ballroom for dancing and cards.

Celeste had not once glanced in the direction of the Earl of Wessex, but she could feel his striking eyes boring a hole in her back. She turned her attention to her charming partner, as Lord Elkin spun her the length of the room.

"Are you enjoying your visit to Sherborne, Lady Rivenhall?"

Time to work. She sighed, wishing she were normal.

"I most certainly am, Lord Elkin, though I find the appeal of Hartford Hall is due more to the company than the weather."

The handsome man looked down at her, a lazy smile spreading across his face. "Why, Lady Rivenhall, if I were inclined to blush, my face would be positively red. But as I am not, perhaps you would enjoy a tour of my home."

"Any room in particular, Lord Elkin?" she teased.

The man quirked a brow and swallowed his lust. "I have

my favorite. However, I am more than willing to show you anything you wish to view, my dear lady."

She laughed, enjoying their banter. "Your study—one hour?"

"My bedchamber is more . . . private."

Celeste flashed her most seductive smile. "Not with seventeen drunken gentlemen wandering the same hall. The ground floor will be deserted in an hour, making it less likely that we shall be overheard."

"Overheard?" His hot eyes drifted to her lips. "Do you make noise, Lady Rivenhall?"

The waltz ended, and she stepped out of his arms, saying, "No, my lord . . . but you will."

Celeste turned her back on Lord Elkin, but she could distinctly hear him mutter, "Bloody hell," as she walked off the dance floor.

She waited the requisite hour and stopped at her bedchamber door. "Remember, fifteen minutes precisely, Marie."

"Yes, I shall remember."

Celeste entered the darkened hall and could hear doors closing as the many houseguests retired. She hugged the darkness and flew down the stairs, rehearsing what she would say if she were seen. She gave a silent prayer of thanks for the empty corridors and slipped into the study before her apprehension could stop her from entering.

Lord Elkin was already there, staring into a small fire just bright enough for them to see one another when they made love. She leaned against the door and smiled provocatively, hating herself all the while.

"I was not sure you would come."

"You underestimate yourself, Lord Elkin."

"John."

"John," she said slowly, allowing him to watch his name roll from her lips. She sauntered toward him, never taking her eyes from his.

"Do you have any idea how desirable you are, Lady

Rivenhall?" he asked, taking her hand and leading her where he wanted her to go.

"Men find me attractive, but unfortunately, I rarely desire the men who are drawn to me."

His lower lip caressed her knuckles as he kissed the back of her hand while seating her on the large settee. "And do you desire me, Lady Rivenhall?"

"Celeste, and I did not travel all the way to Sherborne for the sunshine, my lord."

Lord Elkin settled next to her, causing her to slide toward him. He looked at her lips and her breasts, returning once again to her eyes.

"Then I shall have to make the trip well worth your while," he said before slanting his mouth over hers.

She allowed herself to be taken by the kiss. The man was experienced, knowing exactly how much pressure to use, how slowly to circle her tongue. She returned the embrace and allowed a soft moan to escape her. He nipped her lower lip as he pulled his head back and stared into her eyes, brushing an errant golden curl from her forehead.

"You taste just as I imagined you would, Celeste."

She leaned forward and kissed him, unable to look at the desire she had purposely stoked, burning in his eyes. He groaned, and she felt his muscular arms circle her waist, pulling her into his body.

Her breasts pressed against his chest, drawing his attention and his mouth to her neck. She glanced at the clock over his head. Seven minutes. Damn! He would have her disrobed in that amount of time.

But then again . . .

She pushed against his shoulders with her gloved hands. "Take off your jacket," she breathed. All too eager to comply with her request, he shrugged off his Bath superfine and began pulling at his elegant cravat.

"No." She met his eyes. "Let me." She pulled his cravat slowly from his neck and then kissed the exposed flesh.

Celeste smiled as she leaned back to run her hands up his muscular torso, taking her time in unbuttoning his silk waistcoat. His breathing was becoming ragged, and his breath caught when the last silver button gave. He was watching her hands, but when she reached for the top button of his shirt, Lord Elkin grabbed her wrists.

"My turn," he whispered.

His blue eyes held hers as his hand lifted her skirts and traveled leisurely up her calf and over her knee to her garters.

He moaned, closing his eyes. "Have you been wearing lace garters all evening?"

"Of course. I could not possibly wear my lace drawers without them."

"Bloody hell," he said, taking her mouth in a hungry kiss.

And then they heard it, the unmistakable sound of gunfire. He released her abruptly. "What in God's name . . . ? Damn! I must see to this, Celeste." He shrugged on his jacket and bent down to kiss her one last time. "I'm sorry."

"Please, do not apologize. I shall see you in the morning." He strode to the door, but stopped when she added, "And do be careful, John." A smile lifted the corners of his mouth, and then he opened the door and was gone.

The moment the door closed, she locked it and rushed to his desk. She searched the papers piled in neat stacks and, finding nothing, reached for a hairpin to unlatch the desk drawers to search for the Lion's seal.

And then she found what she had come for in the second drawer from the bottom, a list of arrivals and departures of naval vessels. She had no idea if Lord Elkin was privy to this information with his position as committee chair, and upon finishing her search had found no link to the French. She would turn in the papers and let Falcon decide if the man was a traitor.

Celeste's forehead creased with worry. She rather liked Lord Elkin and hoped that he was not the man she sought.

To the casual observer, the small tavern appeared nothing more than that. A tavern tucked away on a side street by the docks, letting rooms to the passengers awaiting their departure.

But he knew better.

He had followed the diminutive man from the hallowed halls of Whitehall and had observed him making his way to this tiny tavern, nervous as a fox in a room full of hounds.

Initially, he had been confused by the man's apprehension and thought it stemmed from the rather sordid reputation of this particular section of London. But as he continued sipping a tankard of ale in a darkened corner of the establishment, the truth became clear.

A smile spread across his face as he watched a weary traveler make his way to the rooms upstairs, followed shortly thereafter by another.

Both men.

But the man he observed did not appear interested in the young men who cleared the tables of the dining hall. The man stood at the bar speaking with a tall and rather muscular man a few years his junior. He chuckled when the clerk made his way upstairs, followed, not more than five minutes later, by the other man.

He himself had seduced women from his chambermaid to his brother's wife, but never had he dreamt that it would be necessary to seduce a man.

Might be a bit of a lark, he thought to himself. After all, women had been panting after him for as long as could remember, why not a man?

But perhaps what men lusted after differed from what women desired in a lover. He decided to test his hypothesis by making eye contact with a young man seated two tables down from his own. The dandy held his gaze, a hint of a smile pulling at the corners of his lips.

No, precisely the same.

He laughed aloud, saying, "Another pint," to a barmaid, who had evidently been employed for an illusion of propriety, before settling to wait for the clerk to finish taking his pleasure.

Three-quarters of an hour later he watched the small man wander back into the crowded common room of the tavern and settle in his original seat. Quitting his dark corner, he strolled up to the bar with gleeful anticipation.

"Woodson! My God man, what are you doing in this part of town?"

The dark man suppressed a laugh that was threatening to burst through when the clerk choked on a sip of ale, bringing on a violent fit of coughing. When the man finally found his breath, he sputtered, "I . . . I came to see a friend off at the docks."

He held the clerk's eyes and nodded, adding just a *touch* of doubt. "Really?"

"Yes," the man rushed to say. "America."

"Ahh." As if that explained everything. "Never mind," he said, clapping the short man on the shoulder and making sure his hand lingered a moment too long. "We are both here now. Let's enjoy a pint at a table, shall we?" he suggested, allowing a seductive smile to spread across his handsome features.

Woodson's brows furrowed, and the dark man could see the speculation dancing in the clerk's eyes. Damn, his talent was wasted on espionage. He should have been an actor treading the boards at Covent Garden.

But then again, acting was not nearly so exhilarating.

"Certainly, sounds like a capital idea," the smaller man answered eagerly.

The clerk seated himself, but rather than take the seat opposite, the dark man sat next to him, allowing the man's knee to brush his muscular thigh.

"I imagine you are very busy keeping Lord Wellesley's affairs in order?"

"Well, I'm not the only man to see to Lord Wellesley's affairs, my lord." The smaller man lowered his pale blue eyes in feigned humility.

"Come now, Woodson. Everyone knows Lord Wellesley would not walk if you were not there to tell him where to place his feet."

"I do try to assist his lordship." The fair man smiled and gave a weak laugh, inordinately pleased with himself. "I dare say Wellesley is a saint compared with your taskmaster."

"Damn right, old man, which is why I'm having another pint," he said, placing his fingers on the man's hand. "Did you want another?"

When the flustered clerk nodded, he lift his fingers to call for two more drinks, but he did not miss the small tremor that ran through Woodson, or the fact that he was staring at his profile while he spoke with the serving girl. He gave the woman a coin for the ale and rested his forearms on the filthy table, giving the small man the full force of his smile.

"Now, where were we?"

Fourteen

Aidan listened from the darkened sitting room as Lord Elkin left the study.

He had to admit with reluctant admiration that the lady was very good at her profession. She had handled the amorous lord with ease and was at this very moment conducting a methodic search of the man's study.

Aidan had already searched the study and removed any sensitive documents, replacing them with false papers he had prepared before his arrival. If he wanted to identify her contacts, he needed bait, but not at the expense of the men on the peninsula.

He smiled to himself, allowing her a few moments' privacy before pushing the adjoining door wide on oiled hinges. The lady's back was turned as she concentrated on the materials in the mahogany desk, so she did not hear him enter. He leaned a shoulder to the doorframe and crossed his arms over his chest.

"Find anything?"

Lady Rivenhall spun around with a swish of silk. Her

green eyes reflected her surprise, and he noted with more than a little satisfaction that she gripped the edge of the desk for support. And when she made no other movements, he asked, "No knife today, Lady Rivenhall? But I suppose that would have been somewhat difficult to explain when Lord Elkin was lifting your skirts."

She raised her chin. "Quite true, my lord, but at present I would give anything to have brought my dagger with me."

Her composure irritated him, and Aidan felt an overwhelming need to discomfit her. He held her gaze, pushing off the doorframe and stalking toward her.

"Did you find anything of interest, Lady Rivenhall?" he repeated as he stepped closer. She leaned back, and he saw her shiver, whether from fear or a chill he could not say.

"No," she breathed.

Aidan decided to convince the treacherous woman that any documents she found were vital to the success of the British war effort. And, to be truthful, he was rather keen on seeing those lace drawers.

"You will forgive me if I doubt that you have come away empty-handed." He stopped a yard from the desk and looked down at the captivating lady. "Take off your gown." But when she held his eyes and made no move to comply, Aidan said evenly, "You may remove your gown"—he raised a brow—"or I will do it for you."

Lady Rivenhall glanced at the locked door, and he could see her quick mind working through her alternatives. And when she came to the inevitable conclusion that there was no means of escape, her pale eyes returned to his and he felt a grim triumph pulse through him.

Her hands fell to the laces of her luxurious gown, and Aidan could feel his anticipation building as each golden tie gave. He searched for a distraction and an explanation for his unconscionable desire for this woman.

"Very nicely done with the pistol, by the way. Got Elkin out in a hurry, and yet you say you found nothing to interest France? I must confess, I'm disappointed."

Her fair head snapped up, and she glared at him. But the

lady said nothing and continued unlacing her gown, stepping out of it and tossing it at him when she had finished.

Her nipples hardened against her abbreviated chemise, and he tried desperately not to notice as he searched the silk gown. He shoved his hand in the hip pockets, and just when he thought she had not found the documents, his hand grasped the stiff brocade panel of her bodice.

Clever.

He feigned ignorance and tossed the gown across the desk. He could now prove her treachery, but Aidan also realized that there would be someone waiting to receive the counterfeit documents. Someone who, if he exposed her, would go undetected.

He stared at her, his decision made.

"Now your petticoats," he whispered.

The lady untied the layers of silk, resentment burning in her eyes. She stepped out of them and lifted the yards of fabric in his direction. He swallowed before taking them, and on a shaky breath said, "Your chemise."

Lady Rivenhall faltered but complied, and Aidan stood in awe as he stared at the most magnificent body he had ever seen. She was perfect, and stood within his reach in nothing more than lace drawers and matching garters that held stockings to long, shapely legs.

Aidan reached out and cupped her breast, unable to stop himself. He closed his eyes and clenched his jaw in a futile attempt to restrain his desire. She fit perfectly in his hand, and he seized her in a gentle caress.

His other hand slid around her waist and pulled her flush against his body. He could feel the heat of her through his shirt, and his hands fell to her flawless backside. He grabbed her, enjoying the feel of the lace drawers that provided provocative glimpses of creamy, white skin.

"These drawers are *French* I presume?" he asked, the lace sliding as he moved it over her silky curves. However, when she did not answer he leaned back and made the mistake of looking into her pale green eyes. He saw in them a vulnerability that belied her bravado.

He should have felt nothing, no compassion, no need to ease her distress, but he did. He felt an overwhelming desire to kiss her fear away and make love to her on the study floor.

I must be going mad.

"Get dressed," he said, disgusted with himself.

Aidan turned his back on the woman and ran both hands through his dark hair, thinking that if the little traitor cracked his skull open it would serve him bloody right.

The Earl of Wessex was feeling far less charitable the following morning.

He watched as Lady Rivenhall took a turn with Lord Elkin while he himself was stuck strolling the garden with two eligible young ladies on either arm. Unfortunately, returning from Albuera a war hero had incited every matchmaking mama to push her daughter in his direction. Aidan sighed to himself when the young chit to his left pressed her plump breast firmly against his forearm.

"The gardens are quite extensive, are they not, my lord?"

"Quite," he said with a polite nod.

The brunette found it necessary to add to the conversation. "What of your gardens in Wessex, my lord?"

But he hesitated in answering when Lord Elkin's butler spoke with his employer then led the man out of the gardens and toward the house. Lady Rivenhall smiled radiantly as she accepted the man's apologies for leaving her, and then sat down on the nearest bench, apparently intending to await his return.

"My mother was rather fond of roses," Aidan said absently. "If you will excuse me." He bowed and left the two girls to their chatter. The gravel crunched beneath his black Hessians as he made his way to Lady Rivenhall's side.

"Lady Rivenhall, would you care to stroll?" he asked loudly enough for other guests to hear, making it impossible for the woman to deny him.

She rose from the stone bench on which she had been

seated, her smile contradicting her flashing eyes. "I would be *delighted,* my lord."

He offered her his support, and she curled her elegant hand around his forearm. Images of those hands roaming over his body flashed before him, and Aidan forced himself to remember who, and what, she was.

They walked a while longer before he said, "I'm surprised that you enjoy *English* gardens."

She stiffened. "I am quite found of the English countryside, Lord Wessex. My father and I spent our summers with my uncle at his estate in Suffolk."

"And what of your mother?"

"She died when I was but three."

"Pray tell, my lady, is your father a traitor as well, or are you the only member of your family led to betray your uncle and your country?"

"My father . . ." she began with such ferocity that he was taken aback. She closed her mouth, finding her composure. "My motivations are my own, my lord."

For some inexplicable reason her reserve infuriated him.

"I beg to differ, Lady Rivenhall. When Englishmen die by your hand, your motives concern us all." He took a steadying breath and forced his jaw to relax before continuing. "Which brings me to the point of this charming promenade."

The enigmatic woman stared at some spot on the horizon as they continued toward the larger fountain. Her hair sparkled in the afternoon sun, and he could scarcely turn away from her extraordinary features.

"Lord Elkin is a close friend of mine, and I will not allow him to be used. When he asks you to his bed, and we both know that he will, you will refuse him."

Lady Rivenhall's eyes burned with anger when she halted on the gravel path and turned to look up at him. "I shall bed whom I wish, when I wish, Lord Wessex. And rest assured that you will not be consulted on the matter."

"Lord Elkin—"

"Lord Elkin has no information that is of interest to me,

as you well know. So if I choose to bed him, it will be entirely based upon my attraction to the man himself."

"And I thought you were attracted to short men with aspirations of conquering the world."

Lady Rivenhall took his arm, and they turned back toward the house. "Well, I do admire a man who sets goals for himself. However," she added with a bright smile, "as of late, I find myself attracted to tall men with muscular bodies and piercing blue eyes."

Aidan glanced in the direction of her gaze and cursed as Lord Elkin walked back to the garden with a determined stride.

"John is not to be toyed with," he warned.

"Let us allow John to determine if he wishes to become my plaything." Lady Rivenhall's eyes slid to his. "And if you have proof that I am a traitor, then by all means turn me over to Whitehall. Otherwise, leave me to my amusements."

"You forget, I do have proof, Lady Rivenhall," he whispered as he bit into her arm with his fingers. "You interrogated me at Albuera, if you will recall."

The lady batted her eyelashes and said with feigned innocence, "The Earl of Wessex was injured at Albuera, which is no doubt the cause of his confusion. I can assure you, my lord, that I have never left England. I can't imagine why he would be saying such things, except perhaps that I refused his advances." She looked away. "I can be very convincing, Lord Wessex, particularly if men are conducting my interrogation."

Aidan rocked back on his heels, unbalanced by shock. He watched her adjust her sky blue day gown and then look up to greet John Elkin.

"Sorry to have kept you waiting, Lady Rivenhall."

"Do not concern yourself, my lord. Lord Wessex has been quite amusing in your absence." She held Aidan's eyes before turning them on their host as if she adored him.

"Has he?" John asked with hostility dancing in his 'piercing blue eyes'. "Well if you will excuse us, Wessex. I believe I shall show Lady Rivenhall the river."

"Not at all," Aidan said, unable to conjure a reason that would prevent his friend from leaving with the lethal Lady Rivenhall.

Celeste's heart was thundering in her ears as they started for the water. She could feel the Earl of Wessex staring after her as surely as she felt the sun warming her face.

She glanced back over her left shoulder and saw him standing in the middle of the gravel path. His fists were clenched at the sides of his graceful legs, and she could see his chest rising and falling beneath his cerulean jacket.

Celeste shuddered, drawing Lord Elkin's attention. "Are you cold, my dear? Shall I retrieve your cloak?"

"No," she said, turning her gaze and her attention toward her escort. "I just had a bit of a chill."

Lord Elkin glanced over his shoulder. "Has Wessex said something to upset you, Celeste?"

She laughed a bit too brightly. "No, of course not."

"It just seems as though you have a . . . history with Lord Wessex?"

It was a question.

He was asking if they had been lovers. If she had spread her thighs while the Earl of Wessex lay naked atop her, pressing her into the bed. No, he was not her lover. He had merely kissed her and caressed her breast, branding her with his hands and his lips.

Celeste flushed and told the truth. "Yes, John. Lord Wessex and I have a history, but not the sort you imagine. Our encounters have been brief and somewhat hostile in nature, as I am sure you have noted."

They reached the river, and Lord Elkin pulled her against a tree and out of sight of his other guests. His forehead furrowed, and his cobalt eyes locked with hers.

"He has not made advances toward you?"

Images of the previous night flashed in her mind; the earl's strong hands grasping her backside, her breast, his masculine scent filling her mind as he leaned over her.

"No," she said, but she had hesitated too long. She could

see Lord Elkin's jaw pulsing with jealousy, and she hastened to appease him. "The earl's attentions are by no means romantic, my lord." Her smile was seductive when she added, "You are the only man here that holds the slightest bit of interest for me."

His eyes drifted from hers to her breasts and then to her lips.

"Good," he said, kissing her and pulling her into a possessive embrace. Lord Elkin kissed her long and hard and then his lips settled just below her ear. "I spent half the night aching for you, Celeste, and when I finally succumbed to sleep, I dreamt of making love to you."

His mouth descended to the exposed portion of her breasts. He moaned, and Celeste could feel his arousal pressing against her hip. He captured her mouth, his tongue intertwined with hers as his hand closed around her breast.

"John, your guests."

His frustration was palpable. He released her with reluctance and smiled down at her. "I would relinquish my title to be rid of the bloody lot, so that I might spend hours making love to you on this very spot."

Celeste laughed then blushed at the compliment. "But your guests are here."

"Yes they are. Damn them," he said with an amused smile, and Celeste decided that if she were an ordinary woman, she would like this handsome Lord Elkin very much. "I don't suppose that you could wear those lace drawers tonight, Lady Rivenhall?"

"No, I'm afraid not." Celeste's arms drifted around his neck, and she laughed at the disappointment scrawled on his features. "I'm wearing a different pair of lace drawers, as that is all that I possess."

His blue eyes flared bright, and he muttered, "Bloody hell," before slanting his mouth over hers. He kissed her one last time and then, with great reluctance, escorted her back to the manor house.

Fifteen

❦

That evening at dinner, Celeste was seated to the right of her host. Fortunately, Lord Elkin had the foresight to seat the Earl of Wessex at the far end of the table. The young earl appeared engaged by the throngs of females who seemed to follow the man's every move, so Celeste turned her attention to Lord Elkin and the task at hand.

She sat dutifully by while Lord Humphrey droned on about fishing, and on a whim Celeste ran her foot up Lord Elkin's calf. He tensed, but did not turn to look at her. Irritated, she removed her right slipper with her left foot then placed her stocking clad toes on the inner portion of his knee.

Lord Elkin turned his head with a comment about trout and met her eyes, his expression unreadable. He lifted his wine glass and returned to his discussion. Her foot inched higher, and she noted that his breath was becoming short. He lowered his glass and reached for the napkin in his lap. He dabbed his lips and then returned the napkin, seizing her foot under the table with his left hand.

Celeste tried to pull her foot away, but his grip firmed and his thumb began stroking the bottom of her foot in sensuous circles.

Damn! What had she been thinking? It was one thing to tempt the man, but she was waving a red flag in the face of one of the ton's most notorious bulls. Lord Elkin released her foot and his hand returned to his wine glass, but something in the way he moved his lips along its crystal rim told her that he was not thinking of his claret. True, she needed him alone, but perhaps she had gone a bit too far.

Marie had learned that Lord Elkin kept a strongbox in the library, and Celeste needed to gain access. The difficulty, of course, was not seducing the man, but acquiring the key. She had searched John's bedchamber last night after leaving the Earl of Wessex in the study, and had found nothing to implicate the man.

The strongbox was the only other possibility before he could be cleared of suspicion. She needed that key and, unfortunately, Lord Elkin was the only person that possessed one.

Celeste arrived at the boathouse at midnight as agreed and was not surprised to find Lord Elkin already there with lit candles and chilled champagne. The setting was very romantic and should have been deeply moving.

Celeste rarely respected the men she seduced. However, with John she felt guilt digging into her side as she walked toward lush cushions carefully arranged on thick Aubusson rugs. But Celeste reminded herself, as she always did, that she had a duty to perform.

Lord Elkin made no pretense about the reason for their meeting and kissed her soundly the moment she was within reach.

"I promised myself that I would take my time enjoying you. But now that you are here, I'm afraid my need has overcome my sense." John brushed her hair away from her face as he smiled down at her. "You are so beautiful, Celeste," he whispered and then kissed her again.

Celeste settled into his powerful arms and let the slow, sensuous kiss come to its natural conclusion. Lord Elkin pulled away from her and took a step toward the elaborate bedding. He lifted his arm, holding his hand out to her in open invitation.

Her heart began pounding, and she swallowed for courage. Celeste placed her hand in his, but when she stepped toward him, she stumbled, landing hard against him.

"Are you all right, my dear?"

"Oh," Celeste hissed, limping on her left foot. "No, I'm afraid not, John. I believe I have just injured my ankle."

Lord Elkin dropped gallantly on one knee. "Is it broken?"

Celeste hissed in pain as he probed her ankle.

"No, just a sprain, I should imagine. However, I do think it would be prudent to return to the house for some laudanum." She looked into his blue eyes and was taken aback by the amount of disappointment she read in them. "I'm so sorry, John."

"Nothing to be done, my dear," he said, his smile weak. "I'll just take you back and leave you in the care of Madame Arnott."

Lord Elkin bent to lift her, but stopped when Celeste gave an adamant, "No." His slashing brows furrowed with concern. "It would not do for us to be seen coming from the boathouse together at this time of the evening, John. The house is not far, I shall manage."

He nodded, clearly not happy about having her walk to his home unassisted. "If you're sure you will be all right . . ."

Celeste's smile reflected her genuine affection for John Elkin as she pulled him toward her for a kiss. "I shall survive, my lord, just so I might have the pleasure of seeing you in London."

He chuckled and patted her on the backside. "Well, go on, then, or I shall ravage you, injured or not."

Celeste limped to the door and glanced over her shoul-

der to look one last time at the handsome Lord Elkin. He
smiled in farewell, but the disappointment had crept back
into his masculine features.

As she walked to the house, guilt overcame her. Celeste
shook off the weight of it with the toss of her head, reminding herself that she was helping John by eliminating
him as a suspect and that any emotional distress he suffered was nothing compared to the damage Lion could
inflict.

She reached into the pocket of her gown, pulling out
Lord Elkin's keys. They clanked together as she spun them
around the brass ring, looking for one that might fit a
strongbox. She found it. And as Celeste continued toward
the library, she wondered if she would ever be able to forgive herself for the cruel acts of deception she had committed on behalf of the Crown.

John Elkin stood staring out the boathouse windows with
one hand in his pocket and a champagne flute in the other
hand. He exhaled, utterly disillusioned, and admonishing
himself for having hoped that Lady Rivenhall would be the
woman to heal his wounded heart.

He downed a substantial portion of the sparkling liquid,
trying to wash away the memories that bubbled forth of
another stunning woman. John had hoped that making love
to Lady Rivenhall would dull his pain, and that perhaps
she might banish from his mind thoughts of a lady that he
would never possess.

But he had been wrong.

He had been to enough hells in his time to know when
his pockets were being pilfered. And while Lady Rivenhall
was very good, he had still felt the weight of his keys dis-
appearing from his pocket.

John continued gazing at the reflection of the full moon
on the river as he came to grips with the fact that Lady
Rivenhall had never wanted him. She had most assuredly
wanted something, but not him.

A surge of pain crested in the pit of his stomach, lodging

heavily in his chest and he sank to his knees beneath the weight of it. He would remain in the boathouse long enough for Lady Rivenhall to rob him blind—punishment for allowing himself to dream of being loved for himself alone.

Celeste admired the understated elegance of Lord Elkin's enormous library. And while many gentlemen maintained large libraries, not all of them were used. But this one was used, and often. She lifted her right hand to touch the bits of parchment John had, no doubt, utilized to mark his favorite passages. She smiled, turning as she glanced about the room. The bits of parchment were everywhere, like little signposts marking the undeniable presence of John Elkin.

Her heart sank as she walked toward the strongbox, invading his privacy further still. She pushed the musty tomes to one side so that she might access the box mounted in a recess of the oak shelves. She glanced at the door while setting down her candle, then lifted the small silver key.

The lock gave the instant she turned the key, and Celeste was overcome with trepidation. What if she did indeed find some incriminating evidence? What then? But she knew the answer. After she gave the information to Falcon, Lord Elkin would be interrogated by the Foreign Office and eventually put on trial for treason.

Celeste prayed that she would find nothing incriminating as she turned the handle.

She reached first for the velvet cases nestled in the back of the strongbox and was not surprised to find an impressive array of jewels. The cases held emeralds, sapphires, jade, diamonds, and an enormous ruby that she could not help but hold up to the light of her candle.

She smiled at John's impeccable taste and returned the cases from whence they had come. Next, she reached for the papers: legal documents, deeds, investments in shipping and coal, Lord Elkin's will, and a letter.

Celeste removed the communication, noting how worn the edges were, as if it would break apart at the folds if it were opened once more. Celeste held the seal up to her candle but did not recognize it. She carefully opened the letter and began to read.

July 14, 1809
My Dearest John,

To say that I was surprised by your proposal of marriage would be a lie. I had feared that our growing affection for one another would lead to an offer, and I blame myself entirely. It is my selfish desire for your companionship that has led you to declare yourself.

And while your friendship means the world to me, I am not in love with you. I would give any sum to change my heart but, regrettably, I cannot. My heart aches not only for the pain that I shall cause you, but for the loss of my dearest companion.

John, if you can ever forgive my selfishness, I ask that you consider preserving our friendship. Your voice, your smile, your humor brightens the darkest of my days, and I do not know what I would do without them.

I shall reserve the first dance at the Earl of Wessex's ball for you. If you honor me with your partnership, I will know that I am forgiven, and we shall remain companions for the rest of our days.

Your Devoted Friend,
Felicity

Celeste was stunned, and her heart ached for Lord Elkin. The wounded lord was obviously still in love with this woman, or he would not have kept this letter for the past two years. She wondered if John had danced that first dance, or if he had let their friendship dissolve with the sting of her rejection.

Perhaps this woman had set her sights on another man? Felicity . . .

She had heard of a Felicity . . . yes, Lady Appleton. The

woman had some connection to Lord Wessex. She was a close acquaintance of the Duchess of Glenbroke, if Celeste remembered correctly. Perhaps the lady had set her sights on the young Earl of Wessex?

The flash of annoyance that accompanied her thoughts startled her. Surely, she did not expect the legendary Wessex to remain a bachelor. No doubt the man would take a worthy wife once the war had ended. As he should. A strong, young war hero returning to offer for the beautiful Lady Appleton.

Damnation!

Disgusted with herself, Celeste returned the letter to the strongbox. She needed to concentrate on surviving this war, not contemplating the romantic attachments of the very man who was hell-bent on seeing her executed.

She closed the strongbox and pushed the tomes back into position, then made for the door. She blew out the candles with an irritated huff and slipped into the darkened corridor. The house was quiet, and she padded up the stairs without seeing so much as a servant.

Her uneasiness dissipated as she reached the bedchamber door and began contemplating her next assignment. She was thoroughly relieved that, for all intents and purposes, Lord Elkin could be crossed off the list of suspected traitors.

Sixteen

❧❧❧

Aidan sat in the corner of the darkened room, awaiting the arrival of Lady Rivenhall. He rubbed his chin between his thumb and forefinger, but stilled when the door began to open.

"Marie?" the woman asked in confusion. When the door closed, Aidan lit the three-pronged silver candelabra sitting on the table to his left.

"I'm afraid Madame Arnott cannot hear you, Lady Rivenhall."

"What have you done to Marie?"

He saw panic in her lovely eyes, and for the briefest of moments he regretted his choice of words.

"Calm yourself," he said as he rose. "Your maid is experiencing the same sleep I enjoyed at Lord Reynolds's ball. I fear she will have a tremendous headache tomorrow morning, but somehow I cannot seem to muster the slightest bit of sympathy."

He followed as Lady Rivenhall ran to the adjoining room to check on her companion. And when she was satisfied that the woman was unharmed, the lady turned her attention to him.

"How dare you enter my private bedchamber? I shall scream."

"And I will stop you." She glared at him, but Aidan ignored her. "I do apologize for the inconvenience, but I thought you performed your duties in bed, so naturally I began in the bedchamber."

"Naturally." The single word was caustic.

"I'm afraid I shall need to search you once again, Lady Rivenhall."

"Yes, I'm sure that you do," she returned hotly.

Aidan smiled, but he knew it was not a reassuring look. "I shall begin with your reticule while you disrobe."

She hurled the satin handbag directly at his head, and he instinctively reached up, catching the thing in midair. "Let me guess. You had a slingshot as a child?"

"Two," she answered sarcastically.

"I see you still throw very accurately," he conceded before pulling roughly at the pink satin ropes that held the reticule closed.

Inside, he found an expensive gold hair comb, an embroidered handkerchief, and a perfectly balanced knife. Aidan removed the deadly dagger and looked up.

"I was afraid that you had lost . . ." His mouth went dry.

She stood before him, as before, in nothing but lace drawers and matching garters, this time adorned with blue satin ribbons. Her arms were crossed over her breasts, but he knew what they looked like, what they felt like. He imagined what they would taste like as he reached into his trouser pocket, withdrawing a single sheet of paper.

"What have I found in your reticule, Lady Rivenhall?" he asked, his broad smile filled with satisfaction. Her lips were parted, and her blond brows furrowed. "I believe you said I needed proof? It would seem that a dear friend of mine had his office burgled several days ago, and the only items taken were schedules of cargo shipments from his mill."

"No one will believe you," she said, but her apathy sounded forced.

Aidan tilted his head to one side. "Surely you don't believe you are the only one who can be convincing, Lady Rivenhall." He lowered his voice a notch. "I don't understand. The woman invites me to her bed and then begins questioning me about my time in service. My battalion, my commander, their present location, and then I discover this"—he held up the forged document—"in her reticule and became suspicious."

When she said nothing, he backed her toward the bed and shrugged out of his russet jacket. He pushed her onto the mattress with a forceful shove and watched her breasts sway with the impact. Aidan dragged his gaze to her wide eyes.

"But you see, Lady Rivenhall, I have a bit of a dilemma," he continued as he crawled over her, grabbing her right wrist and carefully removing her ingenious gold ring. "I could turn you over to the local magistrate on the morrow so that you can be held over for trial. However . . ."

He rocked his hips against her femininity, concealed only by the light fabric of her thin, silk drawers. His words became harsh as he ground his hardened shaft against her in a vulgar display of masculine longing. He took care to conceal his disgust at the crude behavior, knowing that his actions were necessary.

"However, I find you have something I want." Her eyes were locked with his as though mesmerized and unable to look away. He dipped his head and pressed his lips to the hollow of her neck. "You see, it has occurred to me that you must be rather extraordinary in bed to have become the whore to Napoleon himself."

"I have *never* been Napoleon's whore," she spat.

Aidan lifted his head and stared in disbelief. "You expect me to believe that the emperor keeps such a tempting treat at his side without ever having had a taste of you?"

"He tried," she began, but stopped abruptly as the earl grasped her chin and forced her to look up at him.

"He tried, and what?"

She jerked her chin from his grasp, but he turned her toward him once again, waiting for his answer. "I slapped him," she said when she realized he was not going to relent.

He gave a burst of laughter. "You struck the most powerful man in the world?"

"Yes," she answered, her fair brows furrowed in irritation.

"Yet you remain alive?"

"The emperor . . ." Lady Rivenhall took a deep breath to ease her rising anger before she began again. "The emperor enjoyed it."

Aidan pushed back a bit in order to see her beautiful face more clearly. "What do you mean, he 'enjoyed it'?"

The earl watched color rise from her chest all the way to the tips of her ears, but she did not look away. "The emperor became . . . he found . . ." She sighed and spoke in a rush. "The emperor became aroused when I beat him."

Curious and more than a bit skeptical, Aidan asked, "How?"

The stunning woman closed her eyes, embarrassment tinting her cheeks to a beguiling shade of pink. "On the . . . on the posterior."

"Nude?"

"No!" she shouted, as if offended. "Both of us remained fully attired."

"And he would find *satisfaction* in this?" Aidan was dumbfounded.

"Yes, well . . . I was required to say . . . things."

"What sort of 'things'?"

She closed her eyes, mortified. "I am half English, and he . . . he enjoyed for me to beat him and say . . ." She trailed off.

"Say what?" he prompted.

"That he would never have me, nor England."

Aidan attempted to comprehend the pleasure in that, but he was at a complete loss. "So the emperor has never . . . ?"

"No! I think it was the *not* having that he"—she gestured with one shoulder—"enjoyed so much."

Aidan shook his head. "Leave it to the French to muck up the simplest of pleasures," he muttered, rolling halfway off the woman.

"There is nothing 'simple' about pleasure, Lord Wessex. You English have such prudish concepts of sensuality."

"Prudish?"

"Yes," she said, pulling her hands from his slackened grasp and pushing him away as she lifted herself from the bed. He followed, pinning her to the wall between his muscular arms.

She ignored the implied physical threat and continued. "I have found that the higher a man's station, the more he enjoys being dominated by a woman in the bedchamber, and conversely, the *lower* a man's station, the more he savors dominating. It has been an invaluable insight when seeking information."

Aidan couldn't conceal his disbelief, which for some incomprehensible reason seemed to irritate the woman. Her eyes narrowed, and she was clearly offended by his skepticism.

"Kiss me," she commanded.

Never had a paramour demanded to be kissed, but Aidan eagerly complied. He bent his head over hers, his black hair skimming her forehead. He began softly, roaming leisurely over her soft lips and then effortlessly slipping his tongue between them to taste her.

Aidan wanted to make her ache for him, an Englishman. He sucked and tasted every corner of her delicious mouth before finally pulling away. A lazy smile spread across his features as he looked down at her, waiting patiently for her eyes to open.

"Prudish?" he asked arrogantly.

The woman's dazed eyes fluttered open. "And *that* is your preferred method of lovemaking, Lord Wessex?" Her tone indicated that she was unimpressed.

Aidan's smile was full of sensual promise as he stared at her lips saying, "It seems to have been more than satisfactory thus far, yes."

"Ah. And would you say that your appetites are similar to other men of your station?"

Aidan shrugged his assent.

"And you would not enjoy having your lover in control?"

Aidan looked at her askance. No gentleman would be stimulated by such wanton behavior from a gently bred lady. "No," he answered with confidence.

But before the word had passed his lips, Lady Rivenhall had grabbed his waistcoat and pushed him against the wall, causing him to grunt with the impact. Her lips devoured his mouth in a savage kiss that thrust her tongue into battle with his. The sensation sent a surge of heat spiraling from his abdomen to his groin.

Her hands dove into his thick hair, pulling him closer and deeper into her mouth. She stripped him of his waistcoat and pushed him down on the large bed. His expulsion of air was due not only to the forceful impact with the mattress, but to the feel of Lady Rivenhall stretched out along the entire length of him.

His body was responding to her wild caresses, his shaft growing, hardening. She ground her hips into his as she kissed him. Her hands grasped the top of his shirt, and she yanked, sending the ruby studs that held the garment in place flying. He moaned with pain and pleasure as he felt her nails scrape his flesh.

The temptress untucked his shirt and began trailing kisses along the hard muscles of his chest, pausing to nip at his nipple. His skin jumped at the sensation, and Aidan reached to pull her against his aching cock, but the siren pinned his arms to the bed and smiled.

"No," she ordered, and for some unfathomable reason he complied.

Her tongue laved its way downward, following the lines that crisscrossed his belly. Aidan swallowed hard and discovered that he was holding his breath, willing her to proceed lower.

Her hands quickly unfastened the buttons to his trousers, her tongue tasting him all the while. He watched in wonder as her golden head descended. Aidan shuddered with pleasure as desire began to ripple and lick at his senses.

He groaned as her soft lips pressed the sensitive skin just above the nest of black curls revealed by his gaping buckskins. Her hands rubbed his abdomen as her lips sent him to new levels of ecstasy. Aidan's mouth opened, and his eyes closed as he eagerly anticipated her next caress.

And then she was gone. His eyes opened in frustration, only to see the vixen looking down at him with contempt filling her light eyes.

"You're all the same." She bent down to retrieve her discarded garments. "So easy to control."

It took several moments before he was able to speak.

"Have you never," he began on a heavy breath, "lost control, Lady Rivenhall?"

"To a man?" She laughed, but the sound was anything but amused. "I have never had that luxury, my lord."

Aidan stared into her aqua eyes, trying in vain to comprehend her meaning. He wondered once again what had driven this beautiful woman to betray her country. He tried to imagine a plausible explanation, but there was none. His anger boiled to the surface, and he felt an overwhelming need to make her quiver with desire for her countryman.

His right arm darted out, and he had her on her back before she had time to step away from him. She struggled, but his arms tightened about her waist as he looked down into her eyes.

"Let us see if I can thaw the ice that flows through your veins."

Aidan covered her mouth with his. He savored the feel of her bare breasts against his chest as he consumed her lips. His tongue glided into the heat of her mouth, and she sucked in a breath. He circled her tongue, giving her senses no respite from his sensual demands.

He shrugged out of his gaping linen shirt without lifting himself from the heat of her enticing form. Her breath was becoming shallow, and desire reached deep into the pit of his stomach.

He released her mouth and burned a trail down her neck, reveling in the taste of her nipple in his mouth. Aidan shuddered when she cried out with pleasure as he laved and suckled one breast and then the other.

Her head fell to one side, and he doubted that she was aware of the rhythmic rocking of her hips against him. He moaned his masculine need and grasped the delicate lace of her drawers, ripping them from her slender hips.

The siren's garters were fastened at mid-thigh, holding silk stockings to her shapely legs. She made no attempt to remove them, and the thought of having his head between those silk-clad thighs sent him to even greater heights of anticipation.

He kissed the sleek skin just above her garters, but when he saw her sex, plump and wet, ripe to be tasted, he was forced to grit his teeth or climax then and there.

Celeste was floating.

His touch had ceased to burn and was now causing her body to ache and throb in the most unlikely of places. She could feel the moisture gathering between her legs, but when he dipped his head and tasted her, she very nearly leapt off the bed.

His tongue laved and explored, and she began to feel feverish. She could not breathe, and when his mouth closed over a sensitive portion of her femininity, Celeste cried out in a series of soft moans. She felt as though she was falling, but knew she remained firmly on the bed. Her thighs spread of their own volition, and then she crashed, shattering into a thousand pieces that fractured into even more.

She pushed him away, unable to take another moment of this delicious torment. She heard him remove his trousers, but just as she began to breathe again, he was on top of her, holding her arms over her head. He looked down at her with lust burning bright in his green eyes, but all she could think of was how breathtakingly desirable he was as he braced himself above her.

The muscles in his arms were mesmerizing as they

strained to hold his body above her. His lean, long form
made her hands yearn for their freedom, and his handsome
features and striking coloring held her enthralled. But it
was the weight of him pressing her into the mattress that
caused her to buck against his shaft.

"Please," she breathed, not sure what she was asking.

The handsome earl groaned and placed the head of his
satiny sex at her entrance. He held her gaze and intertwined his hands with hers before thrusting into her. She
closed her eyes and bit her lower lip to take her mind off
of the pain, and when she opened them again he was looking down at her in utter disbelief.

His brows were creased with confusion, and his raven
head shook ever so slightly. "How . . . how can you be a
virgin? You did not . . . Napoleon . . ." His emerald eyes
were troubled as he murmured, "I'm sorry."

Celeste could feel him inside of her, around her. The
pain was nothing to her need to have more of him. "It's
done, my lord." Instinctively, she rocked her hips, causing
him to shudder in her arms. "Make it worth the sacrifice."

He pulled away from her only to fill her again. She
moaned with pleasure each time he returned, and then she
began meeting his thrusts, impatient to be filled. She watched
the muscles covering his abdomen contracting in a motion
that they had been created for. His strokes were coming faster
and deeper, and she could see him holding back.

"Show me," Celeste whispered in his ear.

His restraints broke and he crushed her into the bed with
a masculine authority she had never imagined. He plunged
into her over and over again, his hips rolling, reaching for
her womb. His eyes drifted closed, and she watched his
breathing shorten until, with one forceful thrust, he
stopped breathing altogether.

Every muscle in his elegant body strained to push
further into her, and for the first time in her life, Celeste
fully understood the power she held over men.

Seventeen

Two of the most powerful men in all of Britain sat in the comfortable elegance of Viscount DunDonell's drawing room. The dark brown and burgundy in the room bespoke a masculine presence, while the faint smell of tobacco confirmed it. Light from a fire filled the room as the longtime companions drained the contents of their crystal snifters.

Daniel looked up from his glass and stared at the man who had shattered all of his dreams. He desperately tried to avoid the Duke of Glenbroke, for the mere sight of the man sent his soul into battle. His heart yearned for Gilbert's wife, while his head told him that she was not, and never would be, his. But he wanted her still, and the guilt and jealousy were killing him.

He had known Sarah Duhearst for as long as he could remember and had always imagined her as his bride. But then she had met Gilbert and all his childhood imaginings had evaporated in the blink of an eye.

"How are the bairns?" Daniel asked in order to remind himself that Sarah was a mother and the wife of another man.

Gilbert's silver eyes lit from within, and Daniel wondered where the elusive light came from. "Sebastian is eating us out of house and home, while little Constance has developed her mother's exquisite aim."

The viscount laughed, a part of him happy for his friend, while a smaller, more insistent part envied him intensely. He sighed, anxious to be done with their business.

"It's all settled, then?" Daniel asked in a throaty brogue.

The duke nodded, following the change of subject. "The baron has assured me that the mining has been completed and they are ready to transport the moment you arrive."

"I assume the warehouse has been properly prepared?" Daniel lifted the heavy leaded snifter to his lips and allowed the brandy to warm its way down his throat.

"Yes, the manager has been told that the warehouse will house barrels of wheat to be used by the military. Wellesley will be able to transfer the supplies to his vessels when he is ready to set sail for the peninsula."

"Do we have a date?"

"The twenty-ninth."

Daniel's brows rose, and he gave a whistle of admiration. "Less than a month. Wellesley's an ambitious man, I'll give him that."

The duke's face hardened. "We need him to be, or Napoleon will be in London by winter."

The viscount laughed uncomfortably. "Surely you jest, Your Grace."

His enormous friend crossed his legs, and with a shake of his head said, "No, we have obtained information confirming that if Napoleon defeats our troops in Portugal, he intends to sail for England."

Daniel's heart lurched then dropped somewhere in the vicinity of his stomach. "How reliable is this information?"

"Very. I'm told that our most highly placed operative sent the details of his stratagem. The emperor intends to invade before winter has taken hold."

"Bloody hell."

"Quite," the duke concurred and set his glass down with a melodious ping of crystal. He sat forward, spearing Daniel with his gaze. "DunDonell, I need not remind you of the importance of success. Only three people know of your commission: the baron, Wellesley, and myself."

"Right." Wanting to stretch his legs, Daniel nudged at the wolfhound curled in front of the fire. The hound protested with a low groan, but got up and shook himself awake.

The dog walked toward the doors, and Daniel was taken aback when the paneled mahogany parted as if the hound had summoned a footman to the task. But when he saw his fair friend stroll in as if he owned the bloody place, Daniel gave an indignant huff.

"What the hell are you doin' here, Christian?"

Lord St. John started then flashed his most charming smile—the one that had already earned him a reputation as a rake of the first order. Unfortunately for St. John, Daniel was immune.

"Oh, sorry, thought you were leaving for Scotland. Hunting, wasn't it? Splendid time of year to go—"

"Drop it, Christian, it's after midnight, and I'm tired. What the hell are ya doin' in my house?" Daniel asked, irritated.

Christian cleared his throat, and Daniel rolled his eyes, knowing his friend had gotten into another spot of trouble.

"Well, I was hoping to reside at your lodging for the duration of your stay up north."

"I'm not leavin' till Thursday. But do allow me the pleasure of a guess. Your father?"

His friend's square shoulders fell as they always did when discussing his father, the Duke of St. John. "He seems to have taken a dislike to my latest ladybird."

Daniel chuckled. As the eldest of seven brothers, he himself had dealt with various indiscretions committed by the McCurren clan. However, his siblings' wild oats did not compare to Christian St. John's infamous exploits. Curious, he asked, "Who is the lady?"

"I really don't see what bloody business it is of Father's. I don't see the Earl of DunDonell reprimanding you about the women who warm your bed."

"That is because, unlike you, Christian, *I* am discreet." Daniel's smile held a nefarious glint. "So, who is she?"

"Lady Hamilton."

Daniel raised both brows. "Damn, Christian," he chuckled. "You don't make it easy on yerself, do ya? Your father and brother must be spittin' fire."

Christian walked to the decanter and gave a dismissive shrug. "I'm not the one who is to be a duke, so I've no idea why it matters one whit to either of them."

His friend's blasé attitude annoyed Daniel.

"Very well, you can stay here until I return. But yer not"—he pointed at his fair friend—"I repeat, *not* to bring that woman into this house. My mother would have apoplexy for my bein' such a poor example to the lads."

Christian smiled from ear to ear, lifting his hands in a show of submission. "Never even dreamt of it."

The duke chuckled, and Daniel pointed to the settee. "I suggest you shut yer mouth and sit down before I send you packin'."

His friend did, asking, "Right, what are we discussing?" Christian pulled a cheroot from the inner pocket of his jacket, adding, "Women?"

Gilbert's chuckle turned to out and out laughter, and Daniel could not suppress the grin that pulled at the corner of his lips. "Aye, Christian, that is all we ever discuss."

"I've always suspected you were a bit of a lecher, Daniel. As a matter of fact, I was just discussing the matter with my father not half an hour ago."

Daniel's mouth fell open as he met the impish twinkle in his friend's eye. "You bastard, you know yer father will speak to mine," he said, wanting to throttle Christian, but knowing that he would be laughing the entire time he did so.

• • • •

Aidan Duhearst stood staring at the silk-lined wall as his valet assisted him in donning his gold and green striped waistcoat.

He was tired, having spent a restless night trying to reconcile in his mind the image of Napoleon's mistress with that of the virgin he had just deflowered. The woman seduced men for her own ends. He had seen her do so. Yet, she had most assuredly been a virgin until last night, and had obviously allowed the encounters to remain flirtations.

But did it matter in the least that the lady had not bedded these men? She still extracted the information, still turned it over to the French, still betrayed her country.

But it did matter.

She was not what she appeared to be, and the image of traitor and seductress were now blurred. She was an innocent playing a part. A virgin he had coerced into bed with the threat of imprisonment.

He felt like a bastard.

Aidan was beginning to wonder if he would ever be the man he once was. And while his coercion was unforgivable, the thing he feared more was the intensity of his pleasure in taking her. She had seemed to want him, but if she had said "no," would he have stopped from making love to her?

He was not sure.

A sharp rap at his bedchamber door caused Aidan to jerk his head in that direction.

"Enter," he called and was surprised to see his host stroll in and sink into a chair in front of the blazing fire.

"She's gone." Lord Elkin held Aidan's gaze, adding, "Left for London at daybreak."

"Why are you telling me this, John?"

"Because I should very much like to know what in God's name is going on."

The earl smoothed his hair back before settling into the chair opposite his friend. "What do you mean?"

"Hell's teeth, Wessex, you know damn well my meaning." Lord Elkin sat forward, placing his forearms on his thighs and lowering his voice.

"Last night I arranged to meet Lady Rivenhall in the boathouse. She came at the designated time and conveniently stumbled into me, straining her ankle. She returned to the house for some laudanum. Then I discovered the key to my safe was missing from my pocket."

Aidan shot out of his chair. "Damn it, John, why didn't you tell me you owned a safe?"

Lord Elkin laughed. "Well, that would rather defeat the purpose."

"Have you checked the contents? Was anything taken?" He reached for his emerald jacket and shrugged it on.

"Sit down, Aidan. I'm not quite the fool you believe me to be. The safe has been opened, but the contents remain undisturbed."

"What are the items?"

Lord Elkin shook his head. "Oh, no, I don't reveal the contents until you inform me of the truth."

"I can't, John. I don't have that authority."

"Damnation, man, I chair the committee overseeing naval deployment, for God's sake. If the Crown can trust me, I would think after twenty years of friendship you could too."

Aidan hesitated, but he needed to know if Lady Rivenhall had found anything of importance in that strongbox.

"Lady Rivenhall is not only a French spy, but mistress to Napoleon himself."

Lord Elkin sat back, raising his hands to his temples as if to ease the jolt to his mind. "How could you possibly know this?"

"Do you recall that I was injured at Albuera?"

"Yes." Lord Elkin shifted uncomfortably.

"What I have never told you was that I was captured and interrogated in a French prison by none other than your Lady Rivenhall." Aidan's jaw firmed. "The lady enjoys collecting British noblemen so that they might be hanged before the emperor. I myself escaped while being transported to Paris for just such an amusement."

His host's brows furrowed in confusion. "Why hasn't she been arrested? Have you informed Whitehall?"

"Yes. Unfortunately, the Foreign Office has already investigated Lady Rivenhall and found nothing to incriminate her." He looked at his friend. "But they were not at Albuera. So, John, I really must know what is in your safe."

John's face contorted as he tried to remember. "Nothing of use to her. My will, investments, jewelry, that sort of thing."

"Nothing else?"

Lord Elkin hesitated. "A letter."

"What sort of letter?"

"A private letter that has no bearing on this matter."

Aidan was taken aback by the intensity in his friend's tone. "Very well, John, but I must leave for London immediately. Have my carriage sent to town, will you? And I'm afraid I shall need the use of a horse."

"Have Alfred saddle Samson. He is my fastest mount."

"Thank you, John. And I am sorry. I would have told you—"

Lord Elkin waved away the apology, saying, "I know you would, Aidan."

John watched Lord Wessex leave the bedchamber as he contemplated the information he had just been given. His hand drifted to his pocket, where he touched the letter from the only woman he had ever loved.

Eighteen

❧❧❧

What has happened, *ma petite?*"

Celeste focused her eyes on her companion after having stared out the carriage window for the past two hours. "I don't know what you mean."

"Something has happened, Celeste. I know you too well." The older woman reached out and placed a hand over hers. "What has occurred?"

Celeste fought the tears that welled in her eyes, but once they emerged, the dam broke. She leaned her head on Madame Arnott's shoulder and whispered, "I did something very wicked, Marie."

Her companion stroked her hair and dabbed at her cheek with a handkerchief. "Lord Elkin was not harmed. You did what you must, no more."

Celeste covered her face in shame. "No, not that. I . . ." She paused, not sure she could continue.

"Tell me, *mon amie,*" Marie whispered, rubbing Celeste's back as she leaned into the older woman's shoulder.

"I . . . I bedded Wessex." Celeste closed her eyes and

swallowed a sob when Madame Arnott stilled. "He threatened to turn me over to the Foreign Office if I did not."

Marie kissed the top of her head and resumed rubbing her back in a soft, soothing motion. "Oh, Celeste, you sacrificed your virtue to save English soldiers. This is not wicked."

Celeste pulled out of the comforting embrace and shook her head violently. "You do not understand, Marie. I *am* wicked. I wanted him to make love to me." There, she had said it. "God, help me, Marie. I *wanted* him to touch me. He is so handsome, so noble and brave that every time I look at him, I want to touch him."

"And this is why we leave with such haste from Hartford Hall, *oui?*"

"Yes. I will finish this assignment, and then we shall return to France."

"No! It is too dangerous for you in France. Surely you can see that."

Celeste sniffled and wiped away her remaining tears. "We have no idea how long the war will last, Marie. I am of more use in France."

"Not if you are dead."

"If I am discovered, then so be it. You may remain here, but after this mission, I am for France."

Celeste regretted her words the moment she saw the hurt in Marie's blue eyes. "Of course I shall accompany you to France, Lady Rivenhall."

"I'm sorry, Marie."

Madame Arnott's eyes softened, but the hurt still remained. "I know you are, *ma petite.*"

"The Dog and Duck is just ahead, me lady," the coachman shouted down.

Lady Rivenhall sat up and adjusted her peach pelisse as Marie adjusted Celeste's coiffure. "Am I presentable?" she asked as the landau rolled to a stop.

Madame Arnott smiled. "Your cheeks are pink as if you have spent the afternoon in the sun."

"Thank you," she said, stepping down from the con-

veyance and missing the look of concern that had replaced
her companion's bright smile.

The Dog and Duck's boisterous dining hall gave Celeste
the distraction she needed. The wooden beams and low
ceiling of the room added to the comforting noise that was
far preferable to the seclusion of eating in a private room,
where only Marie stood between her and her thoughts.

"I've made ready the same rooms as before, your ladyship. Nice and tidy, just like last time."

"Thank you, Mister Jones, the rooms were very lovely,"
she said, smiling in appreciation. The old man beamed
from ear to enormous ear, revealing gaps where teeth
should have been. "Now if you don't mind, I should like to
eat."

"Yes, ma'am, the private dining—"

"No, thank you, Mister Jones, your dining hall will be
more than satisfactory."

Marie's head snapped 'round.

"Very well, my lady," the innkeeper said. "Call us if you
have any difficulties."

"That is most comforting," Celeste replied, and the old
man left them to their meal.

"We cannot possibly eat in here." Madame Arnott's tone
was filled with indignation.

Celeste rolled her eyes as she walked into the room. "Do
not be such an elitist, Marie. Has the revolution taught you
nothing?" she teased, sitting at a vacant table along the far
wall.

Lady Rivenhall pulled at the satin ties to her straw bonnet and stretched her neck from side to side. So, it took
several moments for her to notice that conversation had
come to a standstill in the smoke-filled room. Celeste
looked up and saw that the predominantly male patrons
were looking in their direction.

Marie huffed. "This is why we cannot eat in the hall. It
is the same wherever we go. The men, they . . . *covet?*"

"Lust."

"*Oui,* the men, they lust for you. We shall be remembered."

"I do not care, Marie. I am hungry and tired, and I want to sleep. It will take far too long to prepare a meal for us in a private dining room."

"This is not wise."

"What'll you have, me lady?"

Celeste turned to the serving girl, whom she knew to be the married daughter of the innkeeper. "I shall have whatever is prepared."

The woman's eyes widened, and she licked her lips in nervous agitation. "But, ma'am, all we gots is mutton stew and some bread. Me mother would be 'appy to make you—"

"No, thank you. The mutton stew will do very well, thank you. And would you mind bringing a pitcher of ale? I am rather parched from our journey."

Madame Arnott gasped, and Celeste ignored her. She stared at the wooden table, knowing that if she looked at any of the men in the room they would view it as encouragement.

The ale was brought, and she poured herself a large tankard full. Celeste sipped the bitter brew and remembered the many times that she had sat with her troops drinking ale when nothing more palatable was available. Her men had looked to her for strength and inspiration before battle, and she had given them nothing but treachery and deceit.

Celeste had tried to hate all the French, but with every passing year the line between good and evil grew indistinct. The young men under her command had joined the army rather than starve in the streets of Paris.

How could these men be blamed for her father's death?

But it was those men who had suffered for it. The information she had given Wellesley had led to the loss of many French lives. Not the lives of the wealthy men who ordered the death of her father and now sat at Napoleon's side. No, the men who died on the battlefield at Albuera were farmers and peasants, her troops.

Celeste refilled her cup, tired of war and dying and of the enormous burden she carried. If she unmasked the traitor, French soldiers would die; if she did not, English soldiers would die.

Did it really matter?

"Here's your stew, me lady."

Celeste smiled in thanks and ate in quiet contemplation. She scarcely tasted the food, noting only that it was hot and filling. But no matter how much she ate or how much she watched the patrons of the dining hall, her mutinous mind continued producing images of last night.

Of course, she knew what she had done was sinful, but when she thought of being held in the earl's powerful arms she wanted to be wicked all over again. To run her hands the length of his nude body in an attempt to understand why his form enticed her so, why *he* enticed her so.

She had hoped that if she bedded him, her infatuation would be satisfied, would run its course. What an innocent fool she had been. Holding him inside her had only made her body crave more of his exquisite touch.

Despair settled in her chest, and she took another sip of ale, and another, until the emptiness faded. The man despised her. He thought her a spy and would continue to do so. After she had exposed the traitor, she would return to France and continue gathering information for Falcon.

But what if I tell Wessex the truth?

The thought flashed in her mind before she could stop it. She knew what would happen—he would not believe her and in the process of proving her claim, the traitor would escape them. Men's lives were in her hands. It was too great a risk.

And besides, a small voice whispered, she did not deserve a man as fine and noble as the Earl of Wessex. She sipped her ale.

"Need a bit of company, me lady?"

Celeste looked up at the tall man who stood before her.

He was young, blond, and probably considered very handsome for a small village such as this.

"Marie, please go upstairs."

Madame Arnott obeyed, all too familiar with the commanding tone of her lady's voice.

"That's right," the man said with a wink. "Give us some time to ourselves, won't it?" His eyes roved over her with carnal speculation, further blackening her already foul mood.

"Sir, I have invited neither you nor your stench to join me, and I strongly suggest you leave my presence."

The large man planted his palms on her table and leaned toward her, saying, "A woman as fine as you ain't accustomed to sleeping alone." His smile became seductive. "I would be happy to offer me services if you promise not to wake the entire inn when you scream me name."

Celeste's lip curled in a mockery of a smile. "I'm afraid it is you who shall do the screaming."

The burly man's eyes flared with desire a moment before he shrieked in pain. He looked down at her knife cutting into the delicate skin between his fingers. Celeste held her weapon while he held her gaze, withdrawing his fingers from either side of the blade and examining his injury.

"You bi—" he began, and then apparently thought better of it. He walked back to his friends as their laughter rang out through the noise in the dark room.

Celeste wiggled the tip of her knife from the wood of the table and sheathed it to her thigh. She took one last gulp of ale and rose, heading for the staircase with all eyes fixed firmly on her back.

The Earl of Wessex stood at the bar of the Dog and Duck, thankful that he had borrowed Alfred's coat and hat before mounting Samson. The ride was a relatively easy one, and he had overtaken the lady's landau before lunchtime. Aidan had spent the rest of the afternoon at a sedate pace, just far enough behind so as not to be noticed by the coachman.

He slipped into the dining hall just as Lady Rivenhall sat down to eat. Aidan ate stale bread and stared, along with every other man in the room, as the lady downed tankard after tankard of ale.

This had no doubt been a source of confidence for the brave young lad who had ventured so high above his station. Aidan thought that he would be forced to intervene, but the lady had proven just as deadly as always . . . with the possible exception of last night.

A surge of desire swept through him as he watched the woman ascend the stairs. He washed it down with a mouthful of ale and called for another bowl of stew. Aidan waited for his food, trying not to imagine what garments she was removing, trying not to remember the feel of her silk stockings wrapped around his waist as he drove into her, trying not to remember the taste of her flesh as he took her pink nipple in his mouth.

"Another ale," he shouted with a lick of his parched lips.

Is that why the ethereal woman imbibed so much? Was she remembering, or, more likely, was she trying to forget?

He only prayed that he could.

Aidan's morning broke at dawn with the pounding of his head echoed by the banging at his door.

"Just a moment," he shouted irritably as he donned his buckskins and opened the small door. "Yes?"

"The lady's coach is preparing to depart, my lord."

"Well done," he said, tossing the boy a shilling and pulling on his boots and shirt. "Make ready my horse. I shall be down shortly."

"Yes, sir."

Aidan reminded himself that he needed to remain concealed, needed to observe whom she spoke with and where she was staying. He glanced down the corridor before coming downstairs only to see her seated, much as before, eating breakfast. And he had never seen anything more beautiful.

She was breathtaking.

Her golden hair was twisted atop her head with peacock feathers sprouting from a hint of a hat. Her gown was designed to draw attention to her small waist, and when she looked down at her food, Aidan remembered kissing that elegant neck as her pulse thundered with passion.

"Fancy meeting you here," he said before he knew what he was doing. Her mouth parted in shock, and she ceased to breathe. He remembered that as well. "I assume you are traveling back to London?"

"Y-yes. Madame Arnott is seeing to our luggage," the lady said to the table.

The earl sat down in the chair opposite hers and waited for her blue green eyes to meet his.

"What luck. Then might I offer my services as escort?" he said, infusing his smile with every ounce of his considerable charm.

Her eyes divulged her alarm, and he almost felt sorry for her. "No, thank you, my lord, that is not necessary. I'm quite sure you have better ways of occupying your time."

Aidan shook his head. "No, not really."

The stunning woman leaned forward, giving him a tantalizing glimpse of her breasts. "Then let me put the matter in other terms, my lord," she said, her shock having faded. "It will be a cold day in hell before I allow you into my conveyance."

"Then I suggest you don your jacket, my lady," he said, assisting her insistently from her chair. "Because you are about to descend into the mouth of the inferno."

Nineteen

❧

Lady Rivenhall could scarcely breathe as she was escorted outside by the determined Earl of Wessex. His large hand wrapped completely around her forearm, and when she attempted to pull away he discreetly tightened his grip, causing her to lose feeling in the tips of her fingers.

Celeste glanced up at the unshaven lord and knew by the hard glint in his striking eyes that there was no escaping him. She heard a gasp and looked over at her companion, saying, "It appears we shall have a passenger on our journey back to town."

Lord Wessex bowed elegantly and smiled in the direction of Madame Arnott. "Think of me as an *armed* escort, my lady. It would never do to have one of Lord Elkin's guests robbed on their return to London."

Marie glared at the young earl. "How very kind of you, my lord," she said, her tone flat.

"Think nothing of it," Wessex said, helping them into the carriage.

Celeste molded herself to the far side of the landau with

a fixed stare out the window. She felt Marie settle on the lavender squabs to her right, but she did not dare look in her companion's direction for fear that she would make eye contact with the man who now filled the enclosure with his overwhelming presence.

He settled opposite her, and she could have sworn she felt the heat from his legs straight through her skirts. Celeste wiggled a fraction of an inch backward, but continued to stare over the grassy hills outside. Lord Wessex rapped on the ceiling of the conveyance, and they lurched forward to begin their six-hour journey back to London.

Six hours! How would she survive?

Celeste closed her eyes, and when she opened them, she saw a smile spreading across his rugged features. *Damn him.* He was enjoying her discomfort. She wondered if it would be possible to look out the window for the entire journey. She focused on the distant landscape, but it did not help that she could sense the earl's continuous regard.

The trio sat in silence for fifteen minutes before the earl asked, "How did you come to be employed by Lady Rivenhall, Madame Arnott?"

Celeste's gaze darted to Marie's face. Madame Arnott never spoke of that time, and Celeste hated Lord Wessex for making her do so.

"That is none of your affair," Celeste spat ungraciously as she stared into his eyes.

His ebony brows furrowed with confusion, and the matter would have ended there, but for some inexplicable reason Marie answered the man.

"My husband was Lady Rivenhall's cousin," she began, lifting her blue eyes to meet the green of the inquisitive earl's. "When Celeste was but four years of age, French revolutionaries invaded my home and stabbed to death my husband, ten-year-old son, and seven-year-old daughter.

"I had been caring for my ailing mother and returned home five days later to the stench of their decaying corpses. I buried them in the flower gardens of our home and then traveled to Paris to care for a child who had recently lost her mother. I have been thus 'employed' ever since."

Celeste slid her hand to cover Marie's where it rested on the velvet squabs. She squeezed, lending Marie her strength, but a tear escaped Marie and cascaded down her cheek. Celeste quickly looked up at the roof of the landau, blinking rapidly to discourage her own tears.

She turned her head, never once looking at the odious man who had caused Marie to relive the old pain.

"I'm very sorry for your loss, Madame Arnott," he said with such sincerity that Celeste turned to see his face, to see if his features mirrored his tone. "I lost my parents many years ago, and while I would never presume to imagine the pain you have endured, I have felt the loss of family."

Marie nodded in acceptance of his condolences, and then it was the earl's turn to stare out the window. The next two hours of the journey passed in complete silence, and Celeste was convinced that it would have continued had they not stopped to water the horses.

Celeste bolted from the carriage before Lord Wessex could assist her down. She headed for the open fields opposite the stables, desperate to breathe air not dominated by the masculine scent of the handsome earl.

She bent the golden stalks of grass beneath her feet as she made for a cluster of ancient oak trees. Images flashed through her mind of her father being dragged down the stairs, of the French soldiers laughing as she hid in the parlor. Of her father saying, "Conceal yourself, Celeste. Please, my love." His last thoughts had been of her, for her.

But she hadn't returned to her room. She had run to the window and watched in horror as the drunken soldiers mocked her English father. And when that had ceased to amuse them, they had beaten him and finally . . . a captain had pulled his pistol and shot her father in the head while she watched, a coward hiding in the parlor.

Celeste reached the trees and sank to her knees, burying her face in her gloved hands. It had been months since she had allowed herself to think of her father, of that day. She wondered again if he would be proud of her, if she were doing the right thing, if he would forgive her lack of courage that day long ago.

"I'm sorry, Lady Rivenhall."

She heard the soft whisper from above.

Celeste looked up the length of the tall earl standing over her, and on a ragged breath said, "Why should you be? We're French, after all."

The earl sank down on his haunches, and she instinctively flinched away from him as if he would strike her. His eyes flickered with confusion. "I—"

"Save your apologies, my lord, and return to the carriage."

But he did not move, and the longer he remained the angrier she became. Celeste struck out suddenly, pushing him on the shoulders with the force of her anger and causing him to lose his balance and fall on his back. He stared at her in disbelief as he rested on his elbows, still making no move to leave. Rage overcame her, and Celeste flew at him, hitting him in the chest with her fists.

"Stop it."

Celeste swung at his face, but he caught her wrist and rolled her on her back.

"Stop," he growled, now as angry as she.

Celeste attempted to kick him, but the earl responded by straddling her while holding both arms firmly to the ground. Had he shouted or struck her, she would have endured. But instead he bent over her, looking into her eyes as he whispered, "I'm sorry," then bent his head and kissed her so gently she was uncertain if she merely remembered his lips.

Desperate to be comforted, Celeste lifted her head and pressed her mouth to his. He jerked backward, and she could see the suspicion in his striking eyes, but she didn't care. She pulled her arms from beneath his slackened grasp and locked them around his neck, kissing him with all the emotion unlocked by her memories. Her tongue slipped into his mouth, and she drank him in, his strength, his honor, his very soul—and for the briefest of moments she felt worthy of him.

But then the earl tore his lips from hers and jumped to his feet, pacing back and forth in the golden grass, the sun reflecting off his black hair.

"We must talk." He seemed agitated, and Celeste sat up to listen. "We must discuss last night and . . . what occurred." Wessex shook his head and ran his fingers through his hair. "We must discuss what will happen once we return to London."

Celeste shook her head to clear it. "What are you saying?"

The handsome man looked down at her. "You will not be permitted to venture out unless I am informed."

"Not permitted!" She was on her feet, her mouth hanging open.

"Yes, if you require an escort, you will summon me and me alone."

"A bit proprietary, don't you think, my lord?"

The earl stopped pacing and stared at her, anger warming his eyes to a golden green. "No, Lady Rivenhall, it is pragmatic. If you will recall, the only reason you are not in the hands of the authorities is—"

"That you enjoy burying yourself between my thighs."

They stared at one another for several moments before he answered, "Yes."

Celeste closed her mouth and took a deep breath, flaring her nostrils. "Well, my lord, I find your offer lacking in enticement."

"Are you suggesting, madam, that you would prefer the hangman's noose to my bed?"

"Yes, that is precisely what I am saying."

They stared at one another in silence. "You're distraught, Lady Rivenhall. I shall give you one week to reconsider your imprudent answer," the tall man said, striding toward the landau.

"I shall not require a week, Lord Wessex," she shouted at his broad back. "I have given you my decision."

At that, the elegant earl turned and smiled, saying, "Then may God have mercy on your soul." And with a bow he turned and strolled away, leaving Celeste decidedly cold.

Aidan was furious when he reached the carriage and pulled himself to the seat beside the coachman. He needed time to think—a task he seemed entirely incapable of within a furlong of the alluring Lady Rivenhall.

"I shall be riding with you for the remainder of our journey," Aidan said, running his hands through his disheveled mane.

The coachman's leathery skin pulled together in deep creases of concern. "Very well, me lord."

The man glanced down to verify that the ladies had returned to their seats before resuming their journey with a flick of his wrists.

The summer sun should have warmed Aidan, but it did not. He crossed his arms over his chest and focused on the road ahead of him.

He did not understand her.

He had seen her command troops with ruthless autocracy, and on the verge of tears at the distant loss of her companion's family. She was Napoleon's mistress, and a virgin. She pushed him away and then clung to him for comfort.

And God, how he had wanted to comfort her, to make love to her under the shade of that oak tree. Her kiss touched his very soul, and it was that overwhelming demand that had caused him to leap to his feet, to force himself to remember who she was . . . a French agent working on behalf of her emperor.

He would have to speak with Glenbroke upon his return, would have to insist that the duke find another man to follow the enticing Lady Rivenhall. For every time Aidan saw her he remembered being in her bed, holding her in his arms as he pressed into her.

British lives should not be reliant upon his weakening will. He tried to recall the faces of the men he had lost at Albuera, but when he looked into her jade eyes their agonizing screams faded to a whisper.

"Do you have any spirits on hand?" he asked the coachman. The man looked sheepish, causing Aidan to groan. "Good God, man, I'm desperate for a drink, not looking to have you dismissed."

"I've some gin in me basket, if that'll—"

"Perfect, thank you." Aidan reached down and pulled the flagon from the basket under their feet. He took a long draw of the tangy liquid and then offered the driver a sip.

"Women?"

Aidan jerked his head toward the carriage, saying, "Woman."

"Not Lady Rivenhall?" The man sounded astounded by the possibility. "For if 'tis she that grieves ya, then you must be in the wrong. That girl is the sweetest thing that ever did walk this earth."

Even her servants were devoted to the deceptive lady. "Well, if Lady Rivenhall is the finest we have on earth, then I shall be forced to look to the stars for companionship."

As they approached London, the congestion in the streets caused them to slow to a crawl. It took a good hour to reach Mayfair and Lady Rivenhall's lodgings. Aidan jumped down from the carriage and wished that he had not imbibed quite so large a quantity of the coachman's gin.

He handed down Madame Arnott, who promptly made for the safety of the front door. However, when he offered his arm to the younger woman, he held the stunning traitor's hand firmly in his, saying, "I *will* see you again, Lady Rivenhall."

"I think not, my lord."

Aidan released her hand and watched as she made her

way inside. He stared at the door and listened as the landau clattered down the road before turning his attention to the street around him.

"Boy," he called. The messenger was no more than ten years of age and reeked of tobacco. "Head round to Bow Street and fetch a runner." He paid the lad his due, adding, "If you're back within the half hour, I shall double your fee."

The boy smiled, revealing yellow teeth, then tipped his hat and ran as fast as his spindly legs would carry him. Aidan smiled to himself and leaned a shoulder against a lamppost, awaiting the Bow Street runner he would hire to follow the enchanting Lady Rivenhall.

Twenty

Gentleman Jackson's was crowded with amateur pugilists waiting to take their turn in the ring.

The dark man did not unbutton his shirt until the clerk was close enough to appreciate the sight. He smiled, peeling the garment away from his well-defined chest as he said, "Glad you could make it, Woodson. Need all the supporters I can muster, what?"

The diminutive man nodded, his pale eyes drifting downward, lit with anticipation.

"Quite," Woodson agreed, captivated by the sight of the retreating white linen as it uncovered the numerous scars that crisscrossed the dark man's torso, making the one on his jaw look like a scratch.

Annoyed, he clenched his fist and tried to stave off the memories, forcing himself to laugh at the sympathetic horror that had replaced the smaller man's lust. He ran a finger along one of the larger of his raised scars, still pink from its all too recent infliction.

"You think this ghastly? You should see my back." He

laughed. The clerk did not. "It's all right, old man, they don't hurt anymore."

"What . . . how . . . my God, how many battles?"

"Not many." He smirked at the sickening irony. "The majority of my"—he touched the jagged scar on his jaw—"decorations were received after I had been captured."

"Captured!" The clerk gasped, appalled.

"Yes, but not to worry." He winked, not wanting to discuss the matter. "For some inexplicable reason, women love battle scars, run their hands all over them."

Woodson's lust returned as he imagined doing just that. The dark man laughed, causing his stomach to contract into hardened bands.

"The ring is in this direction," he said, clasping his companion on the shoulder. "Did you place a wager?"

"Yes," Woodson replied.

The tall man looked down, giving the clerk his most charming smile. "On me, I hope."

Woodson smiled. "Yes, of course," he said, glancing around the stuffy room that stank of cheroot smoke and sweat.

"Good man. I shall speak with you after my bout. Shouldn't take long," he said with an arrogant laugh.

The clerk would enjoy seeing his dominance as well as his figure, and the dark man reminded himself to take his time in winning the match. He wiped sweat from his face, feeling the scar that traversed his jaw.

He stepped under the rope that had been strung in a square about the room to keep spectators at a safe distance and turned his attention to his opponent. The young buck was large but untried. The dark man smirked, knowing that his experience in battle would always give him an advantage over the dandies that flocked to Gentleman Jackson's.

The bell rang, and the match commenced. He could hear the betting taking place all around him, shouts of encouragement to him but more for his adversary. He did not enjoy physical violence, but he was good at it. Always had been, when it was required.

He waited for the boy to drop his fists and then hit him in the jaw. The boy grunted and jabbed back at him, missing and continuing to move toward him. He waited. The buck now kept his hands high, and the dark man smiled to himself, striking the young man a punishing blow on the side of his soft gut.

The crowd cheered; more shouts, more betting. He waited as the boy lumbered forward and struck at his face. He ducked, but the dandy landed a surprisingly powerful blow on his right shoulder.

His jaw firmed with irritation. *Enough of this.* He advanced, cornering the boy in three strides. He could see the fear in the young buck's eyes as the boy flailed his arms as if uncertain how to protect himself.

The dark man paused, and then with exceptional speed hit his opponent square on the nose, breaking it with a spray of blood across the beige tarp.

The match was called, and a physician summoned to see to the boy's wound. The victor smiled and made his way to the stunned clerk, whose jaw hung open as he watched the blood pouring from the dandy's nose and onto the canvas.

The dark man rubbed his shoulder, reprimanding himself for allowing the blow.

"Check my shoulder, old man. Make sure nothing is broken."

Woodson shook himself from his daze. "Y-yes," he said, looking at his companion's shoulder as if it were a venomous snake.

The dark man let his head fall back as he took air into his lungs. He closed his eyes and then felt the clerk's tentative fingers probing his muscular shoulder.

"Well done," a fellow pugilist offered with a slap on the back.

"Thank you," the dark man said, opening his eyes and smiling when he caught Woodson staring at him.

"Seems intact, my lord," the clerk pronounced with a guilty start.

"Excellent. I'll just go bathe, and then we can pop over

to White's and collect our winnings," he said, making his way to the bathing rooms and leaving Woodson to his own imagination.

A half-hour later the dark man returned, cleanly shaven and attired in fresh garments. "There you are. Let's dash over and pick up our winnings, shall we?" As they walked, he asked, "Are you attending Lord Hambury's ball Friday next?"

"No, I'm afraid I was not invited, my lord. Are you?"

"Unfortunately so. Being a decorated veteran, I seem to get invited to all these bloody events. Oh, well, never mind; undoubtedly be a tremendous bore anyway. I'm only attending out of fear of offending Lord Hambury; the man does have an eligible daughter with a substantial dowry." He waved the thought away. "But I never could stomach the ladies of the ton." He turned to the clerk. "How about you?"

The man turned bright red. "Oh, I never . . . that is to say—"

"Don't tell me you have a ladybird tucked away in Cheapside?" The dark man laughed. "Never mind, your secret is safe with me, old boy. Always found a mistress a bit of a nuisance myself, but to each his own, I suppose."

"Well, I—"

"Ah, here we are," the dark man interrupted.

They entered White's, and he collected five hundred thirty-two pounds in winnings, while Woodson sheepishly retrieved twenty-seven. Suddenly, the dark man wanted to be free of the clerk's company, so he said the only thing he knew would rid him of the man.

"It's a bit early yet, but how about we celebrate my victory with two of Madame Florentine's most skillful whores?"

"No, thank you, I . . . there are one or two things I had hoped to complete for Lord Wellesley before tomorrow."

"Got the ladybird on ice, do you? Well," the dark man

said, clasping his companion on the shoulder a shade too long. "Perhaps next time."

"Yes, next time," Woodson said, full of hope. "Good evening, my lord."

"Evening," he answered, and when the clerk had gone, he considered that two whores would be just the thing to celebrate his victory . . . and his progress.

Thursday morning the Earl of Wessex awakened to a knock at his bedchamber door. He glanced at a clock on the mantel—nine in the morning. *Good Lord!* Aidan groaned and cursed his butler for waking him at such an ungodly hour.

"Yes, what is it?" he demanded, flinging the door open in nothing more than his dressing gown.

"You asked to be notified if you received a communication from Mister Brown." Aidan's butler lifted a polished silver tray that held a single sheet of paper.

"Thank you," he said, dismissing his servant with an apologetic nod.

Aidan ripped open the seal of the missive and sank into a red leather chair near the window. The message consisted of one line of script.

My Lord,
   The lady in question is preparing to attend Lord Hambury's ball.

>   *Sincerely,*
>   *Mister Brown*

Aidan had no notion how the runners received their information, but he was grateful and would reward the man well. His brow furrowed in thought as he sat down to pen a letter to his sister.

He yanked once on the velvet cord and lit a candle, dripping wax onto the back of the folded paper. He pressed his seal into the hardening paraffin just as his servant rapped on the door.

"Have this delivered to the Duchess of Glenbroke as soon as possible." And just before the man left, Aidan added, "Oh, and have breakfast sent up."

"Yes, my lord, breakfast is already being prepared," his man said with a bow as he backed out of the room.

Lord Hambury's ball. Why Hambury?

As far as he knew the man held no position that would be of any use to Lady Rivenhall; nor did Reynolds, for that matter. As chair of the committee for naval deployment, Elkin was, of course, an invaluable source of information, but had proved just as tight-lipped as always.

Aidan sighed, seeing no pattern, no logic to her objectives, and for some curious reason that fact made him uneasy. Perhaps his disquiet lay in the fact that the woman had proven quite capable both in France and England, with this one exception. And that was the difficulty . . . there should not be an exception.

Unless . . .

His breakfast arrived, and Aidan poured himself a large cup of coffee to clear his mind. The black brew was too hot and burned the roof of his mouth, but he scarcely noticed.

Unless the lady's targets were not of her own choosing.

He sat back in his chair, knowing he was correct. The woman had been given the names of men she was to investigate. Aidan slathered butter and strawberry jam on a portion of toast, taking a hearty bite.

But who had given her the names? Surely not Napoleon. The emperor's reach was not that far, so there must be another agent already established in London.

But the question still persisted—why these men?

Aidan continued eating while his mind sifted through the possible answers to that question. But one thing remained clear. Lady Rivenhall was not working alone, and if he wanted to stop the transfer of information to the French, then his net would have to become much wider—he now had two fish to catch.

•   •   •

The following afternoon, Aidan sat in the comfort of his club with his closest friends, Daniel McCurren and Christian St. John. The viscount had requested their presence in order to bid them farewell before departing for his estates in Scotland.

Daniel's brogue became thick as he lamented the difficulties of being the heir to an earldom.

"So, the lass looks at me, in the midst of her husband's ball, mind ya, and says, 'Are you DunDonell's heir?'"

Aidan smiled, anticipating his friend's bold lie.

"I say 'Aye,' and then the lady invites me upstairs for a game of hide the haggis while her elderly husband greets their guests downstairs."

Christian rolled his eyes. "Bollocks."

The Scot raised his auburn brows. "Is it?"

"Yes," Lord St. John insisted, as the viscount reached into his cobalt jacket and pulled out a lace handkerchief adorned with the lady's initials.

"'A token of her esteem,'" Daniel said with a wink toward the astonished Lord St. John. "I tell ya, Christian, it is na easy being a peer. You're really quite fortunate to have your brother bearin' the burden for ya."

"Yes, it is far preferable to have nothing to offer a woman." Aidan was momentarily surprised by the depth of emotion in his friend's voice. "And when next I see my illustrious brother, I shall be sure to thank him for the sacrifice."

DunDonell didn't seem to notice anything amiss. He turned to Aidan and said, "So . . . Mister St. John, here, tells me that you've been gallivantin' around the country, which I must say is not a very kind thing to do to your intended, the beautiful Lady Appleton."

Viscount DunDonell took a long draw on his cheroot, thoroughly enjoying himself, and Aidan turned on Christian with irritation, all thoughts of the young lord's troubles forgotten.

"St. John, I do hope DunDonell is the only person to

whom you have confided that ridiculous tale," he said threateningly.

Christian turned to Daniel in silent reprimand, and the Scot burst into laughter.

"I merely told Daniel that Sarah had it in her mind that you would marry Lady Appleton, that's all. And if Viscount DunDonell had continued, he would have said that I told him you were having nothing to do with it."

Aidan's dark brows furrowed. "I never said that."

The two friends stared at one another, and Daniel whistled, sitting forward in his chair. "Now, this is gettin' interestin'."

Both men glanced at the Scot and back at one another. "You most certainly did say that, Wessex," Christian protested. "You sat in your sister's dining room and said how annoyed you were by her entire scheme."

Aidan nodded. "Yes, I was. I don't need my sister's assistance in securing a woman's affections." He sat back in his chair. "Truth be told, I had considered Lady Appleton for my countess before I left for the peninsula." He shrugged. "It was merely unfortunate timing."

Christian's jaw relaxed, leaving his mouth agape.

"My God, you've managed to render St. John speechless," the viscount said. "Could the apocalypse be far behind?"

Aidan studied his brandy snifter, elaborately casual as he said, "As a matter of fact, I am escorting the lady to Lord Hambury's ball this very evening."

Daniel chuckled. "Well done. The lass will make you a fine wife, Aidan. Congratulations."

"I'm just escorting her to a ball. I'm not proposing marriage."

"It begins with a ball, and before you know it, your—"

"Does Lady Pervill have an escort?" Lord St. John interrupted.

Aidan glanced at Christian, wondering at the uncharacteristic intensity of his tone. He shook his head, saying, "No, I don't think so."

"May I propose a toast," the viscount announced with all seriousness as he raised his cognac high in the air. "Here's to two weddin's within the year."

"Oh, shut it, Daniel."

"Sod off, DunDonell," they said in unison.

The viscount's roar of laughter filled the club, and he wiped his eyes before adding, "Now if you gentlemen will excuse me, I have a woman waitin' for my stunnin' figure to satisfy her every need."

Aidan looked at Lord St. John and smiled.

"There is no need to leave, Daniel. Your mistress can call down to the servants for a glass of water," Aidan said, causing Lord St. John to break into peals of laughter.

The enormous Scot rose and tugged at his waistcoat. "Wessex, I shall let that pass as you have recently returned to civilized society and may yet be a bit rusty with the requisite niceties. However, you, St. John, are a bloody bastard, and I have nothin' but sympathy for your bride Lady Pervill."

Aidan chuckled and inclined his head. "Good afternoon, Lord DunDonell," he said, the model of 'rusty' civility.

"And to you, Lord Wessex," Daniel returned with a sweeping bow.

Twenty-one

Celeste often found that the most discreet place to conduct a private meeting was in the middle of an enormous crush.

It had been weeks since she had contacted the emperor, and she needed to send information to convince him of her progress. Celeste took a deep breath and blew out her anxiety as her landau inched toward Lord Hambury's townhome.

The door to her conveyance opened, and Celeste turned her head as a young Frenchman settled on the seat opposite hers. Henri Renault was very handsome and had a rather sordid reputation with the married ladies of the ton, which did little to elevate his status as a refugee amongst the peerage.

Henri was the second son of a French duke who had been guillotined in the early days of the revolution. The duchess had fled with her children to England, where Lord Renault had resided ever since.

But what polite society did not know was that the emperor had offered to restore his family's holdings in exchange for Henri's services. On the surface, Lord Renault was not the most effective of spies, as the ton held the majority of the French nobles in silent contempt and therefore would never confide any important information.

Fortunately for Henri, several of their wives had. And it was this, along with his ability to relay messages from English collaborators, that made the young lord valuable to France.

Celeste considered the man before her. His nose was a shade too large, which only seemed to add to his appeal. And contrary to current fashion, Henri pulled back his long hair into a queue secured at the base of his head. The style made a woman wonder what his golden mane would look like hanging over her head as he made love to her.

But it was his eyes that seemed to hold the greatest appeal. Yellow turned gold when caught by the sun or the light of an intimate fire. Henri allowed his lips to spread into a lazy smile that was meant to entice, but she was used to his flirtations and continued to look at him with indifference.

"So, Lady Rivenhall," he began in French. "Do you have anything to give me?" He glanced at her breasts, his meaning clear.

Celeste refrained from rolling her eyes at his audacity. The fact that she was reputed to be the emperor's mistress did not seem to deter the young rake one whit.

"Everything I have is for the emperor."

The man chuckled and slid onto the seat next to her. His eyes roved leisurely over her face. "The emperor is very far away, Lady Rivenhall." He bent his head and pressed his lips to her neck. "An experienced woman such as yourself cannot be expected to spend the war in a cold bed."

"Are you offering to warm it, Henri?"

The rogue lifted his head, saying, *"Oui,"* and then bent to kiss her mouth. Celeste turned, and his lips fell to her cheek.

"Take care, Henri. The emperor is not one to share, as evidenced by our involvement in this war."

Lord Renault chuckled and lifted her chin so that he might look at her face.

"Lady Rivenhall, I do not know which is more enticing, your exceptional beauty or your exquisite wit." He held her gaze a moment longer and then gave a hiss of regret. "*C'est la vie.* What do you have for the emperor today, mademoiselle?"

Celeste pulled the papers given her by Falcon from beneath her cloak. Lord Renault's brows rose, obviously impressed with the amount of information she had managed to gather in such a short time.

"It seems you have been warming someone's bed."

Celeste did not comment, saying only, "The schematics are for a new cannon that will be produced very shortly. This weapon is far more powerful than anything we possess, so stress to the emperor the need to adjust his battle plans accordingly."

Of course, there was no new cannon, but any additional troops sent to reinforce current positions would mean fewer battalions elsewhere. However, the other information she had given him was real, and was determined to be acceptable losses to the English war effort. Celeste tried not to think of the men who would die protecting these insignificant outposts, but she did . . . at night, when sleep evaded her.

"Very well. You know how to contact me if you find any information of interest to the emperor," he said, his hand drifting to the handle of the carriage door. Then, stopping, he turned to her with a warm smile. "Or if you get cold."

And then he stepped out of her carriage, leaving her to wait her turn at being dropped at the front steps. Fifteen minutes later, her footman handed her down as she alighted from her carriage. The front of Lord Hambury's home was ablaze with torches, and she ascended the wide marble stairs along with two stylishly clad couples.

She pulled her cloak around her and listened to the murmur of conversation spilling into the street from the front entry. She removed her cloak and nervously awaited her turn to be announced.

The neck of her cerulean gown was cut simply to enhance her complexion, but it was the back of the silk concoction that had caused her modiste to squeal with delight the moment she described what she wanted.

She had ordered the gown to be cut so low in the back that it would be impossible to wear a corset. Of course, the moment she stepped onto the ballroom floor the entire ton would be aware of it as well, which was precisely why she had done it. Celeste had only a few short weeks to attract three peers of the British realm. This was no time to be demure.

"Lady Rivenhall," the announcement sounded over the crowded ballroom.

The murmurs behind her transformed into an absolute roar the deeper she walked into the crowded room. Heads turned, and conversations stopped as she searched for her uncle. The Earl of Rivenhall had agreed to accompany her this evening once Falcon had explained the importance of her mission.

Her uncle had been shocked to learn that his brother's daughter had survived his murder. The earl was only now coming to grips with the reality of her relationship with the emperor and the subsequent danger in which she was placing herself. He had felt it his duty to protect her now that her father was dead, and it had taken Falcon a full two hours to convince him of the importance she held in the war effort.

Her uncle had allowed her use of his townhome while he remained in the country, but Celeste was uncertain if he would sit idly by while she flaunted herself for the ton. She would know soon enough, as her uncle was approaching her from the direction of the gaming room.

"Celeste, darling." He bent and kissed her cheek, whispering, "That dress is absolutely obscene."

"I know."

"You look stunning, my dear," he said for the benefit of

the scandalized onlookers. "Would you care for some refreshment?"

"Yes, thank you."

Her uncle motioned to a footman and passed her a glass of champagne. Behind his crystal he said, "Hambury, Ferrell, and Cantor, correct?"

Celeste nodded, and she took his arm. They strolled about the room, and she could feel the eyes of the ton as they walked. Her uncle introduced her to several matrons before arriving at the side of their host, Lord Hambury.

The married lord was bald and had grown fat through the middle.

"Lord Hambury, may I introduce my niece, Lady Celeste Rivenhall."

The forty-year-old lord smiled with an attempt at rakishness, saying, "Enchanted, Lady Rivenhall, and why is it that we have never seen you in town before tonight, my dear?"

"I have been abroad, my lord, but fearing for my safety, my uncle insisted that I return to England." She smiled affectionately toward her uncle, whom she scarcely remembered, as if he were her father.

"Quite right, Lady Rivenhall. Who knows where that mad Frenchman will invade next? You're better off here at home, what?"

"I couldn't agree with you more, Lord Hambury," Celeste said with her most radiant smile. "And now if you will excuse me, my lord, I believe my uncle wishes to introduce me to his acquaintances." Her uncle turned, and they began to walk away when the rotund lord called after them.

"Might you have a waltz available on your dance card, Lady Rivenhall?"

Celeste cringed at the thought of those bloated fingers wrapped around her waist. "I believe I do, Lord Hambury," she said, writing his name on the card dangling from her wrist.

As they walked away, she felt her uncle's eyes on her.

She looked up and was surprised to see sorrow touching them. "I am truly sorry, Celeste. I cannot imagine what you have endured these past four years."

A lump formed in her throat, and she eased it down with a sip of champagne, saying, "No, you cannot."

The moment Lady Rivenhall was introduced, the dark man knew without a doubt that he had found the emperor's mistress. The girl was exquisite, and he, along with every other male in the gilded room, imagined what she would look like nude and in his bed.

For now he would have to content himself with holding her in a waltz, rather than beneath him in bed. However, he would need to tread carefully, for the woman was the paramour to Napoleon himself, and for good reason, he thought as he stared at her backside.

"What I wouldn't give to get my hands on that," his companion murmured.

The dark man chuckled and smiled his agreement, but then he was startled by a familiar voice. "There you are, my lord. I have been looking for you so that I might introduce you to my cousin."

He shrugged at his friend and offered his arm to the admiral's wife. "Of course, Lady Davis," he said, concealing his rage.

They strolled in the direction of the less-populated gaming room. "I told you *never* to speak with me in public, Sophie."

The girl was expecting his anger and attempted to appease him. "What choice have you left me, darling? You refuse to see me in private." She caressed his arm, and he glanced around to see if anyone had noted the intimacy. "I love you, and I know that you love me. If it is my husband that concerns you, I shall leave him. Anything, darling, I shall do whatever you wish."

He smiled down at the ugly woman. "Very well, dearest, meet me in the gazebo at midnight, and we shall discuss what is to be done." He patted her hand affectionately and whispered, "Now go."

The girl ambled into the ballroom, oblivious to the hard set of his jaw or the steely glint in his eyes. He downed his remaining refreshment and forced himself to set the delicate crystal flute on the nearest table. He walked into the ballroom and awaited his waltz with the stunning Lady Rivenhall.

"Our dance, I believe," he said with a bow, as the disappointed throngs that surrounded her watched helplessly as he led her to the dance floor.

He pulled Lady Rivenhall into his arms and was thankful that he had removed his gloves. His bare hand rested against the flesh exposed by her provocative gown, and she felt just as he had imagined she would, smooth and very, very soft. His shaft was awakening, and he reminded himself to smile politely.

"I understand that you have recently returned from the continent, Lady Rivenhall."

"That is correct, my lord. Austria, to be precise," the girl said. She seemed nervous, and he hoped that he was affecting her. He pulled her a shade closer to his body as they twirled the length of the room.

"I, myself, returned from the continent not four months ago."

"Really?"

He laughed. "Of course, it was the peninsula, and I'm afraid the only memento I came home with was this." He tilted his head so that she could clearly see his scar.

Her fair brows furrowed, and she said, "I'm so sorry, my lord." And for the briefest of moments he thought that perhaps she was.

He lowered his hand a half-inch on her back as his desire increased with each turn of their waltz. It occurred to him that the best way to keep an eye on his competition was to keep her close, preferably very close.

The waltz was coming to a close, so he seized his last opportunity. "Lady Rivenhall, have you managed to see the Royal Theater's production of *The Merchant of Venice*?"

"No, I have not," she said with an encouraging smile.

Confident, he looked directly into her eyes, asking, "Then might you do me the honor of accompanying me Saturday next?"

"Oh, I'm afraid I shall need to consult my uncle, my lord. I fear we might be returning to his country estate at any moment," she answered, smiling up at him and causing a surge of lust that emanated from his belly and settled in his cock. "Might I send word as soon as our plans are settled?"

The waltz ended, and he left his hand on the exposed portion of her back as he guided her toward her uncle. "I would be delighted to receive any communication from you, Lady Rivenhall," he said with a seductive smile.

Felicity sat with her cousin, awaiting her dance partner for the next waltz. She was still heated from her quadrille with the Duke of Glenbroke, and she took a sip of lemonade to cool herself. She discreetly adjusted her chartreuse gown and turned her attention toward her amused cousin.

"Look"—Lady Pervill indicated the far side of the room—"Lord Summers has not taken his eyes off of you all evening, poor man. I mean just look at him. He's gorgeous—and rich."

Felicity sighed. "Don't be crass, Juliet."

"I can afford to be crass, dearest. A man like that would never make me an offer, and I must say that if he had enough sense to fall in love with you, then he is worthy of my admiration."

"It is sentiments such as those that keep me in your company, Juliet."

"Come now, Felicity. Tell me what is wrong with this one. I know Lord Summers has made you an offer, and, as always, you refused him. That makes seven, and I must warn you that wagers are being placed at White's."

Felicity shuddered at the thought of her private affairs

being discussed in public, and with a heavy sigh, said, "Why people are interested in my personal affairs, I shall never know."

"Well, Felicity, that is rather the point. You have no personal affairs—no scandal, no lovers locked away, not even an illegitimate child."

"Juliet!" she admonished, placing her hands on her burning cheeks.

"I'm sorry, dearest, I was only jesting. But I do not understand your refusal of Summers. I'd murder someone for an offer from the man."

Felicity's heart lurched, and guilt washed over her. Her cousin was only a year younger than herself, but had received not one offer for her hand.

"I told you, Juliet. I am not in love with him."

"Nor the other six?"

Felicity lifted her lemonade to her lips. "Nor them."

"Then who *are* you in love with?"

Felicity rolled her eyes in frustration and with uncharacteristic temper, said, "My God, Juliet, you are like a hound on the trail of a fox. I have told you time and time again that you shall be the first to know when I develop a tendresse for a gentleman." She brushed her skirts of imaginary crumbs, adding, "Perhaps if you concentrated on your own affairs, we would not be discussing my offers, but yours."

The moment she looked up into her cousin's cornflower blue eyes, Felicity regretted her outburst. She reached out to touch her hand, but Juliet pulled away. Her cousin's eyes filled with tears, but stubborn to the core, she refused to let them fall.

Instead, she lifted her head, her anger clearly overwhelming her hurt as she stared at Felicity. "Point taken, cousin. Now if you will excuse me, there is a wall that lacks a bouquet."

Felicity started after her wounded friend, but the Earl of Wessex arrived at her side, stopping her.

"Lady Appleton, I must apologize as I will be unable to

dance our waltz." He seemed distracted, frantic even, which was so unlike the elegant Lord Wessex that she became uneasy.

"Is there something wrong, Aidan?"

He stopped looking about the room and smiled down at her. "I'm sorry, Lady Appleton, everything is fine. I do hate to leave you . . ." He was peering over the heads of the crush. "Ah, I see just the fellow to partner you for our waltz."

Felicity waited to be introduced to the gentleman. The orchestra began the opening chords and couples started toward the dance floor. It was so kind of the earl to find her a partner, she thought, as she adored a lively waltz.

"Here he is," Aidan said, prompting Felicity to turn. "Lord Elkin."

Her heart stopped, and then lodged in her throat. She met Lord Elkin's piercing eyes and noted that he was just as stunned as she.

"Thanks, old man." Aidan Duhearst slapped him on the back and then turned to Felicity. "I shall return as soon as possible, Lady Appleton."

Felicity smiled, but Wessex was already gone, leaving her alone with the one man she had thought never to see again. He raised his arm, and she took it, staring at the polished mahogany floor all the while.

Her heart was thundering in her chest, and she could scarcely hear the music. He stood as far away from her as was possible when he took her in his arms and began twirling her about the floor.

Lord Elkin stared over her head, and the awkward silence was more than she could bear. "I take it from your countenance that you had no idea it was I for whom the Earl of Wessex begged your assistance?"

His eyes met hers for the second time in two years, but he said nothing, spinning her around a corner. His large hand burned her waist, and with sudden clarity she recalled the other times that they had danced together, not like this, but with the comfortable ease of friendship.

"When you left for the continent, I never thought to see you again," she said, regretting the loss of her closest male companion.

"Nor I you," he drawled, his deep voice audible only to her. She had almost forgotten the rich reverberation of his voice and was forced to take a steadying breath so as not to cry in full view of the ton.

"I would have thought that two years would be enough time—"

His jaw tensed. "It was not."

The waltz was coming to a close, and Felicity knew she would never again have an opportunity to regain the one friendship she regretted losing. She fixed her eyes on his.

"John, you have had two years to overcome your anger and embarrassment at my refusal." His brows furrowed, and he looked at her like she belonged in the madhouse. She ignored him, continuing, "I should think that in time . . ."

His midnight blue eyes remained fixed on her face as the music stopped, and he bowed. "Is that what you thought, Felicity? That I have refused to see you these last years because I was angry?"

She curtsied, confusion tangling her tongue. "Well, yes."

Lord Elkin escorted her to the periphery of the dance floor and looked down at her one last time. "I have not seen you for the past two years, my dear, because it is entirely too painful."

He held her gaze a moment longer, and it was then she realized that John Elkin was still in love with her. Her eyes burned as he bent to kiss her hand. His lips lingered, and he turned without a backward glance, leaving her completely devastated.

Felicity made her way to an alcove she had seen in the music room and prayed that it would be vacant. It was, and she sank into the cushions behind a potted plant and gave into her tears. Never would she have imagined that she had injured her friend so deeply. She dabbed at her eyes with a lace handkerchief and could feel that, despite all her efforts, they were swelling.

John had been the first man to ask for her hand, and in truth his proposal had frightened her. It was not until then that she understood men often mistook her friendship for more intimate feelings. Since John Elkin's offer, Felicity had taken great care not to form close attachments to eligible gentlemen.

But this stratagem seemed to have had the opposite effect. The more she withdrew from the gentlemen of the ton, the more they seemed to be intrigued by her. After John Elkin, she had been honored with six more offers from men who were sworn bachelors.

The latest, Lord Summers, was known, affectionately of course, as 'the widow's peak'. The man was breathtaking, and she supposed that if she were to marry, he would be an excellent husband. He was wealthy, titled, kind, handsome, and, if the gossip were true, a very skilled lover. What else could a woman hope for?

Love.

She was not in love with him, nor Albright, nor Jones, nor Quincy . . . nor John Elkin. She was such a horrible person to injure a man as fine as John. Perhaps she should reconsider the man's suit, she thought, and then gave into a new wave of tears.

"There you are! The orchestra is warming up for our . . ."

Embarrassed, Felicity turned her face from Lord Christian St. John. "I'm afraid I shall be unable to join you, my lord."

Christian said nothing, but she could feel him standing over her. She swiped at her eyes, ashamed that she had wept in public. He remained and, irritated by his continued presence, Felicity looked up at him.

"Just leave me, Christian." She could see the shock on his face, and her cheeks flushed with humiliation.

"Has someone—"

"No! Just leave me." She held his gaze. "Please, Christian."

Discomfited, the young lord said, "I'll get Juliet," then dashed out of the music room.

Felicity groaned, recalling her last encounter with her cousin. She closed her eyes and forced herself to steady her breathing. If she looked at the floor and walked very quickly, perhaps she would make it outside before anyone noted her distress.

She rose, determined to do just that, when Lord St. John returned. "Juliet is dancing with Lord Barksdale." His blond head tilted to one side. "Where are you going?"

"Home, my lord," she said, starting toward the music room door.

Lord St. John followed in something of a panic. "But . . . but . . ." Then his ice blue eyes sparkled in triumph. "You can't go home unescorted."

"Quite true, Christian, and as my coachman and two footmen are just outside, I shall be perfectly safe."

They were in the main salon, and she must have looked worse than she had imagined. A small murmur began as she sliced through the crush, and she knew without a doubt that she would be the topic of speculation in many a lady's drawing room the following morning. Felicity picked up her pace and then felt Lord St. John patting her hand.

"I'm quite sure that your grandmother will be right as rain in a week or two," the young lord said, at such a volume and with such conviction that it passed through her mind, and not for the first time, that Christian had missed his calling.

The expressions of the society matrons changed before her eyes from disapproval to polite sympathy, and at that moment she could have kissed Lord St. John for his kindness and ingenuity.

Twenty-two

The dark man sat in the gazebo listening to the distant gongs of midnight. He glanced down at his timepiece and noticed that it was five minutes fast. He adjusted the time, winding the pocket watch until the delicate spindle could be twisted no farther.

The young lord enjoyed the music drifting toward him, but he rolled his eyes when he heard Lady Davis clomping down the gravel path moments before he saw her. The stupid chit ran into his arms, and he was thankful that it was dark so he would not be subjected to her face. Sophie kissed him and in an amorous state after his waltz with Lady Rivenhall, he returned her embrace.

"Oh, darling."

"Shhh," he ordered, not wanting her voice to impede his fantasy.

He dove into the girl's bodice, squeezing her nipples to hasten her readiness to receive him. He unbuttoned his breeches and sat on the stone bench, but before he could remove her drawers the girl had sunk to her knees and took him in her mouth as he had taught her to do.

The man moaned, but he wanted to imagine himself buried inside of Lady Rivenhall. He pulled her up, ripping away the girl's drawers, and guiding her to straddle his aching cock. He grabbed her around the waist and pulled her down hard, impaling her to the hilt. She gasped, but he knew she enjoyed it. He lifted her and pulled her down again until the girl had the rhythm he preferred.

"That's it," he encouraged, lifting her slippered feet to the bench and causing her to sink farther still.

The tall man closed his eyes and envisioned Lady Rivenhall. He reached out and grasped the girl's breast and then, with brutal abandon, thrust until he came into her in a devastating climax inspired by the alluring lady spy. His eyes remained closed as the last tremor subsided, and then he opened them, looking at Lady Davis and remembering why he was here.

"I warned you, Sophie, never to speak to me in public."

"I know, darling, but I wanted you so much," she said, wiggling on his cock and smiling. "I did not think you would be too angry."

He lifted her off his lap and buttoned his gaping trousers, then walked behind the girl and kissed her just below the ear, saying, "Oh, but I do mind," just before twisting her neck until it gave with a familiar dull crack.

The dark man took a step backward so that Lady Davis's weight would not come to rest on his boots, then straightened his waistcoat and returned to the ballroom with ample time for his quadrille with Lady Hillary.

They had strolled the entire length of the garden, and the Duchess of Glenbroke had had enough. She stopped on the gravel path, lit only by a distant lantern, and turned to her husband.

"Right, Gilbert, what do you want?"

The Duke of Glenbroke chuckled, looking down at her

with one of the most alluring smiles the ton had to offer. "Always to the point, aren't you, my dear?"

Sarah nodded decisively. "Quite. Now why have you brought me out here?"

"Why do you think I have brought you here?"

"To tell me something you do not want overheard."

"Ahh," he said with a knowing look. "Well, my darling, it might surprise you to learn that I am not the least bit interested in the latest on-dit."

Sarah eyed her husband with suspicion. "But then why else would you have brought me to the far corners of the garden, Gilbert? I'm freezing."

The tall man bent down and seized her gloved hand, kissing the back of it with an ease gained only by experience. "That should be obvious, my dear."

Sarah shivered, unsure if it was due to the cold, or to something much warmer, much more consuming. "I should refuse you for failing to consider the elements."

The handsome duke burst into laughter and looked into her eyes, shaking his head from side to side. "I have never been refused due to weather."

Sarah's temper flared at the reminder of his many conquests. Regardless of their nuptials, women still attempted to gain her husband's bed. "Then go find yourself a more robust companion." She spun round, intending to head for the house. "You certainly have had enough offers."

Her husband grinned, obviously pleased with her jealousy. He reached out, grabbing her upper arm and pulling her into his body.

"Oh, sweetheart," he whispered, brushing her hair from her face as he looked down into her eyes. "You know the moment you threw that figurine at me, I was ruined for other women." He bent his head and hovered over her lips. "I'm so hopelessly besotted that I could not even wait until we were home to taste you."

Sarah dared not look at him; if she looked at his perfectly constructed face, looked at those masculine lips, she would forgive him anything. "But I'm cold," she protested weakly.

His amusement faded, and his gray eyes shone silver in the moonlight, causing her stomach to flip. "Then perhaps you will allow me to warm you?"

He bent his head and seized her, teasing her with his tongue as he took his time in tasting her. Her husband moaned, and the sound of his baritone voice caused her to press closer to his lean body. Her hands reached around his neck, and she pulled him down while standing on the very tips of her toes. Her husband was a tall man, a muscular man, and it would take her several glorious hours to properly explore his masculine beauty.

She was beginning to do just that when she heard a distant thud. Sarah broke their embrace and turned her head in the direction of the noise.

"Gilbert," she said, as her husband kissed down her neck. "What was that?"

"What was what?" She could hear her husband's sensual need, and she very nearly forgot what she was asking.

"What was that noise?"

"I didn't hear anything." His lips fell to the swells of her breasts.

"I heard something."

"I'm sure that you did," he said, ignoring her.

Irritated, Sarah pulled back and pushed on her husband's solid chest. "No, I'm serious, Gilbert. I'm certain I heard something."

He slackened his grasp on her waist, and his head dropped in frustration. "Yes, you said, Sarah. But what would you like for me to do?"

"I don't know. Go and—"

She was interrupted by a piercing scream. Gilbert turned to her. "Remain here," he ordered, taking one step in the direction of the disturbance.

Sarah seized his hand in hers. "I'll be damned if you're leaving me in the garden alone, Gilbert de Clare."

Her handsome husband looked down at her, the slightest of grins lighting his striking features. They strode forward, arriving at the gazebo to find a woman with her face buried in her companion's neck, his arms wrapped protectively around her.

The young man directed the duke's eyes with his own to the crumpled figure lying on the floor of the wooden structure. Sarah's intake of air was audible to her husband, and Gilbert instinctively put his arm around her shoulders.

"Some madman must have wandered in off the streets and attacked her."

"Yes," Gilbert said, causing Sarah to poke him in the ribs. He looked down with a question in his eyes, and she glanced toward the other couple. Understanding her meaning, her husband said, "Why don't you take the ladies inside and inform Lord Hambury of this tragic event?"

"Of course, Your Grace," the young lord said, offering Sarah his other arm.

"No!" Sarah clutched her husband's lapels as if in a panic.

Gilbert's muscular arms tightened. "It's all right, Sarah, you will be perfectly safe. Go with Lord Kerry."

Sarah rolled her eyes and hit him in the back, hard. "No! Please don't leave me," she said sounding pathetic.

Gilbert's confusion appeared to be concern to the other man, who offered, "I shall be back in a moment, Your Grace," as he lead the distraught young lady into the safety of the house.

"Thank you," the duke said to the retreating figure. Then, pulling away from Sarah, he asked, "What is it?"

"You took long enough in getting rid of them."

"Forgive me, Duchess, for thinking you would be distraught at seeing a dead woman lying on the gazebo floor. Had I known dead bodies were a common occurrence for you, I should not have bothered."

"Don't be ridiculous, Gilbert," Sarah said as her husband examined the body. "You know very well that I have never seen a corpse before this very moment. And don't call me Duchess. You know I hate it."

"Lady Davis," her husband said, dusting off his hands as he rose. "She has a broken neck, but I see no evidence of a fall, which leads me to believe that she has been murdered."

"I was afraid of that, but that is not what disturbs me."

"Murder does not disturb you?" Her husband's dark brows rose as he looked down at her.

"Of course it disturbs me, Gilbert, but that is not the point."

"It was for her," he said, jerking his head in the direction of the still figure.

The duchess sighed. "Do you recall kissing me?"

Her husband smiled and stared at her lips. "Every detail," he said in his most seductive tone.

Sarah ignored the heat blooming in the pit of her stomach. "When you kissed me, we were standing at the back entrance to the garden. No one came in or out of that gate."

"Then the murderer went back inside." His stunning eyes reflected his understanding. "The murderer is one of us. Bloody hell!"

"Bloody hell, indeed."

"What the devil is wrong with you?" Lord Christian St. John asked as Aidan watched the ton's rakes clamoring to dance with the provocative Lady Rivenhall.

"Nothing," Aidan said, wondering what the woman had been thinking in wearing such a scanty gown. Weren't spies supposed to be discreet? Well, the dazzling Lady Rivenhall would have attracted less attention had she arrived wearing a French flag.

But that was the point, he supposed. To attract very specific attention, and he had no doubt that she would be successful. Lord Hambury would be no match for her wiles. The aging lord was of less interest to Aidan than was the person who had sent Celeste to investigate him.

So Aidan sat watching and observing her suitors, wondering which one, if any, was her French collaborator.

"I thought you were supposed to be dancing with Lady Pervill."

Christian shrugged. "I was, but I've no idea where the girl's taken herself."

"I can't seem to find Lady Appleton, either."

"Oh, she returned home."

Aidan turned toward his friend. "Nothing wrong, I hope."

"No, no, she felt a chill coming on and thought it wise to retire and get some rest. I escorted her to her carriage."

"Thank you, old man," he said, feeling guilty for so woefully neglecting his duty as escort. Aidan turned again to the reason for his distraction and decided to follow a different tack. "Excuse me, Christian."

The Earl of Wessex cut through the ring of gentlemen surrounding the stunning woman and stood directly in front of her. "My dance, I believe, Lady Rivenhall."

It was not.

"But . . ." a dandy protested, but by then Aidan had the woman half the distance to the ballroom floor.

"You're hurting my arm," she whispered through clenched teeth.

"Good," he said, swinging her around, but they had not taken a full turn of the floor before a commotion began near the beveled doors leading outside.

A woman screamed, and the music stopped altogether. People began to mill around the back of the house as whispers of an attack rippled through the crowd.

Lord Hambury pushed his way toward the stairs, hoping to squelch the inevitable rumors. He put his arms up to silence his guests.

"Ladies and Gentlemen," he said, his tone somber. "I'm afraid there has been a tragic event here this evening. A lady has fallen in the garden and regrettably has died from her injuries."

The ton gasped collectively, and someone yelled, "Who was the lady?"

"Gentlemen, I'm afraid that the lady's family has yet to

be notified. I believe it would be best to wait until they can be located and informed of the accident. Now, if you would assist the ladies home, I would be most grateful."

The Earl of Wessex was in shock as his sister and her husband made their way through the confusion to his side. Sarah looked around, clearly not wanting to be heard, and Aidan knew by looking into his sister's eyes that the information was not good.

"Lady Davis has been murdered. Gilbert and I found her. And, Aidan, we were standing by the garden gate . . . No one entered or left by it."

His hand tightened on Lady Rivenhall's wrist as he comprehended what his sister was telling him.

"You see what this means, Aidan. The admiral's wife was killed by someone at this ball."

Wessex's eyes shot to the beautiful traitor, and she shook her head as if to deny the reality of the situation, but he knew that she was denying any involvement.

Gilbert glanced at the woman on Aidan's arm and seeing her distress offered, "May I escort you to your parents, Lady . . . ?"

"Rivenhall."

"I'll take her."

Gilbert held Aidan's eyes and then with one curt bow said, "Good evening, Lady Rivenhall."

Aidan pulled the lady's wrist, and he could feel her slippers sliding on the dance floor as she attempted to resist him. "My uncle—"

"Will know soon enough the identity of the woman in the garden."

They were at the front entrance, and the cool night air struck his face, but failed to ease the heat of his temper. He found the lady's carriage and all but threw Lady Rivenhall inside.

"Get in."

Aidan followed and then rapped on the ceiling, causing the conveyance to lurch forward. His eyes must have burned with rage because the woman pressed herself into the corner of the coach.

"I know nothing of the events that occurred here this evening." Aidan continued to stare at her, and the brave lady added, "I swear it."

The earl leaned forward. "You expect me to believe that the wife of a British admiral is murdered in the very home where a French collaborator is actively attempting to obtain information, yet said traitor had nothing whatsoever to do with the murder?" He met her pale eyes with contempt. "You're not that good a whore."

Her face contorted and then went blank as she sat more erect. "I don't give a damn if you believe me or not."

Aidan's jaw pulsed. "I know you have been given a list of men to investigate." The breathtaking spy blinked in surprise, but recovered with practiced speed. He grabbed her arm, saying, "And I will have the truth, Lady Rivenhall."

"Unhand me," she demanded, and the earl glanced down at the silver pistol glinting in the candlelight of the landau.

"I see you have graduated from knives, but you forget . . ." Aidan leaned forward and pressed the barrel of the pistol to his chest, never taking his eyes from hers. "I'm well acquainted with firearms."

The woman's luxurious lips lifted to one side in a contemptuous sneer. "And you forget, my lord," she said, cocking the pistol, "so am I." Aidan held her jade gaze and saw no hesitation, only the woman who had ruthlessly commanded her troops at Albuera. "Now remove yourself from my carriage."

Aidan swallowed his frustration and glared at the callous woman. "Certainly, Lady Rivenhall," he said, reaching for the door and alighting from the landau, taking care never to turn his back on the deadly woman. "Until next time." He swept a bow, replaced his beaver skin hat atop his head, and waited for the carriage to clatter out of sight.

•   •   •

The moment Lord Elkin heard of the woman in the garden, he began to search the ballroom for Lady Appleton. But the more the crowd thinned with no sign of her, the more his heart thundered in his chest.

Surely, he had just missed her leaving, he told himself, but his disquiet did not ease. He started toward his carriage then realized that she lived a mere two blocks to the east. His feet began moving in that direction, all his thoughts centered on confirming that she was unharmed.

He dodged partygoers and horses, and with each step his trepidation grew until he found himself in a near dash to her townhome. Lord Elkin bounded up the stairs and banged the knocker against the brass plate.

His heart was pounding from exertion as well as fear, and he knocked again, longer this time. The door opened, and an annoyed butler looked down his nose at him.

John pushed past the servant, who immediately called for two footmen to throw him out on his ear.

"Felicity!" he shouted, and then louder, directed up the decorative staircase. *"Felicity!"*

Lady Appleton appeared from the salon in a blue dressing gown, holding a book in her right hand. Her golden hair fell about her shoulders, and her mouth hung open in alarm. He closed his eyes and took a deep breath to slow his pounding heart.

Thank God.

"John, what has happened?" she asked, grasping his arm and leading him into the salon. "It's all right, Merryweather."

Felicity guided him to a chair near the fire and rushed to the sideboard, pouring him a substantial amount of scotch. She held out the fiery liquid, and he was shocked to see that his hands were shaking when he reached for the glass. The beautiful woman sank down on her knees, placing her delicate hands on his.

"John, what has distressed you so?" Her large eyes held her concern, and he was so overcome with relief he scarcely knew where to begin.

"There was a woman killed at Lord Hambury's home this evening. The lady's identity was not revealed, and when I could not find you"—he held her fawn-colored gaze—"I came here."

Felicity dropped her head and pressed her cheek to the back of his hand. John placed his drink on a nearby side table and began to stroke the back of her hair, and then he remembered she was not his and never would be.

John rose, leaving Felicity in a confused pile on the Aubusson rug. "I . . ." His brows furrowed. "I should leave, Lady Appleton," he said, and then started for the salon door.

His hand was on the polished brass knob when she said, "Wait."

John closed his eyes for a moment before turning to face her. "Why?" His eyes met hers. "What are you saying, Felicity?"

She shook her head. "I don't know."

They stared at one another as she rose to her feet.

God, she's beautiful. He walked toward her, and when he was close enough to see the golden flecks in her light eyes, he whispered, "Don't do this to me, Felicity. If I've no chance of winning you, don't torment me with hope."

"I . . . am very confused, John," she said, her eyes drifting to his lips.

It was all the encouragement he needed. John bent his head and just before covering her mouth with his, said, "Then allow me to enlighten you."

Her lips were as sweet as the woman herself, and he thanked God for giving him this moment. She felt so perfect in his arms that he tightened his hold, but she tensed, and he knew he had reached too high.

Lady Appleton placed her palms on his chest and stared at his cravat. Her forehead creased as she struggled for the words to convey her thoughts.

"I don't know what I can offer you, John." Felicity looked into the depth of his eyes. "I just know that I do not want to lose you again."

John pulled her to his chest and rested his chin atop her head, wondering if he could ever be a friend to Lady Appleton, wondering if he could ever sit by and watch her marry another man.

They held each other for a very long time, both afraid to let go. But finally, he withdrew and made for the door, knowing that if it took her a lifetime to sort out her feelings, he would wait.

Twenty-three

❧

At three o'clock in the morning the streets of Regent's Hill were deserted. Celeste kept to the shadows, thankful that the moon was no more than a sliver.

She peered around the corner the moment she heard a carriage come to rest in front of the house she had been observing. She waited until the gentleman had ascended the stairs and his coachman had passed before making her way across the dark street.

Her newly acquired clothing made it a simple task to slip over the outer wall, but as always climbing to the second floor proved arduous. Celeste slithered through the gentleman's open bedchamber window just before he entered through a door on the far side of the room.

The man wore nothing more than a white cloth tied around his waist. His well-defined chest still held beads of water, which clung to the blond hair that disappeared in an orderly line beneath the low-slung cloth. The young lord stopped abruptly, and Celeste glimpsed a dangerous man the instant before he recognized her.

"Ah, Lady Rivenhall. What an unexpected pleasure." He tucked his long blond hair behind his ears. "Have you come to assist me in bathing?"

Celeste blushed, despite trying not to, and threw her hat on the nearest chair. "No, Henri. I have come to speak with you about the events at Lord Hambury's ball."

The handsome man was smiling now and walked toward her, looking her over from head to toe. His assessment made Celeste squirm. She tugged at her breeches and wished she had worn a jacket, but the stable lad from whom she had stolen the garments did not possess one.

Lord Renault walked behind her, and she felt his hand on her backside as he said, "Until this very moment, I had never realized how buckskins cling to one's form. And what a fine form you have, Lady Rivenhall."

Celeste knocked his arm away and used the tone she took when speaking to her troops. "Did you do it?"

His golden eyes met hers. "Murder Lady Davis?" He shook his head, sending his fair hair to rest on his muscular shoulder. "No, I have never even met the unfortunate lady."

Celeste held his penetrating gaze to ascertain if he was lying. He was not. The man was too close, and she could smell his masculine scent, feel his power. She backed up, saying, "I want you to find out who did kill her and if we are responsible."

The Frenchman walked toward his bed and removed his towel, standing before her completely naked. Celeste wanted nothing more than to turn away, but she did not, knowing that if she did it would be seen as a sign of weakness. Instead, she forced herself to look at his thickly muscled form. His shaft stood ready to take her, and she could understand why women fought to gain his attention . . . and his bed.

When they both knew she had seen what he wanted her to see, he said, "Very well, I shall pump a few of Lady Davis's maids for information." The Frenchman smiled seductively. "Will that satisfy you, my lady?"

Celeste raised a brow. "It might satisfy me, Monsieur Renault, but the maids are a different matter altogether."

The young man's laugh was deep and rich as he slipped under the lush velvet counterpane.

"Now, Lady Rivenhall." He rested his head on his palm, supporting his weight with his elbow. "Unless you intend to join me, I shall need all of my strength for my inquiries." Celeste rolled her eyes and he laughed harder. "I will contact you as soon as I have any information."

Lady Rivenhall nodded her understanding and made for the door, but Henri stopped her. "The window, if you don't mind."

Celeste looked into Monsieur Renault's sparkling eyes. "Why?"

The man shrugged. "I get a much better view of your exquisite backside when you bend over, *oui?*"

Lady Rivenhall yanked open the Frenchman's bed-chamber door, and peals of baritone laughter escorted her out.

It had been one week since Lord Hambury's ball, and Felicity found herself sipping tea with her dearest friends.

"Gilbert is determined to have me increasing by Christmas, and while I adore my children, the twins are not yet one year old. Is it terrible of me to want another year without a babe in the house?"

"Of course not, Sarah. You really should allow Mrs. Cox to assist you more."

Sarah sighed. "You sound like my husband, Felicity."

"Well, I have a bit of news," Juliet began. "Two bits of news, actually. The first is that I heard a rumor that Lady Davis had recently taken a lover." She paused for emphasis.

"You're joking," Sarah said in disbelief.

Lady Pervill shook her light brown curls. "I'm not. I went to school with her niece, Elizabeth. You remember, the girl with the crooked teeth and spots on her face."

"Juliet," Sarah said trying to draw her friend's attention back to the present.

"Oh, yes, poor Elizabeth Davis," Felicity said, remembering. "How is dear Elizabeth? Still spotty?"

"Juliet."

"No, actually, she seems to have outgrown the spots, although her teeth are still as crooked as the local magistrate."

"Well, do give Elizabeth my regards the next time you meet up with—"

"Juliet!" The cousins turned in unison. "Who was Lady Davis's lover? He may very well have been the man that killed her."

"I am not a simpleton, Sarah. I had thought of that, but Elizabeth said that Lady Davis told her she had been forbidden to reveal his identity, even to her closest friends."

"That's incredible." Sarah poured the others more tea.

"My God, Juliet, I can hardly wait to hear your second bit of news," Felicity said, a touch wary.

"Well," her cousin began, lifting her shoulders in excitement. "Lord Barksdale kissed me at the ball."

Knowing that Juliet had not received much notice from the eligible men of the ton, the duchess asked excitedly, "And what did you think of your first kiss?"

"I liked it. As a matter of fact, I liked it so much that I kissed him on the carriage ride home."

"Juliet, the man will think you forward," Felicity warned.

"Yes, I believe that is what Lord Barksdale finds appealing about me." Her cornflower eyes sparkled with mischief as she challenged Felicity to comment further.

"Do you have feelings for Lord Barksdale?" Sarah probed.

Juliet considered it. "I enjoy Robert. He is handsome and charming and a great deal of fun, but it is not as though he has made an offer."

"Then you should refrain from kissing him until he does," the duchess advised with a smile full of dimples.

"How then am I to gain any level of proficiency?"

Lady Appleton sighed in resignation and returned to her cucumber sandwich.

Sarah turned her attention on Felicity and behind her cup said, "Christian informed me that he saw Lord Elkin arrive at your home, Tuesday last."

Lady Appleton blushed, causing Juliet to protest. "Felicity! And here you sit lecturing me on proper behavior. Why did you not tell me? If you will recall, one week ago today you swore, and I quote"—Juliet softened her voice to emulate her cousin—"'If I take an interest in a particular gentleman . . .'" Her voice reverted to her own. *"You will be the first to know."*

Felicity took a bite of cake, giving her time to form an answer. "I have not 'taken an interest' in Lord Elkin. We are acquaintances, that is all."

The other women sent meaningful glances to one another, but it was Sarah who asked, "How many times have you been riding with Lord Elkin this past week?"

Felicity straightened the napkin in her lap, stirred her tea, added more cream to her cup, stirred again, then coughed, saying, "Three."

Juliet's mouth fell open. "You have not seen the man in two years, Felicity. Then you spend three afternoons with him? If you have not taken 'an interest' in him, then what in God's name are you doing?"

"Juliet," Felicity admonished. Then, when she saw her cousin would not relent, she answered, "I don't know, precisely." They waited. "John is a very good friend."

"A good friend! Oh, that is very romantic. I'm positively swooning."

"Juliet!" Sarah warned.

Needing to relieve her guilt, Felicity closed her eyes so she would not have to look at them while she spoke. "If you must know the truth, I believe he is still in love with me."

Sarah placed her hand on Felicity's. "And have your feelings for Lord Elkin changed?"

"I don't know. He had been gone for so long, and I don't want to lose his friendship for a second time. John makes me . . . lighter. I do love him."

Sarah held her gaze and said with all tenderness, "You do the man harm if you are not *in* love with him, Felicity, no matter if you wish to retain his companionship or not. If you are not in love with him, you must tell him so."

"Perhaps I will grow to love him. He would make an excellent father."

"An excellent father!" Juliet could not be contained. "Do you hear your own words? You are not buying a horse, Felicity. The man you marry should sweep you off your feet, should make you want to swoon when he walks in the room—"

"Don't be ridiculous, Juliet," Felicity snapped. Sarah looked over her cup at the cousins while they argued.

"I am not being ridiculous, Felicity. Sarah could scarcely pour her own tea when she fell in love with Gilbert."

"Do make your point, Juliet."

"The point, cousin, is that when you meet the man you are to marry, you should feel . . . something!"

"I do. I feel friendship, and respect, and I enjoy every moment that I am with John. You have been in society long enough to know that is more than most women of the ton can hope for. I have been out in society for three years, Juliet, and it is time I start a family of my own."

"Then why, if you are so keen on starting a family, did you not accept his offer the first go 'round and save the man two years of heartache? I'll tell you why, because you are not in love with him."

Felicity slammed her teacup down, shattering the thin bone china. "Enough, Juliet," she said. "I am so tired of your schoolgirl fantasies. Not every woman is lucky enough to have the man she loves love her in return. Most women simply have to make the best choice available. Excuse me." Lady Appleton stood, then walked out of the room, leaving the other women staring at one another in shock.

Twenty-four
※

Gilbert de Clare, Duke of Glenbroke, sat atop his mount as the animal sliced through the morning mist, which clung to life in the recesses of the riding trail before being burned up by the ascending sun.

"With the murder of Lady Davis, Whitehall will be forced to reevaluate your suspicions of Lady Rivenhall. So, until—"

"Whitehall can sod off," Aidan said harshly. "The Foreign Office all but called me mad when I brought forth my assertion."

Stunned by his brother-in-law's uncharacteristic show of temper, it took Gilbert several moments to respond. "Aidan, men's lives hang in the balance. She must be watched."

His brother-in-law took a steadying breath, his emerald eyes staring at the horizon. "Then hire a runner, or convince Whitehall that the woman is dangerous. Either way, I am finished. I find that I lack the objectivity needed to do the job."

The duke turned his head and sent Lord Wessex a speculative glance. Aidan Duhearst, who rarely raised a brow at the intrigue of the ton, was disconcerted, and Gilbert wanted to know why. He directed Apollo closer to the earl as a group of riders passed them on Rotten Row in Hyde Park.

Gilbert waited, having learned long ago that allowing a person room to speak often provided more answers than a direct question.

"Lady Rivenhall is . . . difficult."

The duke's face remained placid, but his mind was reeling. "And have you tried to control her as we discussed? Did you seduce her?"

Gilbert did not turn toward his brother-in-law, but he did fall back a half pace, watching him from the corners of his eyes. The earl's jaw tightened, and the easy elegance with which he rode was replaced with jarring rigidity.

"Yes," he said finally before clamping his jaw shut.

"And this disturbed you? Aidan, the woman is Napoleon's mistress."

"She was a virgin."

"What?" the duke said, jerking his reins and eliciting a snort of protest from his mount.

The earl's horse slowed to a stop, and Lord Wessex glanced about at the riders that had begun to turn their heads with curiosity.

"You heard me."

Gilbert gave Apollo a squeeze with his thighs, and the pair was once again ambling down the path. "How is that possible?"

Aidan rolled his eyes.

"Damn it, Aidan, you know my meaning. Then she is not Napoleon's paramour?"

Aidan shook his head beneath his beaver skin hat. "You would not believe me if I told you. Regardless, Gilbert, I am unable to contain the woman. If information were passed to the French due to my inadequacies, I would never forgive myself. Tell Whitehall that if they wish to investigate the lady they can handle the matter themselves."

The pair rode in silence for several minutes, each man lost in his own thoughts.

Gilbert contemplated the situation.

If Lady Rivenhall was indeed a French collaborator, and after meeting her, he readily believed the woman capable, then it was crucial that she be watched. However, the woman would be more likely to contact the French without the Earl of Wessex nipping at her heels.

"Very well, Aidan, I shall speak to my contact as soon as is possible."

Aidan's shoulders relaxed visibly. "Thank you, Your Grace," he muttered, continuing down his path.

"Very well. Tell the boy we will begin a second, more thorough investigation."

The duke sat back in his chair, suspicion narrowing his eyes as the old man's sinewy hand moved a rook.

"Who will you assign?"

"Fredricks."

"He's in France." The duke sat forward and stared at the old man. "You're keeping information from me, my lord."

"Am I?"

"Don't be vague, Lord Falcon. I have seen the maneuver too often."

The old man chuckled. "I suppose you have, Your Grace."

"The prime minister will want to be informed." Gilbert positioned his knight, waiting for the explanation that was being formulated behind Falcon's sharp eyes.

"Wessex has complicated the situation enormously." The old man sighed.

"What situation?" Gilbert knew he would be told only what was deemed necessary.

The old man leaned forward. "Has it never occurred to the Earl of Wessex that his escape from Albuera was rather . . . unencumbered?" The man gave a raspy chuckle.

"I mean to say, the French are fools, but not that bloody incompetent."

The duke's eyes widened. "Are . . . are you saying that Lady Rivenhall is—"

"Yes, a double agent recruited by myself seven years ago after her father was murdered by the French. She was only sixteen at the time, but if you have seen the girl then you know why she is now in favor with the emperor himself.

"Her father, Lord Rivenhall, was the liaison officer at the British embassy in Paris when he met her mother, a French noblewoman. They married and remained in France to be near the lady's family. Unfortunately, the lovely woman died suddenly when Lady Rivenhall was but three.

"I watched that little girl grow more stunning with each visit to the embassy, and when her father was executed before her very eyes, I offered to bring her here. She refused." For the first time in Gilbert's remembrance he saw emotion in the old man's eyes.

"If her father was murdered by the French, why would Napoleon trust her? Surely, he would question her loyalty."

"Lady Rivenhall is quite resourceful and so beautiful that a man wants to believe what she tells him. She arrived at court in Paris and offered her services to aid in the war effort.

"When interrogated, she told authorities that her father had beaten her all of her life, and that she hated him and his country, which she had scarcely seen."

"They believed her?" Gilbert asked with skepticism.

"Not initially. She was forced to prove herself time and time again. Smiling triumphantly as she witnessed British officers being put to death. Men she knew she could not save." Sadness pulled at the corners of his mouth.

Gilbert waited for the old man to take a sip of sherry before continuing. "At the age of eighteen, Lady Rivenhall caught the eye of the emperor himself. Having any number of officers to attest to her loyalty, Napoleon took her into his confidence."

The old man looked up and held the duke's eyes. "For the past four years Lady Rivenhall has been our most valuable agent. If not for Celeste, the Earl of Wessex would have been dead two times over."

"How so?"

"Not only did Lady Rivenhall arrange for the earl's escape, she also gave us vital information Lord Beresford needed to win the battle of Albuera. If not for her, your brother-in-law would most assuredly have died there."

The duke's blood ran cold. "What can we do to assist Lady Rivenhall in unmasking this traitor?"

"Nothing! You must do absolutely nothing, Your Grace." The old man spoke with fervor. "Only the two of us know of her existence, and it is imperative that it remain so. Since Wessex's escape, the emperor has watched Lady Rivenhall very closely.

"I suspect he has allowed the girl to come to London as a test of her loyalty. If she is suspected in any way, she will be killed, and the traitor will continue his activity." The elderly man shook his head. "No, better she be believed a French spy than suspected as a double agent."

"Are you suggesting that I am not to inform even the Earl of Wessex of her identity?"

"Particularly Wessex. With this man, this Lion, walking amongst us, it is too dangerous. Time and time again, he has accessed privileged documents contained within the walls of Whitehall. I, myself, took the precaution of destroying Lady Rivenhall's file in order to protect her. Lion believes her to be Napoleon's mistress. He will trust her, but if there is even the whisper of suspicion . . ."

"My brother-in-law would never divulge the lady's identity." The duke's voice was harsh, insulted.

"No, not intentionally, but remember this." He paused to emphasize the importance of his point. "In every ballroom, at every soiree, every event of importance held in London, there will be a French collaborator present, watching.

Some we know. Many we do not. One amiable glance from the decorated Earl of Wessex, the man she is suspected of helping to escape, could put the girl in danger and send the Lion into his den." The old man sat back, straightening his mundane waistcoat.

"You will inform Wessex that the Foreign Office is satisfied with its investigation. That you personally have had a look at Lady Rivenhall's dossier and are in total agreement with the findings." The old man pierced him with a glance. "You must trust me in this, Your Grace. We cannot allow this leak to continue, even if it means sacrificing Lady Rivenhall."

"I am not sure that Wessex will let the matter rest. The girl seems to have disconcerted the man."

"Wessex?" Falcon asked, surprised. "The boy is as steady as a rock."

"Quite, but the fact that Lady Rivenhall was a virgin when he came to her bed seems to have confounded our young earl."

The old man chuckled. "Well, well, well, the lady is more skilled than I gave her credit for. She managed to become Napoleon's mistress without ever having bedded him. Quite amusing, that. Well, never mind. Inform your brother-in-law that the situation is resolved and that he is to give Lady Rivenhall a wide berth."

"He will not be happy."

"Yes, well, none of us are happy about the war, Your Grace. Cunningham's been complaining about the embargo all week, says he can't procure the proper parchment to write my missives, as Whitehall is being rationed. Can you imagine?" The spymaster chuckled, moving a pawn. "Checkmate. Now"—the old man rose—"if you will excuse me, Cook is preparing her special beef stew and has threatened to give it to the dogs if I'm late to supper."

Gilbert stood watching the old man shuffle down his marble corridor and then bent his head to study the chessboard, thinking that if they wagered on the outcome of their weekly chess match, Falcon would be able to purchase enough beef stew to fill Hampton Court.

"Aidan, you will soil your garments." Sarah flicked crumbs off of his Bath superfine with one hand while bouncing her ten-month-old daughter on her right hip.

Aidan looked down at the boy, who sat happily on his lap. He spooned bread pudding into his nephew's tiny mouth and asked, "You would never think of soiling my garments would you, Sebastian?"

The boy mumbled through full cheeks.

Aidan laughed and accommodated the boy with another spoonful of the dessert. He watched his nephew's crimson lips close around the spoon, so sure that his needs would be met.

"Do you ever wonder why Father did it?"

"Went to war?" Sarah asked still bouncing Constance on her hip.

"No, at Lincelles." Aidan stared at his nephew. "Why he charged the French line."

"No, I have never wondered. It was his duty. Father was a very brave man."

Aidan tried to stave off the irritation he felt every time he was reminded of his father's bravery, because he knew his irritation would inevitably be followed by guilt. His father had been the best of men.

Everybody said so.

"Mmm," Aidan said, wishing he had not broached the subject.

Sarah reached for a spoon and began feeding Constance before her twin brother consumed the entire bread pudding. "I don't know why you of all people are asking me. You have fought in far more battles, and just as bravely I might add, as Father ever did." Sarah smiled, her cheeks pulling into dimples. "Bravery must run in our family."

Sebastian burped, saving Aidan from having to agree. "I see that you take after your boorish father," he said, tickling his nephew on the neck and eliciting a laugh that always made Aidan wonder if the babe had lost his ability to breathe.

"Aidan, you really are so good with children. Perhaps you should think about having your own."

The earl glared at his sister, saying, "Thank you for the oh-so-subtle probing into my personal affairs, Sarah."

The duchess reached for the bread pudding and with a frustrated huff, said, "Well, Aidan, here I thought I had made you a wonderful match and you let Lord Elkin steal your bride right from under your nose. I mean really, how are the twins to play with their cousins if there are no cousins to play with?"

Aidan lifted a brow toward his sister. "Foolish me, I thought it was my happiness you were concerned with, sister dear. Perhaps I should just pop 'round the corner and produce a playmate for the children."

"Oh, cork it, Aidan." Sarah wiped her daughter's mouth. "What about Juliet? Perhaps I was a bit hasty in my assessment. The girl really needs watching, and you can be absolutely pedantic at times."

"Pedantic!" he protested.

"She needs a steady hand, Aidan. You would cringe at some of the things the girl says in public." Sarah sighed.

"What things?" he asked, not really caring.

"Just the other day, she was telling Felicity and me a rumor about Lady Davis's lover. We have tried time and time again to discourage her predilection for gossiping—"

"Who was he?" Aidan interrupted.

"No idea. Juliet said the admiral's servants never saw the man clearly. He was tall and wore a hat that obscured his face."

"Then how do they know this man was her lover?"

Sarah blushed. "They heard them. Well, to be accurate, Lady Davis's niece heard them when she was visiting."

"How often did this man visit the admiral's wife?"

"Aidan," Sarah said, her eyes narrowed. "Why are you so interested?"

"Just curious," he lied.

"You are never just curious, Aidan." Sarah patted her daughter on the back. "As a matter of fact you cannot abide gossip."

"It is not gossip, Sarah." Aidan placed his nephew on the black marble floor. "The lady was murdered by one of the male members of the ton."

But his mind was not on Lady Davis's mysterious lover, it was on the woman who very likely commissioned the murderer to obtain the information so valuable to France. His mind was on Lady Rivenhall.

Twenty-five

 ❧❧

John Elkin sat opposite Lady Appleton in a private box at Vauxhall gardens.

They had enjoyed the musical concert and were finishing a dessert of strawberries and cream infused with brandy. The young lord dabbed at his lips and touched his pocket for the thousandth time that evening.

"Are you all right, John?"

Lord Elkin smiled at Felicity over a silver candelabrum. She was breathtaking tonight. Her burgundy gown was cut to perfection to complement the simple elegance that defined the woman who wore it. Large ruby ear bobs dangled over the graceful neck he longed to kiss, and his chest constricted painfully the longer he gazed at her.

"No, Felicity, I am not all right. I have not been all right since Lord Hambury's ball." Her fair brows creased, and he knew that if he did not act now, he would never find the courage again.

John rose and walked to her side, bending on one knee. She gasped, but he tried not to notice her surprise. He took a steadying breath and then said the things he had wanted to tell her for two years.

"Felicity, I have loved you from the first moment I met you. You are my dearest friend and the desire of my heart."

"John—"

"Please, hear me out." She had tears in her soft brown eyes, and he had no idea of their meaning. "I know that you were not in love with me two years ago and might not love me still. But, my sweet Felicity, I swear to you that I would spend every hour of every day ensuring your happiness. I am well aware that neither I, nor any man, deserves you, but . . ."

He reached into his jacket and pulled out the box containing a ten-carat, yellow diamond betrothal ring. "I hope now that you comprehend the depth of my esteem and that you might consider me worthy enough to be your husband." His heart was on his sleeve. "Marry me, my dearest Felicity."

Her gloved hand was covering her mouth, and tears streamed down her lovely face. The lady glanced at the engagement ring and then stared into his eyes. John held his breath as he waited for her answer.

"I . . . I thought that if this moment came, I would not hesitate." Felicity placed her hand on his cheek and crushed his heart with her gentle caress. "I thought I would be able to say 'yes' to the dearest man I have ever known."

John struggled to rise to his feet against the weight of his pain. He turned away from her and closed his eyes in a futile attempt to protect himself. But it did not work. He was bleeding with each word she uttered.

"John, it is I that am not worthy of your esteem, and if I could turn my traitorous heart in your favor . . . I thought with more time . . ." His chest ached as she stifled a sob. "Forgive me, John," she said, and then Lady Appleton ran out of their box, leaving behind her a broken man.

As a gentleman, he should go after her, but he hadn't the strength. Her carriage was just down the crowded path, and he knew that she would be safe. He, however . . .

John sank into his chair and opened the box that held all his hopes and dreams. He stared at the sparkling diamond and snapped it shut, hoping to seal his pain within the confines of the black velvet box.

Lord Elkin sat alone for a very long time, but the longer he sat the more stifling the private enclosure became. He threw back the heavy blue curtain and stepped into the cool night air. How could he have let this happen? How could he have allowed himself to feel the pain of it for a second time?

How could he not?

Lord Elkin reached his carriage, climbed in, and rapped on the roof.

"Where to, my lord?" his driver asked.

"Just drive."

His arms were crossed over his chest as he stared out the window. He tried to allow the rocking of the carriage to soothe him, but he remained restless. He didn't want time to think, to be alone.

A brothel?

"My club," he decided, but as they made for his club on St. James Street, he began to worry that someone would see his pain beneath the bright lights.

And then he saw it.

"Stop," he called to his coachman.

The driver positioned the carriage where he always did when dropping Lord Elkin at Whitehall. It was two o'clock in the morning, but surely someone would be there. And if not, John could catch up on his correspondence; work would be the perfect distraction. He jumped down from his landau, his greatcoat billowing behind him.

"Evening, Lord Elkin," the night watchman offered.

"Evening."

His Hessians clicked down the empty corridors, and as he approached his office, his brows furrowed in confusion. He stared at the light shining from beneath his door. The charwoman, no doubt, he thought to himself.

But when he opened the door he knew he had been mistaken. His eyes collided with the dark man searching his desk. He recognized the young lord immediately and knew in an instant that he was staring at the face of their traitor.

Had his shock not been so great, had he walked more softly, had his mind not been distracted, perhaps he would have reacted more swiftly.

But he did not.

And when the bullet entered his chest, he was surprised that he had time to look down at the wound before dropping to his knees on the cold wooden floor. He turned his head and watched the man leave, and then the room began to dim.

And as his lifeblood pumped out of his body, the last thought that eased him into unconsciousness was *Felicity*.

The Earl of Wessex read the missive a second time as his carriage rumbled down the empty streets of London toward Whitehall.

> *My Lord,*
>   *The lady in question has left her home dressed as a scullery maid and has arrived at the Foreign Office, where she remains. I shall wait across from the front entrance to receive instruction.*
>
>   *Yours,*
>   *Mister Brown*

The runner emerged from the night shadows the moment Aidan's carriage came to rest.

"Where is she?" The earl's tone was terse.

"Inside. The night watchman would not allow me to pass," he said, his eyes offering an apology.

Aidan slapped the bulky man on the shoulder. "Couldn't be helped, Mister Brown. If the lady emerges before me, detain her."

"Right," the man said, full of determination.

Aidan dashed across the street and up the stairs. "I am the Earl of Wessex. Perhaps you will recall my accompanying my brother-in-law, the Duke of Glenbroke, on the premises."

The watchman searched his memory, and unwilling to anger both a duke and an earl the man said, "Yes, I do recall you, my lord. What can I do for you?"

"I need to be given admittance."

The gangly man hesitated. "My apologies, my lord, but I'm afraid I must ask why."

Aidan gave the watchman a friendly smile. "Well, it involves a lady, but I'm afraid I cannot say more."

The man flashed a licentious grin. "I've got women problems meself. Seems me wife has found out about the other women." Aidan laughed his understanding and the watchman added, "Just let me know if I can be of assistance."

"I will, and thank you," Aidan responded, and then slipped past the man and into the hallowed halls of the Foreign Office.

Aidan did not know where to begin, but he surmised Celeste would need light to conduct her search. He glanced at the floor as he rushed down the long corridors, but when he saw a door was ajar he rushed in the room and nearly slipped as his boots slid across the wooden floor.

He looked down, stunned by the massive pool of blood, and then he saw him. John Elkin lay on the floor, his face a ghostly gray. Aidan fell to his knees and gathered his lifelong friend in his arms.

"John!"

His eyes flickered open and Aidan saw the recognition in them. "John, who did this?"

Lord Elkin struggled to get breath, but only managed to gurgle as blood settled in his lungs, the sound pulling Aidan back to the peninsula. He clutched his friend to his chest, knowing that there was nothing he could do to save him.

He grasped John's hand, lending him his strength as they held one another's gaze, and then . . .

"No! No, John!"

John's eyes dimmed, and Aidan knew that he was alone.

He held his friend until the warmth disappeared from his hand, replaced by the cold that now settled in his own chest. Aidan closed his friend's lids over empty blue eyes and set him gently on the floor. Tears streaked down his face, and he swiped at them, welcoming the rage that replaced his sorrow.

Where is she?

His jaw pulsed as he made his way through the maze of corridors to notify the night watchman. The man gasped when he saw the blood covering Aidan's shirt and buff buckskins.

"Lord Elkin has been murdered. You will find his body in his office." His tone became fierce. "And as you failed to protect him in life, I expect you to protect his body in death."

"Yes, my lord," the man said, terrified.

Aidan took the stairs two at a time and stood before Mister Brown with fists clenched at his side.

"Where is she?"

The man stared at the blood on his garment and hesitated when he saw the rage hardening Aidan's eyes. "The lady . . . is in your conveyance, my lord. She came out just after you went in."

Aidan's hand was opening the carriage door with the last of the runner's words, his thoughts on the traitor inside. He flung the door open and slammed it shut. Lady Rivenhall was startled, but when she took in his appearance and looked into his burning eyes she became alarmed.

"You bitch!" he said, and in one swift move he had her by the hair at the nape of her aristocratic neck. She cried out, more from fear than pain, and as he stared down at her, Aidan realized that she was not the only one to blame for John Elkin's death.

He was culpable as well.

He had known what the lady was and had not watched her closely enough, had not contained her enough. The heat of his anger was replaced by a chilling numbness. He reached down and removed her knife and retrieved the pistol from her reticule, then fell to the opposite side of the carriage, shouting "home" to his driver.

The carriage lurched forward, but Lady Rivenhall did not stir, sensing like a cornered rabbit that any movement on her part would trigger his wrath. She sat up with deliberate fluidity, and Aidan could feel her staring at him. He ignored her, keeping focused on the passing buildings and not his overwhelming guilt.

They traveled the remaining distance to his home in silence. Aidan dragged her out of the carriage by her wrist, and then they were in his entryway. He ignored the distress in his butler's eyes as his man viewed his blood-soaked clothing. "Have a bath drawn."

His foot hit the staircase, and Celeste balked. "What—"

"I advise you to remain silent, Lady Rivenhall," he growled, "as I am very close to striking you." Aidan continued up the stairs and when she stumbled, he did not even pause.

She scrambled to her feet and followed him to his bedchamber, unable to do anything else. Aidan opened the door and dropped her to the carpeted floor, her chambermaid costume tangling around her. He removed his cravat and gazed at the blood-soaked silk.

John's blood.

He threw it at her, wanting her to feel the evidence of what she had done. The deceitful woman picked it up, her brows furrowed with feigned confusion.

"What happened?" she asked, looking up at him.

"Spare me the theatrics, Lady Rivenhall," Aidan ripped off his jacket, followed by his waistcoat and shirt.

He lifted his arms and stared at the lines on his wrists where the blood had stopped covering his skin in favor of soaking his jacket. His gaze lingered on his hands, completely covered with John's blood. *His responsibility.* Aidan removed his boots and finally his bloody buckskins.

The traitor averted her eyes, angering him further. He wanted her to see John's blood and wondered what she had seen when she shot him, wondered how John had reacted. He would have been surprised, no doubt. Aidan reached down and grabbed her upper arm, hauling her to the smaller room.

"You will bathe me," he commanded and then sank into the steaming water.

Lady Rivenhall reached for a cloth, knowing better than to question him. The water turned a sickly pink as he submerged his hands in hopes of loosening the blood that had dried beneath his fingernails, but when she reached for his face, he pulled away.

"You have . . . blood . . . on your face." Aidan stared at her as she pressed the white muslin to his cheek. "Where did . . . the blood come from?"

The woman was a consummate liar, and he hated her for what she had done. But he hated himself more for not having stopped her.

"My garments were soiled when I held the man you shot, as he died in my arms." Her face paled, and he had to admit that she was very convincing.

But he knew better.

"Who? What man?"

Aidan's eyes cooled to green shards of ice. "John Elkin."

The woman jumped to her feet and placed both hands over her mouth to stifle a cry of distress.

"No," she whispered, tears welling in her eyes.

"Save your performance for court, Lady Rivenhall." Aidan rose with an angry splash and stepped toward her. "We both know what you are."

The treacherous woman turned to face him, her golden head shaking in adamant denial. "No, I—I'm not responsible," she protested, closing her eyes.

Aidan could feel her chest pounding with fear as he grabbed the bodice of the disguise that had given her access to Lord Elkin's office.

"And I suppose you were at the Foreign Office just tidying up?"

A tear rolled down her cheek as she whispered, "I never saw him."

It was more than Aidan could bear. He pushed her against the wall and stared deep into her black soul. "Don't you dare pretend to grieve the man you've just murdered."

"But I didn't," she breathed.

Aidan snapped. He pulled back his fist and swung, smashing the mirror to the right of her head.

He did not look at her, could not look at her when he lifted the woman and threw her in the water, saying, "Bathe in John's blood."

He retrieved a silk bathrobe from his bedchamber and walked back to the woman. Lady Rivenhall had her arms wrapped around her legs and her fair head rested on her knees. She was crying.

Sickened by the performance, and more so with himself, he said, "Here," throwing the robe at her feet.

She stepped out of the tub and removed her wet garments as she dried herself. Aidan tried not to notice how her nakedness affected him, and concentrated on how she used her body to lure men like John.

"Get in bed," he ordered, indicating his bedchamber with a toss of his head.

The lady complied, and Aidan followed, not bothering to bind her for he knew he would not sleep. He blew out the candles and stared at the darkness for hours, listening to every tick of the clock.

The blame for John's death could be placed squarely on his shoulders, but it would not happen again. Come morning, Lady Rivenhall would be unable to do more harm.

Celeste lay on her side pretending to sleep, but she was awake and watching the turbulent earl through shuttered lashes. He lay on his back with his powerful arms bent at the elbow as his hands cradled his head. She could not see his beautiful black hair, but his eyes were open, and he stared at the brocade canopy that covered the enormous bed.

She watched him for an eternity and when she saw his stunning eyes shimmering in the dark, she could bear it no longer. Celeste reached out and touched his chest gently, but he grabbed her wrist, and even in the dim light of the moon she could see his forehead drawn with suspicion.

But he needed comforting, so she sat up on her knees and placed her free hand on his face. He encircled that wrist as well, leaving her with but one option. Celeste leaned her head toward his, knowing that he could stop her and knowing also that he would not.

Her mouth covered his in the most tender of kisses, and slowly he released her arms. Her hands fell to his lean shoulders as she stretched the length of his muscular body, but he did not touch her. Celeste relinquished his lips and pressed her mouth to his neck, then his chest. Each caress was meant to comfort and soothe. Her hands skimmed his body, and when next she lay atop him, he returned her kiss with equal tenderness.

His arms slid around her waist and with one smooth motion she was on her back. The earl covered her mouth and then shifted to her neck. Celeste was thankful to the dark for giving them this respite, and she arched against him when he took her nipple in his mouth. His large hands covered the expanse of her ribcage, reminding her of his masculinity, his power.

One hand slid down her belly, and his fingers searched her feminine folds, and he groaned when he felt how ready she was to receive him. He returned to her lips, and when she spread her thighs and offered herself, she could hear his breath catch.

The handsome earl eased into her with one long stroke that she thought would never end. He withdrew with equal leisure, and she heard herself moan pleadingly.

The Earl of Wessex bent his head and kissed her as he stroked in again, his tongue mirroring the movements of his hips. He continued his easy rhythm until Celeste could tolerate no more. She lifted her body to meet his thrusts, but he refused to increase his cadence. Celeste wrapped her legs around his waist, taking him deeper.

"Please," she begged, but he was unrelenting.

And then she felt the wave that stole her breath as she built toward an enormous crest. Celeste dropped her arms to her sides so she could enjoy the pleasure washing over her. He plunged deeper, faster, and she was begging him with each cry to end her torment. He did, and thrusting home, she exploded with white lights streaking across the dark.

Celeste could feel her body reach for him, and it was then that he lost control. She could hear it in the masculine moans that were coming now with each powerful thrust he made, and then he shouted, and she could feel herself being filled as he came into her.

She could feel his heart pounding in his chest when he collapsed atop her. Celeste ran her fingers through his thick hair and kissed him on the neck, tasting the salt from the layer of sweat that covered them both. He tightened his arms around her and held her close until his breathing slowed.

And then with a suddenness that startled her, Wessex raised himself off of her as if she had burned him. He stared down at her, but it was too dark to see his features. Then he was gone, off the bed and pacing the room. He snatched a robe and fumbled for the dressing room door, leaving her alone in the cold darkness of his cavernous bedchamber.

Twenty-six

❧❧❧

The Earl of Wessex returned an hour later, bathed and, as always, impeccably dressed. He held a large box in his hand, which he tossed onto the bed.

"I want you ready to leave in half an hour," he said with apathy, scarcely looking at her before he withdrew the way he had entered.

A maid came into the room with a breakfast tray and announced, "A bath is ready, my lady."

Celeste blushed and knotted the tie to the silk robe. Mortified, she followed the girl to the bathing room and saw steam rising from the lavender-scented water.

"You'll need to wait a moment, ma'am. The water is a trifle hot at present."

Celeste stuck her foot in the water and gritted her teeth. "I'm afraid I do not have the time. The earl expects to leave in half an hour." Where they were going, she had no idea.

She sank into the water and hissed in pain, but the distressed maid grabbed the pitcher from the washbasin and poured the entire contents into the bath. The cold water swirled around her and Celeste smiled in gratitude as the bath water became bearable.

The maid lathered her hair with lavender soap as Celeste bathed her body, and within moments the task was complete. She rose from the tub, and the girl's eyes widened when she saw how red Celeste's skin had become.

Lady Rivenhall grabbed her hand, saying, "It's all right. It's not your fault. Now fetch the undergarments in the pink box on the bed and assist me in dressing."

The girl bobbed a curtsy and rushed from the room. She returned with an exquisite chemise adorned with silk roses and Chantilly lace. The man certainly knew how to purchase women's clothing, Celeste thought with cynicism. The gown the earl had provided was a bit too large in the bosom, and she could only imagine whom he had peeled it from. But it was a flattering shade of blue, and she was thankful to have it.

Celeste glanced at the clock, fear clutching her throat. She had eight minutes remaining.

"Do what you can with my damp hair and pass the toast, please."

Celeste reached into the desk she was seated in front of and withdrew a single sheet of paper. She dipped a pen in the inkwell and wrote a short note to Marie, saying that she was well and that she would contact her as soon as was possible.

She sealed the communication before the ink had dried and handed it to the maid, who was still fussing with wet strands of gold. Celeste lifted the teacup and swallowed a large sip of tea to wash down the dry toast, and was in the entryway with one minute to spare.

Wessex looked at her with sunlit eyes, but there was no warmth in them. His ebony brows pulled together, and he walked toward her and gazed at her chest.

"You're all red."

It was a statement, not a question, and she was not sure if he wanted an explanation, but she gave him one anyway.

"Yes, my lord, I'm afraid I did not have time to allow the bath water to cool to the appropriate temperature."

His eyes flashed greener, but she was too tired to try and interpret his mood. Lord Elkin's murder had been weighing on her all night, and she was feeling the effects. She brushed past him and stepped into the carriage without benefit of his assistance.

Aidan Duhearst settled opposite her and shrugged off his greatcoat as the carriage rocked forward. Her stomach flipped at the sight of him in a black jacket and gold waistcoat adorned with large emerald studs that perfectly complemented his striking eyes.

The young earl sat erect, and Celeste was reminded of the first time she had seen him emerge from the prison at Albuera. His jaw held the same determination that she had seen that morning, and Celeste could not help but wonder why.

"Where are you taking me?"

His eyes were as cold as the gems they resembled. "I'm handing you over for questioning to Colonel Lancaster at the Foreign Office."

Celeste could not breathe as panic seized her lungs.

"No!" she said, but the earl dismissed her with a turn of his noble head.

Lady Rivenhall stared at his profile as she searched for a way to stop him. If she were in jail, the traitor would go unchecked. Her years of work in France . . . the men who would die . . . she was too valuable an asset for Britain to lose.

Celeste dropped to her knees and placed her hands on his thighs.

"Please, I beg you not to do this. I will warm your bed every night if you desire it." Her mind focused on the only explanation he might accept, the only explanation that might soften his resolve. "Please, my lord, I do not want to die."

The earl was clearly appalled at her undignified display as she groveled before her captor. Celeste's mind was racing. She thought to seduce him, but rejected the idea in favor of his pity.

"Please, don't do this. If last night meant anything . . ." A mistake. His face hardened, and the man seized her arm with punishing force.

"Get up," he said in disgust, throwing her on the squabs.

The carriage slowed, and he was on the ground before it had come to a full stop. The earl offered his hand so as not to cause a scene and then propelled her up the wide steps of the Foreign Office.

"Please, you've no idea what you're doing," Celeste said in desperation.

The earl stopped one step above her and looked down with regal authority. "I know precisely what I am doing, and if I had done my duty long ago Lord Elkin would still be alive."

Her heart ached for him. "I had nothing—"

"Don't." He grated his teeth.

When they entered the busy corridors of the massive building, Celeste tried to appear an ornament at the handsome earl's side. She averted her eyes and hugged his arm as they proceeded forward, but they had not gone far when a familiar voice caused her heart to leap to her throat.

"Wessex," the old man said with a jovial smile. He walked forward and offered the earl a shaky hand. "Well, well, well, haven't seen you since, when . . . the Duke and Duchess of Glenbroke's wedding ceremony?"

"Yes, I believe that's correct," the young lord said, anxious to be getting on his way.

"And who have we here?"

Falcon turned his eyes on Celeste with no hint of recognition and no indication of the steely intelligence she had witnessed throughout their meeting just last night.

"This is Lady Rivenhall, my lord. If you will excuse us?"

Celeste curtsied. "My lord."

"Charmed," the old man said, patting the Earl of Wessex on the shoulder as he began to walk with them down the congested corridor where the Foreign Offices were located. "I was just coming to have breakfast with my nephew. Would you like to meet him?"

"I'm very sorry, my lord—"

"Here we are," the old man sang, completely ignoring the earl's protests.

Falcon ushered them into an empty office that Celeste knew was not his own. The old man slapped his hand on the oak desk in the first display of temper she had ever seen in the decorous gentleman.

"What in God's name are you doing here?"

The earl's brows furrowed when he realized that the elderly lord was not speaking to him, but to her.

"Lord Wessex forced me to accompany him. He is quite determined to turn me over to the authorities."

"Damnation, boy," Falcon barked. "I told you the matter of Lady Rivenhall was being addressed. You've no idea of the damage you have done."

The stunned earl looked first to Falcon and then to her as the old man settled in a wing-backed chair.

"Sit down," he ordered, pointing to the settee, but the young lord did not move quickly enough. "Sit!"

Dumbfounded, the earl sat.

"Well, Wessex, it would appear there is nothing to be done but explain the entire situation."

"He will not believe you," Celeste warned.

"My dear, Lord Wessex is not the sort of man to allow emotions to cloud his judgment. He will assess the matter properly once our position is clarified," the older man said with unwavering certainty.

The earl concentrated on Falcon, prompting him to speak.

"Lady Rivenhall works for me as an English collaborator obtaining information from the French and sending said information across the Channel."

Lord Wessex glanced at her, clearly skeptical. With the deference appropriate for an elder, he said, "If you will forgive me, my lord, Lady Rivenhall has a way of making men believe what they wish to believe."

"Quite, which is precisely why I recruited her. Lady Rivenhall has been passing vital information to this office for the past four years."

Celeste could feel the earl's eyes on her, but she stared at the intricate designs in the cerulean carpet, unable to bear his revulsion at the things she had been forced to do.

"She . . . Lady Rivenhall is an English agent as well as Napoleon's mistress?"

"Yes." The old man nodded. "Our most highly placed operative. Lady Rivenhall has given us the names of Napoleon's most trusted advisors as well as passing French battle plans for Fuentes de Onoro and Albuera."

The earl's head snapped round so that he could look at her, and then he bolted from the settee and walked toward the window with long, elegant strides. He planted his palms on the windowsill and bent his head. His broad shoulders rose and fell with his increased breathing as Falcon continued his verbal assault.

"Yes, my lord, if not for our Lady Rivenhall you would have died on that peninsula. Not to mention your escape. Who the hell did you think gave you that key?"

Wessex stared out the window, his back to them as he said, "That does not explain why the woman is in England."

The woman. The indifference of his words stabbed at her heart, making her wince.

"The Foreign Office has uncovered a traitor, I'm afraid. The man has been passing information to the French for several months. We've managed to narrow the list of suspects to five peers, and Lady Rivenhall has been asked to investigate them before Lord Wellesley launches an all-out assault on the peninsula in two weeks' time."

"How did she explain her absence to Napoleon?"

The old man chuckled. "As you say, the girl makes a man believe what he wants to believe. Lady Rivenhall managed to convince the emperor that it was his idea to send her to England in order to acquire information for France."

Celeste's eyes remained on the earl's back as she willed him to understand.

"And these five men, one was Lord Elkin?" Wessex asked.

"Yes." The old man sighed. "Made me angry, that. I was meeting with Lady Rivenhall at the time." Falcon paused in contemplative silence. "I always liked that boy. Never mind, best way to avenge his murder is to find the bastard who did it. Lady Rivenhall has two weeks to investigate the remaining lords, and you are going to help her."

"What?" Aidan spun round, his question a rush of air.

Celeste closed her eyes, trying not to hear the note of aversion in his voice and trying not to feel the pain of it.

"My boy, we are running out of time. And, quite frankly, the girl needs assistance."

"Not mine," the earl said bitterly as he made for the door, but Falcon's next words stopped him cold.

"Then you intend to allow this man to pass information that will most assuredly lead to the death of thousands of English soldiers—men you fought beside?"

"Don't," Wessex hissed, his hands clenching, "speak of things you know *nothing* about!"

"Ah, but I do know of the losses on the peninsula, my lord. I lost a grandson at Vimeiro, and I will be damned if I will allow other men to die because I have not done my duty to the Crown."

Celeste's mouth hung open as the two men stared at one another.

"Find another man," the earl said and then, looking into her eyes, added, "I've done my duty."

Celeste felt as though he had struck her. She sat, unable to move, as the young earl turned and departed the small office with a slam of the door.

"Wessex will come 'round, my dear," the old man said with the utmost tenderness. "How long have you been in love with the boy?"

"What?" Celeste looked up. "I'm not in love with Lord Wessex."

Falcon graced her with an indulgent grin. "My dear lady, I have not been given this post by coincidence." The dignified gentleman rose on shaky legs. "You are in love with the Earl of Wessex, and you have been for quite some time."

"I most assuredly am not, my lord, but it does not signify as I prefer to work alone."

"I'm sure that you do, Celeste, but after the events of last night, I'm afraid I cannot allow it."

"A Bow Street runner, then?"

The old man offered her his arm. "I'm sorry, Celeste. Your fates seem destined to intertwine."

"And how do you plan to convince the earl of that, my Lord Falcon?"

The stately man chuckled. "I, my dear lady, plan to win an intriguing game of chess.

The Earl of Wessex spent the day in a daze. He had ridden his horse mercilessly all afternoon and now found himself staggering up the steps of Manton's.

"Good day, my lord. Would you like your regular range?"

"Yes, Alfred," Aidan said as he was led by the footman to his customary position at the far end of the row. He nodded to Lord Deaver on his left, and removed his riding gloves.

The servant returned with the box containing Aidan's dueling pistols. He removed the weapons from their red velvet casing and admired the quality of the craftsmanship. The sterling silver mechanisms had been polished to perfection by the man who now loaded the first of two pistols.

"My lord," the man said simply as he handed the loaded weapon back to Aidan, who then lifted the firearm and with steady aim hit the target dead center. Unfortunately, the target happened to belong to Lord Deaver, who looked at the crack shot Earl of Wessex with a raised brow.

"Sorry, old man." Aidan reached for the second pistol, taking time with his aim. He squeezed the trigger, hitting the wall a good two feet above his own target.

"I must say, my lord, you are by far the worst shot that I have ever had the misfortune to witness." Aidan rolled his eyes and turned toward his sarcastic brother-in-law standing just behind him. "You do, of course, realize that you are aiming for the black mark at the center of the target?"

"Yes, Your Grace, and if you would do me the honor of sodding off, I could get back to my amusement."

"I don't think that is a sound decision, my lord."

"Why the bloody hell not?"

"Well, firstly, from the smell of scotch wafting from within five yards of you, I would say that you have little chance of hitting the broad side of a landau, much less your target. Secondly, I believe you have frightened Lord Deaver here."

Lord Deaver grinned, saying, "Damn right. Thought I would have to duck that last round."

"So, dear brother-in-law, I have come to fetch you for dinner, assuming, of course, that you are able to eat."

Aidan looked up at the silvery eyes of the Duke of Glenbroke. "Far be it from me to reject such a gracious invitation." He turned to the footman. "Thank you, Alfred. I believe that will be all for today."

"Thank God," the duke said. "Now." The oversized man squeezed his shoulder. "Can you walk or shall I carry you?"

"Why the hell my sister married you, I shall never fathom."

Gilbert de Clare chuckled, saying, "Nor shall I."

The two men sat several hours later watching the Duchess of Glenbroke withdraw from the dining room. Aidan called for his third cup of coffee, and when it was brought the duke dismissed the six footmen with a wave of his hand.

"You knew, didn't you?" Suppressed rage vibrated in Aidan's voice.

"Yes," the duke said. "I would have told you if I could have, Aidan. But it was done to protect Lady Rivenhall."

Lord Wessex's forehead knotted in anger. "And I suppose my following an English operative was very amusing for you both."

"Aidan—"

"And your suggestion that I seduce her . . ." He shook his head, unable to continue as regret and shame overcame him. "Have you any idea what you have done to me, Gilbert?"

The duke leaned forward on his muscular forearms. "What would you have had me say, Aidan? I was not aware that Lady Rivenhall was working for England. I needed to identify her contacts, but you were determined to expose her. I merely gave you a reason not to."

"And that is why you suggested I bed her?"

"Yes."

"Damn you, Gilbert," Aidan said, gripping the side of the table while his jaw pulsed in rhythm with his anger.

His brother-in-law waited, allowing Aidan's temper to cool. "Lady Rivenhall needs—"

"No!"

The duke's notorious temper flared. "You owe the woman your life, Aidan, and now that this traitor has turned to murder, you would leave her unprotected?"

"Why me?"

"You already know who she is, the importance of her mission. The fewer people that know of her existence the more likely she is to succeed. Why are you so resistant?"

Aidan exploded out of his chair, knocking it to the floor. "Leave it, Gilbert."

The duke's initial confusion faded and was replaced with steely determination. "Very well, Lord Wessex. I believe your commission as a lieutenant in His Majesty's service does not expire for two months, is that correct?"

"You bastard."

The duke rose to his feet and removed a sealed document from the pocket of his blue jacket, raising it in Aidan's direction.

"I hereby order you on behalf of His Royal Highness the Prince Regent to assist Lady Celeste Rivenhall in the performance of her duties until notified otherwise."

Aidan snatched the missive and crushed it in his hands. The royal seal crumpled into several pieces that fell to the polished wooden floor of the immense dining hall. He turned for the door when the duke's words resounded in the room.

"You will be contacted when you are needed."

Aidan spun 'round and gave an exaggerated bow. "How thoughtful of you, Your Grace. I am breathless with anticipation."

Gilbert de Clare stared after his brother-in-law as he slammed his dining hall doors with such violence the sound echoed throughout the room. He sank down on the cushion of his chair and lifted his cognac to his lips.

The door opened gently, and his wife walked toward him. "From the manner in which my brother left, I take it the interview did not go well."

Gilbert raised his hand to her and pulled Sarah between his thighs. "No, I'm afraid not," he said, resting his head against his wife's chest as his arms slid around her waist.

She smoothed his hair back and kissed him on the forehead. "It's not your fault, Gilbert. Aidan will recover."

"No," the duke said, kissing the swells of his wife's breast. "I don't think he will."

Sarah clicked her tongue in indignation and pushed on his shoulders so that she could see his face. "Why on earth would you say such a thing? Of course he will come round. Lady Rivenhall saved his life, after all. He just requires a few days to get over having been deceived, that is all."

"No." Gilbert pressed his lips to her neck.

"Why not?"

"I'm afraid your brother has fallen in love with Lady

Rivenhall." He was kissing her breasts again, and his right hand cupped the tantalizing mound in his palm.

"How do you know?"

"Because, my dear, that is precisely the same look I had when you were driving me wild with wanting."

Gilbert pulled her in his lap and ended their conversation with a searing kiss before taking his wife upstairs and worshiping her with his body.

"How is she?" Sarah's dark brows were pulled together with concern.

"Not well," Juliet sighed. "She has not left her bedchamber for three days. I'm afraid she blames herself for Lord Elkin's murder."

The duchess sighed, saying, "How could she possibly blame herself?"

"Lord Elkin proposed to her that evening, and when she refused his offer, he made his way to Whitehall."

"But he might have planned to go to the Foreign Office either way."

"I know."

Their voices became a murmur when Lady Appleton stepped away from the bedchamber door. Felicity looked at the breakfast tray that had been brought two hours earlier, and her stomach lurched.

How could she *not* blame herself for John's murder? The fact remained that if not for her, Lord Elkin would not have gone to that building, to that room. She slipped back into bed and pulled the counterpane over her head to block out the offending morning light. Unfortunately, it could not block her last words to John Elkin from her memory. He had poured his heart out to her, and once again she had rejected him.

Why hadn't she accepted his offer? Why hadn't she had the courage to say yes and make her dear friend her husband?

Felicity felt the tears begin again. She pulled her knees to her chest and let them fall, wondering if she would ever be able to forgive herself. However, she was brought out of her grief by a small crack.

Lady Appleton sniffled and sat up, unsure if she had heard something. She listened and a few moments later heard a second clatter coming from the direction of the window.

She walked toward the balcony at the back of her London townhome, and saw a yellow hatbox with silk flowers adhered to the lid. Confused, and more than a little curious, Felicity opened the French doors and bent down to the retrieve the gift.

She brought the box to her bed and opened it. Inside on a white muslin cloth sat a tiny orange kitten with an indigo satin bow tied round its neck. The kitten blinked against the light, displaying big blue eyes.

Felicity picked up the minuscule cat and was amazed by the delicacy of the animal's ribs. She brought the kitten to her cheek and smiled at the smell clinging to its soft fur, new and fresh and innocent.

The kitten gave a tiny meow, and Felicity smiled in spite of her black mood. She placed him back in the box, noticing a note folded in half that leaned against the side of the package. Felicity picked it up, opening it with one hand so that she could stroke the kitten under the chin with the other.

The letter had only a few lines of script.

A few weeks ago this animal did not exist, and in a few short years he will no longer be with us. Therefore, it is your responsibility to enjoy the time you have together, and cherish his memory when he is gone, for the time of his passing is not of our choosing.

Tears flooded her eyes, and although the letter had no signature, Felicity would have recognized the cramped handwriting of Lord Christian St. John anywhere.

Twenty-seven

❦

Lady Rivenhall was seated to the right of Lord Ferrell at the Dowager Duchess of Glenbroke's dinner party, as previously arranged.

His head was turned as he spoke to a plump young girl with crooked teeth and spots on her face. "Lady Davis," she heard him say as the dark man bobbed his head, and Celeste knew that he was turning to make his introduction to her.

She pulled her gown to tighten the bodice against her breasts and smiled with a touch more than polite interest, but less than seductive intent. However, she was unprepared for the impact of his stunning smile when he recognized her.

He turned toward her like a man who was comfortable with his body and said, as if they had never been introduced, "Lord Anthony Ferrell. How do you do? No walkway mishaps, ruined parcels, or twisted ankles, I trust."

Celeste glanced at the deep cleft in his strong chin and then at his dark eyes. They were brown and surrounded by lashes so long and thick any woman would envy them. His golden complexion contrasted starkly with white teeth, and she could see that he was enjoying her perusal of his all too handsome features.

"Lady Celeste Rivenhall. And no, Lord Ferrell, since our inelegant introduction on the Pall Mall, I have remained blessedly intact."

His dark eyes flared to a deep brandy, and his smile broadened as he said, "Yes, you have." His gaze drifted down her body and back to her face in a not so subtle assessment. "You're even more beautiful than when last we met, Lady Rivenhall."

Celeste made light of his comment, saying, "You really should not flatter ladies so outrageously, my lord."

The dark man held her gaze and lifted a brow. "I don't. I make a point of never complimenting a woman unless the remark happens to be true."

Her soup was placed before her, but he did not relinquish her gaze until he had been served as well. They turned toward the lobster bisque and ate the creamy concoction with unbridled appreciation.

"And how are you finding London?" he asked between spoonfuls. "I believe this is your first time in the city?"

Celeste displayed a charming smile. "I adore London, particularly the cultural pursuits that are unavailable to one residing in the country."

Their bowls of bisque were removed in favor of the second course, quail eggs topped with beluga caviar. She lifted an egg slice and placed it in her mouth, closing her eyes as she noted how the saltiness of the caviar was the perfect complement to the earthy tones of the egg. When she opened her eyes Lord Ferrell was staring at her lips, and Celeste remembered how much men enjoyed watching a woman take something into her mouth.

"What pursuits interest you most, Lady Rivenhall?" the man asked with a lazy smile.

"I enjoy the theater, of course, but by far the most enjoyable aspect of town life is viewing the works of art. I have a private collection at home, but nothing could compare with London. Do you not agree, my lord?" she asked, knowing full well the man had an extensive collection in his townhome.

He looked at her in triumph, saying, "Did you know that my mother was an Italian countess from Venice?"

Celeste lied with a shake of her head.

"It so happens that she collected works of art from all over the continent and brought them to England when she married my father."

"Then you are a very fortunate man, my lord."

The quail eggs were replaced with a salmon fillet in a lemon caper sauce.

"Yes, I am, Lady Rivenhall." He smiled seductively as he leaned toward her. "Would you care to view the collection?"

"Might I?" Celeste asked with unconcealed enthusiasm.

The sultry man chuckled at her fervor. "Shall we say Thursday? We could share dinner and then take our time exploring the collection."

"I'm afraid Thursday is impossible, my lord." Celeste allowed him a moment of disappointment before adding, "However, I am available tomorrow evening."

His eyes flared at her eagerness to be alone with him. "Seven?"

"I shall count the hours," Celeste said, allowing a sensual glint to linger in her eyes.

The remainder of the dinner party passed in a blur. She had accomplished her goal, and now her mind wandered to her inevitable meeting with the Earl of Wessex.

She had not seen him since he stormed out of the interview with Falcon, and she could not help but wonder how he would react when next he saw her. Would he still be angry, or would he have reconsidered her role in the events leading to Lord Elkin's death? Would his beautiful green eyes still reflect his disdain of her? The sight of which would shatter her heart, because it was a disdain she could not help but share.

•   •   •

Lady Rivenhall returned home to a barrage of questions from Madame Arnott.

"Well?"

Celeste stood still while her companion removed her garments. "I am to be shown his collection tomorrow evening at seven."

"And do you think this Lord Ferrell is capable of espionage?"

Lady Rivenhall laughed. "I think Lord Ferrell is capable of a great deal. I'm just unsure if collaboration is one of them." Celeste sank into her desk chair covered in yellow gingham as Marie removed the pins that held her intricate coiffure. "I shall have my answer tomorrow."

She withdrew a piece of paper from the top drawer and hesitated before writing the short note to Lord Wessex. Celeste blotted the page and handed the message to Madame Arnott.

"Marie, have this delivered to the Earl of Wessex." Her companion started for the door, but Celeste added, "And do not be seen doing so."

"*Oui.*" Madame Arnott slipped out of the room, leaving Celeste alone with her fear . . . and hope.

The Duchess of Glenbroke gave her husband her arm as the duke escorted her into the cathedral for Lord Elkin's funeral service.

Sarah's stomach tightened as she passed through the heavy doors, hating to lose a man as honorable and kind as John Elkin. She sighed when Gilbert seated her in the front row as befitting their station and then settled in next to her.

The pews filled quietly with mourners, and she stared at the casket, wanting nothing more than to have the painful ceremony over with. A gentleman dressed in black settled to her right, and she turned to make her introduction. But when she saw the familiar face of Viscount DunDonell, she gave him a subdued smile and squeezed his hand in an affectionate welcome home.

Lord DunDonell had been seeing to his estates in Scotland and had recently returned to London. And although Gilbert would never discuss the matter, Sarah suspected that the viscount had been sent to meet with the northern gentry to secure much-needed funds for the peninsular campaign.

"How are you, Daniel?"

The viscount glanced back several pews, saying beneath his brogue, "Very well, Your Grace, but I am wonderin' why the hell St. John has brought one of the ton's most notorious widows to this ceremony." His eyes returned to hers. "Pardon, Sarah."

Gilbert chuckled, his silvery eyes settling on her, causing her heart to skip. "That is precisely what my wife inquired. However, I believe her exact words were 'bloody hell.'"

Sarah hit her husband in the stomach with her elbow and turned to look into the sky blue of Daniel McCurren's eyes. "I believe Christian said the lady was acquainted with Lord Elkin."

The viscount's auburn brows narrowed. "Lady Hamilton is 'acquainted' with half the male members of the ton."

"Is she acquainted with you, my lord?" Sarah asked, the picture of innocence.

"No, a few of my brothers, no doubt, but not me. However, I'm afraid it will take a full week for Christian's father to recover from this little escapade."

"You would think the Duke of St. John would be used to it by now," Gilbert said.

"Aye, you would, but the poor man keeps prayin' that Christian will settle. Unfortunately, St. John's antics are becomin' more and more frequent."

Sarah's eyes narrowed. "Why do you think that is, Daniel?"

Daniel shrugged. "I've no bloody idea." The viscount looked over her shoulder to the opposite side of the cathedral. "How is Lady Appleton?"

"Better, but Felicity still blames herself. Did you know

that John proposed to her the night he was murdered?" Sarah asked.

"Aye, Gilbert told me. Rough, that." Daniel's striking eyes held his concern. "Please convey my sympathies to Lady Appleton."

"I will," she whispered, just as the bishop took his place behind the ornate altar so that the mourners could grieve the loss of a dear friend.

Twenty-eight

The Earl of Wessex sat in the corner of Lady Rivenhall's carriage, having gained access from the stables as planned.

The landau rolled to a stop in front of the lady's townhome, and he stared at the red lacquered door with trepidation. He had not seen Lady Rivenhall since the morning after John's murder, and Aidan was unsure how he would react when he did.

He should feel gratitude and admiration for the woman who had endangered herself to save him, not this incomprehensible anger that rumbled deep in his chest every time he thought of her. Lady Rivenhall had lied to him, yes, but she had done so for the good of the country. How then could he hold that against her?

But he did, and he could not understand why.

Lady Rivenhall emerged from the door, and Aidan felt like he had been kicked in the gut. She was a ruby jewel in the sooty London night. Her vermilion gown appeared to have diamonds adorning the bodice, and she sparkled brighter than the few stars visible in the night sky.

Her footman handed the lady up, and only when the carriage door closed did she turn to look at him. "Good, you've worn black."

"As ordered," he said, trying to compose himself.

Lady Rivenhall lifted her perfect chin, a flash of irritation dancing in her pale eyes. "If you will recall, my lord, I did not ask for your protection. I have managed to survive for four years alone in a pit of vipers and remained unharmed."

"Thus far, Lady Rivenhall," he pointed out.

She surprised him by laughing and turning to stare out the window. "Yes, well, the present is all that I have."

Aidan's forehead creased as he attempted to decipher her meaning. He stared at her delicate profile, not knowing what to say, how to convey his appreciation. He leaned forward, placing his forearms on his thighs as he cleared his throat.

"I want to . . ." She turned her head to look at him, and he lost all of his thoughts. She was so beautiful, so . . . brave. "Albuera . . . I . . . I want to—"

Lady Rivenhall cut him off as she shoved a document in his direction. "Here is the floor plan of Lord Ferrell's home. I will dine with him at seven o'clock, and then we shall view his collection. Begin your search in his study, moving on to the remaining portion of the ground floor."

"What about the servants?" he asked, dropping the topic, which the lady obviously wished not to discuss.

Lady Rivenhall smiled coolly, a touch of cynicism lacing her melodic voice. "It has been my experience that men who hope to bed a woman dismiss the servants after dinner. Leave the bedchamber and upstairs to me. I will call for my carriage when I have completed my search."

Aidan gave a crisp nod as they arrived at Lord Ferrell's front entrance, but then he took her meaning. "You don't expect me to wait in the carriage for your return?"

"That is exactly what I expect, my lord. Falcon may have forced me to bring you along, but that does not mean I want you here." And then she stepped out of the carriage, walking into the home owned by one of the ton's most celebrated rakes.

Aidan wadded up the paper in frustration and waited for the landau to pull around back before slipping into the darkness. He clung to the side of the house, pausing when he saw Lady Rivenhall being seated in the dining room to the right of her host at the long mahogany table.

His jaw clenched when he saw Lord Ferrell grin with anticipation. The man knew women and how to manipulate them to obtain what he desired. His predatory eyes never left Lady Rivenhall, and Aidan could not force himself to move. Every instinct shouted at him to protect her, to force his way into the room and drag her back to the safety of Madame Arnott.

But he could not.

Aidan took a calming breath and reminded himself that the lady had been managing men such as this from the time she was sixteen. He stared at the beautiful woman, and in that moment realized that he had been at war for nine months, but Lady Rivenhall had lived amongst the enemy for four years.

Aidan found himself wanting to ease her burden and moved on to find the study. He picked the lock of a side window and prayed that Lord Ferrell did not allow hounds to roam free at night. He slid the sash open, listening for servants as he climbed into a small parlor. He referenced the crinkled paper and found the study two doors down the corridor.

He felt his way across the room and lit a lamp atop the organized desk. The man had stacks of accounts arranged in neat piles along the far side of the desk, and it took a good half hour to go through all of them. In the end he found supply shipments, troop estimates, dates of departures—but no Lion's seal.

Lord Ferrell was certainly intelligent enough to pull off collaborating with the French, but was he a traitor?

At this moment, Aidan very much hoped that he was.

He folded the documents and put them in his jacket, extinguishing the lamp and leaving the study exactly as he had found it. The corridor was empty, just as Lady Rivenhall had predicted, and he moved easily throughout the ground floor.

He was searching the ballroom when he heard the couple enter at the opposite end of the long room. Aidan concealed himself behind a potted shrub in a dark alcove and watched Lady Rivenhall take small, even steps as she admired the paintings on the wall. She walked toward one particular portrait and stopped.

"These are exquisite, Anthony." *Anthony?* "This one puts me in mind of Rembrandt."

Lord Ferrell's baritone laughter raised Aidan's hackles. "Well, it should, Lady Rivenhall. It is Rembrandt." He could feel the man's arrogance wafting across the room.

"Well, then I'm to be commended for my keen eye."

Anthony Ferrell strolled in front of the enchanting lady and lifted her hand to his lips, saying, "And what lovely eyes they are."

Aidan heard a muffled snap and glanced down at the injured plant in his fist. He dropped the leaves in the pot just as the bastard said, "The finer pieces of my collection are housed upstairs."

Lady Rivenhall stared into Lord Ferrell's mud-colored eyes. "Are they?"

He nodded and pulled her toward him with the hand he had failed to relinquish. "Yes, in my bedchamber," the rogue said, just before bending his head and kissing her.

Aidan could feel the blood surging through his body. He closed his eyes and forced himself to remain rooted to the floor. This was necessary, he reminded himself.

"I . . ." Celeste began, causing Aidan to look at the pair. Her hands were on his chest, keeping the rake at a distance. "I'm not sure that is wise, my lord."

The bastard placed her hand on his arm, adding a seductive smile. "Come and view my collection, Lady Rivenhall," he enticed. "I have no further expectations.

Desires, perhaps," he kissed her hand, "but no expectations."

Lady Rivenhall nodded her assent, and the dark man led her out of the ballroom and toward his snare.

"Damnation!" Aidan muttered and hastily searched the remainder of the ground floor.

He found nothing and glanced at the floor plans to locate the blackguard's bedchamber. Aidan took the stairs two at a time and made his way down the corridor, slowing as he approached the large double doors.

Light streamed from beneath the mahogany door as he strained to listen to the muffled conversation taking place inside. Aidan glanced down the hallway, then pressed his ear to the cold wood and heard . . . nothing.

He pressed harder, squinting as he strained to listen. He could hear something now. A soft rustling seemed to be emanating from the right side of the bedchamber. His brows furrowed as he raised his head, wondering if a woman's gown would make just such a sound as it was being removed.

Aidan rested the back of his head against the wall and peered up at the ceiling. He should be waiting for her in the carriage, he told himself, but for some reason his feet would not move in that direction.

Falcon had ordered him to protect Lady Rivenhall, so he would remain here in the event that she needed his assistance. Not that the lady needed assistance in seducing a man. All she need do was walk into a room and any man would be mesmerized, as Ferrell had been in the ballroom.

Bloody hell!

The man probably had his hands all over her. Aidan could scarcely control himself in her presence, and he was far more civilized than Anthony Ferrell. What if the scoundrel was forcing her?

Oh, God!

Aidan removed his pistol and gave Lord Ferrell's bedchamber door a resounding kick. He glanced about the room as he entered and froze at the sight of Lady Rivenhall braced above a semi-nude Lord Ferrell.

He met her blue green eyes, and his stomach seized. Whether from pain or anger he was not sure, and did not wish to know.

"Pardon the intrusion. I thought that you might need my assistance. I see that I was mistaken."

Aidan spun on his heels and made for the door when the lady stopped his progress, saying, "Well, you are mistaken, my lord. I very much need your assistance, although I've no bloody idea why you are here when I specifically requested that you return to the landau."

"What—?"

"Take off his trousers while I search the room." Lady Rivenhall sat at the writing desk and searched the small drawers.

Aidan wandered to the side of the bed and looked down at Lord Ferrell, who had yet to utter a word. He was unconscious and bare from the waist up. Lord Wessex smiled with amusement as he removed the man's trousers and covered him with the counterpane.

He walked back to the efficient woman, saying, "I see that it was your ring and not your knife that was your weapon of choice this evening."

Lady Rivenhall took a sheet of paper from the desk and began writing. "Be quiet," she said as she wrote. "Now, if you would search the room, we can leave before daybreak."

"Yes, general," he said, unaccustomed to taking orders. "And you will be . . . declining invitations to tea?"

Celeste didn't spare him a glance. "I'm writing a note to Lord Ferrell telling him how much I enjoyed the evening, and what a magnificent lover he was, so on and so forth. It will keep our lively young lord from contemplating why his claret was so powerful. However, I am not sure that I will be able to explicate a broken door." Lady Rivenhall gave him a pointed look that made him want to smile.

Aidan shrugged, not feeling particularly remorseful.

"I've found several incriminating documents. Finish your letter, and I will drop the information off at Falcon's office after I see you safely home."

Lady Rivenhall scribbled a large *C* at the bottom of the communication, and he was once again reminded that she was very good at her trade. He wondered how many other letters she had written as he claimed her upper arm.

She rose from her chair and then turned to face him, wrenching her arm free of his grasp. "I realize you have grown accustomed to hauling me about, my lord, but I will not tolerate any more of your abuse. If you wish to escort me downstairs, then do so as the gentleman you profess yourself to be."

Guilt washed over him, stiffening his spine. Aidan dropped his eyes and bowed his apology as the lady brushed past him and made for the door. He caught up with the angry woman before she had reached the stairs.

Lady Rivenhall stopped and peered down to the floor below, verifying that they were alone in the expansive entryway. They stole toward the back of the house and exited through the conservatory door.

"What did you discover?" she asked when they were nearing her carriage.

"Troop estimates and supply routes, and dates for departure of various military vessels."

"But no Lion seal."

"No."

Lady Rivenhall spoke to her footmen as if they were her French soldiers and then they settled in for the return trip to town. She stared outside, her fair brows creased as she concentrated on the matter at hand.

"Lord Ferrell did not strike me as the sort of man to betray his country."

"And how did our handsome lord strike you, Lady Rivenhall?"

She shook her head in disbelief. "How dare you speak to me in such a manner? Other than saving your miserable life, on several occasions, would you mind enlightening me as to how I have offended you, my lord?"

Aidan thrust his long legs in front of him and crossed his arms over his chest. "Well, let me think. Perhaps it is that you have lied to me at every moment of our association."

The lady lifted her chin and turned her head to study the passing trees.

"Or that I have been forced by my own brother-in-law to aid you in your inquiries. Or that a dear friend was murdered in the process of this investigation."

She flinched, turning to stare at him with pain contorting her exquisite features, causing Aidan to regret his harsh words. He held her light gaze and leaned toward her, his heart thundering in his chest.

"Or that you have endangered your life for the past four years when you should have been the toast of London."

Her brows furrowed.

"Or that you continue to endanger yourself. Or"—he reached for her hand and drew her to him—"that you have allowed men to touch you when the only man who should be holding you in his arms is me."

Aidan kissed her, his arms banding around her in an embrace meant to possess, to brand. Her fingers curled at the nape of his neck as she returned his kiss, devouring his mouth and his soul.

She gave a soft gasp of pleasure, and he was lost. He stroked her tongue, drinking her in. She bit his lower lip, sending a flash of heat to ignite his burning desire. His mouth fell behind her ear, and he raked his teeth down her neck.

Lady Rivenhall yanked off his jacket and threw it on the far side of the carriage. He ripped off his cravat as he tugged at the laces of her bodice. Aidan stared down at her exposed breasts and shuddered at the sight. He lifted her onto his lap, bending her backward so he might have better access to the luxurious mounds.

"You're so beautiful," he whispered.

His mouth closed around her nipple, and he suckled her

in a rhythm meant to enflame. She cried out, arching toward him, and he moaned with expectation. His hands dove under her skirts as he lifted them to reach his goal. He stripped away her drawers, and she opened her thighs for his ministrations.

Aidan touched her thatch of curls and slipped a finger between her moist petals. He suckled her breast with each stroke of his finger, and she began to anticipate his thrusts. His shaft was aching, and her rhythmic movements were bringing him precariously close to the edge.

He lifted her right leg and pulled it across his chest so that she was straddling him. He unbuttoned his breeches and yanked at the flap, exposing his arousal. Lady Rivenhall met his eyes and he impaled her. He moaned and grasped her backside with both hands, plunging deeper into her soft folds.

Aidan had intended to stimulate her, to cause her to crest before he found his pleasure. But she began riding him with her own need driving her and all thoughts washed away on wave after wave of ecstasy. He grabbed her slender hips and pulled her down as he drove into her.

And when she began crying out with each thrust, he knew he was lost. His hips instinctively increased their pace and within moments he fell into the abyss, dragging her down with him.

At ten o'clock the following morning, Aidan found himself walking the corridors of Whitehall in something of a daze.

His intimacy with Lady Rivenhall had shaken him to the core, and he was having a difficult time finding his footing. He clutched the papers he had found in Lord Ferrell's home and tried desperately not to remember the feel of Lady Rivenhall in his arms, the feel of being buried deep inside of her.

Aidan had bedded his share of ladies, but never had he felt such an overwhelming need to possess, to claim a woman as he did Lady Rivenhall. He realized, of course, that his obsession with the lady was fueled by the unusual circumstances in which they met.

Had she been another debutante at Almack's, the intensity of his feelings would not be this profound. But she was more than beautiful. She was courageous, daring, intelligent, and honorable, and he could not stop thinking about her, could not stop wanting her.

Aidan found himself at Falcon's office. "Morning, Cunningham. Is the old man in?" he asked Falcon's capable assistant.

"'Fraid not. Just went to dine at his club."

The earl handed the man the documents from Lord Ferrell's study, saying, "Please give him these papers the moment he returns."

"Of course."

Aidan thanked him and headed down the corridor. He paused at the room where John had been killed, noting that a fine carpet had been laid over the blood-stained wood. He stared at the floor and vowed to avenge his friend by seeing the traitor hanged.

Wessex emerged from the gloomy building and stared at the blue sky. He allowed the sun to warm his face, and he felt a new man by the time he settled into the warmth of his carriage. He sighed, wondering when it would all be over, wondering even more what would become of his relationship with the addictive Lady Rivenhall.

Celeste had spent the morning admonishing herself for allowing her body to control her mind.

She should never have allowed herself to make love to the Earl of Wessex. She had just begun to forget the feel of his muscular arms around her, his large hands wrapped about her waist as he entered her body. She had almost forgotten the look in his emerald eyes that made her feel the most desirable woman in all the world. She had almost forgotten the sound of his moans as came into her.

Damnation!

Celeste shook away her thoughts and dabbed perfume

behind her ears. She glanced down at her lilac day gown, and decided it was the perfect attire for Lady Cantor's musical tea. She pinched her cheeks and rose from her chair.

"Has the carriage been brought round, Marie?"

"*Oui.* Now you will be careful?"

Lady Rivenhall laughed. "I will be perfectly safe," she said, kissing her companion on the cheek.

Celeste arrived at the musicale a quarter of an hour before the performances were to begin. She gathered a plate of assorted fruit and sweets and sat toward the back of the room, waiting for the daughter of her hostess to launch the event.

The biscuits were superb, and Celeste was on her third when a man settled in next to her.

"You're late," she said, her tone testy.

Henri Renault shrugged and took a large bite of cucumber sandwich. "Forgive me, Lady Rivenhall. I was tutoring our hostess on the fine art of pleasing a man with her mouth." He chuckled. "Of course, if Lady Cantor knew that I spent last night plowing her daughter, she might not have been so willing to pleasure me."

The Frenchman threw his sandwich on the bone china in disgust. "This English food is enough to make one ill. I would kill a man for some pâté."

Celeste watched her hostess enter the room and look toward Monsieur Renault with longing. "Might we begin before the music starts?"

"Very well," he said, his smile subtle. "The man you are looking for is tall, dark haired, young, and, according to a chambermaid, handsome but not nearly as handsome as me."

Celeste rolled her eyes. "No name?"

"No."

"No carriage bearing a crest?"

"The man rode a horse, no markings of any kind. This man is thorough, clever, and bold." Henri smiled. "I like him."

"I will be sure to convey your admiration. If you discover a name, do let me know."

"Oui."

"Now, go away before these ladies believe you are more than a libertine trying to seduce me."

"Am I succeeding?"

"No."

"Then it will be my pleasure to keep trying."

Henri Renault stood, smiling at her with sensual promise that would have made most women swoon, but having seen the green eyes of the ebony earl burn with desire, Celeste found other men decidedly lacking in masculine appeal.

Twenty-nine

The dark man gave three sharp knocks on the door to Lord Wellesley's outer office and entered without being invited.

Wellesley's clerk, Woodson, was bent over some papers and took several moments before lifting his head. His eyes registered his surprise, but the clerk sat up and smiled toward his visitor.

"Oh, hello. What can I do for you?"

"Nothing, really," the dark man said, fiddling with his watch, which was buried in the pocket of the waistcoat that perfectly complemented his eyes. "I was just heading to my club for dinner and wondered if you would care to join me."

The clerk's brows rose. "Oh, uh, well . . . I'm afraid I have quite a lot of work left to do this evening."

The dark man strolled around the desk, placing one arm on the back of Woodson's chair and planting the other firmly on the desktop. He bent down to peer over the clerk's shoulder, making sure he was close enough that his breath would be felt on the man's neck.

"Surely these papers can wait a few hours, old man," he said, pressing his muscular chest against the clerk's back as he looked more closely at the documents.

"I . . . uh . . ."

The dark man rose, clasping the clerk on the shoulder and rubbing his thumb back and forth. "You've got to eat sometime, Woodson," he said, releasing him just as the little clerk was tasting his desire. "Come on, we'll return in no time," he encouraged, walking toward the door.

The clerk's eyes darted about the papers on his desk and then up at the dark man, who presented his most devastating smile.

"Very well, but I really must return within the hour."

"Certainly."

"It will just take a few moments to tidy my desk."

The dark man leaned a shoulder against the doorframe in a manner that displayed his powerful legs to their advantage. "Very well."

Woodson had expected him to leave, but when he did not, the clerk busily stacked documents and locked them in the cabinets behind the desk. He made sure to appear bored, but his eyes took in every detail of the smaller man's movements, where and how items were stored, if a key was required to access the documents.

"Ready," Woodson said some five minutes later.

He smiled down at the clerk, and they left the office together. The familiar sounds of the congested London streets assaulted them the moment they emerged from the sanctuary of the extensive building.

He cut through the crowded walk as the clerk attempted to keep up with him by dodging determined pedestrians. But the moment they ventured into the street Woodson said, "Damn," as he stepped in a pile of horse manure. He kicked his right heel on the curb to dislodge the offensive material as the dark man waited impatiently for him to finish.

"The oddest thing happened yesterday." Woodson concentrated on his filthy shoes.

"What was that?" he asked, not caring.

"Yesterday, I was hailing a hackney at this very spot when a Frog came up to me and asked if I worked at Whitehall."

The dark man tensed, his mind spinning. He waited as they started across the street.

"The Frenchman said that he had attended Lord Hambury's ball, where he had met a gentleman working at the Foreign Office, but he could not remember the man's name. And I must say he described you rather well, although I suppose it could have been Lord Eubanks or perhaps even—"

"What did this Frog look like?" The question was casual.

"Tall, fair hair tied back in a queue."

He shook his head. "No, I don't recall speaking to any Frenchman at Hambury's. Must have been some other gentleman."

Woodson kept his eyes on the cobblestone street to further avoid any offending heaps, so he missed the tension in the dark man's jaw.

The two gentlemen sat in the duke's study, their weekly chess match long since complete.

Gilbert noted the gray pallor of the elderly man and wondered if the stress of his unenviable position was taking its toll. The traitor still remained active, and with Wellesley due to depart in eleven days, the situation was becoming desperate.

"Where are you with the investigation?" Gilbert asked as he handed Falcon a scotch and took his ease in his favorite leather chair.

The old man lifted unruly brows. "Not very far, I'm afraid. We have just discovered incriminating evidence at Lord Ferrell's home. I have men watching his movements as well as the others, but thus far the gentlemen have done nothing to implicate themselves further.

"Lady Rivenhall and the Earl of Wessex will search

Lord Cantor's home Sunday next. The man gives his staff the morning off so they might attend services, and the house will be empty."

"And if they find nothing?"

The old man lifted his crystal tumbler to his lips and took a long draw of the fiery liquid.

"Then she will go back."

Gilbert's silver eyes narrowed. "Who will go back?" he asked, already knowing the answer.

"Lady Rivenhall will depart for France and the emperor. If the traitor is not found, she will be invaluable in supplying Wellesley with information. And if the traitor is caught, the man will be in custody and unable to identify her as an English agent to the French. Either way she leaves for Amsterdam in ten days' time."

Gilbert stared at the carpet and then tossed back the remainder of his scotch. "Does she know?"

"Yes. She sent a letter to the emperor last week, along with intelligence information we had supplied."

The duke held the old man's gaze. "Wessex's escape, Beresford's victory at Albuera, the information she will supply Wellesley . . . the French are not stupid. She will eventually be caught."

Falcon sighed. "I know."

"Then why are you sending her back?"

"I'm not. She asked to go. Demanded, really."

"Why?"

The old man set his empty glass on the small side table to his right. "The girl feels responsible for not having saved more men. Penance, I suppose."

"You do realize that Aidan Duhearst is in love with her."

"Yes, and she him, which makes these events all the more tragic."

"What can we do?"

"Nothing we can do, Your Grace. If the traitor is not found, England needs Lady Rivenhall in France."

"And if he is?"

The man shrugged his sloping shoulders. "It is her decision to make, but the girl knows her value to the Crown. And if I were to wager, I'd say this war is far from over."

Celeste was having her hair braided in preparation for bed when a maid rapped on the door.

"Yes," Celeste said without moving.

The young girl entered and, with a curtsy, said, "The Earl of Wessex to see you, my lady."

Her spine stiffened, and she stole a glance at Marie.

"Send him up please, Ruth."

"Yes, ma'am."

Madame Arnott looked down at her, appalled. "The earl should not be permitted in your suite, Celeste."

Lady Rivenhall rose and reached for her dressing gown, tying it about her waist with quick, impatient tugs.

"Really, Marie. I have already bedded him, so what difference does it make if he sees me in my nightclothes?"

"It is not proper."

"Yes, well, I have done many improper things. At least this one will allow me to stay in the comfort of my nightclothes rather than dress just to meet with the man in my parlor. You may retire, Marie, thank you."

"But—"

A knock at her door caused Celeste to stare at her companion. "Enter," she said, and without turning to greet her guest added, "Goodnight, Madame Arnott."

"Good evening, Lord Wessex," Marie said before leaving with obvious reluctance.

Celeste took a deep breath and turned to greet the enticing earl. She avoided his mesmerizing eyes. "Good evening, my lord. What is it that I can do for you?"

Aidan Duhearst remained silent, forcing her to look at his handsome features, his striking coloring, his alluring lips before he used them to speak.

"I wanted to discuss last night."

Celeste's heart pounded against her ribs as she searched her mind for a means of self-preservation. "I assumed that you had given the documents to Falcon this morning. If you had difficulty you should have—"

"That is not what I am referring to, Celeste."

"Then what are you referring to?" She spoke to his black Hessians.

"I am referring to what occurred afterward. In the carriage."

Celeste could not breathe, and she was becoming light-headed. She walked to her dressing table and sat on the cushioned stool, removing her ear bobs.

"What do you mean?"

Aidan stood behind her and spoke to her reflection in the dressing mirror. "You know damn well what I mean." Her head snapped up, and she held his gaze, wanting to be anywhere else when he said, "It was a mistake, Celeste." She pinched her lips together so they would not quiver. "I—"

"Surely, you do not think I expect you to marry me after a mere dalliance, Lord Wessex?" she scoffed. He looked stunned and she was glad, prompting her to continue. "You've introduced me to the pleasures of the flesh, and I wanted to experience more." Celeste shrugged as she stood, walking to her bed. "I knew when I accepted this mission that there would be sacrifices that would be made."

Wessex laughed. "So, last night was a sacrifice?" he asked arrogantly, knowing that she had desired him as much as he had wanted her.

"No," she said, needing to hurt him. "Last night was research for future assignments. You've taught me many things, Lord Wessex." She took off her robe and grabbed a tome for protection. "Next time I need to bed a man, I now know what will satisfy him." Celeste smiled and slipped under her counterpane, adding, "And me." His mouth fell open. "Now if you will excuse me, I really would like to read."

But when Aidan did not leave, she looked up from her

book. His black brows were drawn over his striking eyes, and he appeared perplexed.

"Was there anything else, my lord?"

"No, I just wanted to clarify the . . . situation."

"Consider yourself absolved, Lord Wessex."

Celeste attempted to smile, but an errant tear spilled over her lashes. She looked down at the book so he would not see her distress, but the tear fell, wetting a page of text. She concentrated on the blurry words, but she could hear him walking toward her.

She turned the page just as the earl reached the side of her bed, but the earl did not reach for the book. His hand caressed her wet cheek with the backs of his fingers.

"I'm sorry, Celeste. It was a mistake."

"I know," she whispered, and more tears were soaked up by ancient words.

His large hand took the book from her grasp, and she stared at her empty lap. He sat on the edge of the bed and lifted her chin, forcing her to look at him. "Too much has passed between us. You are employed by the Crown. You . . ." He paused. "You would leave again. I couldn't . . . It would never work."

"I know."

He wiped the moisture from her face. "I'm sorry."

Celeste nodded. "I know."

They stared at one another. "We were never meant to be," he whispered and then kissed her gently.

Celeste closed her eyes and gave her lips to the warmth of his mouth. It was a lover's kiss, and her heart filled with the enormity of it. She pulled off his jacket, not allowing herself to think.

"Celeste." He lifted her chemise and stared at her breasts. "You could be killed."

"I know," she said, pulling him on top of her as she kissed him back. Celeste curled her arms around his neck, clinging desperately to this single moment of happiness.

He tore at his garments, and she felt cold until he lifted the counterpane and stretched out on top of her. He stared down at her, his expression conflicted. His mouth was drawn to hers, and she could feel his heart thundering in his chest.

He consumed her, tasting her mouth, her nipples. She moaned when his palm covered her breast, and he feasted on her flesh. His hands fell to her hips, and his tongue separated her petals, drawing out her desire. He laved and suckled, and just when she thought she would scream, he was on top of her.

The handsome earl looked down at her with such desire that she shuddered with anticipation. He thrust into her, taking both their breaths away. His elbows were planted to either side of her head, and she grabbed his muscular arms as he drove her toward the headboard.

Celeste locked her ankles around his waist, eliciting a masculine moan. "Oh, God, Celeste."

His sensual excitement sent her to the edge, and she began to strain against him. And then she fell. "Aidan," she whispered in desperation, but he caught her, and they fell together.

They spent hours exploring each other, neither willing to ponder the reasons they should not be lovers. Celeste fell asleep with the warmth of him curled against her back, and for the first time in her memory she was content.

Thirty

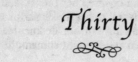

The dark man paid the hackney and stepped into the dirty streets of London.

Music from a bawdy ballad drifted toward him as he made his way to the front entrance of the bordello. The moment he walked in women sat up, smiling their interest. He settled at a corner table and found a pretty blonde whore in his lap.

The girl wiggled her rounded backside against his cock, saying, "What can I get for you, me lord?"

He smiled into her bright blue eyes. "A drink and some information. I'm meeting a friend of mine. A Frog, long blonde hair."

"Oh, Violet just took him upstairs. Nice looking bloke." Her hand began rubbing his cock. "Not as pretty as you, though."

The dark man smiled. "Get us some refreshments, and I'll take you upstairs and make you forget every man you have ever rogered."

"I bet you will." The girl laughed and left to retrieve

their drinks. He glanced about the dim room to see if he recognized anyone. He did not. The girl returned with two glass tumblers, and he said absently, "Fetch a cheroot, would you?" before reaching into his jacket and pulling out a bottle of laudanum.

The girl returned to the bar, and the dark man put two droppers of the drug into her drink. He knew from experience the amount needed to keep a woman conscious, but not cognizant.

He stood when she returned. "Finish your scotch so we can go upstairs."

The whore tossed back her drink with the ease of experience and led him up the narrow staircase. "Which room is my friend in?"

"Violet's room is that one. This is mine," she added. The doxy opened the door and stumbled into the room.

"Take off your clothes," he ordered, knowing that soon she would not be able to do so.

He removed his jacket as he watched the whore peel away the layers of her clothing, revealing pink nipples crowning small breasts and an exceptional backside.

"Back in a moment." He glanced down the hall. "Where's the privy?"

"End of the corridor," the girl said, fighting to stay awake.

The dark man closed the door then slipped into the room across the hall. He tilted his head to one side so that he might better view the sight displayed before him. The noise from downstairs faded and was replaced with the cries of the whore bending over the small bed. The Frenchman was looking down, watching himself enter her feminine flesh.

The fair man spoke with a French accent. "You like that, don't you?"

"Oh, yes," the girl breathed.

Lord Renault stood naked with both feet planted on the floor. His eyes roved over the girl and then he gave an appreciative slap of her backside. The girl lifted herself, meeting the man's thrusts. He groaned his pleasure and grabbed her hips, plunging deeper until his moans of gratification mingled with her feminine cries. His head fell back, and his body tensed as he held himself inside the doxy, grunting his release.

The Frenchman's eyes snapped open the moment he heard the pistol being cocked behind his head. He came off the girl and raised both hands in a show of submission. The whore made for the door, but the dark man stopped her with his eyes.

"Don't," he warned, aiming a smaller pistol at the girl who now cowered in the corner of the room.

"Might I at least face the man that is to rob me?"

He looked down at the Frenchman's muscular body and knew from his investigations of the man that he would be a formidable match.

"No, I think not." The musky scent of sex lingered in the room, and his heart began pounding in his chest. "And I'm not here to rob you, Monsieur Renault. You have been looking into my affairs, and I would like to know why."

The Frenchman laughed. "Ah, now I see it. You are Lady Davis's lover. *Non?*"

The dark man waited.

"I was asked by a certain lady to investigate the matter of her death. See if certain parties were responsible, *n'est-ce pas?*"

"*Oui,*" the dark man said in French. "And what have you told the stunning Mademoiselle Rivenhall?"

"Nothing. I had hoped that we might come to some sort of . . . arrangement. That we might work together. Share the fruits of our labor, so to speak. What do I care that you have killed a stupid English cow? We both labor for France, *non?*"

"That is where you are mistaken, Monsieur Renault. I work for no one," the dark man said, pulling the trigger and splattering the Frenchman all over the filthy counterpane. The whore pulled air into her lungs to scream, and he shot her in the forehead before a single sound escaped her lips.

The dark man bent over the Frog with a knife and after a moment made for the door. He confirmed that the corridor was empty before slipping into the room across the hall.

"Now where were we?" he asked the pretty blond strumpet that lay naked on the bed.

The girl attempted to smile, but the laudanum he had given her was making her groggy. He stripped off his clothes as footsteps thundered up the stairs, and his heart began to race with excitement.

"Spread your thighs," he whispered.

He heard screams and curses as he drove into the harlot. He stroked her knowing that they were searching for him, wondering if they would suspect him. He reached deeper, his excitement building.

"Put your ankles on my shoulders," he ordered as he planted his feet on the footboard to give himself the leverage he wanted. He drove harder, deeper, and when the door opened the thrill of being hunted was so stimulating he forced himself to prolong his climax so he could feel the danger a moment longer.

The door closed, and the light in the room dimmed as he exploded into the whore. He thrust again, extracting every drop of pleasure before collapsing on top of the girl. His head lay on her breasts, and he smiled, reminding himself that he should not be taking such risks. The dark man turned his head and nipped the strumpet's nipple to wake her up. It was not yet two in the morning, and he was determined to get his money's worth.

Lady Rivenhall awoke to a dark room with a fully clothed Aidan Duhearst warming her back. He rolled Celeste onto her stomach and stretched out on top of her, pressing his arousal against her backside. Warm tendrils unfurled in her stomach, and she smiled to herself, pleased that he had woken her before he left.

"Haven't you had enough this evening, my lord?"

He grasped her wrists and bent to whisper in her ear. She turned her head, wanting to feel the heat of his breath as he said, "Expecting someone?"

Celeste's heart stopped, and ice coursed through her veins. The deep baritone voice that caressed her ear was not that of the Earl of Wessex. Her sluggish heartbeat doubled. She jerked her body against the man, but she was pinned beneath his weight.

"Don't scream, Lady Rivenhall, or I will be forced to harm you."

Celeste attempted to devise a means of escape, but all she could think was that she was going to be raped, and she could do nothing to stop it.

"What do you want?" she asked, afraid she already knew.

"We have matters to discuss," the man breathed. "You have been looking into my personal affairs, and I'm afraid I cannot have that sort of interference, even by the emperor's mistress."

The man pressed his shaft against her, and she shuddered. She closed her eyes and tried to think past the fear and revulsion. How did he know who she was? And then she realized.

"Why did you murder Lady Davis?"

The man chuckled. "I see that your mind is just as intriguing as your body. Very well, but what do I get for telling you?" His hand made its way up her bare leg.

"The gratitude of the emperor."

The man's hand lingered on her hip. "I would rather have yours."

"You won't get it."

The man pressed his hips into her. "Don't be too sure, my lady. As a matter of fact, that is the reason I killed Lady Davis. The stupid cow was threatening to identify me if I quit her bed." He leaned closer, and Celeste could feel his lips skimming her ear. "The lady was exceedingly appreciative of my skill."

"And Lord Elkin?" she asked, feeling a bitter rage pushing to escape.

"Careful, kitten," the man warned. "John Elkin was in the wrong place at the wrong time. I was attempting to retrieve information for your lover, the emperor, when Elkin returned to his office. Unfortunate, but there you have it."

"And what do you want of me?"

Celeste could hear the blood surging in her ears, through his silence.

"I want a great many things from you, Lady Rivenhall, but I shall settle for an alliance. The profits from the information we retrieve could be shared. Together, we could see a great deal of blunt."

"The emperor pays me well enough."

"Yes, the lover who sends you into the Lion's den provides for you, but how long will that last, Lady Rivenhall? Or do you enjoy the danger of it?" The man released her wrist to cup her breast, and she could feel his lust as his breath began to shorten. "The stimulation?" he whispered.

"The emperor is not finished with me yet, so I advise you to remove your hand before he hears of this incident. And as for your proposal . . . I work alone."

"Yes, you do." The man laughed, confusing her. "So my dear lady, I suggest you consider my proposition before you reject me out of hand, and as a token of my sincerity I offer you a gift."

Celeste felt something cold next to her right hand. She reached for it and touched a small box.

"Next time you want to investigate me, Lady Rivenhall, make sure the gentleman you send is more worthy of the task."

"Next time?"

"Yes." Celeste could hear the satisfaction in the traitor's voice. "I put a bullet in Henri Renault's brain no more than two hours ago."

Her mind seized, and she started when he took her earlobe in his mouth. "Mmm." He sighed, and then she felt the tip of his nose caress the nape of her neck as he inhaled her scent. "I will see you very soon, Lady Rivenhall."

She was shaking as she heard the man leave by way of her balcony. When Celeste was sure he was gone, she rolled over and lit a small candle. A ball of light illuminated the room, and, full of trepidation, she reached for the tiny box. She separated the lid from the base and fought waves of nausea as she gazed down at the contents—a lock of golden hair spattered with blood.

Thirty-one

~~~~~~

Aidan sat reading the *London Times* over a slice of toast and a soft-boiled egg. He did not want to think about the hours he had spent making love to Celeste, so he sipped coffee and turned to the financial pages.

The embargo had hit everyone particularly hard, and the price of common goods had become exorbitant. Goods such as wine and wheat, which were normally reinforced by a continental surplus, now had been priced out of reach for the common man.

The disgruntled masses had caused some unrest on the east end, and the situation did not appear to be ending anytime soon. Aidan salted his egg and dipped his toast into the soft yolk. He placed the portion of bread in his mouth without taking his eyes off the article he was reading.

The French had attacked a shipment of food stores on the twentieth, just two days before. Aidan considered whether the wheat and barley being grown on his lands in Wessex were the most efficient use of his property. He reached for his pencil and noted the price per barrel of corn, of coal, and dairy products. The country was going to have to become less reliant on foreign imports, and Aidan planned to capitalize on his investments.

He laid the paper down and sliced several pieces of sausage. Aidan wiped his mouth and took another sip of coffee as he tried to imagine England after the war. How it would change, and how it would stay the same. Would the country squires even note the difference?

Then he froze as something tickled the back of his mind. Something at his estate? *No.* He reached for the paper and looked again at the articles he had been perusing and stopped.

The French had attacked a shipment of food stores on the twentieth.

And then he knew in a rush more clear than a summer's sky. The twentieth had been one of the dates on the documents he had retrieved from Lord Ferrell's study.

"We found you, you bastard," Aidan mumbled toward the paper.

A smile spread across his face. The bloody traitor must have passed the information to the French before they had retrieved the papers from his home. Aidan took one last gulp of coffee and rose from his chair, anxious to speak with his brother-in-law.

Aidan caught up with the Duke of Glenbroke at Tattersall's. The duke was examining the withers of a white Irish jumper. It was not particularly pretty to look at, but Gilbert was known for his judgment of horseflesh.

"I'll take him," the duke said to the small man at his elbow. "I want him prepared for travel by Thursday."

"Yes, Your Grace." The man bowed and led the horse away.

Gilbert was grinning from ear to ear when he turned toward Aidan. "Damn fine piece of horseflesh. Going to have him cover my black filly, Delphi." He paused to enjoy the moment as he looked over the horses being led in a circle round the gravel paddock. "What is so urgent that you would track me down in the middle of the afternoon?" He raised one brow over steely eyes, sharpened by acute intelligence.

"We've got him."

The duke jerked his head back in shock. "You're serious. You've found the traitor?"

Aidan nodded and was unable to suppress a smile. "Yes, Your Grace."

His brother-in-law lifted his arm to indicate that they should walk. "Did you find the Lion seal?"

"Not exactly, no."

"Then how can you be sure, Aidan?"

"The information Lady Rivenhall and I retrieved from Lord Ferrell's home was forwarded to France. Every transport ship on that list was intercepted, and there are too many ships for this to be coincidence. The man must have sold the information before we were able to retrieve it from his study. There is no other possible explanation."

The duke reached his carriage. He paused, and Aidan could see him taking the information in, weighing the validity of his claim. And then the enormous man gave a lazy smile. "We have our man."

Aidan nodded. "We have our man."

The earl slid off the back of his mount and tossed the reins to a footman. He was on the stairs to his townhome when a messenger came barreling up behind him.

The boy bowed and on a gulp of air asked, "Might you be the Earl of Wessex?"

Aidan stilled, contradicting his heart, which galloped in his chest. "Yes."

The boy stuck out his arm with a letter clasped firmly in his hand. Aidan reached into his red brocade waistcoat to retrieve a piece of silver, tossing it to the boy before he walked into his home. He glanced down at the communication as he ripped it open and instantly recognized Celeste's handwriting.

My Lord,

I would very much appreciate your coming to my home as soon as is possible. There has been a development in our investigation that I feel I am unable to manage on my own.

Yours,
C

Aidan could not imagine a situation in which the lady would not be able to cope. His heart was pounding as he bounded down the stairs, stopping the stable boy who had just taken charge of his mount.

He arrived at Lady Rivenhall's home in ten minutes' time. The butler answered his knock and directed him to the parlor. Aidan remained on his feet, his black Hessians wearing a hole in the thick carpet.

The moment the door opened he should have been relieved, but he was not. One look at the dark circles under Celeste's haunted blue green eyes told him that she had not slept. He ate up the distance between them and grasped her by the shoulders in a gentle caress.

"What happened?"

Lady Rivenhall, commander of troops, mistress to Napoleon, English patriot, collapsed against his chest. Aidan's heart contracted, and he tried to slow his breathing as his arms banded around the slender woman.

"What has happened, Celeste?"

"He came to my bedchamber after you left," she whispered, so softly that he could scarcely hear her.

"Who?" Aidan asked, more sharply than he had intended.

"The man who killed Lady Davis and John Elkin. He . . . ." She hesitated, causing his heart to stop.

"Did he touch you?"

"No," she said, looking down. "Yes, he touched me with his hands and offered an alliance."

Aidan pulled her closer into his chest, not wanting her to see the rage blazing in his eyes.

"He gave me this."

Aidan took the small box and opened it, staring at the contents in confusion. The box contained a lock of blond hair splattered with blood. "I don't understand, Celeste. Is this your hair?"

Lady Rivenhall shook her head as she looked up at him. "No, it belonged to my French operative, Henri Renault. The man shot him." Celeste held his eyes, and Aidan guided her to the settee. "It is all my fault. I asked Henri to discover who killed Lady Davis. I thought that the French would know, that they would be able to discover information that we could not."

"You are not to blame, Celeste." Aidan rubbed her arms and bent his head to kiss her on the cheek. "Renault was a French spy."

Lady Rivenhall lifted her head and stared at him. "He was a man, Aidan. Henri thought he was a patriot, just as I do. I was fond of him and will mourn his loss."

"Forgive my callousness, Celeste," Aidan said, wondering what toll had been taken on this woman as she lived amidst her enemies for four long years. "Now, I'm afraid I must leave you for the moment, but I promise to return before luncheon."

"Where are you going?" Panic tinted her words and tugged at his heart as he ached to protect her.

"To speak with the Foreign Office about arresting our traitor," Aidan said, smiling for the first time since entering the house.

Thirty-two

❧❦❧

Celeste waited in the dubious comfort of a hired hackney at two o'clock in the morning.

The old man groaned as he pulled himself up and then looked for a clean spot on which to sit. Finding none, he sank into the middle of the seat opposite hers.

"Thank you for meeting me on such short notice, Lady Rivenhall. I apologize for the late hour."

Celeste waved away Falcon's apology and waited for him to begin their meeting.

"We would like for you to search Lord Cantor's home on Sunday as planned. However, I wanted to be the first to inform you that we arrested Lord Ferrell at his home last night. He came willingly, but denied all charges of collaboration and is being questioned as we speak."

"What proof was cited in the charges?"

"The information you retrieved from his home was used by the French to attack the vessels listed in the documentation."

Celeste's brows furrowed, and her mouth hung open. "I . . . am astonished."

"Why? We knew one of these men was the traitor, Celeste."

"Yes, however, Lord Ferrell . . . He did not seem the sort of man . . ." Celeste's thoughts flew to her bedchamber. "Did he admit to killing Lady Davis and Lord Elkin?"

"No. As I've said, the man denied every charge." The old man grasped her hand and looked at her with sympathy softening his features. "It is sometimes difficult to believe, Celeste. I have witnessed it time and time again. A timid man can be a murderer and an angelic beauty . . . a spy for the Crown."

"Yes, but often an honest man is merely an honest man."

Falcon sat back. "Then you think we have made a mistake?"

"No." She shook her head. "I am unsure."

"We are sure, Celeste. You've done what you have set out to do, and owing to you, Wellesley can launch his attack with the advantage of surprise." The old man sighed, showing his age. "Are you still determined to leave in one week's time?"

"Yes." Celeste stared out the window.

"Have you told him?"

Celeste's stomach seized, and her head snapped round to the sherry-colored eyes of the observant old man. "No, and neither will you."

"You don't have to go, Lady Rivenhall. You have done enough."

"It is never enough," she said, her exhaustion clear. "Men will continue to die, and I will continue to try and stop it."

"There are other operatives in place, Celeste."

She smiled with sober affection. "As highly positioned as I am?"

Falcon said nothing, and they sat in silence, listening to the night noises of the park.

"You will be captured this time."

Celeste closed her eyes and concentrated on an owl hooting in the distance. "I know."

She heard Falcon shift, but he surprised her by kissing her on the forehead as he stroked her hair. "Do not leave without saying good-bye."

Celeste grasped the old man's forearm and leaned her cheek against him in an awkward embrace. "I won't."

Neither moved, unwilling to say good-bye just yet. Then the old man coughed and pulled his arm away. "I had best be getting back to Lord Ferrell."

She nodded her understanding, and then the dear man was stepping out of the carriage and Celeste knew that she would never be able to bid Falcon farewell.

Aidan pulled at his stockings, feeling a complete idiot. His gold satin breeches and burgundy jacket were the height of inelegance, and he longed to shed them.

"Why precisely are we dressed in this abhorrent manner?" His question held his irritation.

Lady Rivenhall was concentrating on picking the lock of Lord Cantor's desk drawer, and he shuddered to think how she had acquired that particular skill. She was dressed as an upstairs housemaid with no adornments of any kind, and Aidan could not help but note how beautiful she was.

"You, as you well know, are dressed as Lord Cantor's footman, and I must say you have never looked quite so"—she looked him over, searching for the appropriate word—"frilly."

Aidan raised an eyebrow at her impertinence, saying, "And you, my dear, have never looked quite so drab."

"Thank you, my lord." She added a caustic grin. "Now, do remember, if anyone enters the study, try to look guilty, as if we have had a bit of a tumble."

He glanced at the delectable lady as she bent herself before him. "That should not be a difficulty."

"Good," she said, pulling out the drawer in triumph. "Now, if you don't mind searching the study, I'll just look upstairs."

Aidan strolled forward and sat in Lord Cantor's leather chair. He began reading through countless numbers of meticulous records littering the desktop, and Aidan could not help but admire the middle-aged baron. Every *T* had been crossed and every shilling was accounted for.

Lady Rivenhall returned half an hour later, only to find Aidan propping his legs on the oak desk as he concentrated on the latest mining records.

"Find anything?"

"No." She shook her head. "And you?"

He looked up at her fair features and said, "I found no seal, but have a look at this."

Her small hands reached for the paper, and he watched her forehead crease in delicate lines as she read. He was smiling to himself when she finally looked up.

"It is a mining report, coal, sulfur . . . what of it?" She shrugged, handing back the paper so that he might replace it.

"And this?" Aidan handed her a second paper.

She sat down in the chair in front of the desk, taking the document from his hand. "Dates for transport of mined materials to a holding house near the London docks. All appears perfectly respectable."

The earl smiled, inordinately pleased with himself and thankful for his studies at Oxford. "The materials being mined by Lord Cantor are the raw materials required for producing gunpowder. Our industrious baron is a munitions broker."

"You're joking." Her aqua eyes shimmered with intelligence as she contemplated the implications of his discovery. "We must give this information to Falcon as soon as possible."

She headed for the door with papers in her hand, but Aidan was obliged to stop her. "I'm sorry to disappoint, Lady Rivenhall, but I refuse to be seen in public in Lord Cantor's livery."

The lady took in his attire and, with a nefarious grin,

said, "But, my lord, you could make the dandies of the ton absolutely green with envy."

"Come," he said, rolling his eyes as he seized her arm.

The short distance back to Lady Rivenhall's home was spent in silent contemplation. Aidan gratefully changed back into his normal attire and joined Celeste in her parlor.

"What I cannot comprehend is why a munitions dealer would be on this list of men to be investigated," Lady Rivenhall began as she settled into the settee. "Surely, the Crown would know if he had been supplying the enemy with gunpowder."

Aidan's brows rose. "Yes, they would be aware of it, as every departing vessel is searched for contraband. Therefore, we can assume he has not." He pulled Celeste to her feet. "So, we turn over the innocuous documents to Falcon and are finished with these bloody inquiries," he whispered as he slanted his mouth across hers.

His lips had barely begun to warm when she pushed against his chest. "Lord Wessex, now that the investigation is over, you are no longer obligated to provide my protection."

Aidan tensed. "Meaning?"

She turned her back to him. "Meaning that with the conclusion of our inquires our association is . . . ended."

His lungs seized, and it took a moment before he could draw enough air to say, "Our 'association'?"

The lady turned and met his eye, brushing a golden strand from her lovely face. "Do you prefer dalliance? Either way this will be the last time—"

Aidan interrupted, not wanting to hear the words that would inevitably follow. "If you are still angry about the last evening . . . about my legitimate concerns with this liaison . . ."

"I'm not angry with you, my lord. Quite the contrary. I would like to take this opportunity to wish you a long and happy life."

"This is not amusing, Celeste," he said, alarm constricting his throat.

"No, it is not."

"What the bloody hell do you—"

"I'm leaving."

Aidan's heart stopped. How could this be happening again? Why was he not enough?

"Where?" he whispered, staring down at her and trying not to feel anything.

She stepped away from him, and he let her go.

"France. It has already been arranged. I came to England to capture a traitor, which we have done. When Lord Wellesley launches his attack, he will need the information that only I am able to provide."

Aidan could not move, could not breathe. "It's suicide, Celeste."

She stared at him. "It's no different than your fighting at Albuera, my lord."

Her formality wounded him. "It is very different. You are a woman."

"Yes, thank you for pointing that out, Lord Wessex, but I doubt the emperor would have me as a man."

"The emperor! You cannot be serious."

"I've already written him."

He was speechless, and it took several moments to find his tongue. "When?"

"I leave for Amsterdam Friday."

"Five days?" he asked in disbelief.

"Yes. Marie has already begun to pack our luggage."

He took a step toward her, but she took a step back, maintaining the distance between them. "Why are you doing this, Celeste?" Aidan asked, holding her gaze.

"Why did you fight for your country?"

Aidan shook his head and took another step forward. "I was not running away from something. You are."

Anger flashed through her eyes, and she looked up at him, saying, "Oh? And what might that be?"

"Me," he said, his arms banding about her. He kissed her with every emotion he felt—anger, confusion, and desire.

He felt her melt against him for a moment before she

tore her lips from his. "Really, my lord, your arrogance knows no bounds." She was a bit breathless as she made for the door. "Now if you will excuse me, I really must begin—"

"Marry me." The words escaped him in desperation, and his heart was thundering in his ears. He stared at her back, waiting to have his heart torn from his chest.

She turned, tears swimming in her aqua eyes. "Don't . . ."

"Marry me, Celeste."

She reached for the door. "I can't."

Aidan, who had scarcely been able to stand a moment ago, leapt for the door, preventing it from opening. "Don't go to Paris, Celeste. You have done your part. Stay here," he whispered down to her. "Stay with me."

Her fair head was turned down, and he knew that she was crying. Aidan bent his head and kissed her just below the ear. "You saved me once before, Celeste." He paused. "Marry me and save me again."

She turned, throwing her arms around his neck, and then he could breathe again. Aidan closed his eyes and pulled her to his chest. He smiled and stroked her back as she soaked his shirt.

"Say yes, Celeste."

"Y-yes," she said on a hiccup of air.

Aidan laughed at her ineloquence. "Near enough. Now go tell Madame Arnott you are to be a countess and not a spy." He kissed the tears from her cheeks and stared into her beguiling eyes. "We shall talk in the morning when you are rested."

She nodded and left him alone in the sun-filled parlor. Aidan expected to feel the weight of an offer, forced from him to keep her in England, to keep her alive. But he did not feel heavy at all. Quite the contrary. She had chosen to stay . . . with him, even as duty called her to France.

Celeste had saved his life, had haunted his dreams, and now would sleep beside him every night. He smiled to himself. She would certainly hold his attention in bed. In that respect they were the perfect match, and had been from the moment he first touched her.

Aidan gathered his hat and the documents from Lord Cantor's home and made for the door. The butler raised a brow at the wide grin on Aidan's face before saying, "Good day, my Lord."

He smiled down at the man and placed his beaver skin hat atop his head.

"Yes, yes it is." And then the Earl of Wessex was out the door and lifting himself into his carriage. "Whitehall," he shouted to his coachman.

Aidan's smile faded, and the noise from the busy streets blurred into a constant hum as he considered his interview with Falcon. The spymaster would not be pleased at losing his most highly placed operative, but Aidan did not care. Celeste would be safe.

The outer office was empty, so Aidan walked across the room and knocked on Falcon's door, all the while wishing that Cunningham had been there to soothe the old man's wrath.

"Enter."

Aidan stepped into the small office, his Hessians announcing his arrival. The old man looked up from the stacks of papers before him and removed his glasses as he sat back in his chair.

"Might I assume that this is an urgent matter, Lord Wessex?"

Bad start.

"It is," Aidan said, holding the man's eyes and preparing himself for the inevitable confrontation. "I have come to inform you that Lady Rivenhall will not be boarding the ship to Calais Friday next."

Falcon's eyes narrowed, and Aidan saw a flash of the very formidable man he must have been in his youth. "Oh, and why is that, my lord?"

Aidan lifted his chin, bracing himself for the man's outrage. "Because the lady has consented to be my wife."

The old man raised a brow as he lifted himself from the

chair. He said not a word and walked around the desk, coming to stand directly in front of him.

"I knew I could rely on you, boy. Steady as a rock. Steady as a rock!" Falcon broke into a broad smile and shook his hand in ardent congratulation. "Thought I was going to have to hold the girl against her will." The old man laughed. "Celeste is extremely stubborn, as you well know."

Aidan blinked, feeling suddenly as though the world were topsy-turvy. "You're pleased that we are to be married?"

"Pleased! Damnation, boy, why do you think I partnered you with the lady in the first place? Always knew the girl would want to return to France. Needed something to keep her here, didn't I?"

"You mean you . . . you anticipated my offer?"

Falcon shrugged modestly. "Don't know if 'anticipated' is the correct word. More of a hope, really. That girl has had more men than I can shake a stick at attempt to seduce her, and not once did she bat an eyelash. But the night you discovered her at Reynolds's ball . . . well, the girl was fit to be tied."

"Are you suggesting that she was in love with me then?" Aidan could not believe it.

The old man chortled. "Good God, man, how should I know if the girl was in love with you? But she was attracted to you, of that I was certain."

"But I thought she was a French agent." Aidan's tone held his skepticism.

"Yes, but she knew that you were not, and that your behavior stemmed from a sense of loyalty and patriotism, which she admired greatly. In that, at least, you are a perfect match."

A perfect match. Aidan smiled. "Yes, I suppose we are."

"So," the old man began with a grin. "When is the happy day?"

Aidan shook his head. "We have not discussed the matter."

"Take some advice from an old man." Falcon's sherry-colored eyes looked anything but old. "The woman will want to delay the wedding until the perfect flowers are in season or some silly nonsense, but put your foot down. Three months at the most. That is all any man should wait to have the woman he intends to make his wife."

Aidan laughed, "Three months?"

"Less if you can manage it, but I think that sister of yours will cause problems for you."

"Always has."

"I can only imagine." He smiled. "Now, go back to your betrothed and keep the girl out of danger. A woman that beautiful and clever will be pursued by the ton's most notorious rakes until the day of the ceremony, if not afterward."

A surge of possessiveness overcame Aidan, and he was startled by its intensity. He bowed, saying, "I can assure you, my lord, that will not be a difficulty."

Falcon laughed and sat behind his desk. "A rock."

Thirty-three

※

Oh, Aidan," his sister said, flying into his arms. "I am so happy for you."

"I believe I told you, dearest."

The duke's comment, accompanied by his smug grin, earned him an orange hurled at his head. He caught it, having grown accustomed to his wife's fits of irritation.

Aidan laughed. "You really should stop tossing things at your husband, Sarah."

"Glenbroke is enormous," she said, lifting her elegant hand in the direction of her husband. "One or two dents will hardly be noticed."

"Do you promise to examine me later, darling?"

"Only if you are very, very good."

The duke chuckled at his outrageous wife, as Sarah turned to Aidan, all smiles. "A Christmas wedding. Oh, it will be perfect. We shall have less than six months, but I'm sure we can manage."

"You have three."

"Three!" Sarah all but shouted.

"Very well, two."

The duke laughed, and his wife glared in his direction.

"What I really want is for you to take Celeste under your wing. She has been in France for the past several years and will need to be reintroduced to her peers."

"She is very brave, your Celeste."

Aidan sobered. "Yes, she is, but she need not be any longer."

"Well, old man. I believe this calls for a tall drink of congratulations." He handed Aidan his finest brandy. "I must confess, I thought Daniel would get shackled—"

"Shackled!"

"My apologies, darling." The duke bowed in Sarah's direction just as an apple went sailing overhead. Gilbert pretended not to hear the loud thud as the fruit hit the mahogany paneled wall of their dining room. "I felt sure Daniel would be the next to take the path to matrimonial bliss, to wedded jubilation, to—"

"Very amusing, Your Grace." Sarah attempted to appear annoyed but only managed affectionate exasperation. "At least give us the pleasure of announcing your betrothal at our ball on Wednesday."

Aidan laughed at the desperation in Sarah's emerald eyes, eyes that matched his to perfection. "Very well, sister dear. If Celeste is amenable, then Gilbert may announce our betrothal Wednesday evening."

Sarah bounced up and down and clapped with excitement, prompting Aidan to add, "The sooner the announcement is made, the sooner the preparations can begin for the wedding."

The duchess grunted her disapproval. "Three months. Really, Aidan, people will think you were forced to marry Lady Rivenhall."

Aidan felt warmth spread through him at the thought of his bride increasing. "Perhaps I am," he said, teasing his sister as if she were still ten years of age.

Her mouth fell open, and the duke chuckled. "Well, if you are going to make such indelicate comments, darling, you should anticipate such answers." Gilbert's silvery eyes fell to his. "You do not, do you?"

"What?" Aidan asked, playing the innocent.

"Need a hasty wedding?"

Aidan smiled, his dimples contrasting with the wicked glint in his eye. "Three months," he answered, calculating that if his sister believed there was indeed a need for a hasty wedding, she would not hound him for the next three months. "Until Wednesday, Sarah." He bowed. "Your Grace."

He took his leave, delighting in the fact that he had rendered his talkative sister utterly speechless.

Celeste was polishing off her second glass of scotch when the Earl of Wessex arrived. She set the tumbler down by the decanter and ripped open her reticule, pulling out a sprig of mint. She chewed voraciously and spit the mangled leaf into her handkerchief.

She searched for a place to dispose of the soiled cloth and in desperation stuffed the white linen between the cushions of the settee. Her smile was perhaps a bit too bright as she awaited the arrival of her fiancé. Truth be told, she was having a bit of difficulty comprehending that the Earl of Wessex, the legend, was indeed her betrothed.

Was she truly that fortunate?

No, the earl had made the offer to keep her from returning to France, of that she was sure. He had proven his honor by attempting to protect her yet again. Oh, the earl was attracted to her. She knew that by the way he looked at her, touched her.

Therefore, the question remained. Could she accept this marriage? For her part, Celeste knew she would never find a finer man in all the world. He was breathtakingly handsome and had only to enter the room to make her weak in the knees. He had offered his life in defense of his country, and she would always admire him.

No. If she were honest, she would admit that she more than admired Aidan Duhearst. Celeste knew beyond all doubt that she had fallen in love with the Earl of Wessex. But he was not in love with her.

How could he be?

The door opened, and Celeste fixed a polite smile on her face. Aidan's forest green jacket was of the finest quality, and his black trousers and boots made his powerful legs appear as long as she knew them to be. She blushed, and he gave her a lopsided grin, revealing those dimples that made her stomach flip.

"Good evening, Lady Rivenhall," he offered, bowing elegantly.

"Good evening, my lord," she said, feeling awkward. Celeste tugged at her cerulean gown and suddenly wished that she had left her hair down. She felt exposed and vulnerable.

The earl walked forward, standing before her, and Celeste had never felt so small. She looked up into his clear green eyes and for just a moment she thought that perhaps he was pleased with their arrangement.

"You look lovely, Celeste," he whispered as he bent his head and kissed her. His hand drifted to cup her cheek, and the warmth of his bare hand startled her. His lips were equally warm, and he grinned. "Mint." He smacked his lips with brows pulling together in contemplation. "And brandy?"

"Scotch," Celeste admitted.

His baritone chuckle reached into her, and she shivered as he said, "I'd better have another taste." His lips met hers again, but this time his warm hands pulled her flush against his body. His tongue persuaded her mouth to open, allowing him to slip inside.

He surveyed her mouth, and Celeste heard a soft moan that she realized was her own. His hand splayed on the small of her back as he drew her closer. She could feel his arousal against her hip, and Celeste closed her eyes, remembering the absolute pleasure of feeling his power braced over her as he drove into her body.

"Definitely scotch," he said with a teasing smile meant to put her at ease.

But it did not.

She stared up at Aidan Duhearst and realized that she wanted to marry him, wanted it more than she could have thought. She had always dreamt of a quiet life where she was not forced to do horrible things, a life with many children and a home somewhere in the country.

Tears welled up in her eyes as she thought of her father and the children that would never know him, of walking down the aisle alone as she made her way to take her wedding vows.

Aidan looked down at her, concern creasing his forehead. He wiped a tear from her cheek with his thumb, asking, "What troubles you, Celeste?"

She avoided his all too perceptive gaze. "I was just thinking that my father will not be here for my wedding."

"Nor mine," he said, with such sadness that Celeste looked up.

"Sarah told me that your father died in battle?" she asked, realizing that she knew very little about the man she was to marry.

"Lincelles."

He looked away but she saw his pain, prompting her to ask, "How long ago?"

"He left me . . . us, when I was ten." He shrugged. "After my mother died, he joined the fight against France. He led the charge at Lincelles and died there, leaving the earldom to me."

Celeste was overcome with sympathy. "I am so sorry, Aidan. He must have loved her very much," she said.

Aidan lifted his head and stared at her as if he had never seen her before. He blinked. "Who?"

"Your mother," she said, confused. "Your father must have loved your mother very much to have grieved her so deeply, to have gone to war rather than face life without her."

Her fiancé stared, his eyes glistening with tears. "Yes, he

did." And then he laughed, contradicting his sadness and confusing her further still. "Yes, Father adored my mother. He was not the same man after she died."

"I'm sure losing your mother was difficult for all of you." They stared at one another. "I know how difficult it is to lose someone. I am sorry, Aidan."

"So am I." But she knew that he was not referring to himself, which made her tears start anew. "You could not have saved your father, Celeste," he whispered. "And no matter how many traitors you expose, nothing will change the simple truth that you are not, and never were, to blame for his death."

Celeste could scarcely breathe. His words reached down to the darkest part of her, spreading light there for the first time in years.

"Thank you, Aidan."

He wiped a tear from her cheek and then turned and offered her his arm. "Now, let us go to the ball before your nose resembles a raspberry." Celeste smiled through her tears and followed him to their betrothal party.

For the past two days the Duchess of Glenbroke had come to Celeste's home, interrogating her—it was the only appropriate word for it—on her favorite flower, color, composer, dance, jewels. However, the most enjoyable part of these afternoon teas was hearing of Aidan's childhood.

Hearing of the boy who loved his parents and spent his days hunting and fishing and concocting horrible ways in which to torture his younger sister. A young boy who had shouldered the loss of his father and the devastating responsibilities that followed, a man who requested a commission in His Majesty's cavalry in order to follow in his heroic father's footsteps.

"He was wounded several times," the duchess had said with sadness contorting her features. "We had hoped he would return home after the first battle." Sarah sighed. "Albuera was the worst, of course. He had headaches for months after his return."

Celeste had not been able to breathe, and upon seeing her distress, the duchess had come to her side. "He is all right now, Celeste. I'm sorry, I thought you knew."

But she had not.

The thought of the world losing a man like the Earl of Wessex, of her losing a man like Aidan . . . She glanced over at his masculine profile as he stared out the window. They were approaching his sister's home on Grosvenor Square.

"Ah, here we are. Now, I must warn you. Sarah will wait until the last possible moment before asking Gilbert to make the announcement. She has always enjoyed a good secret and will not relinquish it easily."

Celeste grinned, saying, "I would never think of ruining the Duchess of Glenbroke's enjoyment."

They shared a conspiratorial smile, and Celeste relished the moment of closeness.

He handed her down, and as they ascended the stairs the butterflies in her stomach multiplied with each step toward the front entry.

Tonight, she would be the center of attention, and she could not help but squirm under the anticipated scrutiny. For so long she had been avoiding attention, avoiding attachments. She had moved in society in Paris, of course, but never like this, never in the open and never without a goal.

Celeste glanced at her fiancé, and he squeezed her hand, dissolving all of her doubt with his comforting smile. It was at that moment that she realized, truly understood, that she was not alone, that she would never be alone again. She would be his countess and his wife, and in return, he would be her husband and confidant.

They entered the Duke of Glenbroke's home, and Celeste's mouth fell open. Roses in various shades of pink covered every column within view, and the duchess's generosity and acceptance was all too much. Her chin began to quiver, and Aidan inclined his head toward hers.

"What is the matter?"

"Pink roses are my favorite flower," she offered as a weak explanation, unable to voice her overwhelming gratitude and disbelief that she would soon be his bride.

Aidan smiled broadly, and she knew that he was pleased with his sister. "I'm so glad that you are enjoying them."

Enjoying them. His family's generosity astonished her. They walked into the ballroom, and she could not believe the vastness of the long room. It seemed as though the entire ton could be accommodated quite easily within these paneled walls. Hundreds of candles lit the enormous chandelier overhead, and the Austrian crystal sparkled prettily across the polished wooden floor.

"It's beautiful," she whispered.

Her fiancé leaned toward her, saying, "It does not compare to you, Celeste." She pulled her gaze from the exquisite chandelier to take in the exquisite man she was to marry. He smiled, his dimples displaying his amusement.

A waltz by her favorite composer began to play, and Aidan met her eyes with his. "My dance, I believe."

He led her to the floor, and before she could form a coherent thought, she was in his powerful arms. Their movements were fluid as she moved anywhere he wished her to go. Celeste marveled at how he managed to maneuver her about the floor while continuing to stare into her eyes. His colorful gaze flared, and she wanted nothing more than to take him to her bed and fulfill the promise she saw reflected there.

"Bloody hell, Celeste. Meet me in the west wing in half an hour, third door on the right."

She nodded as the waltz ended. He led her to the edge of the floor and whispered, "Half an hour," with a desperation that mirrored her own.

Celeste noted the time and spoke with Ladies Pervill and Appleton as the minutes dragged along. She danced a quadrille with the duke and a waltz with Lord Reynolds. And finally it was time to make her way to Aidan.

Making her excuses, Celeste all but ran up the stairs. She opened the door and scanned the room, disappointed that she was the first to arrive. But then the door was pushed closed and Aidan was pressing her against the wall.

Their mouths tangled in desperate battle, and he moaned when his hand closed around her breast. He tore his lips from hers and pulled her across the room to a large chair. His eyes burned bright as he sat down, guiding her between his legs.

His hands lifted her skirts and she could feel his fingers curl around her legs just behind her knees. "Take off your drawers," he said on ragged breaths.

He watched as she eagerly complied, and the instant Celeste had finished his large hands were trailing up the backs of her thighs. He lifted her skirts and carefully pulled her onto his lap. They stared at one another as he positioned her knees to either side of his lean hips. He grabbed her backside and kneaded the soft mounds.

"Oh, God, Celeste. I have never needed a woman as much as I need you."

He pulled at his breeches, exposing his maleness, which stood rigid and ready to take her. He grabbed her buttocks and squeezed, saying, "Come down on me, Celeste."

He held her gaze, and their desire crackled in the small bedchamber. She sank down and felt his arousal breech her entrance but she continued her downward descent, holding his gaze all the while. He filled her slowly, and she felt every inch of his penetration.

His hands drifted to her hips, and just when she thought she had taken all of him, he thrust upward, taking her breath away. He closed his eyes and groaned, then opened them on a ragged breath. "Ride me, Celeste."

She was unsure of what to do. She rose on her knees and sank down again, causing him another groan of pleasure, and she reveled in the power of controlling their lovemaking. Celeste was mesmerized as his breath caught when she stroked him again. He was hers to control, hers to pleasure.

Her hips rolled as she lifted off of him, and he grunted with delight. He tried to hold her gaze, but the more she learned what pleased him, the more his eyes drifted closed. Her own breaths were becoming short, and even though she ached to prolong their joining, her body hungered to be filled by him.

Her head fell back as she rode him, and when she looked at Aidan, his eyes burned hotter than she had ever seen them. His hand firmed on her hips and he took control of the rhythm. He lifted her and held her firmly in place as he thrust deeper into her. His eyes closed, and his pace increased. Watching him so close to his pleasure, knowing that she was the woman he desired, sent her over the edge.

She cried out as her body was seized by wave after wave of delight that caused her to quiver in his muscular arms. He drove into her several more times, trying desperately to prolong her ecstasy, but he was lost. He came into her with such intensity that he shook for several moments.

Her fiancé stared at her then grasped the back of her head, pulling her toward him in a passionate kiss.

"I don't think three months will do, Celeste. I'm afraid I will not be able to keep my hands off of you."

"Two?"

"One."

"Your sister will have a fit of vapors."

"Sarah never swoons. She is much more likely to throw something." Celeste laughed, and he gave her another playful kiss. "There is a washroom just in there. I shall return to the ballroom first."

Celeste nodded and reluctantly ended their intimate contact. She started toward the washroom when Aidan's voice stopped her.

"Celeste, I . . ." Something akin to confusion passed over his features. "I shall see you downstairs."

She pushed away her disappointment. "I'll be down shortly."

Aidan nodded, and then she was alone.

Celeste entered the washroom and righted herself, all the while wondering what he had meant to say. She went out into the corridor and was glancing down to verify that her flounces had not been crushed, when she was grabbed from behind and pulled into a small parlor.

She attempted to scream, but a large hand muffled her cry. "I only wish to speak with you, Lady Rivenhall," the man said, blindfolding her. "I believe I told you that I would contact you again."

Celeste stiffened, her mind racing as she felt the silky cloth tighten against the back of her head. Lord Ferrell was in custody. Could they have made a mistake? She strained to see as the man turned her to face him, but her sight remained as dark as the moment.

"I must say I admire your technique. If you are able to satisfy a rake like Wessex then you must be very skilled indeed." The man's tone was appreciative, and Celeste had no doubt he had seduced many ladies of the ton.

"Is that how you retrieve your information, my lord?" Celeste drawled in her most superior tone.

"The majority of the time, yes." The man pushed her against the door, and she was surprised by how solid he was. "I do so enjoy obtaining the information, and from the way Wessex made you moan, Lady Rivenhall, I take it you do as well."

A wave of nausea came over her as she imagined this man listening to her intimacy with Aidan. She fought it back, determined to know who this man was and what he had to offer.

"What do you want?" she asked, ignoring his advance.

"As I said in your bedchamber, I would like to join forces. With your powers of persuasion and my connections, we would be able to target certain individuals who could prove quite useful."

"Divide and conquer?"

"Collude and profit."

"I do very well alone, my lord."

He chuckled, and she could feel his breath on her cheek, his eyes on her body. "Yes, I'm sure that you do, but why do twice the amount of work when we could share resources?"

The question hung in the air. "No," she said finally, pushing against the wall of his chest with the palms of her hands.

The man did not budge, saying "Before you issue a hasty refusal, my lady, you should consider that I am on the verge of uncovering information that will make me a very rich man."

"Then why do you need me?"

"You have the ear of Napoleon himself. I want the emperor told that it was I who uncovered Wellesley's battle strategy."

Celeste froze, unable to take air into her lungs. "You're lying."

"I shall have the admiral's invasion plans by the end of the week."

Her heart was racing as she imagined the men who would die if this traitor were to succeed. "The emperor would reward you handsomely for such information."

"And you, Lady Rivenhall." He leaned closer, the heat of his lips hovering over hers. "Will you reward me?"

Celeste raised her chin and played the part she had played for the last four years. She sneered, saying, "I'm the paramour of an emperor, not an Englishman."

"And the Earl of Wessex?"

"Is useful," she finished.

"Yes, I believe I heard how useful the young earl was to you. Very well, we shall meet tomorrow evening, eight o'clock at the ruins at Holborn."

The man was no simpleton. The ancient ruins stood at a barren hilltop, and anyone approaching would be seen instantly. She would have to consider her options carefully.

He continued. "I want five thousand pounds a year and an estate in France in exchange for Wellesley's tactics and departure dates."

"I shall need to authenticate the information."

"I would expect no less, Lady Rivenhall. And do bring the required documents from your lover, or you shall leave empty-handed."

"I would expect no less, my lord Lion."

The man chuckled. "Well done, Lady Rivenhall, very well done." She felt his fingers against her cheeks. "I'm pleased that you realize with whom you are dealing," he said, dropping his fingers to caress her forearm until he held her hand. "Until tomorrow," he said, pressing a kiss to the back of her glove.

Celeste heard the click of the parlor door and she struggled to remove the blindfold. She yanked the door wide, desperate to catch a glimpse of this traitor as she stepped into the dim hallway, but it was already empty and she remained unenlightened. Her brows furrowed as her mind bounced about like dandelions in the wind. Music from the ballroom drifted toward her as she slowly made her way down the corridor.

What was she to do?

If she told Aidan of the liaison he would insist upon accompanying her, endangering himself as well as the outcome of the meeting. *Falcon*—she would speak with Falcon. The old man would be concerned for her safety, but he would understand the importance of keeping this information from France, no matter what the individual sacrifices. Aidan would not be objective. And while he did not love her, his offer was proof of his desire for her safety.

His offer!

Celeste flew down the stairs, panic constricting her throat. She searched frantically for her fiancé, and then they saw one another through the crush. Aidan smiled, and her heart lurched. He looked up, nodding as she reached his side. Celeste followed his eyes up the curved Italian marble staircase.

The Duke of Glenbroke stood with champagne glass in hand, waiting for the ton to gather round so that he might announce their betrothal.

"No," she whispered. If the traitor knew that they were betrothed, knew that they were aligned . . . "Stop him, Aidan," she said, turning toward her fiancé.

He laughed, assuming she was jesting until he saw the panic in her eyes. "What are you—"

Celeste placed both hands on his forearm. "You must stop him, Aidan. Please."

Confusion and hurt gathered in his stormy eyes.

"Ladies and Gentlemen, I would like to thank you all for coming here this evening . . ."

She swallowed her tears as he stared down at her, his mouth a grim line. "Aidan, you must stop him from making the announcement. Please, Aidan. Please."

"As you know, the duchess and I have been happily married for over a year . . ."

Aidan did not move, and Celeste released him, making for the staircase. He grabbed her upper arm, saying, "Very well, Lady Rivenhall."

"However, tonight we would . . ." The duke paused as Aidan ascended the staircase. The enormous man tilted his head and Aidan whispered in his ear. Gilbert's brows rose ever so slightly and he straightened with a bright smile spreading across his features.

"We would like to welcome you to our home and thank you for your generosity and friendship throughout the past year."

The crowd clapped and smiled indulgently as the duchess joined her husband at the head of the stairs. He whispered in her ear, and she smiled brightly, looking out over the crowd. When her eyes settled on Celeste they stilled, and her smile seemed to fade. Celeste's chin quivered, and she turned, pushing her way toward the front entrance.

She was waiting for her cloak when Aidan reached her, pulling her into the cloakroom. "Get out," he snapped at the footman. The man bowed and left them amongst the silks and furs. Aidan turned on her, anger burning in his green eyes. "You were leaving?" His voice shook with fury and betrayal. "You end our betrothal after . . . after . . ."

He closed his eyes and took several calming breaths, pain clearly etched on his handsome face.

"Aidan," she said, placing her hand to his cheek.

His eyes flew open, and he seized her arm. "Don't touch me," he grated through clenched teeth. "Am I allowed the honor of an explanation, Lady Rivenhall? Or was I to guess, as I watched your carriage retreat down Pall Mall?"

Tears welled in her eyes and she ached to confide in him, to comfort him and to be comforted by him. But she knew that he would try to protect her, that he would follow her and endanger the mission.

"I find that I need more time to consider your suit."

He pulled back as if she had struck him. She watched confusion and pain harden into bitterness. "Take all the time you need, my lady." He leaned forward so that they were level with one another. "For the offer will not be made again."

Aidan waited to see that he had hurt her as much as she had injured him before exiting the cloakroom with a re-sounding slam of the small door. Celeste sank back against the greatcoats and wraps, covering her face. '*You have given enough,*' he had said, but it seemed that she would have to sacrifice the only thing that had ever truly mattered . . . him.

Thirty-four

⤞⤟⤞

The Earl of Wessex awoke at four o'clock Thursday afternoon, the result of having imbibed in the solitude of his study for the majority of the previous evening.

Aidan was submerged in a hot bath, his head threatening to split open at any moment, when his washroom door did. The Duke of Glenbroke strolled in and sank into a small chair, which looked even smaller as the enormous man balanced himself on the spindly golden legs.

"Right. What is going on, Aidan? I was forced to listen to your sister's conjecture all evening, and I refuse to do it again tonight."

Gilbert leaned back with his arms crossed over his chest and Aidan knew his brother-in-law would not leave the room without an explanation. The only difficulty was that he did not have one.

"I haven't the foggiest notion."

Gilbert's luminescent eyes narrowed, and his arms fell to his sides. "What do you mean, you don't know? You're in love with her, aren't you?"

Aidan shrugged. "Lady Rivenhall ended our engagement, not I." He ran his hand through his wet hair, admitting to himself, "And, yes, I am in love with her."

"Then go and get her," the duke said, as if the woman were the *London Gazette*.

Aidan lifted his arms from beneath the surface, splashing water onto the carpeted floor.

"And just what am I to do, Your Grace?" he asked with irritation. "Drag her to the altar?" He lay back and placed a cloth over his eyes. "I'll not beg a woman who doesn't want me."

Although Aidan could not see the man, he could feel the duke studying him.

"If you love her, Aidan, you should drag yourself across hot coals to make her your wife, or you will regret it for the remainder of your days."

Aidan did not remove the cloth from his eyes for fear that the duke would see the depth of his despair. "Thank you for dropping in, Gilbert. Close the door on your way out."

The duke remained several more moments, and Aidan knew he wanted to say more. But what else was there to say? He had made an offer and she had refused him. It had happened to many gentlemen before him. Aidan removed the damp cloth from his eyes and stared at the silk-covered walls. His pride had been bruised, and would eventually recover.

But as he remembered holding her in his arms, he wondered if his heart ever would.

Lord Wellesley's clerk had made his way to the front steps of Whitehall when he remembered that he had not brought one of the estimates needed for his meeting with his lordship.

The admiral preferred meeting over a leisurely luncheon in the privacy of his home, which made it damned inconvenient for Woodson. He had spent the majority of the morning pulling files and organizing the documents requested by Lord Wellesley, and inevitably he had forgotten one.

The small man muttered a curse and turned back toward his office. He was running through a mental checklist, considering what other items may have been left behind, when he entered the small room and stopped in utter surprise.

His large friend stood with his back to the door and his hands in the cabinet containing the files. He would disarrange them, Woodson thought with irritation, and then asked, "What are you doing?"

The dark man turned with the devastating smile that never ceased to paralyze the clerk with its sheer beauty.

"Woodson! There you are. Been looking for you everywhere; thought we might dine together."

The clerk's brows furrowed as he stared into the striking eyes of his handsome colleague. "But you knew that I was meeting with Wellesley for luncheon."

The tall man chuckled and came around the desk, draping his arm over Woodson's shoulders. The clerk could feel the man's power in every muscle of his bulky arm and chest.

"Not luncheon, old man, dinner."

"Oh, well, yes." Woodson attempted to think. However, it was difficult when he was so near a man of such masculine perfection. "But why were you looking in my files?" he asked as he set down the documents in his hands and went round to retrieve the estimate he had forgotten.

"Just curious," the dark man said, and then stood behind him, planting one hand on the wall to the right of his head. "I thought we might go to that pub down by the docks."

Woodson's heart was pounding, and he closed his eyes in a futile attempt to steady it. "Why . . . why do you want to go all the way down there?"

The handsome man leaned down and whispered in his ear, his hot breath causing gooseflesh up and down Woodson's arms. "I think you know why. The same reason I was there the first time."

Woodson could scarcely think, scarcely believe . . . but

the man continued, "And unless I miss my guess, we will do very well together."

The clerk tried to answer, but all of his thoughts were focused on remaining upright.

"Midnight. Will you come?"

Woodson managed to nod, and the heat of the man left his back. He heard his door close, and it was several more minutes before his breathing became regular. He picked up the documents on his desk and made for the door, but with each step his mind cleared and his brow began to furrow. And by the time he reached Wellesley's home, it was an all-out scowl.

Lord Wellesley was enjoying a plate of kippers when the clerk entered the room with a deep bow. "Have you brought everything, Woodson?" the man asked, motioning to a chair on his right.

"Yes, my lord."

Confused by his assistant's tone, the admiral looked up, saying, "What the bloody hell's the matter? You appear as though you've eaten a rotten egg."

"I don't know. That is to say, I'm not sure."

"What in God's name are you babbling about, man?"

Woodson took a deep breath, making his decision. "Do you recall that a spy has been selling information to the French for the past five months?"

Lord Wellesley scowled. "It is hardly a fact I might forget, as the traitor has cost me several battles."

The small man turned a bright shade of pink. "Of course, my lord. Please forgive—"

"Do get on with it, Woodson."

"Well, I . . . I believe I might have just identified that man."

Lord Wellesley's silver utensil dropped to his plate as he stared at the clerk in shock. A smile spread across his features, and he gave a boisterous laugh.

"Oh, well done, Woodson. Our lord Falcon has been determined to unmask this man, and my clerk announces over luncheon that he has identified the traitor. Jolly good, Woodson, jolly good. Who is the bastard?"

The clerk told him, and the admiral's eyes filled with skepticism. "The man is a bloody war hero! Killed countless Frenchmen on the peninsula and was even captured."

"Nevertheless, my lord . . ."

Wellesley's hands balled into fists. "Very well, I shall inform Falcon of your suspicions, but if you are correct, Falcon will want to string the man up himself."

"You have made the correct decision, my dear. You can explain everything to Wessex after we have this man in custody."

Celeste stared at the fire as Falcon tried to soothe her from his chair in the modest study. Aidan had not spoken to her since their parting at the ball. He had not even sent a note demanding an explanation, not that she could give him one, but she wanted him to ask for one nonetheless.

No, the Earl of Wessex had well and truly washed his hands of her at last. She would welcome his anger if only to see him again.

"I'm sure you're correct," she agreed, not believing it.

"Now, here are the land transfers and bank documents, all forged with Napoleon's seal. You are to sign them in this man's presence in exchange for the documents he is selling. You have done this a hundred times, Lady Rivenhall, so I need not remind you of the importance of this exchange."

Celeste nodded, the numbness making her agree to anything. "I'll not disappoint you, my lord."

Falcon stared into her eyes. "You could never disappoint me, my dear, but as you have refused my offer for an armed escort . . ."

"It's too dangerous. If he sees anyone, he will call off the exchange."

"I don't like it."

"You have no choice, my lord, nor do I." Celeste rose

and retrieved her reticule. "I shall return as soon as the exchange is complete."

"Take care, Celeste."

She smiled down at her mentor. "I've done this a hundred times, remember?"

"I know," he said with such sadness that her brows furrowed with confusion. "And I am truly sorry."

Their eyes met, and she knew she would cry if she remained, so she did not. She turned and left the study with a new sense of determination. She was determined to identify this traitor, determined to save English soldiers, but perhaps most of all she was determined to make the old man proud of her.

The Earl of Wessex spent the remainder of Thursday afternoon on Rotten Row.

He walked his horse and greeted acquaintances, hoping to drive Celeste from his mind. He sat listening to Lord Christian St. John, who had, along with Lord Barksdale, accompanied Ladies Pervill and Appleton to the park.

"The man was reciting Hamlet's soliloquy, skull in hand, when an orange came flying out of the pit, knocking it to the floor." Christian paused at the amused chuckles of his companions before continuing. "So Kean turns to the audience and raises a brow, saying, 'It would appear I'm in need of a fresh skull.' Then he looks down at the offending patron and says, 'Yours seems to be sufficiently hollow.'"

The quartet roared with appreciative laughter, and before Aidan had time to consider his feminine company, he asked politely, "Did you go with Lady Hamilton?"

Christian's laughter died as Lady Appleton turned a dull red, while Lady Pervill's mouth hung open in undisguised shock. Lord Barksdale stared in disbelief that Aidan had spoken of Christian's mistress in the presence of gently bred ladies. Aidan turned and met the stormy Nordic blue eyes of Lord St. John's. Christian rarely got angry, but when he did it was well deserved.

"My apologies—"

Aidan's words were cut off by an explosion in the distance and then another. Christian leaned over and steadied the women's horses, and then a third explosion, much larger, sent black smoke billowing into the air.

The riders turned to look in the direction of the docks, and a low murmur of speculation sped through Rotten Row. Aidan watched the smoke with a sense of dread and started toward the disaster.

"You won't be able to assist, Aidan," Christian called after him.

Aidan ignored him, knowing that he was right, but he was not going to the docks to offer assistance. Something, some terrible thing was drawing him there. The crowds thickened the closer he drew to the scene of the explosion. Smoke was everywhere, and he pulled his cravat over his face to filter the filthy soot.

Sailors were dragging bodies from a warehouse as the fire brigade attempted to control the inferno. "What happened?" he asked a sailor.

"Don't rightly know. She just blew," the man shouted back over the shrieks of panic.

The fire flared, and timbers collapsed, sending onlookers scattering. Aidan steadied his horse, and when the horror had subsided, he found himself near a carriage displaying a crest covered with soot.

Aidan's heart began to race, not from the carnage around him, but from an internal panic that was even now numbing his limbs. He brought his mount alongside the carriage and called up to the coachman, who was clearly beside himself.

"Who is your employer, sir?"

The coachman pointed in the direction of the burning warehouse. "He was only going to be a moment. Told me to wait here." Aidan nodded patiently, as he had seen men similarly stunned after the heat of battle. "Told me to wait."

"Who told you to wait?"

"Lord Cantor. Told me to wait here. He'll be back in a moment."

A small explosion sounded, sending Aidan's mount rearing up in fear. But Aidan made no attempt to control the animal, as he no longer had command of his body. He fell to the street and rolled beneath Lord Cantor's carriage a moment before the horse's hooves crashed down on the exact spot where his head had just been.

Aidan stared as his mount bolted, and then staggered to his feet. He was covered in soot and dirt as he watched Lord Cantor's warehouse burn to the ground. People pushed past him to assist the dead or dying. Alarms sounded, and people cried out with grief.

But Aidan did not hear any of it.

He stepped away from the treachery before him and turned in the direction of his home. His brows drew together in confused shock only to be obscured by black soot.

This was not a coincidence. The ships on Lord Ferrell's list had been attacked, and this . . . Lord Ferrell was in custody. He could not possibly have known about the information retrieved from Lord Cantor's study.

Only three people knew of both sets of documents: Aidan, Falcon, and . . . Lady Rivenhall.

I need time to consider your suit.

Pain cut through him, sharper than an enemy sword. How could she have done this—betrayed her country, betrayed him?

Falcon. Would Falcon believe him? Yes, given the evidence the old man would come to the same, inevitable conclusion, no matter how painful.

I have already written the emperor. I leave for Amsterdam Friday.

Aidan's memories propelled his feet forward. He pushed aside the pain and searched for a hackney, but the explosion at the docks left the streets empty the farther he traveled away from the inferno.

Celeste had been using him. Aidan laughed harshly. She

was very good at her profession; always had been, from the first moment he had set eyes on her in that interrogation room until now. How many other men had she convinced of her affection? How many other men had made an offer for her hand, an offer to spend the rest of their days loving her?

He lifted his head against the pain that was threatening to bring him to his knees. He spotted a hackney down the road, and his jaw clenched with determination and anger. He needed to see her, needed to unleash his pain on her.

"Hyde Park." The driver eyed him suspiciously until Aidan tossed him some coin. "The remainder when we arrive."

"Yes, my lord," the man said, having decided that, despite his appearance, he was a member of the quality.

Aidan stared out the window but saw nothing. The hackney bounced with every irregularity in the road, but he welcomed the violent jarring. He needed a distraction, needed to slow this simmering anger that was threatening to boil over, for he feared what he would do to her when it did.

The conveyance reached the park, and Aidan gave the driver the directions to Lady Rivenhall's home. "Stop here," he said, not wanting to wait while the driver turned the hackney about.

He paid the coachman and walked across the street and up the steps, banging on Lady Rivenhall's door with his fist rather than using the brass knocker. The butler appeared and was startled to see the familiar Earl of Wessex in such a state of dishevelment.

"My lord?"

"Lady Rivenhall, where is she?" he asked, pushing his way into the house.

"I'm afraid her ladyship is out, my lord. Perhaps—"

Aidan looked through the man as he brushed past. "Celeste. Celeste!" he shouted.

Madame Arnott came down the stairs with alarm in her

faded blue eyes. "She is not in residence, my lord, so kindly refrain from shouting."

"Where is she?" he asked, with such ferocity that he surprised not only Madame Arnott but himself.

Marie glanced at the butler and then guided Aidan into the parlor, closing the door. She eyed him skeptically.

"Why should I tell you, Lord Wessex? You are obviously overwrought."

Aidan caught sight of himself reflected in the mirror over the fireplace. The upper portion of his face was black with soot that ended in a line where his now filthy cravat had been. He removed the white silk from around his neck and began cleaning his face as he gave the only answer that would convince Madame Arnott to reveal the lady's location.

"She is in danger, Marie."

The older woman's eyes grew wide with alarm. She turned toward the fireplace and twisted her handkerchief in her hands. "I thought she might be. I told her not to go."

Aidan paused. He could not move as a sense of dread ripped through him. "Where is she, Marie?"

Indecision contorted her features, and then with a rush, she said, "The ruins of Holborn. She is meeting him at eight."

I leave for Amsterdam Friday. He glanced at the clock, six forty-seven.

"Who is she meeting?"

"I don't know." Marie shook her head. "I swear I do not. Please, do not let anything happen to her, my lord."

Aidan turned and was running out into the street as he searched for a conveyance, any conveyance. He hailed a hackney and pulled out his watch when the black lacquered coach rolled to a stop.

"The Foreign Office," he shouted. He would have just enough time to speak with Falcon and obtain a pistol before heading for the ruins.

He headed down the empty halls, arriving at Falcon's

office. Lord Cunningham sat poring over documents and looked up the moment Aidan entered.

"I need to speak with him."

"I'm afraid he is not in at the moment." The man laughed. "He rarely is."

"Damnation!"

"Perhaps I could be of assistance?"

Aidan considered his options as he stared at the large man, stared at the jagged scar that had been earned, like so many others, on the continent.

"I have reason to believe that Lady Rivenhall is working for the French."

The assistant looked stunned.

"She cannot be trusted and should no longer be considered one of our operatives. The lady is at this very moment meeting with a man to exchange information vital to the British war effort."

"My God!"

"I require the use of a horse and a pistol."

The man nodded, saying, "I'll have two horses brought round immediately."

"Two?"

"I'm going with you. Just let me send a messenger to the old man," he said, withdrawing a pistol from his desk.

Lord Cunningham left the room and returned not five minutes later. "It's all arranged. The horses are being brought around."

"It's not necessary for you to accompany me."

"Yes, I realize that, my lord, but the fact remains that there will be two of them to your one. And I should never forgive myself if something were to befall you."

Aidan nodded as images of those under his command flashed in his mind's eye. "Very well."

The men mounted and started in the direction of Holborn. Aidan wondered what he would feel when he saw Celeste, for at the moment he felt nothing. He had been forced to choose between the woman he loved and his country, and the choice had been too difficult, leaving him hollow and very, very cold.

Falcon returned to his office annoyed with the prime minister for insisting a written report of Lady Rivenhall's operation be sent to Wellesley. Being forced to reveal Lady Rivenhall's operation was dangerous enough, but to put the information in writing, where anyone could read it, was completely negligent.

He opened the door to his outer office thinking how much easier his job would be if not for the interference of government officials who would not know a French agent from their backsides.

Falcon puffed his exasperation. Still it was the prime minister who had made the request. He would satisfy the man's dictate by sending a communication to Wellesley requesting a meeting. He smiled. One or two vague pages, he decided. And if Wellesley was too busy to receive his report . . . well, he could hardly be blamed. Yes, a meeting would be better. A meeting to be scheduled *after* Lady Rivenhall had trapped the elusive Lion.

"Cunningham." Where was the damn boy? "Cunningham!" he growled, walking to his office, sure his assistant was there. He opened the door and saw that the room was vacant. Sighing, he sank into his chair and pulled open his desk drawer.

Empty. Not a single sheet of paper.

"Damn this embargo." He paused, summoning the energy to lift himself from the comfortable leather. He placed his hands on the arms of the chair, blue veins bulging near his enlarged knuckles. With a grunt, he rose then waited a moment to be sure of his balance before walking back into the outer office.

But just as he reached his assistant's desk there was a knock at the door. He considered not responding, but as he pulled the right drawer open the scraping of wood announced his presence.

"Enter."

The door opened so slowly that Falcon stopped his search out of mere curiosity. His brows furrowed as he waited, but when Wellesley's diminutive clerk entered the room he smiled in greeting.

"Woodson, just the man I need." His eyes fell to the desk drawer and he pulled out several sheets of parchment.

"Yes, my lord, but—"

"I need to arrange a meeting with the admiral first thing in the morning." He closed the drawer.

"I would be happy to arrange the appointment, my lord, but first I must speak with you."

"Oh, damn!" Falcon cursed himself.

He opened his assistant's drawer and pulled out the sealing wax and began rummaging through the official brass seals used by the Foreign Office. The others, the more discreet seals, were under lock and key in a very secret compartment in his desk. However, today he needed his official seal to prove that he had attempted to contact Wellesley.

"Admiral Wellesley sent me to inform you, well, suggest really, that I believe I know who—"

Falcon listened halfheartedly as he placed a seal on the desk and reached into the draw for a second try. "You know what?" he asked pulling out another seal.

He glanced down at the flamboyant image of the Lion just as Woodson said in a rush, "I believe I know who the traitor is."

Falcon felt a flash of heat that he was old enough to recognize as rage.

Cunningham had been the one to identify the five suspected traitors. Men with sensitive positions in the Foreign Office, men that the Lion knew would have privileged information. Men whose homes would be searched and the information brought back to his office, to Cunningham's hands.

The bastard had Falcon doing his work for him, retrieving information that he could then sell to France. Lion even had the impudence to place his traitorous seal ten feet away from him.

"Cunningham," he hissed through clenched teeth.

"Yes, but how did you—"

"Where is he?"

But then he remembered. He pulled out his gold watch from his waistcoat. *Dear God!*

Celeste.

He had kept her file hidden with the others, had burned her dossier months ago. And if Cunningham had found the files, he would not have gone to this meeting. He would have known that it was a trap.

Still, Falcon could not be sure.

"Find Wellesley. Have him dispatch ten soldiers to the Holborn ruins immediately. They are to protect Lady Rivenhall at all costs. Kill Cunningham if needs be, but be sure the lady is unharmed. Go!"

The clerk turned, and he could hear him running down the corridor. Falcon sat down in the traitor's chair, praying that his stupidity had not cost Celeste her life.

As the busy streets of London faded, replaced by the gentle hills of the countryside, Aidan began to have doubts. Perhaps he could take her to Wessex, keep her isolated until the war was over, keep her by his side so she would not be able to gather information to sell to his enemies.

But she had made her choice, the night of their betrothal ball. And while Lady Rivenhall might be attracted to him, might even harbor some affection for him, it clearly had not been enough.

He had not been enough.

"There it is," Lord Cunningham said.

Aidan looked up and saw the withered chapel with the sun setting behind it. It stood alone, a mere remnant of what it once had been, much like himself. His soul had been all but destroyed by war, only to be resurrected for the briefest of moments by his love for a woman. And, he had envisioned, her love for him.

As they approached, he saw her horse grazing beside the ruins, verification of her betrayal. Aidan clenched his jaw and let the freezing numbness take over. They dismounted some distance away and moved stealthily through the underbrush and outer walls. Candles flickered in the uppermost room, and he knew she was there. He could feel her presence.

"I'll go first," Cunningham offered, his pistol drawn.

Aidan nodded, not bothering to pull his firearm and wondering if she would try to shoot him. He stared at the large man's back as they made their way up the winding staircase, avoiding decades of debris while they ascended.

When they entered the uppermost room, they could see that she was alone. Lady Rivenhall turned from what had once been a window and stared at him as she tried to work out how he had come to know of her treachery. The fading sunlight lit her hair to a breathtaking gold. Aidan reached for the support of the wall behind him as Lord Cunningham lifted his pistol toward her.

"Lady Rivenhall, we have come to place you under arrest for treason."

The lady tore her eyes from Aidan and turned to Lord Cunningham. "What are you saying? I am no traitor."

Aidan could bear her lies no longer.

"We know, Celeste. Your associates killed Lord Cantor this afternoon when his munitions warehouse was set alight. Only three of us knew of that facility, and I'm relatively sure that I did not pass along the information." His voice was quiet, his eyes awash with resentment and pain.

"Aidan, I—"

"Save your breath, Lady Rivenhall." The sun reflected the tears streaming down her face, and the sight clawed at his heart, making his bitterness grow. "You have played me for a fool one too many times."

She swiped at her tears as if she could stop them. "If you think after Albuera, after I assisted you in escaping, after everything we have . . . if you have so little faith in me, my lord, than I am well rid of you."

Lord Cunningham stood beside her now and laughed, saying, "Well, you must admit, Lady Rivenhall, that you

are rather good. I myself was quite convinced you were a
French collaborator when we danced at Lord Hambury's
ball."

"Why would you possibly have thought . . . ?" Celeste
turned to look at Lord Cunningham, and Aidan saw her understanding flash across her face. "You knew. You took the
documents from Falcon's office. Why? Why would you
betray your country?"

"Why?" The man shook his head, as Aidan tried to comprehend what was happening. "I fought for this country,
killed for this country. But when I was captured by the
French, this country let me rot in prison rather than pay the
pittance of a ransom for my return."

"The Crown does not pay blackmailers for the release of
prisoners," Aidan said, reminding him. "Paying ransom
would merely encourage more assaults on British citizens
worldwide."

Lord Cunningham's blue eyes hardened to ice, as he
turned his gaze from Lady Rivenhall to Aidan, as if seeing
him for the first time.

"A pity for those prisoners, don't you think, my lord?"
The man ran his hand over the scar that marred his otherwise handsome features. "I received this during one of my
interrogations."

"Why did you kill Lady Davis and Lord Elkin?" Aidan
asked, changing the bitter subject.

The man smiled and wrapped his left arm around Lady
Rivenhall's waist, pulling her flush against the left side of
his body. He bent down and whispered in her ear as he
trained the pistol on Aidan.

"You know how much I enjoy taking information from
women."

Aidan watched Celeste shudder in Lord Cunningham's
arms and instinctively took a step toward her. The traitor
cocked his pistol, and Aidan stopped in his tracks, knowing that he could not save her if he were dead.

"As for John Elkin . . ." The man shrugged. "As I've

told you, he was in the wrong place at the wrong time. Much like the two of you."

In the moment that Lord Cunningham brought the pistol to her back, Celeste lifted her pale eyes to meet Aidan's, but there was no fear reflected in them, only forgiveness.

"No!" Aidan shouted, but his cry was muffled as the pistol fired.

What had he done? Oh, God, what had he done?

Aidan stared down at the woman he loved as her yellow bodice turned red, soaked with her own blood. He met the eyes of Celeste's killer who drew a second pistol as Aidan lunged at him. The pistol fired, and the bullet slammed into Aidan's left shoulder. But the burn of the wound was nothing to the grief that consumed him.

They were well matched in size and strength, but Lord Cunningham rolled atop him and struck him on his newly inflicted wound. Aidan cried out, the pain blinding him. The tall man took the opportunity to place his knee, and all of his weight, on Aidan's shattered shoulder.

Aidan struck out, but his left arm was useless. Lord Cunningham wrapped his hands around Aidan's neck and began to squeeze. Aidan choked, knowing that he would soon be dead. The thought should have struck fear into the very recesses of his soul, but it did not. Without Celeste at his side, with her death squarely on his shoulders, he was not sure that he could survive anyway.

The evening sun began to dim, and stars began to dance about the small room. He could feel his eyes drifting closed as his mind faded into darkness, then Lord Cunningham's grip eased.

Aidan looked up in confusion as he heard the man struggling to breathe. And there, lodged in his throat, was a very familiar dagger. The man's hands went to his throat, and his blue eyes grew wide just before his last breath escaped his body.

Aidan hauled himself up, his left arm dangling as he ran to Celeste's side.

"Celeste." He pressed his hand to her ribs to stop her life

slipping through his fingers. "Celeste, don't leave me. I'm so sorry, my love."

Her eyes fluttered open, and she smiled. "It is not your fault, Aidan, no more than the death of the men under your command. This is war, and sacrifices must be made."

"Not you."

"And why am I more precious than any other person?"

"Because I love you."

Tears filled her eyes as she looked up at him. "And I love you," she said, her eyelids struggling to remain open.

Aidan scooped her up into his arms, oblivious to the blood between them. "No, Celeste. Stay here." Distant footsteps sounded on the stairs. "No!" Aidan gripped her closer. "No!" he shouted, and the moment she died, so did he.

Soldiers entered the darkening chamber, but Aidan was so lost in his grief that he did not hear the boots scuffing the stone floor as the men lifted Lord Cunningham's body from the room. They returned moments later to take Celeste from him, but he could not let her go. His first instinct was to hold on to her until his sorrow killed him and he could join her.

"My lord," he heard above his head as the young captain touched his right shoulder. Aidan kissed his love for the last time, then allowed the soldiers to carry her from the room.

He stared at the blood pooling between the stones, and when the room was empty, he saw a flash of light from the corner of his eye. He looked down at her dagger and bent to pick it up. It was cold and held none of the warmth from her hand. He walked to the window and looked down at the rocks below.

Why had he lived?

Why hadn't he died in battle like his father? What made him worthy of God's mercy?

He had thought he understood, thought that he had sur-vived to spend his days loving her. Making her happy, vanquishing the memories of her father's murder with the laughter of their children.

He stared at the rocks.

The truth was he was no more worthy of survival than he had been of the blissful contentment he felt in her arms.

He was alone again. But unlike the loss of his parents, this wound would never heal. Celeste had saved hundreds of soldiers, but with her death, she had killed him. He would never be the same.

"Lord Wessex."

Aidan turned and fought his constricting throat to answer the young soldier that had entered the room. "Yes."

"I've been sent to inform you that Lady Rivenhall has a faint heartbeat and has been—"

Aidan brushed past the boy as he stumbled down the stairs of the ruin. He could not breathe as hope swelled painfully in his chest.

"Where is she?" he demanded of the commanding officer.

"Lady Rivenhall has been taken to the Duke of Glenbroke's townhome. A rider has been sent ahead to summon his personal physician."

Aidan was on his horse and galloping toward London before the lieutenant finished speaking. The sun had set, and the dark road ahead was barely visible, but he dared not stop.

He could not.

Thirty-five

❧

The Duke and Duchess of Glenbroke stood anxiously at the bedside as the doctor pulled the counterpane over Lady Rivenhall's chest.

The physician sighed heavily, saying, "I've removed the bullet and closed the wound. There appears to be no damage to vital areas, but she has lost a great deal of blood. Provided the wound does not fester, we should know by morning if she will survive."

Sarah stared at the pale woman lying in her bed. "Is there nothing more we can do?"

The doctor shook his head. "We will know by morning. I shall return then."

The duke clasped the physician's hand. "Thank you for coming, William."

"It was my honor, Your Grace. I only wish that the circumstances were not so grave."

The doctor turned to exit the room, but was startled to see the disheveled Earl of Wessex blocking his path.

"Aidan." Sarah rushed to her injured brother, but he did not respond, did not even seem to notice her.

He skewered the doctor with his eyes, saying, "If you leave this house tonight, I will hunt you down and kill you in the street."

"Wessex!" the duke admonished as Sarah gasped at her brother's pronouncement. "Mr. Albright, please accept my apologies—"

"Don't apologize for me, Gilbert. I am quite serious."

The doctor stared at Aidan warily, and Gilbert placed a gentle hand on the elderly man's back as he said, "Let me show you to a guest room just down the hall, Doctor Albright, then perhaps you might see to Lord Wessex's shoulder. We shall notify your household of your stay, and please do not hesitate in calling for anything you require."

As Gilbert left the room he stared at his wife in silent communication. Sarah watched helplessly as her devastated brother lifted Lady Rivenhall's right hand in his and carefully lay down beside her.

"Celeste, my love, I'm here. Please, forgive me," he whispered. "Please, forgive me, dearest. Please. I'm so sorry."

Tears welled in Sarah's eyes as she watched her brother caress the woman's forehead with his hand as he kissed her softly on the cheek. Sarah lifted her arm to touch him, soothe him, but realized nothing could help his pain until morning.

She left the room and walked downstairs, calling for her cloak when she arrived in the entry. Her husband arrived a few moments later, his dark brows furrowed above silver eyes.

"Where are you going?"

"To pray."

Gilbert pulled her into his powerful arms and kissed the top of her head, saying, "I'll go with you."

Aidan glanced up as the first rays of light filtered through the part in the velvet drapes. He looked down at Celeste with benefit of the light to see if she appeared improved. She did not. He had spent all evening staring at the rise and fall of her chest, convinced that if he watched, he could will her to take another breath, will her heart to keep beating.

Aidan squeezed his eyes shut and rubbed his bandaged shoulder with his fingertips. "What would I do without you, my love?"

"No idea," came a weak answer. Aidan's eyes snapped open, and he stared in disbelief and hope. "Get yourself killed, I would imagine."

He laughed and tentatively placed his hand on her pale cheek. "Not likely, with your deadly propensity for knives."

The corners of Celeste's lips lifted in a faint smile. Tears filled Aidan's eyes because he knew, in that moment and without a doubt, that she would survive. He bent his head and kissed her, pouring every ounce of himself into the gentle caress.

"Marry me?"

A spark came into her blue green eyes as she said, "I thought that 'the offer would never be made again.'"

Aidan kissed her knuckles. "Things have come to light that have forced me to reevaluate that particular declaration."

"Such as?"

"You are the bravest, most noble woman that I have ever met, and I would be a fool to let you leave this house without a ring on your finger."

"So you are admitting that you are a fool." She smiled tremulously, saying, "Perhaps I should reevaluate my original reply."

He kissed her softly and stroked her hair, staring into her eyes. "My God, Celeste, I thought I lost you," he said soberly.

"How can you have lost me when you just found me?"

Aidan stared at her and waited for the constriction in his throat to ease before whispering, "I love you."

Tears filled her eyes and spilled from the corners, cascading toward her golden hair. "Oh, Aidan, I think I loved you from the first moment I saw you."

His smile reflected his heart. "Well, I most assuredly did not love you. Wanted you, yes. But, my God, I had never seen such an evil woman in all my days." She laughed and then caught her breath at the pain.

Terrified, he shouted for the doctor, but Celeste put a reassuring hand on his. "I shall be fine, Aidan." She smiled. "But perhaps you should leave so that my stitching does not tear."

His anxiety eased the moment the doctor entered the room. "Very well, Lady Rivenhall," Aidan said with an arrogant drawl. "I have errands to run."

"Do you?" she asked with a raised brow. "And what might those be?"

"I have to find a parson and a ring because you, my dear, are getting married today."

Celeste flashed him the most enchanting smile he had ever seen. "Your sister will have a fit."

Aidan bent down and kissed those delicious lips, and with an impish grin said, "The duchess can host the announcement of our first child."

Epilogue

With a brandy glass in one hand and a pocket watch in the other, Falcon determined that he had several more minutes to converse before he would need to resume his work.

He nestled into the corner of his wingback chair and stared over his desk at the two men that had been so instrumental in plugging the leak at the Foreign Office.

"Damned embarrassing, having my own clerk turn out to be the traitor," he mumbled. The Duke of Glenbroke chuckled at the irony and Falcon pointedly ignored him, continuing, "Well, never mind, caught the blackguard in the end."

"I believe it was my wife who caught the 'blackguard,' my lord."

Falcon's old eyes sparkled as he turned to stare at the elegant Earl of Wessex. "Clever of you to avoid waiting for a wedding. I always knew you were a bright man." He sipped his brandy, asking, "How is the countess?" as if she were an ordinary woman.

"Busy." Lord Wessex's tone was touched with pride and

Falcon felt a deep satisfaction in orchestrating the match. "My wife insisted that she continue to aid the war effort by tending to the wounded. However, she has agreed to stop her ministrations once she is increasing."

The duke's left brow rose. "Are you making an announcement, Aidan?"

"Not yet." Lord Wessex grinned from ear to ear. "But rest assured that I am dedicating myself to the task."

"I am quite sure that you are." Glenbroke laughed at his brother-in-law's obvious enthusiasm.

"As a matter of fact," the earl said, standing, "I must be off to retrieve my wife from the hospital before her patients refuse to relinquish her."

"Celeste is more than capable of defending herself, my lord."

"Wessex is newly wed." The duke leaned forward to gather his gloves and beaver skin hat from atop the desk. "Let the man enjoy his illusion of control, before the realities of married life set in."

"Quite right." Falcon met amused silver eyes as the duke rose to his feet. "It would be cruel otherwise."

"Good day, my Lord Falcon." Glenbroke bowed in sarcastic deference to the ridiculous title, then clasped his brother-in-law on the shoulder before ushering him into the hall.

The door clicked shut and Falcon stared at his mahogany desk thinking how fortunate Britain was to have such men. His gaze drifted to the right and he lifted the first of three pristine files, opening it. He could feel himself grinning as he made the final notes that would conclude this dossier.

A great weight lifted as he closed the document, forever filing it away in his heart. Falcon allowed himself a moment of victory, a moment to feel the pure joy of absolution.

And then, reluctantly, he cast his eyes on the other two. The women of Whitehall were as necessary as the war itself, but the need for both was painful. He picked up the top folder, running his hand over the heavy parchment as he spent several minutes in prayer. He set the first file down gently, protectively, and then reached for the third much larger and infinitely more complex dossier.

He sighed, too old, too experienced in the art of war not to recognize the devastating toll this covert service took on the women he'd recruited. Lady Celeste Wessex's happily-ever-after was the exception rather than the rule. The majority of his agents, both male and female, would die—were, in fact, already beyond saving. He had to believe that their sacrifice was not in vain, not when they fought and died for the one ideal Falcon himself would kill to protect—a free and peaceful Britain.

CONTINUE READING FOR A SPECIAL PREVIEW OF
SAMANTHA SAXON'S NEXT NOVEL

THE LADY KILLER

COMING DECEMBER 2005
FROM BERKLEY SENSATION!

PARIS, FRANCE
OCTOBER 17, 1811

Nicole closed her eyes, but she could still see the image of General Capette sprawled across the mahogany desk, blood pouring from the ragged wound in the back of his head. She could still smell the gunpowder drifting through the luxurious fifth floor suite she had just been given admittance to clean.

Her eyes snapped open as she turned toward the fearsome crack that splintered the gilded doors nearest the ornate brass locks. Nicole froze, astonished by the transformation of the amiable French soldiers who had searched her moments ago.

They entered the cavernous room with their pistols drawn, but it was not their weapons that made them lethal. It was the coiled muscles, the hard set of their features, and the cold that had settled in their eyes.

"What has happened here?" the lieutenant bellowed as he ran toward her, the sound of his black polished boots bouncing off the carved panel walls.

Nicole opened her mouth to explain but she had no words to describe the horrific scene she had just witnessed. Blood trickled on the inlaid wooden floor and she dropped to her knees, scrubbing at the sticky liquid before it was absorbed into the tiny crevasses.

The tall man lifted her from shock with a firm grip on her upper arms. "Mademoiselle!"

Nicole jumped, startled into answering by his shouting.

"I . . . I was airing the general's room when a man . . ." She pointed to an elongated window and the second soldier rushed toward it, leaning out.

"There is a rope hanging from the roof," he reported to his superior.

Nicole felt a calloused finger lifting her chin and she was forced to look into the hard hazel eyes of the young lieutenant.

"Describe this man," he said, the muscles in his jaw throbbing.

"Fair hair." A tear streamed down her face as she forced herself to continue. "Tall, handsome. He . . . He shot the general and climbed onto the balcony."

"Gaston." He glanced at the other man. "Search the roof. I'll take to the street. Mademoiselle"—his eyes darted back to her the instant that they were alone—"you must remain here until I return."

"No!" she protested, desperate to get out of this room. "Do not leave me here. What if—"

"Do not fear, mademoiselle," the lieutenant said, patting her hand as if she were a child awakened by some gruesome dream. "This man will want to get away from the hotel as quickly as possible."

He turned to go but Nicole grabbed his arm. "Please, don't leave me," she whispered.

The lieutenant looked down and sighed with frustration, propelling her out the damaged doors and toward the servant's staircase. They had descended two flights of stairs when they rounded a corner on the third floor and very nearly collided with an elderly butler holding a laden dinner tray.

The lieutenant scarcely stopped, leaving her with the bewildered servant, saying, "I must go if I am to capture the general's murderer."

But Nicole knew he would never capture the assassin.

General Capette was so reviled by the French themselves that Napoleon had assigned bodyguards to protect his most victorious commander. The objection to the general, it was commonly agreed, was in the barbaric manner by which he achieved those many victories. Murderous men such as Capette were hardly the harbingers of *liberté*.

There had even been rumors that the general had raped a chambermaid at the hotel, which undoubtedly was the reason Nicole had obtained the position a mere eight days ago.

"General Capette has been murdered?" The old man stared at her blood-spattered apron in disbelief.

"Yes." Nicole nodded. "A man climbed from the roof onto the balcony."

"Are you injured?"

Nicole's chin began to quiver. "No." She was not injured, but she would never be the same.

The old man turned to escort her to the kitchens, but, needing to be alone, she stopped him. "Your supper is becoming cold. I am unharmed, I assure you."

Nicole could sense the butler's apprehension, so she descended the stairs before he could protest further. She continued her brisk pace until a mixture of aromas wafted up the stairwell from the direction of the noisy kitchen.

Slowing, she stepped onto the landing and cautiously pushed the door inward. The deafening sound of metal pots, rapid chopping, and shouting greeted her as she walked in. Colorful fruits were piled everywhere as pastry chefs agonized over the finishing touches to their evening's creations.

She continued walking, trying not to disturb the kitchen workers during the most chaotic portion of their day. They would learn of General Capette's murder soon enough; she envied them their last moments of ignorance.

The back door of the hotel came into view, and Nicole felt the tension ease from her shoulders. She had no wish to start sobbing like a child in front of the entire kitchen staff, but she feared if she did not leave soon, she would.

Exhausted, she opened the white door and lifted her face to greet the cool autumn breeze before stepping onto the uneven cobblestone street that ran the length of the fashionable hotel. The door closed behind her and she walked toward the Seine, just as she did every night.

She stopped only once, to remove her shapeless lace cap and bloody apron and toss them both into the river. Even in the dark, she could see the powerful current carrying them away. Nicole watched from the embankment until the white cloth was swallowed by the dark waters beneath the Pont Neuf.

Nicole turned north toward her apartment, reaching into the pocket of her black muslin dress. Engraved silver glinted in the moonlight as she removed her pistol and absently reloaded the exquisite weapon.

The streets of Paris were very dangerous at night.